DEATH
AND
BETRAYAL

SEELEY JAMES

Published by
Machined Media
12402 N 68th St
Scottsdale, AZ 85254

DEATH AND BETRAYAL: A Jacob Strearne Thriller, released February 18th, 2020
Print ISBN: 978-1-7333467-1-9
ePub ISBN: 978-1-7333467-2-6
Distribution Print ISBN: 978-1-7333467-3-3
Sabel Security #8 version 2.33

Formatting: BB eBooks
Cover Design: Jeroen ten berge

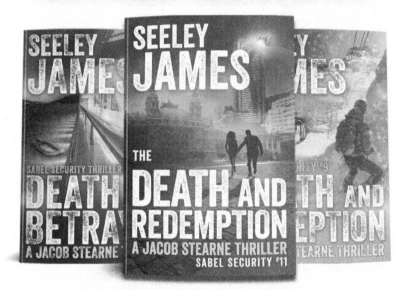

For my granddaughter
Jenee

CHAPTER 1

THE MAN THEY CALL RA took a deep breath and tamped down his growing agitation without betraying his emotions. The general controlled a good deal of money. Ra could put up with the general's emissary a while longer. Ra said, "We're talking about an auction for the most advanced weapon system the world has ever seen. An auction your general could easily win. What concerns could he possibly have?"

The emissary inhaled to create a dramatic and smug pause.

Ra resisted the urge to glance over the sea toward Monaco's harbor. He was dying to see if his darling's tender was on its way back from town, but he wouldn't allow himself to be distracted.

"The general does not believe you have what you claim." The emissary said in his heavily accented English. He gestured with his arms wide, encompassing Ra's superyacht. "I do not see it here on your little skiff."

Behind his left shoulder, the emissary's sycophantic lieutenant smirked.

The dig was childish. The *Savannah* was the biggest yacht in Monaco, a present to himself after making billions in commodities. An all-American yacht for his all-American success story. So American, in fact, it was too big to dock in the harbor. Sure, it was post-season, and the *Numina* would drop anchor due east of him in a matter of weeks. Until then, the *Savannah* reigned supreme. He felt like gutting the slimy emissary for his rudeness. Instead, he smoothed his Kiton sport coat and puffed up his thin frame.

"Don't be a fool," Ra sneered. "If I kept Alvaria onboard, sleezy generals from around the world would send commandos to take it from me. In case that's what you're thinking, rest assured, I have security. We call them 'the dogs.' You've met two of them." He gestured to two bulky men in black suits standing close by. "Fido and Rover. Spot keeps watch with a rifle in case someone approaches uninvited. There are more. Benjie, Yeller … I have a whole kennel."

Ra turned his back on his guests and checked the harbor. He couldn't wait for his darling to return but he needed to conclude this delicate business before then. He didn't want her to see the kind of men he dealt with. The emissary wore a ludicrous uniform without insignia yet festooned with medals. His black hair was greased straight back with what might've been motor oil. The lieutenant dressed and groomed himself to match. The very definition of a toady.

"The general does not believe the system can do what you claim," the emissary said.

"Oh, my misguided friend. Alvaria is the stuff of autocrats' dreams." Ra laid his hands on the railing, keeping his focus out to sea. "Imagine what it can do. At the push of a button, a hundred drones leap into the air, locate their target, and annihilate whoever you choose. Each drone on a single-purpose mission, never stopping until one of them achieves the objective." He straightened up and turned to face the emissary. "No more political rivals. No more annoying reporters asking inconvenient questions. No more adversaries across your western border. Everyone doing as they're told, all under the general's control. As it should be. It's science fiction—and it's here today. Naturally, there will be a proof of concept arranged."

"The general is skeptical you can obtain this system." The emissary crossed his arms and widened his stance. "The Americans have impenetrable security."

"I stand on my reputation. Many times your poor general has failed to pay me in a timely manner, yet I have never failed to deliver what he needs. From rocket launchers to automatic rifles, they arrived on time and under budget. He would still be a lieutenant were it not for me making good on my promises. He knows damn well my word is gold. I have all the right people in all the right places. My plan has been in the works for years. Alvaria will fall into my hands at exactly the right moment. He doesn't need to believe in me. He can wait—" Ra paused for dramatic effect "—until his rival uses it to target him."

To his credit, the emissary didn't flinch.

"Imagine," Ra said, "if Iran acquires Alvaria, they could destroy the ruling classes of Saudi Arabia and Kuwait in an afternoon. The next morning, they could annihilate Iraq's parliament. Your little corner of the world would come next. Then, they invade. The price of oil skyrockets because they would control 24% of the world's production. Sanctions are lifted under threat of an oil embargo. And just like that, the Persian Empire is reborn."

The emissary shrugged.

Ra said, "North Korea wants it to bring Japan to heel. And vice versa. Ukraine wants the Crimea back and—"

"I get the picture." The emissary thought while he took a long, deep breath.

He pressed a finger to his lips and looked at the deck. After a long moment, he lifted his finger and shook it at Ra. "The general does not like the glimpses of the future you have illuminated. He does not want to participate in your auction. Instead of bidding for it, he demands you turn it over to him or he will report you to the Americans. If he doesn't get it, no one will have it." He paused and smiled. "There will be no resurgent Persian Empire."

So that was the general's play? To squeal on him? Ra's world turned red and heat flushed his head. He would have to send a message. A message so strong, no one on his list would misunderstand. He would not allow his endeavor to be seen as a trifle. He had a reputation to maintain. Ra flicked a quick glance at Fido, who sprang into action.

To the emissary, Ra said, "I am most disappointed to hear you say that. On a different subject, do you recall meeting my man Bonham in a café last month? Bonham is my second-in-command. He offered you money to turn against the general. Ah, I see from your surprise that you do recall the encounter vividly. Well, sport, the problem for you is that when you turned him down, your lieutenant did not."

As the emissary's surprise turned to shock, his gaze swiveled to his lieutenant. At that moment, Fido knelt at the emissary's feet and clamped

3

leg irons on his ankles. In disbelief, the emissary looked down at his shackles, then followed the attached chain to find Rover standing at the railing, holding a very large, very heavy stone. "Do you think you can scare—"

"You've been paid," Ra said to the emissary's lieutenant. He held out an old, razor-sharp dagger. "Slit his throat."

The lieutenant stared at Ra in disbelief. "Now?"

"Yes, now. Or die with him. Your choice. Ah. You've seen the light. Good man. Right here, above the collar. Stand behind him so you don't get blood on yourself."

As the young man weighed the knife in his hand and moved behind his former boss, Ra took out his phone, set it to video, and pressed record. The knife slashed through the stunned and wordless emissary's neck. Blood sprayed forward. Rover dropped the rock overboard. The chain's slack disappeared and yanked the emissary's body with it, over the railing and into the deep.

The young man looked up at Ra, who kept the video rolling. The psychological weight of his first murder began to contort the young lieutenant's expression. As he pondered his rapidly changing allegiances, he looked down to find Rover placing leg irons on his ankles. Behind him, Fido stood at the railing with another rock. He looked back at Ra and squeaked, "Why? I did what—"

"I think it's obvious, isn't it?" Ra asked. "You can't be trusted."

Over his shoulder he saw the tender bearing his darling returning from shore. She would be onboard in five minutes. No time for long goodbyes.

He turned back to face the lieutenant as Rover slit the young man's throat. "There are four more of your kind in the general's private guard. He'll be dead by morning, so you'll be in good company."

The stone dropped. The chain tightened. The lieutenant's body flew over the railing into the deep.

Ra looked at the pool of blood covering the deck. He snapped his fingers. A steward appeared. "You see this ugly mess? Scrub it clean."

CHAPTER 2

MY BREATHING AND HEART RATE were as low as I could get them and yet the guard sensed my presence. The ambient glow of city lights from down the hill silhouetted his holstered pistol. He took a long look over his shoulder, stopping two degrees short of where I stood motionless in the blackest shadow of a stone parapet. Another guard watched from above on the bulwark, his gaze sailing into the darkness ten feet over my head.

The first guy turned away from me and sniffed the air. His partner said something in Greek. The first guy sorted through the scents wafting up the hill from the harbor—sea and fish and algae and boats—searching for a hint of something out of place. Something like me. But he didn't smell me. My quick dip off the dock had paid off.

After a long time, the suspicious one replied in their native language.

The human eye registers movement quicker than it recognizes objects, echoes of our primordial ancestors who fled wolves and bears every day. I was invisible as long as I could remain motionless. I let the mosquito crawl on my neck.

The guy in front of me snapped a mic on his shoulder and spoke. The only word I recognized was "Kostas." I'd seen the name on a badge. The guy wearing the badge was one of two guys taking a nap courtesy of the Sabel Darts I'd stabbed into their legs. Which meant alarm bells would start ringing shortly after the guy in front of me realized Kostas was having a bad day.

Thirty feet separated us. Too far to bolt out of the dark in a surprise attack. He would draw his gun and fire before I crossed half that, and I'd been a high-school track star. If he missed, the guy ten feet over my head would get a shot off clean and easy.

The guy above me said something in a tone that sounded anxious. Probably a concern about the health of Kostas and his companion. The guy in front of me faced his partner, which took his gaze directly toward me, up just a notch. He could see me if he tried. And he was trying.

A sneeze tickled my nose.

Mercury, winged messenger of the Roman gods, said, *Wait for it, homie. I gotcha covered.*

I said, *Just what I need.*

Hey now. No need to get all sassy. He stepped into my line of sight, blocking my view of the guard most likely to shoot me.

My snark was justified. On my last mission, Mercury bet the other gods I would die in a hail of gunfire. Why had he gambled with my life? He was short on heavenly cab fare. Apparently, the centaurs' trust funds ran dry fifteen hundred years ago and Uber hasn't reached Mount Whatever yet. He even lied to get me to step in front of armed assassins just to win the bet. With gods like him …

Not that he hasn't helped me. The ratio of lives saved to outright betrayals might be a thousand to one, come to think of it. If he exists—and isn't a manifestation of PTSD-induced schizophrenia like the psychiatrists keep telling me—he can be a great friend. Over my eight tours of duty as an Army Ranger, he'd guided me to heroic victories so many times colonels would fight over which battalion could claim me. Plenty of soldiers, confronted by the existential absurdity of a firefight would glue themselves to my side, such were the legends surrounding my invincibility.

But, being tight with god, while comforting, can create complications. For example, he wears a shamefully small toga, the kind you might find on a male stripper. Thank Jupiter no one else can see him. His morals come straight out of the might-makes-right manual. He still thinks you get promoted if you kill your boss and take over his legions. He didn't catch the transition from "plunder" to "grand theft" either. In fact, if I took half his divine guidance, I'd be serving multiple life sentences. And he's a jealous god who demands thanks and praise at the most annoying times. Like right now.

DEATH AND BETRAYAL

Thank you, I said. *You're the greatest god of all, Mercury.*

Satisfied, he smiled and floated out of the way on those flappy little wings on the side of his helmet. Physics be damned.

The guard in front of me tried his radio again, then waved his companion down off the wall. He pulled a SIG out of his holster and crouched in the kind of shooting stance you see on cop shows. The lights of Corfu twinkled around his dark profile. He looked like a target at a shooting range.

Above me, boots scraped back off the rampart and jogged to the stone steps fifty yards away. He dropped down them two at a time and ran to join his friend. Terrible tactics for them, but perfect for me.

What did I tell you, dawg? Mercury said. *I lined up your adversaries for you. Who's your favorite god?*

Yeah. I rolled my eyes in the dark. *Like I said, all thanks and praise to Mercury.*

Thank you. Now, was that so hard? Why do mortals always hesitate to thank the gods for the bounty—

I tuned him out as guard number two jogged toward his more alert and dangerous partner. The first guy glanced back to make sure the sounds were coming from the person he expected. I pushed off the wall and ran up behind the jogger. I stabbed a dart into his right butt cheek.

Sable Darts carry a non-lethal dose of inland Taipan snake venom that induces instant flaccid paralysis in the victim. They remain alert but unable to move for a couple minutes. The second stage of the dart is a powerful sleep medication that knocks them out for the next four to six hours. Sabel Industries developed them to compete with Taser but the occasional death due to allergic reactions scared off insurers and inflamed a few plaintiff's attorneys. They never reached the open market.

The man I popped went down like wheat under a scythe. I ran over his back as he face-planted on the hillside. The last remaining guard's brain pieced together things that didn't make sense. He worked out why a large shadow had just erupted from his friend's back as I reached him. He was a professional. His instinctive reflex was to aim the gun at any dark or threatening objects. I qualified as both. The muzzle wheeled around to my face.

There wasn't enough time to land the dart in an unprotected location. He had a bulletproof vest and tactical belt. I changed tactics two strides out. I had never played football, but I'd seen it on TV. I did what any offensive linesman would do if the ref wasn't watching: I went for a cut block at his knees.

Bones and ligaments snapped and popped amid the noise of his pistol. All three of his shots went skyward as we rolled down a patch of grass. We banged into a tree. I tried to get the dart in his thigh. As we scrambled to right ourselves, I found an opening for my non-lethal weapon. His watch ended a few seconds later.

"What was that?" The voice came over my comm link slathered in panic. "Mr. Jacob? Mr. Jacob?"

"Fine, Dimitris. I'm fine." I rose and took a deep breath. "Going inside now."

I patted my side pocket to make sure I hadn't lost the ring stashed there. It was still secure in its protective robin's-egg blue box. I made sure the pocket's zipper was closed.

I jogged up the steps to the parapet. Flashing colors from a large screen TV lit up the curtains in the master bedroom on the second floor. The owner hadn't heard the shots through his soundproof windows. Those windows had kept me from eavesdropping the night before. His line of work required a hefty dose of paranoia that usually served him well, hence the windows. Tonight, they sealed his fate.

Entering the house, I took the stairs to the ten-car garage. Everything was right where my informant had told me. In the second bay from the end, next to last year's Bentley convertible, sat ten stacks of wooden crates.

I pried one open at the cost of a splinter. A small, blond toothpick of cheap pine stuck in the base of my thumb. I pulled it with my teeth and peered inside the crate. A rack of Beretta 70/90 fully automatic rifles awaited me. The same model used a few months earlier by a group of deranged murderers hoping to kick off a worldwide religious war through a series of coordinated mass shootings. Ten rifles per crate, ten crates. Where were they going? I snapped pictures of the serial numbers, then tapped my comm link. "Dimitris, I found them. Just like he told us."

"The European Union is in your debt, Mr. Jacob." Dimitris Bakakis, prosecutor for the Corfu prefecture, lowered his voice to a whisper. "Be sure to make the call."

"I'm on it," I said. I dialed 112, the Greek equivalent of 911, identified myself as a guest of Baron Konrad von Frieden, and reported discovering the cache of weapons on his premises. Minutes later, Dimitris's friends from the Hellenic Police SWAT team stormed the Frieden mansion armed with a legitimate, albeit somewhat staged, search warrant.

I stood outside the garage with my hands above my head forming a circle, the prearranged signal that I was one of the good guys. The heavily armed SWAT team swirled past me, securing the sprawling estate and dragging the owner away from the German-dubbed version of *Breaking Bad*. They propped him in a chair at the dining room table, surrounding him with men in full battle-rattle.

Dimitris took a seat opposite Konrad and stared at him for a long, quiet, uncomfortable minute. I stood in the back row, watching the proceedings over some well-armed shoulders. Dimitris hoped to get a blurted confession but expected a silent demand for legal representation from the Baron. His expectation proved prophetic. Dimitris didn't speak the Austrian's native German and Baron von Frieden refused to speak Greek, so they carried on in English.

Dimitris painted a clear, realistic picture of life in prison and offered leniency for information leading to Konrad's superiors in the arms business. Konrad, who chafed at the Greek's informal use of his first name, insisted on a lawyer. Dimitris ignored the request and continued to detail his bleak picture for the millionaire.

Eventually, Konrad leaned in. "You don't understand. Everything in life is a transaction of value. You are inviting me into a transaction whereby I give you names I do not know in exchange for promises you cannot keep. This is of no value to me. I patiently await a different transaction. I will give a man money in exchange for something quite valuable: the truth of my innocence in a court of law. This is what separates little civil servants like you from important men like me—understanding the value in a transaction."

Mercury tapped my shoulder. *Dawg, did you forget about the guest quarters?*

I said, *The Greeks have it handled. Their turf, their search. I've got a date back in the States.*

Mercury said, *Before you try slipping that ring on her finger, you got something important to do. They missed someone special. You need to get your butt down there and see who's crawling out from behind the linens.*

I said, *It doesn't matter who's hiding—*

The officer in front of me gave me a disapproving look as if I'd spoken out loud. I shrugged, backed out of the room, and wandered through the house. There were guest rooms on the ground floor the size of my home back in DC. Outside, a free-standing guesthouse stood a short walk from the main entrance.

Mercury said, *No, homeboy, not the nice guesthouse. Check the little one he uses for relatives.*

Behind the pool cabanas stood an ancient one-room cottage, four stone walls covered in white stucco. Approaching the only door, I heard a scratching noise inside. I opened the door and flipped on the lights. A man was trying to flee the room through a window on the opposite wall. Static cling held a pillowcase to his back. He looked over his shoulder at me with a frantic expression. I recognized him at once.

I said, "Lieutenant Hale?"

CHAPTER 3

IT WAS HIM, ALRIGHT. LIEUTENANT Nathan Hale, no relation to the revolutionary. The finest lieutenant I'd ever served under. He had the unmistakable chiseled chin of a heroic explorer. That chin had confidently led my platoon into battle for two tours. Lt. Hale was the only officer who hadn't curled up into a metaphorical fetal position in his first firefight.

"Jacob?" He flushed red like a stoplight at midnight. "Hey. I, uh, I'm not sure what's going on here."

"You're climbing out the window of a home being raided for illegal arms dealing."

"Is that what's happening?" He looked anxiously over my shoulder at the open door. "I had no idea."

"Then why did you hide in the linens?"

His gaze followed mine to a sheet straggling out of a thin closet. He brushed the pillowcase off his back. "Look, it's not … Don't jump to … I'm not part of that."

My heart cracked. There's a faith soldiers must have—we're the good guys, we did the right thing, we killed the right people, we spared the innocent. I'd seen soldiers lose that faith and go home crushed and broken. I felt for them. I called them, I hugged them, I went to their funerals. It's an easy faith to lose. And one you could lose at any moment—even long after the shooting stopped. There were times I'd be brushing my teeth and remember that time I'd launched a 40 mm grenade into a shack and killed six insurgents. Were they as bad as the intelligence reported? Or were they simple shepherds in a tragic case of mistaken identity? To keep sane, you have to keep the faith.

Plenty of good soldiers mustered out and returned to civilian life. Some went home and got a job and fell in love and moved into a house on the prairie and lived happily ever after. Some went home and self-medicated to block out the abject madness they'd enthusiastically embraced. Some went home and gave up on humanity as being hopelessly flawed and checked out forever. A very small minority of apostates offered up their deadly skills to brutal lords who skirted the bounds of law and morality.

Lieutenant Nate Hale was not the kind to lose the faith.

Yet here he was. Fleeing a crime scene with a small, blond toothpick of cheap pine stuck in his palm.

"Remember Karachi?" he asked.

"We were never in Karachi."

"Officially." His smile twitched and his voice wavered. "We can reminisce as long as no one else hears us."

"Not until 2065, according to regulations."

He nodded. "I saved your ass from that guy with the scimitar."

I stood still.

A moment passed and his recollection caught up with him. "Or, actually, you saved me from that guy. Right. Thanks again."

"How teams work, Lieutenant."

"We dropped a lot of bad guys in our day, huh?" He stretched another weak grin over that once-valiant chin. His gelled hair still held a youthful wave the color of oats.

"That we did. How deep are you, Lieutenant?"

"I'm not in uniform anymore. Call me Nate." His hands flopped at his sides, nervous and uncertain. "How about saving me one more time, Jacob? Whaddaya say?"

"What happened?" I asked. "Nate."

"Well ..." he ran his fingers through his hair. "I had a business opportunity. Import-export stuff. Finished medical products. Did you know Greece is a big exporter of finished medical products? True. Anyway. Good partners, good customers, and I was doing well. Then a big deal came up. I needed extra financing." He blew out a heavy breath. "I got a taste, you know? I saw these guys with tons of money and cars and women and … They aren't any better than you and me. They aren't as smart. They never worked as hard. Never endured as much. Never even served." He closed the gap between us. "Jacob, these guys are filthy rich. They've never faced the shit we've faced. They're just dumb punks compared to you and me. What's wrong with guys like us getting a few spoils? We've done more for truth and justice in one day wearing ACUs than they ever will in their entire lives. They owe us a place at the table."

Nothing he said sounded like my old lieutenant. I stood still.

"I got into something I didn't understand." He stumbled for words. "It was complicated and by the time I figured out what was going on, it was too late. I couldn't get out."

We faced each other for a long time. Outside, the Hellenic Police were making their second rounds. They were checking under bushes and looking into linen closets. Footsteps closed in.

His eyes watered and his fingers splayed out. "Would you at least give your old lieutenant a head start, Sergeant Stearne?"

Mercury said, *He's got a point about the rich guys, dawg. They might be emperors today, but they aren't shit compared to bad-ass you. Dude, think about what you did tonight. You raided an arms dealer with four guards on duty—and you did it single-handed.*

I said, *But what's the right thing to do here? Does he deserve a second chance? He was a damn fine officer.*

Your call, bro. Mercury laughed and slapped my shoulder. *Free will sucks, huh, whiteboy?*

Did I mention Mercury is African, as in black? Makes sense when you think about it. God made man in his image; someone wrote that somewhere. And anthropologists have proven the first humans came from southeastern Africa. Which means a lot of racists are in for a big surprise at the Pearly Gates. But. Not my problem.

I weighed the good things Lieutenant Nate Hale had done when I knew him years ago. Then an image of mass shooters firing on worshippers in churches and temples popped into my head. They had hundreds of Beretta 70/90s stolen from an Italian Army depot. I stopped them from killing thousands of innocent people. The thought of the potential carnage made me ill.

Nations, states, cities, and communities are, at their core, tribal. Historically, tribes have been incited quite easily to war. Arms dealers profit from conflict. The more weapons the other tribe has, the more you need, they tell both tribes. They have no moral boundaries. Whether they're putting machine guns in the hands of child soldiers or arming the strongman's secret police, they sell anything they can get for the highest price possible. As scum of the earth go, they're the scummiest. And, as Nate pointed out, getting filthy rich.

"I'll give you a different head start." I grabbed him by the collar and shoved him toward the door. "I'm a friend of the prosecutor. They offer leniency for the first guy to volunteer. I'm giving you a head start on being the prosecution's star witness."

Nate flipped around to face me up close. "Whoa. Jacob. Shoot me then. Do it here. You don't know this guy. They call him Ra, like the pharaoh, the god of the sun. When you're with him, the sun shines on you. Without his blessing, you have no life."

"Ra?" I scoffed. "He's in handcuffs waiting for his lawyer."

"I'm not talking about Konrad." Nate's eyes bounced wildly, focusing first on my left pupil, then on my right, then back, fearing for his life. "He's third-string. Ra is big. If it goes 'bang' between the Black Sea and the Gulf of Aden, it was delivered by Ra."

CHAPTER 4

WAR IS THE ULTIMATE COMPETITIVE sport. You go into it with plans and objectives, then the bullets start flying and survival—that most primal instinct—picks you up by the scruff of your neck and heaves you across all your logic and morality. Your values are reduced to a pocketful of rubble you'd trade for one extra magazine. No one who plays the game walks away unscathed. Those who live through it do so having relied not on their patriotism but their brothers in arms. Surviving a battle bonds two people together like no other bond in life.

He was using that bond. It pissed me off.

"Remember that pregnant woman the Taliban officer killed when he tried to spray our platoon?" I circled him. "Who sold that guy a rifle? Remember what that al-Qaeda grenade did to the family hiding in the wrong bunker? Who sold those crates of M67s to al-Qaeda? You've seen the kids ripped apart by AK-103 rounds gone off-target. Who sells these guys weapons?" I left a dramatic pause. "Konrad von Frieden."

"Yeah." Nate's head sank. His shoulders fell. A deep sigh came from inside him. As if he'd carried the ethical weight for weeks and finally set it down. "I didn't have a way out. These guys … Jacob, they don't mess around."

"Neither do you." I punched his shoulder. "You're going to tell the prosecutor everything because it's the right thing to do, not because you care about your life. You have a choice between prison for life and doing the right thing. You're one of the good guys. You're going to save the lives of Syrian kids and Afghan kids and Yemeni kids. When you do, you'll be sparing the life of Americans right alongside them."

He perked up. The idea of switching sides appealed to him. He made a life-changing moral choice while I watched. I was proud of him. A soldier might leave the service, but service never leaves the soldier. He was a good man who needed a way out. I gave him one. His appreciation showed on his face.

"You're right," he said. "New mission: bring down Ra. Thanks, Jacob."

He laced his fingers behind his head and turned and walked out the door in front of me. I told him to drop the prisoner posture. I trusted him not to run since the place was crawling with Greek cops. He led and I followed up to the main house.

My thoughts turned to going home to see my girl. Jenny made my heart flutter the way they write about in romance novels. I never knew that was possible. When we lay on my sofa reading books, I felt at peace with the world. Nothing else mattered. They say when you meet the right girl, you just know it. When I met Jenny, I knew it. We didn't argue; we settled disagreements peacefully. We respected each other's ideas. I'd even taken an active role in her recovery and therapy. She was moving from the reorganization phase into the renormalization phase. Although it wasn't easy, things between us were going well.

A few strides later, I pulled the ring box out of my pocket and flipped it open. The big stone glittered in the dark. I had a good feeling about it. My boss, Ms. Sabel, had given me a bonus that reflected the substantial new business my recent exploits had brought in. I'd spent a good chunk of that bonus on the ring. Maybe it was too much. Or not enough. I can never tell.

Mercury said, *She's worth it, brutha. She's the daughter of a Caesar. She could take you places if you work it right.*

I said, *I would never marry for money. Besides, when the opiate lawsuits settle, her big-pharma-dad might not be so rich.*

Ain't nothing wrong with marrying for money, homeboy. He slapped the back of my head. *Don't be so fucking proud.*

I said, *Gods shouldn't swear. It just isn't right.*

Mercury said, *I am the god of ... what? God of what now? Oh. That's right, eloquence. Haven't you noticed? You're using big words like valiant and apostate and existential.*

I learned those words in Ranger School. I thought for a moment. *Maybe not existential. That might've come from you.*

As eloquent as he claimed to be, he now favored street language over oratory. His rationale makes sense. He fired up Roman orators from Cicero to Marcus Antonius, but all that fell apart when Constantine took the empire Christian and the whole Eurocentric world plunged into a thousand years of illiteracy and ignorance. He and the other gods tried everything to regain their former glory. At one point, Mercury befriended a young playwright named Shakespeare and convinced him to write nice things about Roman history in exchange for guidance. Or so Mercury claims. When that didn't pan out, he came to the New World. Now he's using street lingo that changes every other day. To my ear, he doesn't have the fluidity of Kendrick Lamar or Dr. Dre.

Mercury said, *See there, bro? You're using words like fluidity and befriended. You're coming up in the world. Ima make you into a Caesar yet.*

I said, *I got that from reading Attica Locke.*

Nate looked over his shoulder at me. "That's kind of highbrow literature for you, isn't it, Stearne? I thought you read Baldacci."

"Just trying to step it up some." I pushed him toward the side entrance to the main house.

We went inside where a cop checked him in. I parked him in the kitchen and went to find the prosecutor, Dimitris Bakakis.

The prosecutor was still in the dining room surrounded by soldiers. I listened over their armor-clad shoulders. Konrad had thrown caution to the wind and was talking. His silver crewcut glistened under the overhead halogen lights. A substantial man, he spread out with an arm stretched across the back of the chair next to him. He was saying, "This is no threat, Dimitris. I merely predict the future as it will inevitably happen. You should heed my advice."

"You only know his codename, Ra. Yet you expect me to fear him. Why?" Dimitris sat straight, his curly black hair perfectly groomed and shiny. His notepad and recorder laid out straight before him.

"Connections." Konrad tried to repress a smug smile. "From Washington to Brussels to Berlin. Even Athens."

It was a conversation of power, who had it and who didn't. Above my paygrade. I checked my phone. One message from Jenny. Two from Ms. Sabel.

I read the text threads. Ms. Sabel expressed concerns about meeting my parents. She was uncharacteristically insecure about her fashion statement. One might think a young billionaire industrialist who had inherited a huge company after a stellar career as a soccer star would have more confidence. Usually, she had too much. Being worried about what a family of farmers in Iowa thought of her took me by surprise. Then I realized she had been stepping deeper into her executive role every day. Her father had been a larger-than-life entrepreneur who dressed better than anyone in Washington, and she wanted to fill those shoes. Iowa would be quite different from DC, and far outside her experience. She wanted to send the right message, something not too formal or pretentious, and not so casual as to dishonor my parents' hospitality.

Mercury said, *You appreciating me, bro? Under my guidance, you now have Pia-Caesar-Sabel worried about impressing your people. You, a humble farm boy making her, a billionaire, worry. That young woman has never lost confidence in her whole twenty-eight years. Not in the World Cup, not in the Olympics, not ever, because wherever she goes, she owns it. Literally. And, she's the champion, the gold medalist, the greatest of all time. On top of all that, she's not just rich—she's stinking rich.*

I said, *Is any billionaire a Caesar to you just because they have money?*

Mercury looked at me with disdain. *Uh. Yeah.*

It doesn't matter if they're good or decent people, just rich?

Mercury said, *Have you read those books I made you buy about the emperors? Did they seem like they were winning awards for congeniality? Tiberius? Caligula? Nero?*

I texted Ms. Sabel, "They've seen plenty of pictures of you. They follow you on Instagram. They expect you to wear your favorite sports wear. It would mean the world to them if you were comfortable in their home. They invited you to say thanks for remodeling it, not to impress you or judge you. They want to show you that your money was well spent and appreciated."

"Their house was shot up because of me," she texted back. "It was the least I could do. OK, I'll chill about the outfit. When do you get here?"

"Morning. Just finishing up now, heading to the airport."

Next, I read Jenny's text. She left a bunch. She couldn't wait to meet my parents. She wanted to know if I'd get back to Sabel Gardens in time for dinner. That didn't happen so she sent another text telling me to call her after I'd beaten the bad guys to a pulp. And so on. There was a hint of the Adult Attachment Disorder, fear of being left alone, the therapist had warned about. Since Jenny was with Ms. Sabel, I didn't worry about her this time. Overall, it was refreshing to find such positive texts waiting for me. They brought a smile to my face. I unzipped my jacket pocket, fingered the ring box, then zipped it back up.

I started a text-reply when Dimitris walked out of the dining room and down the hallway toward me.

I stopped him. "Konrad's not talking?"

"Talking big like an important man. As if that will save him. But he gives me nothing I can use against him."

"I have just the guy for you. Konrad doesn't know we found this guy. He's on the inside and willing to work his way out."

We moved into the kitchen. I made the introductions and stood next to Nate while Dimitris laid out a few conditions. Dimitris liked the idea of an undercover operative since Konrad was confident about walking. Nate Hale leaned into the mission. He and Dimitris began to see a future together. Nate agreed to terms and shook hands with Dimitris.

Then Nate turned to me and said, "Jacob, you're right about all the innocents damaged by this. If going through the system doesn't work, you have to promise me you'll stop Ra."

"You got it, brother."

"Not a promise. That's too easy." He looked at the ground and thought for a second. "I need you to swear on the blood of our fallen brothers that you'll stop Ra."

Our eyes met. His were resolved like we were about to go to war. I said, "If anything goes wrong, I swear to make them pay."

He slowly began to nod his acceptance. I gave him a bro-hug.

Then it was time to go. I had an important date ahead of me.

Dimitris walked me to the front door. We said goodbye with a handshake.

He looked sad. "You're leaving the country? We're on the verge of taking down the biggest merchant of death in the Middle East, Mr. Jacob. We need you. Not just Greece, but the EU—and all of humankind."

"Thank you for the kind words, my friend. Sorry, but I have plans tomorrow back in Iowa."

"Nothing could be as important as this. The land mines this man distributes are a threat to millions of innocent children. And the way you work, you are worth ten, no, a hundred of my men. You will be honored with parades, this time in Riyadh, Jerusalem, Cairo, everywhere. You must stay to help me."

"The system works," I said and patted Dimitris's shoulder. "Because you are the system. You've got this. Like I said, I have big plans."

He didn't look satisfied.

I smiled and pulled the robin's-egg blue box from my pocket. I flipped it open.

The sparkles blinded him. His eyebrows shot up to his hairline.

"Indeed, you do have the most important of plans." He patted my back. "She must be the finest woman in America if she caught your eye. Best of luck, Mr. Jacob."

CHAPTER 5

BRADLEY HOPKINS SURVEYED THE MEETING room deep in the Truman Building. Right off he knew he would be shunted to the corner with the new guys and the interns. Not because of racism—he hadn't encountered any that he could definitively point to in his time at the CIA—but because of his career choices. Switching careers mid-life was a setback. And six years of sobriety hadn't helped him climb the new ladder either. Just like everywhere else, drinking with the boss worked at the Company. An avenue of brown-nosing he actively avoided.

He checked the nameplates. Secretary of State Lincoln Coulter was positioned dead center on the giant surfboard of a table. CIA Director Cynthia Bergstrom would sit across from him, a setup meant to have them square off like prize fighters. If it came to that, Bradley would put his money on Ms. Bergstrom, the director everyone referred to as the Tasmanian Devil for her whirlwind style of leadership. Not that it would come to that. Pads of paper, special pens, and coffee mugs, all with the State Department seal on them, made it clear who owned the meeting.

Bradley made his way downstream from the big Kahunas. His boss, Collin West, sat at the table five chairs down from Director Bergstrom and two chairs from the end. Collin, always an early bird, pored over the agenda and scribbled notes. He pointed his pen at a wire stacking chair against the wall behind him. A direct order about where to sit. Bradley had hoped to be at the table. Not today. He took the seat.

Two clean-cut young men plopped down next to him bragging loudly about the past weekend. Totally awesome, dude.

After exhausting their recollection of what few scenes they could piece together through the drunken haze, one boy turned to Bradley and reached over with an open hand. "Ryan Wheeling, Weapons and Counterproliferation Mission Analyst."

Bradley smiled politely and shook the offered hand. "Bradley Hopkins."

He didn't want to say his title because it was the same as Ryan's. Only Bradley had kids about Ryan's age. And his cube was three away from Ryan's. He suddenly felt small and unaccomplished.

He was spared from further interaction by the arrival of the important people. The meeting began and immediately fell into the monotoned drone of yes-men and yes-women. Bradley nearly fell asleep while they plowed through the first six pages of the agenda. Not even the brightly colored PowerPoints could keep his eyes open. He leaned back in his chair and let his eyelids droop for just a second. In that flash, he saw his former career. In the sun. Wet grass at his feet. Voices all around him, some happy, some concerned, some yelling, some praising. That's what he missed most: everyone working together toward a common goal. His eyes reopened a split-second after he felt his chin dip. Ryan gave him a glance.

If only he hadn't been forced out of that idyllic career. He'd never drifted off in those meetings, not even in his drinking days. Everything was dynamic, every idea considered, every suggestion weighed, every person treated as an equal until proven otherwise.

But staying there hadn't been an option. The CIA was.

"Albania."

It was the word he'd been waiting to hear, and he almost missed it. He strained to listen.

"…years in the pipeline. This is too important to NATO and our allies to let anything mess it up." The woman speaking was two chairs down from the Secretary of State, which made her a big shot. "We need one-hundred-percent buy-in on this for a perfect execution."

"In what parallel universe does this deal make sense?" Bradley had no idea why he'd leapt to his feet and blurted that out. He'd carefully planned his protest—and this was not the plan. Yet here he was.

His boss glowered over his shoulder. The woman speaking stared at him with unadulterated hatred. "And you are?"

"Bradley Hopkins, Weapons and Counterproliferation Mission Analyst," he replied.

Her nameplate read, *Regina Forrest, Assistant Secretary for Political-Military Affairs*. Which was, as her assigned chair indicated, two rungs down from the Secretary. She was under the Under Secretary. She said, "Thank you for that amusing outburst. Moving on. The shipment will leave next week—"

"Pardon me, ma'am," Bradley couldn't stop himself despite diving into career-suicide territory. "We're talking about the most horrific weapons system of the century. Alvaria is like Tolkien's ring—anyone who has it will be tempted into despotism. Imagine, all your critics dispatched at the push of a button. We cannot let this deal go through. Aside from the fact the Albanians have no need for a weapons system this advanced, they simply don't have the security in place to prevent it from falling into the wrong—"

"They have been vetted and assisted. Everything has been triple-checked. We've gone over this many times in the past two years. Sabel Security has been contracted to safeguard the system. Perhaps you missed those meetings. Thank you for your concern. You may sit down. Now."

"You went over it during the previous administration." Bradley felt his boss's eyes ordering him to sit down and shut up. "You were appointed by President Roche. I doubt very much that a professional statesman like President Williams will—"

"That's quite enough." Reggie Forrest slammed a pad of paper on the table for emphasis. "Who appointed me has nothing to do with it. Now sit down and keep quiet or I'll ask security to remove you."

"That won't be necessary." Collin West, his boss, rose between them, facing Forrest, then turned to Bradley and hissed. "Sit the fuck down."

Bradley dropped back in his chair. For a second he thanked the Almighty that most white people couldn't tell when a black man flushed with humiliation. He wanted to crawl under the chair and dig a tunnel back to his office. He'd planned his objection so carefully, but when the time came, he blew it. He never should've brought up her appointment status.

It was only a matter of time before President Williams replaced everyone from the previous administration. Right now, the Senate had a backlog of confirmations for the top jobs. Forrest would remain in place for a few more months. Enough time for her to ruin his life—and national security.

All eyes left him when Secretary Holden made a joke.

Ryan leaned to Bradley's ear. "Dude, I had no idea you could stand up to brass like that. I'm so glad someone around here has balls. Respect."

Bradley slowly turned to the boy who was holding up his forearm for a bump. Bradley obliged despite loathing the gesture. The boy smiled.

His boss wasn't smiling. He passed Bradley a note. "My office, right after."

He was so fired.

Bradley closed his eyes and let the next hour of posturing roll through his mind like the sound of a stream. To keep his sanity, Bradley repeated the serenity prayer drilled into his head from nearly three hundred anonymous meetings, "God, let me accept what cannot be changed; the courage to change what can; and the wisdom to know the difference."

Alvaria was something he could not change. Time to accept it.

Finally, the pain of tedium ended. The meeting adjourned. It was time to pay for his outburst. Bradley stood. Ryan rose at his side.

Director Bergstrom caught his eye between the many shoulders positioning themselves for a quick exit. She was staring right at him. No, not staring—heading straight toward him.

Collin West grabbed Bradley's arm and tugged it, trying to get his attention. He was speaking in a curt, harsh voice, but Bradley couldn't hear it. The Tasmanian Devil was scribbling something on her pad while pushing through the people separating them. For a second, he thought he heard Ryan defending him to the boss, agreeing with his stand against the Alvaria deal.

Director Bergstrom pushed Collin's shoulder, forcing him to face her. "Find someone who can clone this guy, Collin. I need ten more of him by tomorrow. Now leave us. I need a word with him."

The boss and Ryan didn't wait for an explanation. After they managed to close their open mouths, they scurried away.

Director Bergstrom said, "Glad to see someone around here can stand up to Forrest. But a full-frontal assault is a fool's errand, as you've no doubt noticed. She didn't get where she is by letting people challenge her in open meetings. There's someone I know who can be as ruthless and driven as Forrest. Here, call this number. Let this woman handle the problem. It's her personal cell, tell her I sent you. Tell her what's going down. She'll know what we need done. She's young, but she'll be discreet. No need to bruise egos when we can achieve our result quietly."

She tore a strip of paper from her pad, placed it in his palm, spun on a high heel, and zoomed off. He watched her push large men out of her way. Tasmanian Devil indeed. She'd given him a mission. One he wanted.

He glanced down at the strip of paper. The solution to a national security problem was scribbled in blue ink. He choked. It was a name and number he never would've guessed. He blinked several times and read the name again to make sure his eyes weren't playing tricks on him.

Did it have to be her? Anyone but her. Six years ago, he'd sworn he would never speak to the self-centered, overprivileged, arrogant young psychopath again.

But this was critical. The Tasmanian Devil had ordered him to make the call. World peace hung in the balance. Thousands of lives, democratic process, even freedom itself was at stake. He would have to set aside his personal problems and deal with it.

He wandered corridors for twenty minutes before he worked up the courage to dial the number.

She answered on the first ring. He recognized her voice from the two syllables in hello.

He said, "Pia Sabel? Yeah. This is Bradley Hopkins."

He heard the sharp and sudden inhale of shock and guilt and surprise and regret. Then a pause. Followed by a weak and wavering voice that said, "Coach Hopkins?"

CHAPTER 6

IT WAS ALL GIRL TALK from the moment they arrived at the hangar. Ms. Sabel and Jenny stopped long enough to give me hugs, then went right on. Something about shoes and handbags. I smiled and nodded and said, "Those are nice." The only thing *Hermés* meant to me was Mercury's Greek adversary. If a billionaire and the daughter of a billionaire were talking about it, I couldn't afford it. That was all I needed to know.

Which brought up a problem that had worried at the base of my brain since I started dating Jenny Jenkins. We had a significant socio-economic divide between us. Her father founded one of the largest drug cartels … I mean, largest pharmaceutical companies in the world. He was loaded. How Jenny had grown up relatively normal was beyond me. Probably because she'd taken her mother's side in the divorce.

We trotted up the airstair to Sabel One. Despite having grown up in the same social circle, they only started spending time together after I started dating Jenny.

As we taxied out to the runway, Ms. Sabel took a call that turned her white as a sheet. She said, "Coach Hopkins?"

She left us in the forward part of the jet and jogged to her stateroom in the back.

Which left Jenny and me staring at each other across a small table. I didn't mind that one bit. She bit her lip with a quiver and looked out the window. I'm old enough to know there's no sense in asking, "What's wrong?"

I replayed her conversation with Ms. Sabel in my head and realized they'd both been covering anxiety with fashion talk the same way guys bring up sports to avoid serious topics. Like fashion.

I put my hand out, palm up, two inches from hers. A gesture I'd learned from my grandmother who would offer a hand to hold whenever a painful experience pierced my otherwise idyllic childhood.

I always felt a spiritual connection from Jenny's slightest contact. As if our souls combined when we touched. Without looking at me, Jenny's hand slipped into mine as it had after every one of her therapy sessions. The longest handholding always followed the roughest sessions. The sessions dealing with the killing.

"I love that you've accepted me as damaged as I am," she said without facing me.

I squeezed her hand. Her eyes rose and the gaze from her sparkling hazel eyes met mine.

"What did you tell them about me?" she asked.

"The truth. The Navy let the rapist go on a technicality, he came back for more, you shot him in the eye. Because he hadn't been convicted of anything, the all-male tribunal convicted you. Then the president pardoned you. Everyone outside the Navy calls it justifiable, including my family."

Her hand trembled in mine. She tugged it away. "I changed my mind. I don't want to go."

"Jenny, your psychiatrist said you can't hide forever—"

"Screw her."

"They're not important people. Just two farmers right out of American Gothic. Except my father has hair." I put my other hand on top of hers. "This is not an audition. It's not a judgment. Nothing they can say or do will change how I feel about you. Besides, you said you wanted to know more about me and how I managed not to go crazy growing up in Iowa."

Mercury materialized out of thin air in the aisle next to me. *Yeah, dawg. Iowa is not where you went crazy.*

He was right about that. I met Mercury just outside of Baghdad during a certain-death experience I survived because of his guidance. He claims.

I said, *Holy Minerva, could you just give us a minute?*

Mercury likes to tag along when I'm in the company of Caesars, also known as rich people. He hopes one of them will see him, have a Paul-esque conversion, and spend big on new temples that will restore the pantheon to its former glory. He and the rest of the Roman gods have been reduced to panhandling for centuries. They're jealous of the celebrity-induced expansion of Scientology and hope to leverage my exploits into any kind of renewed fame or notoriety.

"You're right," she smiled and shook the anxiety out of her head. "I was giving in to a little jealousy of Pia, that's all." She held up a hand to stop my rebuttal. "I know, I know, they want to show her the renovations. And having her here takes the spotlight off me, so there's nothing to worry about."

"Right."

Her glowing, mischievous smile returned and lit up the cabin. "That's what I love about you, Jacob. You think of everything to protect my recovery."

We gazed at each other like love birds.

"Before we take this relationship any further, though," she said, "I need to get my career back on track. I need to work. That's the right way to proceed. Renormalize."

I turned to Mercury, *Did she just say, 'before we take this relationship any further?'*

Mercury said, *That's what I heard.*

Damn, I said. *She's right. Those should be her priorities.*

My fingers rolled over the ring box in the pocket of my bomber jacket. Somewhere in my deranged mind, I'd conjured up an image of kneeling in the aisle and popping the big question. My fantasy included champagne and flowers and glitter from heaven, followed by introducing her to my parents as my fiancé, not just another girlfriend. My dream was about to get sucked into the jet engine where the intake blades would slice it into paper-thin strips before the inferno in the combustion chamber vaporized it and spat it out through the high-pressure turbines, leaving nothing but a trail of smoke behind us.

Mercury said, *Dude, what's with the melodrama?*

I said, *I thought her next step would involve me. Why doesn't she see me as the next step in re-normal? Whatever that means.*

Mercury sprawled on the couch, eating grapes and talking with his mouth full. *Cuz there ain't nothing normal about you. She likes you in bed. She's not so hot about you afterwards. Ever notice that? Yeah, you want her to take you seriously, you need to be a Caesar. Mister Big, like her daddy and her mommy. Right now, you're just a boy-toy, she cuddles up in private but doesn't know you in public. Like that time her mom invited you over for dinner and then Jenny cancelled?*

I said, *Why are you trying to shake my confidence? Besides, her mom is the Vice President of the United States. She got called into an important meeting ... probably.* I thought for a moment. *Didn't she?*

Ms. Sabel's voice rose from the other side of the stateroom door. She was on her third call and pissed at someone about something.

"Will she be in there long?" Jenny winked. Then she tilted her head toward the couch. "Are you an eight-miler?"

"A what?"

I figured out what she meant the second after I asked. I'd just revealed my lack of private-jet sophistication. Private planes fly higher than commercial, often around forty thousand feet, just shy of eight miles high. And Jenny loves risky sex. I love sex, but not getting caught. On a company jet. By my boss. Who considers me the brother she never had.

Jenny tugged my hand. "C'mon. You're not afraid of *La Tigresa*, are you?"

She referred to Ms. Sabel by the name the Mexican National team gave her early in her soccer career. Suddenly, the eight-miler club sounded like an organization I should join.

We moved from the chairs to the couch, landing in a heap of entangled limbs.

"Jacob," Ms. Sabel called from the back, "I need you."

My head popped up automatically. I looked over my shoulder. The door was open, but she wasn't standing in it. She hadn't seen us. Yet.

Jenny put her fingers in my hair and pulled me back into a kiss I couldn't refuse.

"Jacob?" Ms. Sabel again.

I pushed back and gazed at one seriously disappointed girlfriend. I said, "I'm on duty. This is a working trip."

"You're choosing her over me?" She looked serious. I started to laugh it off when she scowled. Dead serious. Her doctor had warned me about sudden jealousies.

I shrugged. "Uh. Yeah. She's the boss."

"When are we going to have some time for just the two of us? No one else."

Apparently, the two weeks Ms. Sabel let us joyride on her superyacht were not enough for Ms. Jenkins. Maybe Mercury was right—she didn't want to be seen with me in public. Did I embarrass her, as Mercury implied? No, we'd spent a week working the front lines at the homeless charity together. A great experience that revealed her empathetic side. She'd even posed with me for both publicity pictures. Maybe she was used to trust-fund boys who didn't have to get up in the morning. Nah, she'd once had a promising career as a Naval officer. She knew the meaning of work.

I gave her my I'll-be-right-back look and pushed off and jogged down the aisle.

Ms. Sabel met my gaze as soon as I entered the cabin. Her eyes slid up to my tousled hair, then to my cheek. I remembered Jenny had been wearing lipstick. Movie-star red. I felt myself blush.

"Something's come up," Ms. Sabel said. She pointed to the frantic spread of handwritten notes scattered across the bed. Strands of hair had escaped her usually tight ponytail. Her eyes bounced around the room. She said, "Catherine called. Oh, uh, Catherine De Bolle, head of Europol. Your friend Nate is helping them identify the arms dealers linked to Frieden, but his knowledge of the players only goes so high up. They think this Ra character is someone I know. There's something strategically important at stake here. I need you for this. I can't trust anyone else."

I hesitated before asking, "Are we still having dinner with my folks?"

CHAPTER 7

WE ARRIVED AT MY CHILDHOOD home just in time for dinner. Jenny and Ms. Sabel took it in as if they were entering a museum called "How the Little People Live." It was a plain-vanilla farmhouse with a large porch crossing the entire face, the main entrance dead center, a row of windows on either side, two main floors, and gabled windows in the attic. Various barns and sheds surrounded the brick-paved farmyard on the north side. As we stepped out of Iowa City's only available limo, a massive green machine pulled in from the north forty and parked in front of the machine shed.

My sister Joyce climbed out of a John Deere cab, leaving the hay baler attached. It must've killed her to come in for dinner in the middle of haying season. Autumn days like these called for eighteen-hour shifts, whether your brother comes home or not. There could be an unpredicted rain and whole fields lost. I expected her to be pissed and brusque. Instead, she took off her gloves and met us with a giant smile I found puzzling.

My mother called us inside.

That call on the jet had upset Ms. Sabel like few things I'd ever seen before. There was more to that call than she'd told me. We resolved to spend some quality time with Mom and Dad; we'd worry about the rest of the world when we got back to DC. She managed to set aside all her tension and she greeted my parents with hugs and air-kisses.

Joyce tracked around the bottleneck of formalities at the front door and shoulder-bumped me. She pointed to her tractor. "Wanna see the new Starfire and AutoTrac on that sucker?"

No one loves farm life more than Joyce. I was pretty sure she was talking about satellite guided plowing systems that let her ride along using only a joystick for adjustments. I said, "Let's have dinner first. I missed lunch."

"C'mon." She tugged my arm. "I gotta tell you something."

Mom tugged me the other way and wrapped me up in a hug that she held for a while. Joyce shrugged and slipped by. Dad shook my hand and patted my shoulder.

Mom served wine and cheese in the parlor. Louis Kirby—Joyce's main squeeze for over a year—joined us. After introductions, Sheriff Kirby took a position in the archway between the parlor and the dining room and coughed. Joyce hopped up next to him with a smile good enough for a toothpaste ad.

"We have a little announcement," Louis said.

Joyce dug around in her jeans until she found something. She held out a ring. "We're ENGAGED!"

Mercury squeezed into the nonexistent space next to me. *Does she always take the wind out of your sails, homie? Didn't she throw her last engagement party the same day you were given the Distinguished Service Cross? Whatever happened to that fiancé anyway?*

It took me a while to answer since I'd lost my breath along with my ability to think. *The guy figured out she's her own solar system. Everyone revolves around Joyce. He fled the county. Damn it, I feel like jumping up and yelling at her for raining on my almost-parade, even though she had no way of knowing my plans.*

Mercury said, *You lost your opportunity on the jet, bro. Now you can't ask Jenny on this trip or you'll sound like a sad little brother trying to even up a sibling rivalry.*

I said, *She should've known I was coming home to get engaged.*

Mercury offered me a plate of cheddar and Ritz crackers. *Dude. Why do you think she pushed Louis to give her the ring today instead of next week or month or year?*

We cheered and toasted and hugged and oohed over the ring. A full carat smaller than mine. At least I had that. When the smiles began to strain, we moved to the dining room.

Dad and I found ourselves at the back end of the parade. I whispered to him, "What do you think of Jenny?"

He stopped and turned me by my elbow. "You're not serious about her, are you, son?"

"I'm getting there. Thinking about her more."

"She's the kind would leave you first drought comes along." He walked into the dining room.

Echoes of the Dust Bowl haunted generations of farmers. Some couples had pulled together and toughed it out. Others split up and searched for greener pastures. In terms of my father's farm-speak, few assessments were as damning. But I could change his mind. He'd see.

Mom had gone all out for her special guests using great-grandmother's silver service, a collection of pieces from various families. White linens and crystal goblets adorned the table. Stuff we hadn't used since the Queen of England's last visit.

Mom asked Jenny, "What do you do?"

"In the Navy, I handled high security recovery. Like, when a special encryption device needs to be recovered, I led the team."

"Does the Navy lose a lot of those?"

"Never. But other countries lose things all the time. My team was there to help the US recover things."

Since no one wanted to ask if the Navy would have her back, the conversation dropped into an awkward lull. Jenny filled it by asking my mother, "Were you two high school sweethearts?"

"Oh no," Mom said. "We knew of each other, small town and all. But we didn't travel in the same circles until we worked the same clubs."

"You were a waitress?" Jenny asked, her voice tainted with disbelief.

"Jazz musicians. We ended up in the same band."

"Let me guess—you were the lead singer."

Mom put her hand on Jenny's forearm. "Honey, I'm a tub-kicker."

Knowing laughs went around the table. Jenny and Ms. Sabel looked confused.

"Drummer," I said. "Mom can kick ass on skins."

I took a big gulp of wine and prayed to Vesta my parents wouldn't dive into their long-closeted pipe dream of reviving the *Stearne Family Quartet* with Joyce on trumpet and me on sax. So embarrassing.

Especially the photo album. What happened in Dubuque should stay in Dubuque.

"Why did you go into farming?" Jenny asked.

"No choice after we were busted for smuggling dope."

Wine spewed out across my dinner plate. I blurted, "Busted for wha…?"

"New Orleans fuzz were on us like white on rice. Couldn't breathe." Mom, Dad, and Joyce all looked at me as if I'd forgotten how to count. Mom said, "We never told you about that?"

I mopped up the wine and poured salt on the stains.

Ms. Sabel steered the conversation in a new direction. "How long have you been married?"

When they gave her the answer, I could see her subtracting Joyce's age and coming up with four childless years. "Why wait so long?"

"You need to sow your wild oats before you plant them in rows," Dad said. "We got around a bit. Had some fun before settling into the quiet life. Experiences can hold a marriage together forever."

Mercury appeared at my elbow with a wine bottle and topped up my glass. *Don't ask about the orgies at the Montreal Jazz Fest, homeboy. There are some secrets your parents get to keep forever.*

Yeah, I said slowly. *Ima take your advice on that one.*

Jenny stared at the flowers in the center of the table and said, "Marriage is terrible. It never works out. It's what philosopher's call the Lover's Paradox—despite our intentions, intimacy can't occur without considerable mutual harm. Everyone gets excited about the great big party and the honeymoon, but then it always turns into boredom and betrayal and estrangement before it devolves into a nasty divorce. Then you have to pick sides."

Everyone but Jenny traded furtive glances. We hoped one of us would say something witty to fix it. Jenny kept her gaze on the tablecloth in front of her, oblivious to her transgression.

Dad tried. "Well, we made it work somehow."

"Yeah." Jenny's voice sounded distant. "But you're way out here in the middle of nowhere with nothing else to do."

Another long, painfully awkward silence followed. Then Jenny's head snapped up, her gaze bounded around the table, suddenly aware of what she'd said.

"You've brought us a marvelous wine, Pia," Mom said in the most cheerful voice possible. "Thank you. Where did you get ... Oh, I see, it says Sabel Vineyards right on the label. I didn't know you had a winery."

Ms. Sabel looked at her with a gaze full of astonishment. "Neither did I. I just asked my sommelier to put a case of something nice on the jet just before ... um. You're welcome."

She blushed.

Joyce and Louis began clearing plates while the rest of us sat dumbfounded and wondering how to bridge the wealth-divide and the marriage-divide without digging up new divides.

No one wanted dessert. Louis decided he should check on his deputies and Joyce wanted to roll up some more bales while there was still moonlight. Mom and Dad insisted they didn't need help with the dishes. I led Jenny and Ms. Sabel to our bedrooms.

Ms. Sabel stepped into my room and hugged me while Jenny watched. "I'm so sorry. I had no idea about the winery. The properties division keeps buying ..." She caught a glimpse of Jenny weighing a far more egregious faux pas against her own lack of self-awareness. "Yeah. Well. Tomorrow's another day. It'll get better. I'll let you guys work it out."

Mercury said, *How many wineries do you have, bro? Have you lost count? Sheeit.*

I said, *She didn't mean it like that.*

Mercury said, *Says it, means it. She has so much money she doesn't know what she's doing with it. Why don't you have a winery? You do all the work and yet you fly in her jets. Izzat fair?*

Ms. Sabel backed up a step and patted my chest with sympathy. When Jenny wouldn't make eye contact, she said good night and left.

Jenny stood at the window staring out at the blackness. In the distance, the rack of lights on Joyce's tractor lit up a few acres of hay. She said, "I'm sorry if I embarrassed you. I just think marriage is a sham."

The ring in my pocket felt like a ten-pound river rock. I slipped my arms around her and rested my chin on her shoulder. "Maybe your parents weren't the best role models."

"Dad used his money to buy our loyalty. Everything was a transaction. Want to stay in private school? Tell your mother you're having Thanksgiving with me. Everything involved an anti-mom response."

"Marriage can be a great institution," I said. "A commitment between two people in front of their community and their gods."

I felt her tense in my arms. Every muscle twitched into defensive readiness. "Did you say gods, plural?"

"Slip of the tongue. A commitment between two people and their community—"

She spun in my arms and pressed her hands lightly against my chest. "Is it true? Those things people say about you having some kinda weird religion-thing?"

"We're talking about marriage. Let's stay focused on that." I pulled my hands away, unintentionally expressing a little frustration.

Mercury stood behind her looking shocked. *You haven't told her about me, your personal god and savior?*

I said, *I'm going to. Getting there. This might not be the best time.*

Mercury said, *I am so disappointed. I can't even.*

"What good does it do? It's just a piece of paper." She backed up a step. "Smaller than the prenup by four hundred pages. And don't think about getting married without one of those these days. I'm not talking millionaires here; I'm talking working class too. Things might be all well and good for a few years, then you split up and who gets the 401(k)?"

"OK, slow down." I circled my hands around her waist. "I only went to the therapy sessions that dealt with our relationship. I missed the ones that deal with your perspective on marriage. I'm guessing your father is at the heart of your distrust. Tell me about that."

"He was a cheater. Mom was a captain back then. He had girls coming and going from our house whenever Mom shipped out." She squeezed me harder. "That's why I get a little jealous sometimes."

I turned to Mercury, *Should I mention she looks a lot more like General Thompson than Bobby Jenkins and that her mom and the general served at the Pentagon together for a year before she was conceived?*

Mercury tiptoed toward the door. *Hey homie, I'm gonna come back when you stop dating the wacko-chicks. Remember Yumi, the cop who couldn't handle violence? And Sylvia, currently serving time for art fraud? You really know how to pick 'em. Jenny here's got a lot more problems than you can fix. And those problems are going to get a lot bigger in two minutes.*

I said, *I feel something different with her. Sure, she's damaged. Aren't we all? I can bring her around on marriage. It'll take time, but she's worth it. Why, what's going to happen in two minutes?*

Mercury pulled the door open. *Did I say two minutes? I meant right now.*

Ms. Sabel stood in my doorway. "We have to leave. A sniper just shot and killed Dimitris Bakakis and Nate Hale."

CHAPTER 8

THE MAN THEY CALL RA looked up from the desk in the *Savannah's* stateroom when he heard the ship's tender approaching from Monaco's harbor. Springing to his feet with verve he hadn't felt since his youth, he spun down the spiral staircase to the main lounge. Sure, there were many more contracts and reports to read, but his darling had been gone all day and he simply had to feel her embrace. He had to steal these tender moments when Bonham and the guys weren't around to see him melt like butter.

He stopped in the hallway and checked himself in the mirror. After running his fingers through his salt-and-pepper hair, he tugged his tropical shirt straight. He brushed off a speck of lint and smoothed his white slacks.

She climbed the stairs from the sport deck with a big floppy hat and sunglasses covering her beautiful face. She carried only one bag. An all-day excursion in Monaco and only one bag? For months they'd been an item and she still didn't take advantage of his credit card. He liked that in a way, but he would rather she spent wildly on herself. He liked having her dependent on him for the stuff of life.

She rose to his level, her perfect posture never straining.

When she didn't greet him, he said, "Darling, how good to see you again after all these hours."

He reached around her and pulled her in. She hesitated for a moment then leaned into his embrace. Her sunglasses brushed his chin when she rose on her tiptoes to kiss his cheek.

Something was off.

"All those shops, all that time, and only this?" He peeked in the bag.

"A pair of comfy house shoes? They're too small. Oh. For your mother."

He admired her family bonds. She would never accept gifts from him that would put her in his debt. He bought her clothes that she would wear then later put away as if they belonged to someone else. As if she'd only borrowed them. But she would lavish his money on her mother. The assisted-living facility he provided cost every bit as much as any other girl's shopping splurges. Indeed, he realized, that was what he loved about her. That she put her mother first.

One day he would get her to put him first. Before all others.

"What is it you do?" She pulled out of his arms and tossed her sunglasses and hat on the side table with attitude.

"You know what I do." He circled around her with a question on his face. "Commodities trading and finance. Large scale. Why? What is it? Something's happened since breakfast."

"Why you have violent men for bodyguard?" Her light Japanese accent flared when she was angry.

"There are violent men in the world, my dear. I don't want anything to happen to you." He followed her into the lounge. "Did one of them hurt you?"

"No." She folded her arms and gave him a wicked glare. "Fido beat up Roma boy."

Had anyone else complained about the man he called Fido he would've snapped her neck. Yet his chest felt hollow and his blood cooled, and he felt something he'd rarely felt in his life: remorse. He hated letting that emotion into his being.

She didn't blink. She didn't move.

"It's time for cocktails." He coughed and gave her a smile she didn't return. "Bonham and his girls will be over for dinner shortly. Let's have apple martinis while you tell me what happened."

He snapped his fingers at the unseen staff. A steward appeared and took his order and disappeared. He gestured to the sofa and took his place. She left a space and a chill between them.

The steward appeared with their martinis seconds later. He raised his glass to her. She set hers on the table without a sip.

"A Roma boy asked for money." She held his gaze. "I started to open purse for a few euros. The boy reached for the purse. I was detective. I know purse-snatcher. No problem for me. I pulled the purse back. But Fido grabbed his arm, twisted him away, and smashed fist to his face. Many times. Unnecessary. Then stomp his ribs and yell at me when I pull him off boy."

The man they call Ra hired bodyguards such as Fido to do exactly that kind of thing. In his world, sending a message was more important than preventing a crime or seeking justice. A reputation like his must be maintained. Everyone had to know he would never allow his woman to be trifled with. Yet her disapproval cut him to the bone. He should laugh at himself for being so enamored as to acquiesce to her concerns. And yet he knew he would do what she wanted. He said, "I will speak to him. He should never raise his voice to you."

"What do you do really? Why you need such violent men?"

"You've seen my ledgers. You know what I do." He sipped his martini. He didn't care that it was a froufrou drink Bonham and his men would laugh at. The older he got, the more he liked sweet, light drinks. To hell with what any of them thought. "I take care of the little guys. Those repressed by sanctions and left without a champion. I ship them grain and oil and lumber. Whatever they need behind the new iron curtain of international sanctions. It's not their fault some dictator hundreds of miles away offended some prime minister thousands of miles away. They still need to feed their children and drive their cars. I finance those deals. I end up in some pretty rough places where the bandits and the government are indistinguishable. Strong protection is a necessity."

She picked up her drink and sipped.

"I'll have a word with Fido," he said. "If he ever raises his voice to you or disappoints you, he's gone."

She looked pacified, not satisfied.

"How is your mother?" he asked.

"She does not know me when I call."

"Believe me, darling, I find that the saddest thing imaginable. I trust the specialists I paid for are doing their best."

She moved closer to him on the sofa and took his hand. "We thank you. You are most generous."

She pecked his cheek and snuggled under his chin. When he felt her body close to his, he felt whole. If he believed in such a thing, he would call it a spiritual link. They stayed curled up together while they finished their drinks. Then she went to change. He felt a loss when she walked away, like part of him had been torn off.

He sent for Fido and waited by the railing. The sun was setting and the lights beneath his yacht came on, illuminating the sea beneath him. He looked across the waters at the other yachts. The *Numina* was anchored half a mile east of him. He seethed with jealousy having lost his bid for it just a few weeks earlier.

Denied. That chafed him more than any insult in years.

His yacht, the *Savannah*, might appeal to some. But it was over a hundred feet shorter and lacked a helipad. To the west, a row of Saudi and Russian yachts vied to compete with the *Numina* for bragging rights. A contest the *Numina* easily won. Only twenty ships could best the *Numina*, and most of those only in length, not fittings. He wondered when the new owner would throw a party. There had to be a party to show it off. Invitations to that party would be the ticket of the season.

"You wanted to see me, sir?" Fido asked. Backlit by the salon behind him, the behemoth waited with his hands folded in front of him.

Shorter than average and slender, the man they call Ra never found size to be intimidating. He pointed to the deck in front of him and waited until Fido stepped into his assigned space. He looked up into the bodyguard's face, pointed over the railing, and snarled, "I don't care that you beat a Roma half to death, but if you ever rebuke my darling again, I'll do to you what I did to Hollins. Do you know what I did to Hollins?"

Fido swallowed hard. "Yes, sir."

"Tell me, I want to hear you say it."

Fido cleared his throat before answering. "You cut off his cock and balls and threw them to the fish while he watched."

CHAPTER 9

MS. SABEL'S ANNOUNCEMENT CRUSHED ME.

"They were in the prosecutor's office," she said, "behind closed doors. Theoretically, no one knew Hale was in the building. The sniper fired from four buildings away. Whoever hired him intended to send a message. A big message."

Ms. Sabel explained the travel complications to Jenny while I shoved things in my duffel.

Nate's prediction had happened. My mind replayed Dimitris's plea for help bringing down Ra. Nate's desperate face begged me for a head start. I'd heard the arrogance in Konrad's voice. I'd misjudged the power and reach of the enemy. I'd thought only of my personal issues. Nate's death was on my hands. My blood oath just became real.

I'd sworn to take down Ra should the system fail.

Mercury tossed my phone charger in the bag. *They picked the wrong people, homes. Retribution is your middle name. Whenever justice needs a champion, you are there. Saving the world is what you do.*

I looked him over. *Could you tone it down a notch? I'm not a fan of high expectations.*

Dude! Mercury looked at me like I'd slapped a baby. *You have god on your side. Don't be afraid of no expectations.*

I shook my head, hoping he'd go away, and started thinking. Killing Konrad von-whatever was my first stop on the road to bringing them all down. I was good to go. Nothing else needed to be said. Nothing else needed to be considered.

Until I saw Jenny's face.

We trudged down the hall, down the stairs, and crossed the living room. Jenny complained bitterly with every step. I didn't understand her problem. She'd been a loyal naval officer not so long ago. As such, she should instinctively understand the justice demanded by the dead. We reached the front door.

"You're going with her? And leaving me?" Lots of emphasis on the trailing pronouns. Jenny stood on the porch next to my mother with a glare that could've melted the rest of Greenland.

I tried one last time. "Sabel One only has a secure data line for the main cabin's flat screen. You have neither the clearance nor the need-to-know to see whatever it is they're going to show us. You can't be on the jet. I don't make the rules. I'm sorry."

"You said that," she snipped.

"We're not going back to DC."

"You said that too."

Mom put an arm around my girlfriend while giving me the stink eye. Jenny leaned into Mom's shoulder. Despite her outburst on marriage, my parents now had two daughters and no son. Apparently.

I stepped up to give Jenny a kiss, she turned her face. After a moment's hesitation, I kissed her cheek.

Dad handed me my duffel. I took it, and we exchanged nods.

I trotted down the steps to Ms. Sabel and the limo. We got in and buckled up in silence. Then she said, "Sorry."

"Not your fault." I sighed. "She has AAD, Adult Attachment Disorder, as a result of her Rape Trauma Syndrome. Still in a vulnerable state. But she'll survive and Nate didn't."

"You didn't fail Nate," Ms. Sabel said. "The system failed to protect them. We're the backup to the system, the failsafe."

She didn't know about my blood oath to Nate.

Once in the air, Ms. Sabel connected the secure line to Langley. The big screen rose out of the credenza. We sat and waited while the screen flashed protocols and asked for facial recognition. We faced the camera, then turned to the side, like thugs getting mug shots, so the system could check our ear cartilage.

The face of a middle-aged man appeared. An onscreen ID named him as Bradley Hopkins, CIA. He wore an inexpensive suit and had a sun-dried face with a lot of gray in his hi-lo fade. He had a passing resemblance to Malcom X without the megawatt smile. He nodded at us and started to speak.

Ms. Sabel cut him off. "Coach, I mean, Mr. Hopkins, this must have been a difficult call for you. I appreciate the trust you put in me—"

"Not my idea." His expression didn't change. "Ms. Bergstrom's orders, ma'am. Leave it there."

"OK." She folded her hands in her lap.

I didn't need to glance her way to know Ms. Sabel didn't want to leave it there.

He introduced himself and his "mission" within the CIA. "My specialty is advanced weapons systems, who should get them, and who should know they exist. The companies that develop new systems want to profit from their research immediately by selling them to everyone with money. But our country doesn't want to face some of these systems across a battlefield, so there is always a tug of war going on between government and industry."

"Profit versus national security," Ms. Sabel said.

"Capitalism produces both growth and entropy," he said. "As I'm sure you're aware, manufacturers constantly influence administrations and Congress to allow international sales. These are the ordinary market forces that my mission is directed to analyze and assess. I am tasked with evaluating each weapon system for its potential and comparing that to the government at the intended destination. Will they be good stewards of a deadly technology? As a hypothetical example: if someone should promote it, I would be the guy to advise against stockpiling nuclear weapons in an American-controlled military base in Libya. The country is not stable. The government cannot control the population well enough to guarantee the safety of our weapons."

"So," I said, "someone is trying to sell nuclear weapons to an unstable country?"

"Something worse than nuclear weapons," he said.

"Worse?" I noticed Ms. Sabel wasn't shocked by his statement. She'd heard this presentation before.

"Weapons of mass destruction that harm civilian populations invite the wrath of the entire world. No one has used a nuclear weapon since the pictures of Hiroshima's victims circulated seventy-five years ago."

"So, what's worse?"

"This is the part where I remind you that divulging what you're about to hear to anyone unauthorized can and most likely will result in a death sentence. Should you divulge this information to unauthorized persons while overseas, that death penalty could be executed swiftly and with extreme prejudice."

He'd just given me the federal version of a death threat. His was the real-world version of the old joke, "I could tell you, but then I'd have to kill you." I nodded my acceptance of his terms.

I asked, "Who's the manufacturer?"

"I am not cleared to know that." He hesitated before explaining. "Spies like to get jobs emptying trash cans in top-secret labs. To cut down on that, the companies involved are kept on a separate security level. To do my job, and the job Sabel Security has been engaged to do, we only need to know what it looks like."

"We understand," Ms. Sabel said.

Bradley Hopkins continued his presentation. An engineering video full of diagrams replaced him on the screen. The drawings showed aircraft with folding wings and a jet engine intake encircling the entire fuselage at the rear. No cockpit.

"Autonomous drone swarms." He paused while I digested the phrase. "Alvaria is a swarm of one to five hundred small drones, controlled by collective processing, each capable of destroying everything in one hundred cubic feet around the target. Targeting can be done by facial recognition, in light or dark, and through standard walls. You can add license plates, several known addresses, even friends and relatives with whom your target may associate. It has a range of two hundred miles, and once launched, they're completely autonomous."

I visualized a hundred cubic feet, roughly the interior space of a passenger car. The target and anyone within an arm's reach of him. "Mechanized assassination?"

"It can be used for that," Hopkins said. "In case you missed the term 'collective processing,' that means a hundred drones each with the processing power of a mobile phone, sharing their processing power for exponentially increased capacity and redundancy. If you shoot down one drone, ninety-nine more keep coming. Shoot down another, and the collective, the hive-mind, recognizes the problem and dispatches five or ten drones to eliminate the threat against the main body. If you're the target—"

"Ginsberg's Law of Thermodynamics," I said. "You can't win, you can't break even, and you can't get out of the game."

"Exactly." Bradley Hopkins's expression turned a deeper shade of grave. "Imagine a despotic leader in Kazakhstan, Turkey or Algeria, fearing his ouster, sending out a drone swarm to attack the opposition leadership. Or a prime minister, angry with the free press, sending a drone swarm to annihilate a hundred reporters he didn't like."

He went silent for a moment while he clicked his mouse. "Let me show you the system in action."

A video took over the screen. It showed a man holding a drone slightly larger than a radio-controlled model plane. The wingspan was a foot shorter than his arms stretched out to either side. He folded the wings into the body, leaving the two rudders of the V-tail exposed, and snapped it onto a metal rod ten feet long. The rod was one of ten. Each held a drone. He backed up and displayed a tablet. The picture of a radio-controlled car appeared. The software drew boxes around it, marking and labeling "Unique Identifying Characteristics." When it was done, the software put up a yellow box with boldfaced letters inside, "Target Identified." The operator chose the option to "Destroy." Then he pressed a different button on the tablet. All ten drones shot into the air. Their wings unfolded as they reached speed and altitude. He tossed the tablet on the ground and smashed it with a hammer to prove he wasn't controlling the drones.

He then picked up a remote control for a car the size of a child's wagon. In the background, the drones banked right and separated. They stayed low and went around buildings in the distance. The man sent the car across the large field in front of him, he zigged it left and right as the drones came in from half a mile away. He stopped and started and turned the car, but the drones kept coming. He drove it into a small bunker.

Carrot-sized missiles burst from two drones. The bunker was destroyed. The car came out the other side and went behind a wall. The wall was destroyed. The car kept running.

Then the swarm locked on the car. The drones zeroed in on the target from five different directions at once. A hail of explosions vaporized the small vehicle. When the smoke and dust cleared, only a hole in the ground remained. The drones collected into a V formation and swung around the field as if doing a victory lap. One by one, they peeled off and came in for a soft landing on the grass at the man's feet.

The video stopped and Bradley came back on, as still as a stone carving. He asked, "Scary enough?"

"Enough." I nodded. "But what does this have to do with Konrad von Frieden?"

His glance slid to Ms. Sabel with an unspoken question. She squirmed.

"This is about national security," she said. "Frieden is a separate issue."

"Who is Frieden?" Bradley looked displeased. "Where does he fit in?"

His question and Ms. Sabel's attempt to cut off the conversation told me we were two steps ahead of the CIA and Europol. The Company was searching for arms dealers interested in Alvaria while Europol was interested in the specific dealers most likely to be involved. She wanted to keep those agencies separate to preserve the integrity of her search for Ra.

I understood Ms. Sabel's thinking. I said to Bradley, "Sorry, I confused topics. What is our mission here?"

"Weapons sales take years to develop and entail a lot of politics." He relaxed a little. "Years of planning, ambassadors, trade deals, senators, and CEOs are all involved. Undoing a deal could mean quashing hundreds of jobs, destroying local economies, all kinds of blowback."

"And?" I asked.

"This deal was a fait accompli before someone put it on my desk." He sighed. "Someone, in his or her infinite wisdom, decided to sell the most dangerous technology of the century to the Albanians."

"What's wrong with them?" I asked. "Low corruption, NATO member, nice people."

"Tiny police force, non-existent military, unsophisticated security, per capita income of $12,000, and has been trying to get into the EU for ten years."

"Ripe for theft," I observed.

"A single operating Alvaria System represents $10 billion in research and development. But that's all early costs, software, controllers, and engineering. That rack you saw? The drones cost a couple thousand each."

The implications were obvious. On the black market, Alvaria could fetch millions and tip the balance of world power. Of the twenty-nine NATO members, Albania was one of the smallest five. Pirating the system could increase the entire country's GDP by twenty percent overnight.

"I can't stop the deal," Bradley continued. "I'm just an analyst who recommended killing it. Despite the obvious flaws, smarter people than me have signed off on it. It's going through. A few days ago, NSA picked up some SIGINT about an auction for Alvaria. It hasn't even shipped yet, but people expect it to be on the black market soon."

Ms. Sabel said, "I have a team of people heading to Tirana to help secure the delivery. We will establish the best security possible."

"You damn well better." He looked hard as a rock again. "But that's between you and the State Department. They're hiring Sabel Security for that end. What the CIA requires of you is to find out who thinks they're going to steal the drones."

"We can do that," I said. "So can you."

"The Company has … complications and can't engage on this one," he said. "It would embarrass our NATO ally—I'm told."

We contemplated that for a moment. Then Bradley asked, "Who is Konrad von Frieden?"

I waited for Ms. Sabel to take that one since she'd shut me up last time. She said, "An arms dealer."

"That guy out of Corfu?" Bradley asked. "Too small a player for this deal."

We didn't respond.

"Alright then." He didn't take his hard gaze off Ms. Sabel. She looked at her hands. "Let me know when you've identified the auction's bidders. Don't take any action—the CIA will decide how to handle it. Let me be clear about that. You are only to identify the parties involved. Report in the minute you have them. Are we clear?"

"As day," I said.

Ms. Sabel sat up suddenly. "Coach, before we go—"

"Call me Bradley."

"OK, Bradley. I have to say something. I, um." She huffed. "I've thought a lot about what happened and ... I'm sorry. I hope you've forgiven me."

He drummed his fingers on the desk, then reached for the mouse to end the call. "We're done here."

The screen went blank.

I pointed at the screen, working out a nice way of asking what that last bit was about when she cut me off.

"I need you on this job. It won't be easy."

I faced her. "No problem."

She clearly believed the two missions—my intent to destroy whoever killed Nate and the CIA's interest in an auction for a scary weapon—dovetailed nicely. She thought she was using me. Which she was, but I didn't mind. The CIA's problem would finance my search for Nate's killers.

I pointed to the blank screen. "Something you want to tell me about Hopkins?"

She got up and strode to the stateroom. "No."

CHAPTER 10

DUANE BOYD WAS SHORT, BALD, and wore a wrinkled suit as he rose from behind a cheap desk in the basement of Interpol's international headquarters in Lyon, France. And he was American. I wasn't expecting that. He was the kind of guy who talked louder than anyone else and slapped your shoulder when he shook your hand.

"Count me as a Jacob Stearne cheerleader. I'm a big fan, big fan." He slapped my shoulder again. Then he looked at Ms. Sabel. "You too. Not only am I a huge fan, so is my oldest. I can't believe you quit the beautiful game when you did. You could still take the field and kick ass. You could beat Mia Hamm's record for assists in a couple more games. Maybe catch up with Abby Wambach on goals. Are you going back? Will you? Please?"

"I'd love to," she said. "I thought about it right up until my father died. But then I inherited some big responsibilities, so … not happening."

"Are you ever going to talk about why you left?"

"No."

Her curt answer wiped the jovial smile off his face.

He turned to me out of embarrassment. "So, what can Interpol do for you?"

I said, "I'm looking for background on Baron Konrad von Frieden."

His smile turned into a frown. "You already found him. Everyone knows that. Dimitris Bakakis put a full report in our databases before he was murdered. Every cop with a Mediterranean beat asked for a copy."

"The Greeks released Frieden after the shooting."

Duane Boyd stroked his chin and looked me over for a long time. He motioned to the chairs in front of his desk and tracked around to his side. He said, "First off, Konrad's title is bullshit. The Austrians abolished titles after World War I. He might have a pedigree, he might not. There are claimants to titles who have actual properties and land they can trace back a century, and they say Frieden's an imposter."

"He had a huge house on Corfu," Ms. Sabel said.

"I didn't say he wasn't born rich. He was. He went to all the best schools in Europe and America, then discovered his parents had blown his inheritance by the time he was thirty-something. The only thing they left him was a shipping company. He stuffed the ships full of small arms, pistols and rifles, and took them to embargoed countries like Iran and Iraq. In a few years, he was back in the green. He's been on my radar for a long time. But he is slick. Shell companies and trading partners. No one ever caught him. Then he sold rifles to those neo-Nazis you destroyed— for which the world thanks you, Mr. Stearne—and the rest you know."

He spread his hands, then slapped them down on the desktop as if to say, adjourned.

"Where is he now?" I asked.

"Despite what you see on TV, Interpol is not a police force or an intelligence agency. We don't have cops in uniform or special agents like the FBI. We're a central database for every country in the world, even Vatican City. Police units send their most-wanted lists and look-out-for lists to us and we disseminate them. We categorize by crime, like terrorism or fraud or cybercrime. I am what's left of the arms trafficking group. This is my file on Konrad von Frieden."

He plopped a manila folder on the desk. Inside were three sheets of a paper. One was a standardized form. The other two were handwritten notes.

I scanned them.

"These notes look like they were taken from that documentary—"

"*Killing Tradition: The Arming of Africa.* Yes, that's my handwriting. I hoped someday someone might care. But that's all ancient history. Frieden has been at it a long time."

"You said you're what's left?" Ms. Sabel asked.

"When I started here fifteen years ago, there were twenty-three of us working hard on the fifth floor in a large office. Then, the biggest arms dealer in the world—who also provides more than half Interpol's budget—decided we were far too proactive. We'd alerted a few nations to arms sales in progress, and the deals were quashed. Someone somewhere believed in letting markets ebb and flow because they'll self-correct. That's like defunding the fire department and letting the flames self-correct. Eventually, when all the buildings are reduced to ashes, they'll run out of flammable materials." He rolled his eyes. "Anyway. They moved me to the basement. I was grateful. I have a wife and kids. I needed the job. So. Is there anything else you want?"

We sat in stunned silence. We didn't need to ask which country requested the defunding. The USA sells more weapons than the next five countries combined.

My eyes rolled over the file cabinets behind him and the computer on his desk. He had a lot more information than he was sharing. My muscles involuntarily flexed as I considered beating the truth out of him. I sensed Ms. Sabel going through the same decision in her mind. Her muscles also flexed. We were alike in that we both have short fuses where bullshit is concerned. We also tend to find the quickest, most violent solution to a problem. That doesn't always go well.

Watching us, assessing our intent, Boyd looked slightly frightened. He rolled his chair back a few inches.

After a few seconds, Ms. Sabel decided he was a decent guy and deserved finesse instead of violence. "We're also interested in anything you can tell us about an arms dealer they call Ra."

His eyes squeezed shut as if this were the one question he'd hoped we would never ask. "Do you mean the mythological sun god of the ancient Egyptians?"

Mercury leaned over my shoulder and pointed at Boyd. *Who's he calling mythological, bro? Ra is no myth. I was just playing cards with that sucka a couple nights ago. Won a couple hundred aurei off him too. You can't let people dis the ancients just cuz we're not so popular these days. We're a minority and should be respected.*

I said, *Where've you been?*

Mercury said, *Me and ol' Rosemerta did a little dancing in the*

Ampitheatre of the Three Gauls. Rosemerta was my Celtic consort back in the day. Whenever I came to town, she was up for a booty call. She's still got it, y'know what I'm saying? Man. That was quite the place back when this town was called Lugdunum. You know how many Gauls made sacrifices and prayed to me for success in commerce at that amphitheater? Many, dude. Plenty of Gauls owed their fortune to me. And they knew it. And they were grateful. I said, grateful. Hint, hint, motherfucker.

I said, *I'll get right on that.*

"Sorry?" Boyd said. "Get on what?"

"Researching the Egyptian god of the sun and kings." I stared him down. "In the meantime, what can you tell us about the arms dealer?"

His pale skin shed what was left of its color. After a long, thoughtful look at the desk, he looked at me. His eyes popped to the left, then came back to me. "That's all for today. Lots to do, full agenda. I've got to finish a few things before I take my lunch in the rose garden." He stood up and made his eyes do the pop-left thing again. "Good of you to drop by. I'm a huge fan. Huge. And you, Ms. Sabel. I can't believe I met you. Oh, hey, I almost forgot. I hope you don't mind, but when you made the appointment, I brought in something I'm working on for my daughter. Could you autograph this for me? I'm going to surprise her on Christmas."

He spun around backwards and rummaged through his credenza before coming up with a book. A compendium of the greatest women players dropped on the desk. He handed Ms. Sabel a pen. She flipped it open and fanned to the chapter on her and jotted a note to his daughter, Crystal. Then she fanned a few more pages and stopped on the French captain, Amandine Henry. She noted it was covered with a long screed of good wishes. Ms. Sabel turned back to her page and added a PS to exceed Amandine's word count. She added hearts and Xs. She closed the book and handed it back to Duane Boyd.

Mercury leaned between us. *D'ya see that, bro? That's how Caesars are. Competitive AF. All the time, in everything, they always gotta win. You start thinking like that and we could make a Caesar out of you.*

I said, *In my line of work, the winner lives and the loser dies. So far,*

I'm winning.

Mercury said, *And who's been making that happen?*

Boyd smiled. "Thank you so much. Sorry I have to run, but it's almost lunch time. In the rose garden."

His eyes bounced to the left again.

CHAPTER 11

SECURITY ESCORTED US TO THE street where we immediately got out our phones and looked up "rose garden, Lyon" on the map. Behind Interpol's massive building sits one of the largest parks in Europe. A quarter mile away was a famous rose garden, Roseraie du Parc de la Tête d'Or. The bushes were covered in burlap due to a forecasted frost. We walked around killing time and admiring the burlap.

Boyd trotted up about twenty minutes later with a brown bag.

"Sorry for the cloak and dagger," Boyd said, "but Big Brother is alive and well and living in the bowels of the Interpol building. They track every file that comes in, where it goes, who views it, which folder you put it in, whether it was deleted or copied. Why? Because there are plenty of gangs and cabals who would like to bribe some of us and have their records vanish. Management watches and reports every conversation and meeting. We don't want people to find out we're discussing Ra."

"Who would be interested?" I asked.

"Did I mention there were once twenty-three of me?" He sat and started in on a homemade sandwich. "Ra's connected. Big time connected. If he doesn't have twenty-two of your coworkers sacked, he has you shot from four hundred yards away."

His reference cut me to the bone. Dimitris's sniper had been four hundred yards away. I said, "You're saying Ra ordered the hit?"

"Bare minimum: it required his blessing. Look." He took a deep breath and continued. "I'm thrilled that you care. I hope you take down Ra. He really is a mythical creature. No one knows his real name. No one knows where he's from. He makes deals happen. The biggest deals.

Nearly every illegal weapon delivered in the last ten years, from Odessa to Nairobi, came through him. Don't think he's just another player."

"What about Frieden?" Ms. Sabel asked.

"The Swedish thinktank, SIPRI estimated global arms sales in 2017 at $398 billion. Of that, illegal arms transactions are estimated to be between one and ten billion, depending on the year and the warring nations. Ra's cornered the market on a quarter of that business. He has a big operation. Think of Ra as a multinational company, and Frieden as one of several small arms divisions. There might be six or eight smugglers for each division. Some have a few ships, others have trucks, maybe a plane or two. They each have a piece of Ra's puzzle. If one of them gets shut down, like Frieden, he has five more to take up the slack."

"Who are you afraid of?" I nodded toward the building in the distance.

"Where Ra's concerned, everyone." He glanced around, looking for observers. "A couple weeks ago, the US Assistant Secretary for Political-Military Affairs came to visit. She paid a special visit to my lonely corner of the basement. She asked questions."

"Did she order you to quit looking at Ra?" Ms. Sabel asked, with an incredulous tone in her voice.

"Nothing overt." He shook his head and finished his sandwich. "The questions were carefully crafted as if she were investigating the bad guys herself. And she might have been. I want to make this clear: she might be a good guy in this. But. She asked if there were any reports from any police force in the world about a big arms deal going down. She had all my reports in her hand, she knew my official answer. Yet she asked a hundred questions without ever mentioning Ra—but clearly meaning Ra. I'm not stupid. She was looking to see if I had anything unofficial that hadn't been turned over. I did my best to act like an incompetent bureaucrat."

"Why didn't you trust her?

"No one comes to the basement. Especially big brass from the biggest superpower. That, plus the fact that arms control doesn't fall under her on the org chart. And then, there's the vibe." He shivered. "I felt like a Dalmatian puppy meeting Cruella De Vil."

He wolfed down a bag of chips.

Ms. Sabel and I exchanged glances. Something was coming. Extortion, plea for a job, request for protection, something.

"When stuff comes into Interpol, we code it." He crumpled his brown bag into a ball. "We don't care if Mauritania's police chief's wife complains about the next-door ambassador's dog barking all night. That doesn't get filed, it gets trashed. We preserve a record of it coming in, who evaluated it, and who decided to trash it. Every now and then, some high-ranking arms-specialist from some big police force comes in to check what we're keeping and what we're tossing. Virtually all of them have told me to toss files when they see something about Ra. It's all just a myth. He doesn't exist. Years ago, I set up a special trash can just for Ra files."

He looked at me for a long time without saying anything. It got weird. Then he handed me his crumpled bag. "Would you find a bin for me? I've got a lot to do today. I'll have to find a new job and move to a different country. Because, if you fail, I'm as dead as Dimitris Bakakis."

He walked away at a brisk pace.

I squeezed the bag and felt the SD card inside, his special trash can full of Ra files. I shoved the wadded bag in my pocket in case we were being watched.

Ms. Sabel worked her phone for a minute. She looked up. "Reggie Forrest, Assistant Secretary for Political-Military Affairs. Wikipedia lists defense trade under her responsibilities."

"What does that mean?" I asked.

"We are our own worst enemies," she said in a hazy voice.

"What?"

She looked around and started strolling the park, her long duster trailing in a light breeze. "A point of no return. The CIA wants us to uncover the Alvaria auction bidders. You want to have a word with Konrad von Frieden. I picked you for the assignment because I guessed they would be one and the same. I thought Frieden was Ra."

We walked along quietly, each of us thinking about the mission ahead. We'd taken on serious criminals before. We took on a Russian general and a brainsick president without a second thought. But this time, we were talking about a criminal syndicate with what had to be federal connections. Whether the connections were easily manipulated or corrupt didn't matter. The federal machine destroys anyone and anything in its way. If we wandered in front of the machine, we would be roadkill.

"Boyd took a big risk giving me that SD card," I said. "I can't wait to find out what's on it."

She muttered her agreement and kept her gaze focused in the distance.

Homie, Mercury said, *you're not hearing what she's telling you.*

I said, *OK, what am I missing?*

Mercury said, *I can't be spoon-feeding you this stuff. If you want to hang with Pia-Caesar-Sabel, you've got to think like a Caesar. C'mon now, let's see if you're Caesar-material.*

I said, *Brave is one thing, but this will be different. Is that what you mean? To figure this out, we need to be smart and have a real strategy. Is that what she's telling me?*

Good start, bro. Mercury slapped my back. *Now for the hard part. What's the strategy going to be?*

I said, *Hard?*

Mercury rolled his eyes and stared heavenward. *Why me, Apollo? Why do I have to get the stupid ones?*

I said, *Wait. Bradley Hopkins authorized us to discover the auction bidders. The obvious play is to find Ra and follow him around. He must have a list of the bidders.*

"Exactly," Ms. Sabel said. "If Ra is the biggest arms dealer and Alvaria is the biggest arms deal, he's the key."

"And he's connected to the sniper, so, two birds, one stone."

"I know you're in it for the retribution." She gave me a stern look. "The CIA did not hire us to assassinate anyone, only to identify the bidders."

"Collateral damage. They invented the phrase. I'm not after retribution. Nate asked me to take down Ra if the system failed. I owe it to him."

Ms. Sabel stopped and faced me. "I'm not authorizing collateral damage for any reason."

"OK."

We walked along a lake in silence. Then I asked, "What did you mean about the point of no return?"

"You and I have a tendency to take on bad guys regardless of the law." She watched birds splashing in the water and drew her overcoat tight around her. "In this case, there will be a lot more scrutiny. We've been legally contracted to find the bidders. This Reggie Forrest has more political power than the entire CIA, and there's a good chance she'll have us arrested for interfering with foreign policy. Naturally, if Ra should become collateral damage, she might escalate the charges to murder."

"We've played those odds before. There are always risks."

She stopped and grabbed my arm. "How big a risk are you willing to take? Would you alienate your friends? Would you break up with Jenny to get Ra? What risk is too big?"

"Well, about Jenny." I dropped onto a bench overlooking the water. "I wouldn't give up Jenny."

I unzipped my pocket, pulled the box out, flipped it open, and held it up for her to see.

She stared at it while the gravity of its purpose sank in. "You're going to ask her to marry you?"

"Was."

"Oh." She sat next to me and took my hand. "At your folk's place? And then she threw shade on the institution of marriage?"

"Yep." I sighed. "Right after Joyce stole my show."

We sat in silence for a long time, both staring across the water, watching a pair of swans float by. Swans mate for life. Easy when you have a three-ounce brain and live in the middle of nowhere, Jenny would argue.

I took a deep breath. "We got sidetracked from your point. So. I wouldn't give up Jenny for a mission. But I've risked my life several times. So have you. Wait, I see what you're saying. If I marry Jenny, I'll have to rethink that?"

"Worse." She rose and we resumed our walk. "Since Dad's murder, I've taken on a lot of responsibility. When I take risks, I'm risking the livelihoods of sixty thousand employees who depend on me for their paychecks. They feed their children, pay their mortgages, and care for aging parents with that money. If I take on the State Department, I don't put Pia Sabel at risk, I put sixty thousand families at risk."

Mercury strode between us looking like a philosophy professor thinking heavy thoughts. *And this would be Ginsberg's Law of Thermodynamics again, homie. You can't win, you can't break ... Wait. Maybe I'm thinking of the Paradox of Existential Nihilism.*

I said, *Huh?*

Mercury said, *Existential nihilism teaches that life has no meaning. If that's true, existential nihilism has no meaning.*

I said, *If you say so. But what does that have to do with anything?*

Mercury shook his head as if I were the dumb one. *Dude. There's too much at risk for her to be connected to this. You don't have as much to lose. She wants you to complete the mission. But the mission doesn't exist.*

I looked at Ms. Sabel. "I'll find Ra and keep you out of it."

"I can't ask you to do this, Jacob." She stopped and grabbed my shoulders. "It's a bigger risk than you think. If it goes south, and State comes after you, you can't ever come home."

CHAPTER 12

THE MAN THEY CALL RA waited for his righthand man, Bonham on the sport deck. As the tender approached in the gathering darkness, Bonham stood on the prow, his blazer flapping in the sea breeze, revealing its golden silk lining. An entourage stood behind him.

As the boat bumped the yacht, Ra called out to Bonham. "You have too many people on my little dinghy."

Bonham beamed his handsome smile. "It's a bit tight, but three of us are coming aboard. That should lighten the load. These lovely young ladies have decided to escort your darling to the concert."

The crew tied up and lowered the gangway. Bonham stepped out like a model materializing from a fashion magazine with the confidence and cynicism of privilege. They shook hands enthusiastically while Rover and Spot dragged two men out of the launch and escorted them up the steps to the swimming deck.

Just after they left, Ra sensed the presence of his love at his elbow. Once again, her approach had been silent and unassuming. He slipped an arm around her.

His darling hissed into his ear, "They are prostitutes."

"Certainly not," he said. He gave her a squeeze. "Bonham's a Washington Brahmin and a Dartmouth man. He would never consort with courtesans. These are the artists he sponsors. Or are they ballerinas?" He looked to Bonham. "I forget which day you entertain which girls."

Bonham roared with laughter. "These fine young ladies are candidates for my scholarship program." He faced Ra's darling. "They're in desperate need of mentorship and guidance, my dear. I do hope you'll give them the best advice possible. And this time, I swear, they're all old enough to vote. They've been double-checked."

She stared daggers at Bonham, then at Ra. His heart collapsed. "I swear, darling, this is the last time I let Bonham tag his girls to your schedule. Give them some cash and send them to a club. Do have fun for both of us. The concert will be the most beautiful of the season, I'm sure. I need the space for delicate negotiations or I wouldn't insist. Please."

He helped her to the tender where Bonham's girls welcomed her with laughter and a glass of champagne. The pilot pushed off and the tender disappeared into the night.

Ra and Bonham crossed to the stairs to follow the dogs and their captives. As they climbed, Ra put a hand on Bonham's shoulder. "Don't bring your girls around anymore. I'm getting a little older, wiser, and more appreciative of the finer things in life."

Bonham looked at him with surprise on his face. "What next? Will that little scamp have you redecorate the forward cabin and remove the pole-dancing studio?"

"Already gone, sport." Ra said. He dug his fingers into Bonham's shoulder and hissed, "Don't ever disrespect her again."

"What's happened to you?"

"I met someone who cares about something bigger than exchanging sex for shopping trips. She cares about the people she loves: her family—and me. She deserves respect. The same respect you would show me."

Bonham paled and observed the boss carefully.

Ra stepped ahead and looked over his new guests: Konrad von Frieden and his operations chief, Vassilis Giannoulis. Both men had their feet chained to fifty-kilo stones and their hands tied behind their backs. They stood at attention, Konrad giving his best impression of an aristocrat facing the guillotine.

"One thing, before we start on them," Bonham said in a confidentially low voice. "Fido tells me you chewed him out. I've asked you before to let me pass judgment on my men. It breaks the chain of command when you do it."

The man they call Ra frowned at his friend for a long, drawn out, and uncomfortable time. "Is that all he told you?"

Bonham leaned back and crossed his arms. "It was a simple report, but yes."

Without taking his eyes off Bonham, Ra raised his crew radio and ordered Fido to join him. The large man lumbered down the steps from the bridge. Ra directed Fido to the deck at his feet. "On your knees, Fido."

The large man glanced around at his peers and the captives. Everyone's eyes were riveted to the interaction. Fido lowered himself to his knees. Bonham winced.

Ra grabbed a fistful of the man's hair. "I hate equivocation. I want you to tell dear Bonham why I threatened you. Tell him your transgression. Do it now."

Fido looked up at Bonham with pleading eyes. "I, uhm, I spoke harshly to the lady."

"And why is that wrong?" Ra asked.

"It's not my place to question the lady. Forgive me, sir." Sweat broke out on Fido's forehead.

"I was benevolent letting you off with just a warning, Fido. And yet you attempted to frame yourself as a victim. For that you should be punished. You will choose your own punishment."

Fido looked up at the man they call Ra, then at Bonham, who offered no consolation. "Twenty lashes, sir?"

"That is acceptable. You will administer them yourself. Twenty lashes, each drawing blood."

Then Ra shouted for all on deck to hear. "Nothing short of the full truth will be tolerated. We cannot survive on lies and half-truths. We must ground our operations in empiricism which leads us to realism and that will lead us to success. Without a firm, proven grip on the reality we confront, we can only lose. Is that understood?"

Everyone replied in unison with a robust, "Yes, sir."

He let go of Fido's hair. The big man rose to his feet and left the deck.

Ra turned his attention to his captives. "Now, what do we have here?"

Konrad said, "I don't know why you're upset with me. I've done nothing."

"Nothing? You spent twenty-hours in the custody of a Greek prosecutor. That is something." He turned to Bonham. "Doesn't that seem significant to you, Bonham?"

"Indeed." Bonham smoothed his blazer. "Prosecutors are known for cutting deals with people. Asking them to spy on their employers, fabricate evidence, tell them things that aren't true. Why, the potential for havoc alone casts the dark shadow of suspicion on a man."

Ra walked up to Konrad and looked him over without saying anything. He pushed Konrad's face to the left and examined the man's skin. Then he pushed Konrad's face to the right and continued his examination. When he finished, he sniffed. "They didn't tattoo him, Bonham. Yet I had to spend a significant amount of money on attorneys to get him out. So how can we tell if dear old Konrad is redeemable? Should we allow him to continue with operations? Or will he stab us in the back while we sleep?"

"You can trust me. I've told them nothing—"

"Don't grovel." Ra patted Konrad's cheek. "It's unbecoming. We will decide this. Don't speak until spoken to."

"Well," Bonham said, "Konrad is the most productive smuggler of the lot. And by a significant factor. He has that going for him."

"Yes. But would you bet your life on his past productivity testifying to his loyalty in the future?"

"Now that is sticky." Bonham approached Vassilis, the Greek half of the duo. "What a man might do when his testicles are in the vise of a prosecutor is quite unpredictable. Perhaps Vassilis would shed some light on the subject for us."

Ra tracked around to Konrad's operations chief. "Vassilis, tell me how Mr. von Frieden came to be in the custody of the Greek prosecutor—but before you speak, remember what I said about being evasive. Be sure to clarify even the slightest detail."

"They charged into the compound, sir. They didn't use the prefecture police. Our informants had no idea about the operation. We had no advance warning—"

"That is my point." Ra strode a full circle around the men. "They surprised you by obtaining some highly classified information. My mole tells me someone called them from inside Konrad's house and reported crates of rifles. We know the caller was not a guest as he claimed. How did he know where the remaining arms were stashed? How did he break into the house to report from a specific location?"

"I don't know, sir."

"Konrad," Ra spoke quietly, "do you know who called the police and told them where—in your house—to find crates of stolen Italian rifles?"

"No, sir. I have no idea who—"

"And that, right there, is my problem. Do you understand, Konrad?"

The man looked at Ra with wild eyes. "No. I, I don't."

"How do I move forward? How do I trust an operation—one of my best, mind you—after this tragic and illegal home invasion by the Greeks? The biggest deal of my life is coming in a few weeks. Deal of the century. I need someone I can trust on the job to move things from point A to point B. Until this week, I never thought twice about who that would be. I can't trust the Estonians with something so big. They mess up too often. Same goes for the Egyptians. They're just plain sloppy. But you, Konrad, you run a tight ship. But how do I trust you now? How can you redeem yourself?"

Ra took out a stiletto and held it up. He let light glint off the shiny blade into Konrad's eyes.

"You could have one of your people shadow me twenty-four-seven," Konrad said. "I've nothing to hide."

"That is the problem. You had something to hide and you didn't hide it. No, sport, I'm looking for a different solution. Something permanent. Something reliable that will prove to me you will never betray me."

Konrad shook his head. Vassilis quivered.

"Machiavelli teaches," Ra continued, "that when we find ourselves in a tight spot, we should avoid the values of justice, mercy, and wisdom and rely on cruelty, brutality, fear, and deceit. In other words, fear is a much more effective motivator of loyalty than love or compassion. Did you know that, Konrad?"

The Austrian shook his head violently, his eyes never leaving the knife.

Ra held the dagger in his hand as if he were about to stab someone in the stomach. "This is the V-42 stiletto used by my grandfather in the Devil's Brigade during World War II. I keep it honed razor-sharp in his honor."

Ra raised it above his shoulder as if ready to plunge it into Konrad's chest. He held the pose for a moment as if deciding something. He lowered it. "You know, I think there is a way you can prove your loyalty to me, Konrad. You see, someone is responsible for letting you get caught in the Greek trap. Now, what could you do that would convince me to let you get back to work?"

Konrad looked puzzled as Ra slit open the bindings around Konrad's wrists with a flick of the knife.

Vassilis stared at Konrad, the whites of his eyes big and shiny in the moonlight.

Rover stepped up and unfastened the chains holding Konrad's ankles to the stone.

Ra flipped the blade in his hand, catching and holding it by the sharp end, and offered it to Konrad.

Konrad's eyes nearly popped out. He stared at the knife. He looked up at Vassilis. "You can't be serious. Vassilis is my best friend. We've been together since the beginning. I would never—"

"How disappointing then." Ra tossed the stiletto again and caught it by the handle. "I insist on loyalty. This was to be a transaction of loyalty, Konrad. You do something for me to earn my trust. I bestow that trust in you. A simple transaction. Now I must learn to trust the Egyptians. They're sloppy, but they will be alive next week. And they never hesitate to prove their loyalty."

He turned and took a step away. Rover dragged the chains forward to Konrad's ankles.

"Wait." Konrad swallowed hard.

"Konrad, no!" Vassilis leaned away as far as his chains would let him. "NO!"

Konrad took the knife.

"Just a moment," Ra said. He took out his phone, set it to video, and pressed record. He nodded at Konrad to proceed.

CHAPTER 13

SHORTLY AFTER WHEELS-UP, PIA SENT Jacob to her stateroom so he could sift through Duane Boyd's records on Ra in peace. She had another secure Skype connection appointment. The screen flickered through the protocols again. When the screen produced three video feeds, she quickly checked herself to make sure she didn't have spinach in her teeth, then minimized herself in the corner and focused on the other two feeds.

One was labeled State, as in Department of, and included two professionally dressed women who sat in front of a departmental seal. One of the women was older and sat with the determined demeanor of a worldly leader. The other face was young, bright, hopeful, and lit with naïveté. Pia recognized her from somewhere but struggled to recall where or why.

The other window was labeled Pentagon and included one man with a face seasoned in a boxing ring and four stars on his epaulets.

Pia smiled at him and said, "Hello, General Garret. How are you?"

"Good to see you, Pia." He scowled. "You'll learn about my mood in a minute."

"I am Regina Forrest, Assistant Secretary for Political-Military Affairs." The older of the two women scowled as she spoke.

Pia hoped her shock didn't show. Forrest was the one who quizzed Interpol in excessive detail about the arms dealer they called Ra.

"And you," Pia said to the other woman, "are Eva Gomez, star striker for the University of Southern California, right?"

The petite woman's face lit up at her name. "I graduated last May, though. I have to say this is quite an honor, Ms. Sabel. You're my hero. All those—"

"We'll have time for chit-chat later," Forrest said. "The reason—"

Pia interrupted quickly. "Your expression tells me you have a good deal of unpleasantness to unleash, Ms. Forrest. Before we go down that dark path, I need to know a few things about the people involved on the call. Ms. Gomez, are you an intern?"

Forrest crossed her arms and creased her scowl into a full-blown frown.

"No, ma'am." She smiled broadly. "I was lucky enough to join State as a full-time employee."

"Given your skills on the field, I would give you clearance for this call in a heartbeat. But, for the record, I need to know: has the administration cleared you for this particular call?"

"She is cleared for a certain level," General Garrett said. "But not the highest. Not concerning the subject matter at hand. As much of an asset as she must be to the Assistant Secretary, I too questioned her participation. However, Ms. Forrest insisted. For the purposes of this call, we will refer to the items in question as 'the product' and nothing else. For the record, among my other duties at AFMC, I am JCS's liaison to the PM."

Pia found the idea of bringing Eva to the call highly irregular, but it wasn't her decision.

"Thank you for that explanation, General," she said. A quick glance at Eva made Pia realize the young woman had no idea what the General's abbreviations meant. "I have been briefed on the product. That term will work for me. If you wouldn't mind, could you remind me of those acronyms?"

General Garrett laughed. "Sorry. I'm responsible for Air Force Materiel Command, AFMC. As such, I'm also the Joint Chief of Staff's, JCS's representative to Ms. Forrest's department, Political-Military, PM."

Pia looked at Ms. Forrest. "I'm satisfied then. Proceed."

Ms. Forrest picked up a report on the desk in front of her. "A few days ago, the product was picked up by a shipping company on behalf of the Albanian government. The transport ship went off course and stopped responding to all efforts to communicate with it. Through satellite tracking and air reconnaissance, we have determined the ship made an unscheduled stop off the coast of Tripoli this morning."

Pia waited a moment. When Forrest didn't continue, she asked, "And you presume the product has been lost?"

"Exactly."

"OK. What do you need from me?"

"Sabel Security is your company, is it not?" Forrest used the voice of a TV prosecutor.

"It is."

"And Sabel Security was contracted to ensure the security of the product, was it not?"

"It was."

"Then the State Department expects you to live up to your contract and find the missing product before it falls into the wrong hands. The nation's future is threatened by these events. Nothing less than the balance of power in the world is at stake. You, of all people, have a personal stake in the outcome of this unfortunate event. I've read the contract, Ms. Sabel. Your company is fully responsible for the safety and security of the product and the people handling it. Your failure to provide the most basic security from the outset will be considered a breach of the contract. Failure to act can be interpreted as willful negligence and possibly a criminal act."

Pia felt anger rising in her like a kettle on a burner. She waited a moment to see if Forrest's outburst was over. She glanced at General Garrett who looked angry, yet his eyes weren't on Pia. Eva appeared to be doing her best to suppress her shock at the charges her boss had leveled against her soccer heroine. The young lady was clearly blindsided by the accusations.

Pia took a deep breath, determined to keep her cool. She said, "If you read the terms of the contract, Ms. Forrest, no doubt you read Part I, paragraph 5, sub-paragraph 2, regarding the location and events that trigger the beginning of the terms of engagement. If you've not, I will summarize them for you. Sabel Security stands ready to begin our stewardship of the product the moment it physically arrives in Tirana and is accepted as the authentic product by Sabel Security team lead Miguel

Rodriguez."

Pia waited while Forrest, reeling in shock, thumbed through the pages of the contract in front of her. Eva Gomez looked up at Pia with wide, uncertain eyes.

Pia continued. "I see in the contract terms that the Office of Regional Security and Arms Transfers, whoever they are, contracted with someone else for the transportation and delivery of the product. Sabel Security is still awaiting the authentication procedures before our stewardship can begin."

General Garrett remained stone-faced as he added, "RSAT is the division of Ms. Forrest's department that decided, against AFMC's advice, to use a third-party transport."

Pia could tell when Forrest arrived at the mentioned section of the contract because Forrest's face exploded in crimson.

"We sought advice from your department, General," Forrest said.

"You asked for advice on how to contract a freighter," General Garrett growled. "And they said don't. When your people insisted, we wrote specifications with caveats."

"This isn't helpful," Forrest snarled back. "We need solutions here."

"If I were you, I would turn to General Garrett for revised advice," Pia said. "Materiel is his area of expertise."

Forrest looked at Garrett. "Uh. General. What would you suggest?"

"You were warned, Reggie," Garrett said. "You ignored the advice of subject-matter experts when you went ahead with this project. You refused AFMC's help after that. Now all those dire predictions have come true. Are you asking for my counsel so you can ignore it too?"

"No, sir." Forrest's shoulders caved.

Garrett huffed, then he said, "My advice is simple. The US Government has the capability to track down and recover the product, but none of our special forces are cleared to handle it at this time. Going through all the right channels for approvals and clearances will delay deployment by days if not weeks. There's another obvious reason you do not want to deploy federal agents that I will assume you can easily grasp. On the other hand, Ms. Sabel's people are already cleared and briefed due to the security contract you signed. They're equally capable of doing the job and probably better prepared than any government agency at this time. They have the expertise and the personnel in theater. I would hire them this minute to track down and return the product. Time is of the essence, Ms. Forrest. If the product is in Libya right now, it could be anywhere in the world by midnight. And—your ass is on the line."

"What do you mean?" Forrest asked. "Why not deploy federal agents? What obvious reason?"

"The list of people who knew what was on that ship is very small. There is a good chance the person alerting the thieves is a federal employee. Ms. Sabel is motivated to recover the product and her people could not have been involved in the disappearance."

Pia considered what General Garrett had not said. The insider who tipped off the thieves was likely to be in Forrest's chain of command. Which led Pia to consider why Reggie Forrest visited Interpol. Could someone that high up at State be a part of a conspiracy to steal Alvaria? If so, it would be pretty stupid to make the Interpol visit in person. Forrest couldn't be that dumb. Or was it arrogance?

Forrest took a deep breath, then looked at each participant on the call. "Ms. Sabel, would you accept an amendment to this contract to include finding the product as soon as possible?"

Pia paused a moment to consider whether the CIA contract to find the bidders represented a conflict of interest. She didn't believe it did, although one would certainly delay the other. She would never find the bidders if Alvaria was recovered too quickly. The auction would dry up as soon as the recovery became known. If her team pulled it off, they would be heroes. If they failed, Sabel Industries would lose billions in government contracts.

"I will deploy my people in advance of your amendment. Get it to me by end of day."

"Two things," Forrest said. "One, I want you to take on Ms. Gomez as a liaison to represent my interests in the search. I will get her cleared. Second, how quickly can you recover the product?"

Pia parsed the events and requests of the call. Having an unvetted aide on a secure call then assigning her as liaison was an interesting circumstance. Blaming Pia for the mishandled delivery was either the master plan of an evil mind or the bumbling of an inexperienced and unqualified political appointee. She said, "Remind me of your relationship to former president Chuck Roche."

Forrest clenched her jaw. Her eyes narrowed to slits. "Irrelevant. How long will it take to recover?"

"My team and I would be honored to work with Ms. Gomez on this mission. As for how long it will take to recover something you lost? Quicker if you quit trying to cover your ass and longer if you don't."

General Garrett laughed out loud and clicked off.

Pia clicked off without laughing. She stared aimlessly out the window, considering the gamble she just took.

She sensed Jacob's presence and looked up. He waited in the stateroom doorway for permission to come in. She nodded to him.

Jacob said, "Did it go the way you expected?"

"Yes, in every detail." She tapped a finger to her lips as she thought. "Except for a surprise twist named Eva Gomez."

CHAPTER 14

I STOOD ON THE DECK of Ms. Sabel's tender, staring at the biggest yacht I'd ever seen. It was too big to park in Monaco's harbor, which meant we had to ride in from the city dock. It was painted Sabel blue, a satiny shade of royal blue. On the back of the ship, in large raised letters, was the name, *NUMINA*. I couldn't wait for Mercury to remind me that was what the earliest Romans called the gods. Literal translation: divine will. As I watched, a big chunk of the yacht's back wall, twenty feet tall and forty feet across, rose upward on giant hinges, revealing a cavernous internal bay. Our pilot guided the murmuring boat inside the much bigger yacht. Sport boats and jet skis waited on davits to one side. Opposite them sat a six-person plexiglass submarine with *Seamagine Aurora* emblazoned across its ballast tanks. Next to that, a smaller yellow submarine. I couldn't take my eyes off them.

Mercury stood beside me in his formal toga. The one with the red trim. *Where's your personal submarine, homie? It's time you quit this lousy job and became a Caesar yourself.*

I said, *I like working for Ms. Sabel. I get all the perks and none of the hassles.*

Mercury said, *You should have a megayacht, brutha. You should have a jet. Next time Jenny wants some alone time with you, you don't have to borrow Pia-Caesar-Sabel's little scow. Listen to me, dawg. I'm the god of commerce. Augustus Caesar was a big fan of mine. He listened to everything I told him, and he amassed a net wealth of $4.6 trillion.*

I said, *Back when wealth was gained by pillage and plunder?*

Mercury said, *They call it mergers and acquisitions these days. Same shit, different name. No matter what you call it, it's highly effective, bro.*

Ms. Sabel stepped to my side. "I have a feeling Dad would've approved of buying this new ship, but it's so ostentatious and overwhelming, I feel bad about it. It's just not my kind of thing."

She'd been doing a lot of things lately that were right out of Alan Sabel's playbook. "Why did you, then?"

"Captain Chamberlain turned the *Asteria* into a profitable charter operation and made a case to expand the fleet." She laughed. "We have six yachts now. He wants to take on Carnival Cruise Lines."

"Fleet?" I felt myself getting a little nauseous. Maybe Mercury had a point about my future. Why couldn't I be rich? It would be nice to blow three hundred million on a boat and—instead of it costing me anything—it becomes yet another revenue stream.

"Chamberlain convinced me to add three new ships by telling me how many new jobs I would create."

She shrugged and waved to someone on deck.

I never took my eyes off the submarines during our conversation and missed the welcome-aboard call. A freaking submarine. Two in fact. It occurred to me the wealth gap might have reached a new level of absurdity.

Captain Chamberlain greeted Ms. Sabel with a big grin. He gave me a suspicious glance, as if I didn't belong there. The Englishman must've forgotten who got him the job at Sabel. Though it was the least I could do after I nearly sank his previous charter in a hurricane.

Six staff tied off the craft, looking sharp in their Sabel Yachts uniforms. I followed Ms. Sabel and the captain as he extolled the virtues of his corner in the sprawling empire of Sabel Industries. Something about two helicopters, seven tenders including diving platforms and Zodiacs, two submersibles, two swimming decks … and then I lost track. Or interest.

Ms. Sabel stopped him by tugging his jacket sleeve. "I'm sure it's nice. Is the party ready for tonight?"

Big parties were another part of Alan's style she had been enjoying lately.

"Indeed, mum." From his pained looks, she may as well have stabbed him in the gut. "We have an event that will put *Numina* on the map and line up reservations well into next year."

Judging by the staff armed with champagne flutes and the roses lining the hallways ahead of us, it appeared he had planned a Broadway production to impress her on her first visit.

"Jacob and I have some work to do before the party starts." She squeezed his arm. "I have complete faith in your capabilities, Captain Chamberlain. You have exceeded my expectations. Please extend my thanks to the entire crew."

"I will, mum." He gave me some side-eye as if I were the reason Ms. Sabel wanted to skip the tour.

"How many guests have accepted the invitation to stay the night?" she asked.

"All thirteen guest cabins are filled" he said. "Everyone on your special list accepted. I understood Mr. Stearne is staying with you. Is that correct?"

She didn't answer.

He turned a judging eye my way.

I had no idea what to say. They usually gave me a cabin of my own with the crew. Someone above my pay grade had made changes without asking me. Ms. Sabel always had a long game running. What it was and why it involved making Captain Chamberlain think we were an item was beyond me. All I wanted was to find whoever paid Nate's assassin. Whatever she was doing would lead me to him, so I kept my mouth shut.

Chamberlain coughed and showed us to the owner's deck. Apparently, when yachts get to a certain size, a stateroom just won't do. An owner's deck is required.

While he watched her, Ms. Sabel glanced at me. I had come to read her expressions and understood what she wanted.

I said, "That will be all for now. Thank you, captain."

Chamberlain gave me the kind of once-over I hadn't seen since boot camp. Then he left.

My duffel rested in the corner of the master suite. There was a mirror over the bed. A bit uncomfortable with the arrangement, I shot a look at Ms. Sabel. She didn't return it. Her gaze was focused on a yacht anchored three hundred yards across blue waves.

CHAPTER 15

"WHAT DO WE NEED TO go over?" I asked. "I read all the files on Ra and there's no clue to his identity, but a lot about how to find his subcontractors or department heads, whatever you call them. That's where I plan to start."

She glanced over her shoulder at me before returning her gaze to other yachts nearby. "Bianca ran an analysis and cross-referenced possible suspects. She's narrowed down who Ra might be to one of a few people: Mikhail Yeschenko, Deng Zhipeng, George Falconer, Josephine Seligman, or Ritchie Skaite. I invited all of them to the party tonight."

She watched the gentle waves for a quiet moment. Then she said, "You'll be going after Konrad von Frieden and working your way up the smuggler chain from there. When you get to the upper level, you'll be in the world of billionaires. We have to build a legend for you. We'll make you a Sabel Security executive on paper. There's a certain type who rise to that level. People who are confident and assertive to a fault. They're freight-train personalities who border on psychopathic. Billionaires are not easily intimidated or impressed. They have their own security operations. You won't slip past them the way you did on Corfu. You'll have to walk in the front door."

"No problem," I said.

"Yes, problem," she said. "You're underestimating the assignment. To move among them, you'll need to learn their ways. How to push when shoved, dismiss unwanted questions, lose your patience for effect. How to fire employees on the spot, and always find a way to get the VIP exception even—or especially—when you've been excluded. They need to see you on their level."

Mercury bounced on the bed, landing on his back. *Oh dawg, you are in now.* His gaze rose to the mirrored ceiling. *Hey, look at this! Narcissus would love this place.*

I said, *Not now. I've got to concentrate on what she's telling me. I'm not sure about the messages here.*

Mercury said, *Message? She's sending you a telegram. Or is it email, text, IM? I can't keep track of what mortals use these days. You know damn well what she wants from you.*

I said, *No, I don't. She's building a legend, a backstory, to make me look important. I get that. What she isn't explaining is how my duffel ended up in her room. Did the staff do it on her orders or was it their assumption? If I read things wrong, this could get hella awkward. So. Tell me.*

Mercury jumped off the bed and stood toe to toe with me. He whispered, *She's gonna teach you how to act like a Caesar. If you listen, we're on our way. Next thing—you be DA MAN!*

She was in the middle of saying a guy's name.

"Mikhail Yeschenko?" I asked. "The guy who ran a billionaire's cabal and tried to kill you when you broke it up? He's on the guest list?"

"Make no enemies, as Dad used to say. Your enemy today might be your biggest profit center tomorrow. All is forgiven in business. Oh, but I forgot to mention his ex-wife, Katyonak Yeschenko, as a suspect. She aged out of the gold-digger class and leveraged her divorce settlement into a fortune of her own. She's the biggest provider of finished medical products in western Asia. Aspirin, diabetic tests, pregnancy kits, anything in packaging you can put on a shelf for consumers."

The term caught my ear. Nate Hale had been in the business of shipping finished medical products.

She leaned her back against the glass and gave me a grave look. "Over the next few days, you will accompany me to several events. The first is the yacht-warming party here. Followed by the Young Global Leader's conference in Davos. You'll be rubbing elbows with them, making them see you in a new light. Right now, you're background. Remember the wallpaper at your local movie theater? Of course not. No one does. It doesn't matter, it's just background. And that's how much they care about you. You're wallpaper unless you can buy an office building from them, or sell them a million barrels of oil at half price, or give them a piece of your next venture before it goes public. When you work your way up from Frieden, you can no longer be background. You have to be relevant."

"OK, what do I need to change?"

"Fashion first. You dress like Jacob Stearne, farm-boy-turned-war-hero in jeans and a t-shirt. Billionaires will pat you on the back for your service, but they'll never build you a stadium. You need to step out loud and proud. You're a peacock who wants everyone to know you're in the room and you have the biggest dick."

I choked, having never heard her talk like that. "OK, dress like an asshole—act like an asshole."

"No." She shook a finger at me like a schoolteacher. "They're not assholes unless you get in their way. Remember what Dad was like? You loved him. He charmed everyone and made them feel welcome, wanted, appreciated. First time you met him, you thought you were best friends, right?"

"He was a great guy."

"Did you know he couldn't remember your name until after you saved his life? Until you produced something of value, you were background. And Dad was one of the good guys."

That took my breath away. Alan Sabel had thought of me as an equal—or so it had seemed. Wow. What an act.

Mercury said, *It wasn't an act. He lived and breathed his interest in and love of everyone around him. Just like every Caesar before him. But why remember someone if all they're going to do is sweep the crumbs off your table? Tell me something, homes. What was the name of the waitress who served you at The Bier Baron Tavern last week? Black hair, pierced lip, tattoo on her wrist, remember? She took your order without writing anything down and got everything right. What's her name?*

I said, *I get your point.*

"Do you know how to charm an obnoxious billionaire?" Ms. Sabel asked me.

"Tell them they look fabulous?"

"No. Ask them about their favorite subject."

"How am I supposed to know their favorite subject?"

"Themselves. Just like everyone else." She pushed off and dug into her closet. She sorted through workout clothes. "Ask them how they got started. Ask them about their key to success. Ask them their five favorite films. Whatever they tell you, keep your eyes focused on them and celebrate their answer, no matter what it is." Her voice rose half an octave, pretending to speak to one of her peers. "I never thought of *Blood Diamond* as a top film, but I see you're point. You're a genius!"

She grabbed a wad of clothes and her pink boxing gloves and went into the bathroom.

I changed into my workout shorts. We took the elevator to the gym and passed a below-water lounge with underwater windows. I almost tripped when the nine-foot bignose shark outside caught my attention.

"OK," I said, "I get it. Charm the hell out of them."

"But whenever possible, put them in their place. If Josephine Seligman offers up six films when you ask for five, slam her." Ms. Sabel turned to me with a sudden and angry glare. "I said five, not six. Pay attention." Then she smiled as if she'd just fallen in love with me. "What a great t-shirt!"

I looked down. My t-shirt had a dwarf in camo holding a grenade. Under him was the caption, "Hi-ho, hi-ho, it's hand grenades I throw."

I said, "Thanks, it's one of—"

"I didn't mean it. I know you like them but pull them out of your duffel and have a steward ship them back to your house. You need to dress like a king from now on. My point was, slam someone, then compliment them. Make them live for your approval and they'll constantly try to win it."

We warmed up with her usual routine of pushups, pullups, sit ups. A hundred each. Then jump rope. Followed by weights in large quantities.

When we took a break, she pointed out the portal at the row of big boats lined up in Monaco's bay like an invading navy. "You see those? They're erectile dysfunction statements, more commonly known as superyachts. On each one is a man with a hot-as-hell woman half his age, a team of assistants who only know the word 'yes', a breath-taking narcissistic personality disorder, and a highly effective grasp of how to get things done. They're obsessive about everything. They fawn over their girlfriends like precious jewels, not life partners. Owning a woman becomes life and death itself to them. You can admire them, hate them, analyze them, or ridicule them, but it will never affect what they do. They're like high-speed trains on a track only they can see. Anyone standing next to the rails is a bystander. Anyone on the rails will be crushed. Anyone willing to feed their engines will be given a seat reflecting their contribution. Everything has a value. Nothing, not even a handshake, is exchanged without a calculation of value."

We wound tape around our hands and put on our gloves and headgear. We stepped into the ring. Before I could consider the silliness of having a boxing ring on a yacht, she slapped the timer.

While we circled each other, looking for an opening, she said, "Most of these guys do great things. You can argue they're overpaid, but they're providing jobs and services, improving society, and leading their company into the future."

"What I don't get," I said as she landed three quick jabs, "is why one of these guys would work an arms deal. The guys you're talking about have big, legitimate businesses. Why take a risk like that?"

A blinding-fast uppercut snapped my head back. I bounced on my toes and circled the ring, trying to concentrate on defeating her strategy. Knowing she couldn't directly compete with a man due to the muscle-mass differential, she compensated with speed. Her punches came out of nowhere. I managed to predict and deflect the next couple and pop her with a combination.

She made me pay for leaving my ribs unprotected.

Where all her ideas were leading was still a mystery to me. She had my mission all mapped out in her head but wasn't giving me the full picture. That bothered me. It seemed like acting, a career that didn't interest me. But she was giving me access to her peer group, one of whom might be the guy who'd ordered Nate's murder. For that, I would go along with just about anything. I paid close attention to these details. I wanted to get it right.

"The guy we're looking for is a true psychopath," she said. "For them, it's all about risk. Criminals, soldiers, CEOs all exhibit psychopathic tendencies, but the guy we're looking for is full blown. He'll thrive on the edge. He's doing this because firing a VP isn't satisfying enough. Killing one is better. Squeezing a hundred million out of the bottom line is boring. Taking a hundred thousand from inside North Korea is exciting. What he loves most is getting away with it. It makes him feel superior. Especially if he has a big, legitimate business."

I considered her approach as we traded jabs. My plan was to find Konrad and talk him into introducing me to Ra. Then I would kill the bastard. Problem solved. World saved. Friends avenged—just like Nate asked. But Bradley Hopkins asked us to find the bidders and she wanted to please the CIA. Would she mind if I short-circuited her master plan? I considered throwing that idea out there to test her reaction.

Mercury pointed to her left ear. Unprotected. I landed a punch hard enough to turn her head. But that didn't stop her counterattack. Throwing a left hook blind, she smacked my nose.

Lucky toss.

The bell sounded.

We backed off, panting.

"Why is my duffel in your room?" I asked.

Mercury rolled his eyes. *You know what they say, homes. If you don't ask a stupid question, no one will know how stupid you are.*

I said, *I'm missing a piece of the plan here. There's something she isn't telling me.*

Mercury said, *So what? You're cannon fodder. Do what you're told and don't ask.*

"The crews on superyachts are like one big family," she said. "They'll talk. Word will get back to the other billionaires."

That part confused me even more. Her plan was to profile her billionaire frenemies to find the bad guy, then steal the bidders list from him. That would work. Maybe. So why make them think we're sleeping together? Do billionaires all sleep together? Cuz, I didn't sign up for that.

"We could just track down Ra and kill him," I said. "I vote for that option."

A hint of disappointment creased her expression. "Alvaria is too valuable. Someone else will step into Ra's shoes. The bidders will be back. If the CIA knows who they are, they can stay one step ahead of them."

The bell sounded and we squared off again.

"OK," I said, "you want to know who's buying? It's the Chinese and the Russians. Who else would it be?"

"The Saudis, Israel, Iran, North Korea, Argentina, Venezuela, or basically, anyone in the world. And within China, which faction is it? A Red Army general with a desire for more power could take over with one of these systems. So could an internet billionaire, like Deng Zhipeng."

We traded combinations, mostly deflected.

"Got it." I nodded my acceptance and got a jab in the nose for it.

Ms. Sabel takes no prisoners.

She said, "Are you in?"

I said, "I'm in. Hell, if I can take down an ISIS fighter with an AK, I can take on any billionaire."

CHAPTER 16

I FELT LIKE A KING in my new wardrobe. A gay king, but that always impresses the ladies anyway, so I didn't mind. The slacks were so light and soft I couldn't tell if I was actually wearing them. The tight shirt showed off my significant pectorals and seemed to give me a massage while the bright pattern almost blinded me. The shoes cost more than my parents' lifetime wardrobe budget.

Ms. Sabel and I waited one deck above the main salon while all the guests arrived. The hostess wanted to arrive last. Below us, the party was going strong.

Ms. Sabel wore a sparkly silver gown that flowed like liquid from her right shoulder down to a slit on her left thigh. It kept going to the floor where it brushed the deck. They must've taped the dress to her body in places. Her plunging neckline bared more skin than she'd ever shown before. It looked good rather than provocative because the gods chose to leave her without significant cleavage. She was an athlete after all. Someone had styled her sandy hair with modest waves instead of her usual ponytail. Diamond-encrusted combs kept it back from her face.

She looked hot as hell and she knew it. Sexy-Pia was a different person. Her uber-confidence stretched into a whole new realm. Her smile lit up the room and her swirl held my gaze.

The DJ stopped the music while we waited. Nearly thirty people paused below us amid the hors d'oeuvres and martinis. Captain Chamberlain took the mic, introduced himself and welcomed the guests aboard the *Numina* for its maiden party under new management. Cheers went up. Then he introduced Ms. Sabel and me. Without saying anything specific, he left the impression we were a couple on the verge of engagement. Before I could ask her what that was about, she sauntered down the stairs milking every step for attention and tugging me along behind her. A spotlight found us on the last few steps. Wildly enthusiastic applause greeted us when we hit the floor.

Every straight male in the room fell in lust with her. The women raised an eyebrow of concern that the competition had just gone up a notch.

She pulled me into the center and gave a royal wave followed by a deep bow. She made a short speech about how privileged she felt having such special guests. She pointed to them and named them. None of them blushed. All of them soaked up her praise as if they deserved more. Then she introduced me as the man who had saved her life several times over. She even recounted the time I pulled her from a wrecked car seconds before it exploded.

That was when I noticed the ceiling-to-deck video screens were showing me accepting a *Legion d'Honneur* award from the President of France. I'd saved a Paris church from mass shooters. Just doing my part for humanity. I didn't even want the medal until Ms. Sabel convinced me it was good for business. Which was probably why she had it playing on all the screens. Plenty of potential customers in the room.

Mercury stood next to me in his finest, full-length toga, waving to the crowd. *Can you feel it, homie? This is whatcha call mass adoration. Everybody loves you right now. You're on the verge of becoming one of them, a Caesar.*

I said, *I gotta admit, this doesn't suck.*

Mercury kept waving. *Stick with me, dawg. They'll be throwing you a real Roman triumph. It's not just a noun, it's an event. The biggest ceremony Rome ever threw was the triumph. Senators and magistrates would lead you into the city. In front of you, all the spoils of war, the gold, the slaves, the exotic animals, followed by your officers and your army, and at the end, with rose petals tossed in your path, you in a gleaming chariot. After the noise died down, you would make sacrifices to the gods. Especially me. Then the whole city feasted. Ah, homie, those was good times.*

His description was a bit beyond where we were, but I could get behind his idea of a triumph.

Ms. Sabel tucked her hand in my elbow and steered me in a way that made it look like I was leading. We spoke first to Josephine Seligman, an attractive woman on the downside of fifty. She was originally from Indiana and now ran a private bank in London. We were both Midwestern emigrants; I thought we'd hit it off. But no matter what topic I tried, she kept returning to the uncertainty of the investment markets and how much she hated risk. As an example, she told us about a shipping company she'd been forced to repossess. Then she tried to sell it to Ms. Sabel.

Josephine looked around the room and said, "I don't know how you put up with all these men, Pia. Such egos."

Mercury whispered in my ear and I repeated his words. "Is it solipsistic in here, or is it just me?"

The two women stared at me long enough for me to lose faith in the god of eloquence, then they burst out laughing. Josephine put a hand on my forearm and leaned in. She said, "If you ever need a loan, drop by my London office. Anything you want. I like smart heroes."

Ms. Sabel tugged us away to her other guests.

I turned to find Mercury with his hands out, expecting a little love.

I said, *I can't give you thanks and praise. I don't even know what the joke means.*

Oh, dude. Mercury shook his head sadly. *Look it up. And quit reading Kazuo Ishiguro. Too damn serious all the time.*

Ms. Sabel said, "You passed the first test with flying colors. But then, I started with the easy one. I'm taking her off the suspect list."

"Why?"

"Did you hear her talking about risk? We're looking for a skydiver." She glanced at me apologetically when she remembered Rangers are big on skydiving. "The good news is, if you ever start your own business, you have funding."

The Russian oligarch and international criminal Mikhail Yeschenko pushed two people aside to catch us before we spoke to anyone else. He was short and stocky, like a bulldog ready to fight over the last hunk of steak in the Urals. The blonde supermodel at his side stood six inches taller than him. The supermodel took one look at Ms. Sabel, who added a couple more inches to the occasion, and tucked behind Mikhail's shoulder for safety.

"She must know of your reputation," Mikhail laughed to me as if we were old friends. "She's afraid of you."

I stared at her while talking to him. "How did you land such a hottie? What's your secret, Mikhail?"

Like a true psychopath, he lapped up the flattery.

Without warning, Ms. Sabel pushed me against Yeschenko's shoulder, his arm encircled me while his girlfriend tucked under my other arm. We grinned until the camera flashes blinded me. When the first photographer darted away, another stepped in. We strained our smiles for round two. I recognized both photographers as the kind of paparazzi who had never been allowed near a Sabel party in the past.

I felt the fabric of Yeschenko's jacket. "You've recovered nicely since Yuri Belenov tried to wipe you out."

"He stole little more than my lunch money." Yeschenko's face hardened to death-threat level. "He didn't do as much damage to my operation as you."

"Just business." I gave him my soldier stare. After one too many near-death experiences on the battlefield, a soldier begins to question whether he's on Earth, in heaven, or hell, and then he realizes it doesn't matter. All the tension in his face disappears giving him the look of someone on the verge of sleep. The only unnerving thing about him is the intensity in his eyes. No movement escapes him, no adversary can sneak up on him, his next move will be instantaneous and deadly.

Mikhail flinched, not because I scared him but because he hadn't expected such an expression at a party. A smile of respect spread on his face.

"You should hire Sabel Security to track down Belenov," I said. "I've found him before. I can do it again."

Yeschenko's smile turned genuine. He pushed his index finger to my chest. "That is a great idea. I will take you up on that next week."

Ms. Sabel expertly moved us through the crowd. "Another stellar performance. And this time a more formidable encounter. You'd make a pretty good billionaire."

"But he stays on the suspect list," I said.

"Absolutely. That was an interesting invitation to have us track down Belenov. If he calls, I'll scratch him off the list. He won't want us close to his operation if he's after Alvaria."

Ms. Sabel tapped a well-dressed boy on the shoulder. When he turned around, I realized he was not a child, but an adult not much over five feet tall with the bearing and arrogance of the last emperor of China. I'd never met Deng Zhipeng, but his efforts to woo Ms. Sabel—despite her being nearly a foot taller—were legendary in company gossip.

He ignored me and kissed the back of her hand. Then he asked if she could help him with his permanent residence application since she was a good friend of President Charles Williams. He alluded to problems between the Red Army and his internet company. He hadn't been back to his homeland for some time, fearing a crackdown. She promised to see what she could do.

We wrote him off the suspect list and moved on.

That's when I lost my concentration.

A ghost from my past moved through the crowd. A woman I once loved almost as much as Jenny—until she walked out on me—stood across the dance floor.

When a lover leaves you, not because of something you did but because of who you are, seeing her again is shattering. Every cell in my body felt like ice. Long before Jenny, I'd fallen for Yumi Shibata. We had a deep and meaningful relationship until I had to put down a couple assassins in my backyard. My extreme violence shocked her. She walked out and never looked back.

Yumi looked at a canapé before deciding against it. She looked around the room and found me staring at her. People moved between us, obscuring the view.

Mercury put an elbow on my shoulder. *Sucks to see an old flame at a billionaire party. You know what that means.*

I said, *That she came here to find me?*

Don't you wish? Mercury teased. *No, it means she came here with a billionaire. Don't you hate it when someone dumps you then winds up better off? But shake that out of your head. Turn to the guy on your right and say, 'My sister ships tons of kale to Odessa.'*

I did as my god commanded and found myself in the middle of a conversation with a fiftyish man who had the lean-and-hungry look of a marathoner. My memory rewound and found his name, George Falconer, just as he laughed.

He focused on me as if we were stranded on a life raft with no one else in sight.

"Don't look at me," he said. "We handle every commodity except health food. Too volatile. You know what they say, 'Perishables never die, they just sale away.'"

My laugh sounded as real as I could make it. I asked him, "How many children do you have?"

"What makes you think I have any?"

"You're so good at dad jokes."

He laughed. "You can do better?"

Mercury spoke, and I repeated his words. "Who is this Rorschach guy and why does he paint so many pictures of my parents fighting?"

Falconer roared with laughter and slopped his drink. I liked the guy.

He squeezed my shoulder. "We should get together some time. You're a very interesting young man. How about coffee tomorrow?"

"He can't," Ms. Sabel jumped in. "We're off to Davos tomorrow."

"Young Global Leaders conference? I'm giving a talk there. We simply must have a drink after."

We made plans.

Ms. Sabel turned to the next guest on her list, hedge-fund king Ritchie Skaite. Round and balding, mid-sixties, he looked like he hadn't slept in a week. Beads of sweat sat on his pudgy face and forehead, waiting to drip down. Before I could try my hand at being one of the billionaires, he cut me off.

"Pia, I need your help," he said with a worried look. "This morning, I decided to retire. The stress has been eating at me for years. Last night, I had a Scrooge-dream where I saw my future. I was surrounded by ex-wives and employees with their hands out. All of them waiting for me to die so they could contest my will. When I woke up, I immediately signed

Bill Gates' Giving Pledge. I saw your name on the list. You have to tell me what to do next. I need help with this charity stuff."

She eyed him half with suspicion and half with sympathy. "You've never supported a charity?"

He shook his head. The beads of sweat flew off his face. More formed.

Skaite begged her to show him the homeless shelter she supported in DC. She challenged him to make and serve dinner there. He looked relieved, as if she'd absolved him of his sins. At least he was on the road to redemption.

"Sounds like someone had an epiphany," Ms. Sabel said. "If he shows up next week, he'll be off the suspect list."

We moved on to the last on her list. Katyonak Yeschenko. A lady who knew she was the sexiest woman in the room and had the purr to prove it. Twenty years earlier, she had been the top model in Kiev. Now in her early forties, she was on a mission to get her growl back. Her deep neckline barely contained the polished globes of silicone-under-skin pressed together to form a bottomless fissure. A diamond as big as my thumb sat at the top to help direct viewers. She hugged me when Ms. Sabel started to introduce us.

I didn't see the hug coming. My eyes were still glued to the diamond.

"I know all about your hero, Pia," Katyonak said over my shoulder. "I want him for my man-harem when you're done with him."

At that moment, I understood the true meaning of objectify.

Katyonak dragged me to the dance floor and proceeded to modernize the tango, yanking me to and fro and leading a sexual allegory in twists and turns. I didn't mind. She had an attitude that age would never take away from her. She was more fun than women half her age.

Unwilling to let someone steal her date, Ms. Sabel joined us. The two women sandwiched me with rhythmic thrusts, bumps, and grinds. Not that I minded a whole lot.

Cameras flashed and other dancers gave us some room. I love to dance, but I'd never been a spectacle before and was growing more uncomfortable with the arrangement with each new song the DJ played. I wondered if Ms. Sabel had been taking Ecstasy.

Mercury made it a foursome. *Dawg, you are the man of the moment. You're up on all the celebrity blogs.*

I said, *What is going on here? When did I become a chick-magnet?*

Mercury said, *When you decided to propose to Jenny. Never shoulda showed Pia-Caesar-Sabel that ring. Nothing makes a woman want a man more than knowing he wants someone else. Same goes for men wanting another man's woman, but those feuds usually end up in the hospital.*

I said, *Ms. Sabel's not like that. She thinks of me as the brother she never had.*

Mercury said, *Who cares, dude? Get down with yo bad self. Whatever's going down, it's time to stop thinking of her as Ms. Sabel. She knows you only do that to maintain a formality that will keep your ass from falling in love with her. Personally, I think she wants you to call her babe-a-licious.*

That was not going to happen.

A slow song came on and Ms. Sabel pushed Katyonak off the dance floor. She wrapped herself around me and we swayed. Her hands wandered around in a way that made me uncomfortable. Not because I'm some kind of puritan—my fantasies lean toward the dissolute—but because reading women's signals is a subjective art form. This was one relationship where I didn't want to misinterpret anything.

In my ear, she whispered, "I'm glad you can read my mind, Jacob. It means the world to me that you get what I'm trying to do. Hold me tight."

More cameras flashed and men started lining up to dance with the boss. I peeled away and found a nook where I could catch my breath and figure out what she meant. Everything she did was part of a strategy. If she relied on my mind-reading skills, we were in deep trouble. I didn't want to disappoint, but I wasn't going to cross a line with her that I'd reserved for Jenny. I understood why we spent all day working on building my legend. Things were rolling along just like we'd planned. We'd already eliminated several suspects. There were a few more to go.

So where did the dirty dancing come in? If she was using events to sexualize our relationship, I was back to Ginsberg's Law of Thermodynamics.

Or was it the Paradox of Existential Nihilism? I always get those two mixed up.

That's when a text message came in from Jenny. It read, "WHAT THE HELL IS THIS?"

She linked to a gossip site with a picture of Ms. Sabel and me half an inch from kissing on the dance floor. The headline read, *From Terrorist-Hunter to Boy-Toy on the Côte d'Azure.* The post included a page of pictures with me, Ms. Sabel, and Katyonak in what the photographer had cropped to represent various simulations of group sex.

While trying to formulate a response, I felt the presence of someone directly in front of me. I looked up.

Yumi Shibata said, "Jacob, I need you."

CHAPTER 17

I WOKE ON A COUCH in the living room of the owner's deck at the top of the *Numina*. Had it been a bad dream? Which part? My ex-girlfriend asking for help before glancing over my shoulder, seeing someone, then running away? Or me ducking through a crowd of billionaires, on the run from a Russian cougar and a boss behaving badly? Or trying to get Jenny on the phone so I could talk her off the ledge?

All of the above.

Ms. Sabel, an insomniac who sleeps three hours on a good night, was not around. I showered and stepped out to find she'd straightened up the living room and tossed my clothes around her bedroom. Then she ordered breakfast on the outside deck where heaters kept us from sensing the chilly November air. Clouds had moved in, rain was imminent, and she wasn't talking.

"What was that all about last night?" I asked with an edge I tried—but failed—to soften.

"The reason you feel like a brother to me is because I have your absolute trust. I appreciate it." She touched my arm. "By the way, Mikhail Yeschenko called. He wants you to find Belenov. No one else, just you. I told him you're on a mission. He said it can wait. That means he's off the suspect list."

Then she took a call from Tokyo.

I finished my omelette au fromage and found my duffel neatly packed in her suite. The whole room had been cleaned, the bed made, the furniture polished, and the windows washed without a single word spoken or noise made. The staff on this dinghy would make terrific spies.

We rode one of the *Numina's* two choppers to Nice, where we took

Sabel One to Zurich. From there, it was another chopper to Davos. Ms. Sabel caught up on business calls while we flew. She never answered my question about the night before. We checked into the Presidential Suite at the new Intercontinental Hotel in Davos. She made extra efforts to stay on the phone.

Bored after lunch, I wandered around the hotel complex. A crew set up a reception for the Forum of Young Global Leaders in the ballroom. An unattended guest list on a tablet was too tempting to pass up. I scrolled through six hundred names. A World Champion racecar driver, a famous actor, a well-known entrepreneur, and the leaders of several famous do-gooder organizations caught my eye. There were brochures laid out about the sessions. Some of the people I'd met in Monaco were leading break-outs or giving speeches. To me, it looked like the world's billionaires were grooming the world's next generation of billionaires for something. Maybe they were clearing the way for a global plutocracy.

Mercury leaned over my shoulder. *Dude. Where you been? The plutocracy happened in 1985. Time for you to step up and join in.*

I said, *I prefer to serve my country, defend my constitution, and fight for truth, justice—*

Save it, homes. Mercury looked like he'd eaten something sour. *Truman was the last US President who wasn't a multi-millionaire. Since him, the rest owed their lives to the billionaire class. Now, the billionaires are cutting out the middleman and buying whatever office they want. You can't beat 'em so you may as well join 'em. You can be a Caesar too. You're no smarter or dumber than any of them. You just don't have their confidence.*

I felt a hand swirl a circle on my back. Katyonak whispered into my ear, "You would be my head-of-harem, Jacob. Leave her. She doesn't care about you."

She looked just as good in the daylight as she had the night before. I said, "Ms. Yeschenko, you're in the finished medical—"

"Please, call me Katyonak." She pinned me with sultry eyes.

"—products business. Did you know an exporter named Nate Hale?"

"Nate was a good man. Too bad he made such bad choices in friends."

"Oh? Who were these bad friends?" I asked.

She squeezed my arm, letting her fingertips trail down to my wrist. "Oh, Jacob. Don't concern yourself with those evil men. They ruined poor Nate. He was such a lovely man."

"Do you know those evil men's names?"

"I am not like my ex-husband. I do not associate with men who act like criminals. Nate made a deal. I told him it would go badly. I told him to stay with me a little longer." Her eyes misted. "He would not listen to me. You will listen to me, won't you, Jacob?"

She hooked a finger in my belt loop and tugged me closer.

"Wow, look at the time. I'm running late. Catchya later." I all but ran for the elevators.

It was still too early to call Jenny to fix things. She hadn't been answering my calls anyway. I went back to the suite and re-read everything in Duane Boyd's files about Ra. Nothing new jumped out at me.

Miguel Rodriguez, my best friend from my Ranger days and fellow Sabel agent, showed up with Ms. Sabel's other favorite employee, Tania Cooper. Miguel was six-five, two-thirty with the stoic bearing of a proud Navajo. Tania was a beauty formed from an exceptionally diverse racial lineage topped with wild hair. They had the two rooms next door to Ms. Sabel's suite. Miguel looked at me oddly when I asked if his room had an extra bed. They left me to catch up on their jet lag.

Ms. Sabel came in, wearing another amazing evening dress. Bold, bright colors flowed down it like spilled paint. She worked on some sparkly AF earrings. She looked me over. "Didn't I tell you to send those t-shirts home?"

I looked down. In giant letters, my t-shirt read, "But did you die?" Directly beneath was the Ranger's logo.

"You can't go around looking like that," she said. "There's a new outfit for you in the closet. The reception's in ten minutes."

"Wait a second," I said. "I don't get what's going on here. Jenny's so pissed off about the gossip sites, she won't return my calls."

Ms. Sabel's gaze fell to the floor. She started to say something, then stopped.

SEELEY JAMES

She held up a necklace indicating she needed help. I took it. Ten pounds of diamonds and platinum. I pulled it around her neck and tried to fasten it in back. The clasp was more complicated than anything I'd run across. I guess the maker didn't want it falling off or getting snatched. I had to look it over to figure it out. While I did, it occurred to me that Mercury had a point about the ultra-rich. These people were no better or worse than me. For that matter, Nate Hale was right too. None of them had fought the battles I had. I could make most of them crap their pants just by looking at them.

"It's tough, I know," she said. "And it's going to get tougher."

"Trying to butter me up?" I managed to get the Gustave Eiffel-designed clasp fastened.

"I'm serious, Jacob." She turned to face me. "We have to find who is willing to risk everything to steal Alvaria. I asked you what risks either of us were willing to take."

In my recollection, the conversation had centered on me not losing Jenny. Maybe that was just my perspective.

She looked at me as if I'd forgotten everything. She said, "I told you I can't risk the jobs of sixty thousand employees."

"So?" I hesitated, not sure where any of this fit in. "How are people's jobs at risk if you stop doing things that make Jenny jealous?"

"Can't be helped." She stood in front of me, eye to eye, toe to toe. "There's a lot on the line right now. I know what I'm doing, even if it hurts to do it. I need you to trust me. Please."

I've said no to a lot of women. I've never been able to say it to Ms. Sabel.

We went to the reception and repeated the party on the *Numina* for a larger crowd. This time, Ms. Sabel was the popular one. Every guy in the room and a few of the women asked her to dance. She kept pulling me onto the dance floor. The cameras continued to flash. Her dance moves were even more salacious. I couldn't wait for the next text from Jenny.

I decided to do that thing most people do when their love lives are swirling down the toilet for reasons beyond their control: I drank. Heavily.

Yumi appeared again. Then she disappeared again. Like an

apparition. Given my relationship with defunct pantheons, there was a better than even chance she was a phantom. Since Katyonak and Ms. Sabel were trying to ruin my relationship with Jenny, it stood to reason my mind would invent a spirit from the past to help seal my fate. We humans tend to be self-destructive like that. Besides, Yumi was a blue-collar girl from a blue-collar family. She wouldn't be in a we're-rich-and-you're-not conference in Switzerland.

I woke up in my fancy duds, face down on a couch, a trail of drool running down the cushion. No texts from Jenny. Not even a reply to my many ill-advised pleas for a sign. As I re-read some of my late-night texts, I cringed. Drunk texting should be outlawed. I wondered if I could put a breathalyzer on my phone to prevent a repeat offense.

When I got out of the shower, Ms. Sabel had laid out another over-the-top outfit with a note to join her for breakfast at the event buffet. I put on the costume and went downstairs. While the clothes made me feel funny, they did get lots of compliments. Not just from Katyonak, who repeatedly complimented the fit of my slacks while running her fingers over my butt, but also Josephine and Falconer. Even Deng Zhipeng commented on my sartorial choices.

Josephine Seligman caught me at the entrance and talked up private banking as if I cared. A few familiar faces from the night before complimented me on my "uninhibited" dancing. They walked away snickering. More vaguely familiar people asked me if I would be accepting Katyonak's offer. Apparently, my exploits from last night had gone viral on social media.

From that moment forward, I promised myself, I would never drink again. Until next time.

Mercury cut in line in front of me. *What's better than making a drunken fool out of yourself in front of global leaders, homie?*

I said, *If it has anything to do with evangelizing for the Dii Consentes, forget it.*

Mercury leaned back. *Dude. Think. What's better than acting like a world class idiot in front of the world's idiot class? Getting ahead of them in the money department. You're no good proselytizing for me if you're not rich. Who's going to listen to some homeless wacko on the street corner? You can be rich like them. You can be a Caesar. And I'm the god who can get you there. All you have to do is—*

Ms. Sabel stepped between my personal deity and me, sparing me a lesson on how slaughtering the Gauls will lead to riches. She said, "Feeling better?"

"I've been thinking." I plopped some scrambled eggs on my plate. "I don't get how this kowtowing to the rich is going to help us find Ra. I know, I promised to do things your way, but I feel lost and confused. So, how about we try my way: Go after Konrad and beat it out of him?"

Forever the athlete, she topped her yogurt with a serving of fruit.

Then she clanked the metal bowl loud enough for it to echo in the room. She turned to me, her face flushed with fire in her eyes. She screamed, "That's what I'm SICK OF! Damn it, Jacob! I'm done with you. I've had enough of your BULLSHIT!"

She smashed her bowl on the table, sending fruit and yogurt in every direction, and started to storm away. She stopped three paces later in front of a wide-eyed Josephine. She shouted at the banker, "Do you still have that shipping company you wanted to sell?"

"Uh." Josephine swallowed. "Yes."

"How much?"

"Fifty million. And that's the lowest—"

"Done. Send me the bill and give him the company." She pointed at me with an index finger on the end of her fully extended arm. It felt like a lightning bolt.

Her glare ran down that finger and arm like a deadly laser beam. She said in a voice everyone in the room could hear, "Consider it severance."

She stormed out.

Josephine looked at me, slightly embarrassed. She held out a business card, shrugged, and said sheepishly, "Congratulations?"

CHAPTER 18

PIA SABEL WALKED INTO HER office at Sabel Industries headquarters, tossed her purse on her desk, and crossed to the windows. Her last look at Jacob's face haunted her. The view of downtown Bethesda from the eighteenth floor was just as frightening. It was drizzling, cloudy, and dark. All the leaves had fallen from the trees. Black scratchy branches reached up to her like starving children desperate for help. She leaned her forehead against the glass and watched the ant-people so far below.

Had it been presumptuous of her to think Jacob would grasp and understand her needs? Hurting him had been an unintended consequence.

Tania walked in. "Other than that, Mrs. Lincoln, how did you like the play?"

She turned to face her seasoned veteran. "Did I do the right thing?"

"I did the right thing once. I got busted from captain back to lieutenant. That's why I work here. You get it. The right thing always has a cost. It's rarely pretty." She sighed heavily. "Besides, Jacob was asking for it."

Pia tracked around the desk and dropped into her executive chair.

Tania took a seat opposite her and studied Pia. "Your dad used to tell me to make a decision, then, right or wrong, move on."

"Doesn't make it any easier," Pia said.

Tania handed her the updates for the two Alvaria-related contracts. "Miguel and I are tag-teaming both the CIA contract to find the bidders and the State Department contract to recover Alvaria."

"Why both of you?"

"Make it easier to delay and confuse. Your plan is complicated and it's not going to happen overnight."

Pia's intercom buzzed. Her secretary announced the scheduled call with Reggie Forrest, Assistant Secretary of State. Pia clicked the speakerphone and announced herself.

"I need an update," Reggie said without preamble. "You've spent the last several days hobnobbing with Monaco's elite and drinking in Davos. You should be tracking down Alvaria."

"My people are working on it as we speak."

"I understood you would take personal responsibility. You also agreed to accept my liaison, Eva Gomez."

"I am taking personal responsibility. I told you my people are working on it. Don't waste time making me repeat myself." Pia took a deep breath to control her rising anger. "Send Ms. Gomez over and we'll bring her up to speed."

"She's in your lobby at the moment. She's been there all morning. And she's been cleared for and briefed on Alvaria."

Pia looked up at Tania. After their first encounter, Pia had researched Eva Gomez and discovered she'd recently survived a mass shooting. The last thing she'd intended was to show any disrespect.

"We'll track her down." Pia tilted her head at Tania, who took the hint and moved quickly to retrieve the missing liaison. "We won't reveal our sources and methods to her. That's proprietary and need-to-know. What do you expect her to do here?"

"Since you're obviously not involved in the daily operations, I expect her to shadow you. When you get reports from your agents, she can relay that information to me."

For Pia, it wasn't just an insult; it meant Eva would be an unnecessary layer and potential for miscommunication. What good would it do Forrest when everyone—except Eva—knew Eva was a spy?

Tania returned with the diminutive striker-turned-State Department specialist. Eva entered with a huge smile, still bright, still hopeful, and still lit with naïveté. She carried herself like a soccer star, full of confidence and swagger, with no sign of her recent trauma. Pia shook hands with her and gestured to a chair next to Tania.

"Now that you're all there in one place," Reggie said, "I'd like a status report."

Pia replied, "My project manager has tracked the crew and ship without substantial breakthrough."

"You mean Miguel Rodriguez? Why was he in Davos with you instead of Tripoli where the ship landed?"

Pia noted Forrest's knowledge of her entourage and wondered who the woman's source was. CIA? NSA? NSI? DIA? She said, "If you'd like to micromanage the project, Ms. Forrest, we can turn the project back to you and wait for your people to find it."

"Don't shirk your commitments, Ms. Sabel. Your man wasn't even looking for it. He went to parties with you after you broke up with your boyfriend. I didn't even need to ask the NSA what my contractor's up to. It's on all the gossip sites. Your people should be in Tripoli."

Pia calmly watched Eva's eyes bulge at the caustic exchange. Colleges don't have classes on nasty business conflicts. Naïveté.

"Sabel Security does not need your direction, Forrest." Pia felt her anger reaching a breaking point. "The one place we know Alvaria is not—is Tripoli. The ship never docked, and no cargo was loaded or unloaded."

"How can you be so sure if your man never went there?"

"Because he is not my only employee. We have over two hundred agents securing other corporate assets on Tripoli's docks. Due to high criminal activity, commercial travel of any kind is not recommended. If your thieves unloaded Alvaria there without an army bigger than Sabel's to secure it, they would have lost it to bandits. You can look up general conditions and travel advisories on the State Department's website."

"Well." Forrest paused and snorted. "What is your next step?"

"To foil the thieves and recover the product."

"That's not a next step, that's an evasion. You made commitments to your country. I see no evidence you're doing a damn thing. Going forward, I demand daily updates on everything you're doing."

Her words stung Pia like icicle knives. She said sheepishly, "We're working on it."

They clicked off.

Pia observed Eva Gomez from head to toe. The young lady appeared to be in a state of shock. An expression she would learn to hide soon enough. Of the many problems Pia had encountered as a businesswoman, few had presented as complicated a choice as Ms. Gomez. How should she handle a spy who isn't even aware of her role? Could she trust Eva Gomez? Or treat her as what real spies would call a *useful idiot*? Although that term of art sounded off in this case, a more accurate term would be *useful ingenue*.

"Welcome to the real world, Ms. Gomez." Pia rose and smiled. "We tend to be more direct with each other than college experience may have led you to believe."

"Yeah," Eva said slowly. "True that."

The young woman's upturned face still showed considerable starstruck admiration. Pia felt conflicted about treating her as useful. If she told Eva her strategy, how much of a risk would that represent?

"Tell me something," Pia said. "Have any of your college friends been approved for a security clearance concerning the most dangerous weapon in the American arsenal?"

"Uhm, I don't think so, no."

Pia rose and tracked around the desk. "Out of the seventy-five thousand employees at the State Department, why do you think you were picked for this job?"

Eva shook her head. "Availability? Capability? Loyalty?"

"I'm sure you were loyal to USC's Trojan family while you were there. They gave you a spot on the team, you gave them your best effort. A complimentary transaction that made sense."

"I still am a loyal Trojan, Ms. Sabel." Eva rose. "Always will be."

"Call me Pia." She walked Eva out of the office and down the hall. "Loyalties lean toward the transient in the adult world."

CHAPTER 19

THE MAN THEY CALL RA trotted up the steps from the sport deck behind the woman he loved, hating himself for sounding like a scared schoolboy. "I swear, darling, Pia Sabel means nothing to me. It was a business discussion. We had a couple drinks, nothing more."

"So you say." She crossed the main deck, leading him from the dark to the brightness inside.

"You're being silly." He chased after her.

"Am I?" She stopped and scowled at him. "She's young, rich, and just dumped her boyfriend. All things you like."

"I inquired about engaging the services of Jacob Stearne."

Ra hated the feeling in his stomach. Any other woman in his life would've been shipped back to her mother by now. He wanted to appease her petty jealousies, but an important call awaited him. He had no time for drama. He clenched his fists. How had his darling gotten such a hold on him? Why had he allowed himself to be so smitten with her? She was his weakness.

"What do you want with her boyfriend?" she asked. She took the spiral staircase up to the master suite.

"Are you serious? He's a one-man wrecking crew." He caught up with her and said quietly, "One Jacob Stearne is worth ten Bonhams."

She looked at him with more tenderness than she had in the last twenty-four hours. "You replace Bonham with Jacob Stearne?"

"It would not be easy, but I'm working on it."

"You replace Bonham's dogs?"

"Because it is your wish, I am exploring options." He stroked her shoulder. "These things are delicate propositions, though. No guarantees."

She put her hands on his chest softly and leaned into him. Ra circled her with his arms and felt the warmth of her body. These were the moments he lived for now. He almost laughed at himself. Whipped. A year ago, he would've found the idea inconceivable. Yet here he was, inhaling the scent of her perfume and drifting into heaven.

His reverie was broken by the call he expected. He pulled his phone and shook a playful finger at her. "Don't mention this to Bonham. Not a word, not a hint. It could produce a disastrous preemptive strike."

He kissed her forehead. She nodded and pulled away.

He took the call as he dropped down the spiral staircase. He did not need to speak. He only listened as his informant hurried through incomplete sentences in whispers. When the call ended, the man they call Ra clicked off and said, "Shit!"

There were ways he could handle the new situation. It would take a lot of thinking and careful planning. He texted Bonham, ordering him to drop whatever women he was holding and join him on the *Savannah*.

Fido stood watch on deck. Blood stains streaked the back of his shirt. They were light, but clearly the man had taken his twenty lashes seriously. Ra liked that in a bodyguard. He wondered if Jacob Stearne would take his punishment like a man. Doubtful. Stearne struck him as a man who thought himself equal to Ra. Perhaps Stearne was more than a soldier.

He strolled aft and watched the waves in the moonlight. His gaze traced the line of yachts in Monaco's harbor. He thanked the heavens Sabel's *Numina* was gone. Off to Santorini, he'd heard. Let the throngs of second-class tourists in Greece ooh and ahh over the monster. All that mattered was that things were back to normal in Monaco. His *Savannah* was, once again, the biggest ship at anchor.

Of the many things demanding his attention, though, his woman distracted him the most. If he had the strength, he would send her away. She was a liability that could cost him his life. He should pull a Pia Sabel and dump her in public. He took a moment to admire Sabel's method. When you want to quit someone, do it in public. Make it a spectacle. See it on Instagram. Then you can't be weak and let them back in. Logically, he knew he would have to do that. Having someone hold your love in her hands gave her too much power. A dangerous vulnerability. Yet in his heart, he knew he could never let her go. Her unwavering loyalty to her loved ones lit up his life like no one before. He could trust her with his life.

Bonham's tender arrived. The handsome devil bounded up the stairs to join him.

"Bad news," Ra said. "The CIA is aware of the auction."

Bonham inhaled his shock. "How did they get wind of it?"

"We got greedy, sport." Ra rested his elbows on the railing. "We invited one too many parties. Someone used an unsecured phone. Someone had a mole on their end. Someone got drunk and bragged. There is no way of knowing how they got the news. They're the CIA after all. But it gets worse."

"Dear god. What?"

"They've hired an outsider to uncover the bidders."

"Which means our mole will no longer have a view into their progress." Bonham mimicked Ra's posture on the railing. "It has to be Konrad."

"Why do you say that?"

"It's obvious, isn't it? The Estonians are doing fine. The cops haven't broken down their doors with a search warrant. The Egyptians, Romanians, Cypriots are all accounted for. Who else could it be?"

"It could've been that stupid general. He might've gotten word out in the time between killing his emissary and killing him. Unlikely, though." Ra turned around, leaning his back to the rail, and observed his security chief for a long time before answering. "How do I know it's not you?"

Bonham snapped back a step. He started to answer but stopped himself. He stood up straight like a soldier at attention.

"You are my security," Ra said. "We've had two security breaches on your watch. First Konrad, and now this. You've gotten comfortable in your role, Bonham. You've gotten sloppy. Too many orgies on the *Miss Conduct*. Too much reliance on Fido, Spot, Rover, and the rest."

Bonham nodded.

Ra patted his shoulder, letting his man know he wasn't truly under suspicion. Ra had promised him more money from this deal than the man had made in his entire life. Bonham was a good accomplice at killing people, but he was inept when it came to operations. The business side scared the man. Bonham would never undermine the process.

Ra considered the options for the auction. His calculations put the price tag at $1.5 billion, but it could go higher. The Chinese might scoff, but they would never let the Iranians outbid them. Still, there was a severe problem that needed fixing. That much Bonham could do. But how to handle the eager, anxious, and distrustful bidders? He considered several options before settling on one.

"You are to visit each of the bidders in person," Ra said. "You will let them know there has been a breach. Blame one of the other bidders for drinking too much. Tell them the offender has been cut out of the deal. Let them know we will reschedule when we find an acceptable time and location."

The man's jaw dropped. "We can't push it back. We've worked ages on this. They'll be furious. They won't believe—"

"Are you in favor of letting the CIA crash our party, Bonham?"

"No." Bonham relaxed his stand. "Damn it. You're right. It's too risky. I'll leave in the morning."

"Morning?"

"Tonight. I'll leave right away." Bonham turned and took a few steps, then stopped and faced Ra again. "I assume you expect an act of loyalty?"

Ra nodded slowly. "Choose your own punishment."

"Would bringing you the head of Konrad von Frieden be acceptable?"

"Can you replace $7.2 million in gun running profits?" Ra strode up to him and shoved a finger in Bonham's chest. "I don't want Konrad killed, you idiot. Bring me the head of the man who stood in his garage and called the police."

CHAPTER 20

I SHOULD'VE BEEN HOBNOBBING WITH the next generation of extra-privileged young people. That was the plan. We'd rehearsed it. Ms. Sabel had groomed me for the role. Everything was going well.

Instead, I was escorted to the curb by Jessie, a fellow Sabel agent I barely knew. My duffel landed on the cement next to me. He summoned a cab to take me to the airport. Then he held out his hand.

He said, "Credit card and Sabel phone, please."

I stared at him in wordless shock. Sabel phones are the most prized possessions in the industry. They're proprietary. They use Sabel Satellites for global connections. They have magic tech behind them that makes my brain hurt when they explain it to me. If you leave the company, you have to turn it in. It's an act as traumatic as giving up citizenship. And the credit card was a special issue with no spending limits. It felt like Jessie was amputating my limbs.

He sensed my pain. "Sorry, Jacob. Orders."

I handed over the requested goods. He handed me the latest phone from Apple, a huge step down. No replacement credit card. He shrugged regretfully and walked back inside.

Turning in my phone hadn't been part of the plan. Nor was running around without funding. And getting walked to the curb by a junior guy? None of this was part of the plan.

But I got the message. It was billboard-sized and directly from Ms. Sabel: You're dead to me.

I stood on the sidewalk feeling as if a giant bird of prey had swooped down to wrap me in her wings while she pecked out my heart and brains.

Was it an act? It might have been, except that it didn't feel like one.

No matter how I looked at it, the scenario didn't make sense. Ms. Sabel had gone to great lengths to make me look like an executive on the same economic plane as Yeschenko, Deng, Falconer, and Seligman. We'd worked to eliminate half of the suspects already. We were supposed to narrow the rest down by tomorrow. We were on track to unmask Ra himself. We were winning.

So why the cold dump?

Was it really because I didn't sleep with her? Nah. The only thing that made sense was that she had some kinda plan for me to go it alone. But if that's the case, why take my phone and leave no way to communicate? If this was an undercover mission, how am I supposed to contact Ms. Sabel when I find the guy? She's a brilliant strategist; she would've at least set up plans and backup plans for basic communication. Right? Miguel and Tania had gone with me when I went undercover in Andalusia. They had kept watch and helped out. If this is part of her plan, what happens if I get in too deep and need extraction? Am I supposed to send up smoke signals? That's not how she operates.

Something had gone horribly wrong. Either I'd done something—or not done something—or she'd gone nuts. She had gone nuts before. That possibility was the only one making sense to me.

The iPhone was brand new. I had to set it up before I could use it. Which took a horribly long time when I needed answers fast. Finally, I was able to dial Miguel.

"I can't talk to you," he said. "I need this job. Don't call me."

He clicked off.

My former best friend hung up on me.

I dialed Ms. Sabel. An automated voice told me my calls were blocked. Same when I called Tania. Jenny was so pissed I was afraid to call her.

I got in the cab just as Josephine Seligman came running up. She told me I needed to sign papers in London. Someone would meet me. What did make sense was Ms. Sabel giving me a company as severance. While it seems excessive to most of us, it was pocket change for her. She'd given several of us huge bonuses and extravagant gifts when we did something right. Once, after I saved her life, she gave me a Ferrari. Some terrorists blew it up—but for a couple weeks, I was styling.

The cab drove me off into an overcast morning.

There was no use denying it: I'd been ejected. I was lost. I'd spent my adult life with giant institutions behind me, the US Army then Sabel Security. Now, I wandered the wilderness alone and confused.

I felt like I'd been gutshot and left for dead.

What in Vulcan's name did I do that made Ms. Sabel treat me like vermin? That single question flipped over in my mind as I staggered through a barren, featureless world.

At least I owned a shipping company. Somewhere.

Josephine's VP met me at Heathrow. He scooped me up, took me to the bank, gave me a temporary credit card, and had me sign all the papers. He popped the cork on a bottle of champagne and took me out to a fancy restaurant even though I was in no mood to celebrate. The next morning, his assistant, Mason, took me to Durrës, Albania to show me the company.

Albania. Where Alvaria was going to be shipped. Quite a coincidence. Was it an act after all? Seligman had repossessed the company months ago. Ms. Sabel heard about it yesterday. She only found out about Alvaria a few days ago. There was no way she set things up that far in advance. Was there?

At some point during the day, Jenny called. Short call. Iceberg words. She needed "some space." And not for the first time in our short-but-intense relationship. After everything I'd done for her, she needed space? Who forced her into therapy to confront the two-by-four life had slammed in her face? I'd been working through it with her for months. We were making progress. I thought. Until she needed space.

Maybe I should give her a lot more space. Like half a world.

CHAPTER 21

ALBANIA SEEMED LIKE A GREAT place to get some space from the women in my life.

I read travel blogs during the flight with Mason. Everyone said Albania is a friendly, relatively safe country. On the drive from the airport in the capital, Tirana, we saw nice farms and well-kept buildings. Durrës was a different story. As we pulled into town, I realized the bloggers had been visiting other parts of the small nation.

While it was true the people were nice, and I didn't see any video surveillance or the fist-sized padlocks found in most cities. It was a rust bucket. The sidewalks were strewn with litter. People lived in unfinished apartment buildings with aging rebar extending to a yet-to-be-built second floor. Fire-hazard wiring looped from pole to buildings. Children played in busy streets. Intersections were a libertarian's wet dream: no signage or traffic controls.

Mason, the charming young assistant banker in suit and tie, took me to the office of my new home, Detit Exports. A two-room affair on the third floor of a crumbling building overlooking the harbor. There were no employees in sight. One room was set up like a classroom with six desks facing the front. Behind them was the second room, the owner's office, with a waist-high wall and glass above that. The owner liked to keep an eye on the employees. The windows were dirty, the desks were dusted with papers and forms, the furniture had been secondhand thirty years ago. Three pictures hung on the wall. Each showed a nice, clean cargo ship. Each ship was a bit smaller than the *Numina*. Each picture had that color fade indicating it had been hanging there for a few decades. It was doubtful the boats I owned were still pristine.

Mason explained the company name. The Canadian who'd last owned the place thought *detit* was Albanian for sea-going. It was, in a way. It's a form of *seawater*. Close enough, apparently.

Mason looked around the main room. "They're supposed to meet us here. Perhaps it's lunchtime."

I crossed the room to glance around the owner's office. Sam Spade might step out any minute. A large safe stood open and empty in the corner. A bottle of cheap booze stood on one side of the metal desk. No cap. An inch of brown liquid in the bottom with the distinct look of spit-back swimming in it. It had a label written in what I guessed was Albanian. Behind the desk was a credenza filled with more empty bottles. The last owner had chosen quantity over quality as operations sank into bankruptcy.

Mercury strode in looking smug and satisfied. *We are on our way now, homie! Can you believe this? You got your own shipping company. Whooee!*

I said, *I don't have a company. I have a dung heap in a ghetto.*

Dude, what's with the attitude? Mercury crossed his arms and gave me a scowl. *Aristotle Onassis started with less than this.*

I said, *Who?*

Richest man in the world, bro. You don't know him? Mercury put a finger over his lips and thought. *Wait, he's been dead a while. Seems like yesterday, but I guess it was over sixty years ago. When you're old like me, time flies. Anyway, he was a shipping magnate. He was a refugee in 1922 and a billionaire in 1952. He did it all with ships. We're gonna do the same damn thing. Start thinking empire, baby!*

I said, *Yeah. Right.*

Mercury said, *Get yourself an attitude of gratitude, brutha. You know how many people would love to have a $50 million shipping company dropped in their laps? I don't think you get the scale of the opportunity in front of you, homie. Listen up—the average American makes sixty-three thousand a year. If you saved every penny of that and never spent a dime, it would take you sixteen years to accumulate a million dollars. But it would take you 15,873 years to reach a billion dollars. You're never going to become a Caesar working for someone else.*

DEATH AND BETRAYAL

I said, *I don't care.*

Mercury said, *You're not hearing me. If you have a million dollars and you spend it at a dollar per second, that's sixty dollars per minute or $86,400 per day, you'll run out of money in a little over eleven days. But if you have a billion dollars and you spend a dollar a second, it'll last you almost THIRTY-TWO YEARS! Thirty-two freaking years! And you don't have to pay taxes!*

I said, *Wait, why wouldn't I pay taxes?*

Mercury said, *Beats me, but for the last thirty years, voters have elected guys who gave huge tax breaks to the rich. Nowadays, billionaires don't gotta pay. Anyway, quit whining and let's turn this backwater export into something bigger than Sabel Industries. Then one day, you can drop a billion on a yacht and not think a damn thing about it.*

He had a point there. A billion is a whole lot more than a million. Maybe I could turn this dust bin into a billion dollars. I guess I could've been dumped on the Serengeti with nothing. Even so, gratitude was not what I was feeling.

Ms. Sabel had kept secrets from me. She'd never done that before. Well. Except for that time she shot me. But these secrets were different. Secrets about that CIA guy. Secrets about Alvaria. Secrets about her plan. Why wouldn't she confide in me? The brother she never had.

Fuck her and her secrets. She dumped me on the sidewalk in Davos like a used tissue and blocked my calls. She wasn't my problem to worry about anymore.

Mercury was right. It was time to get rich.

CHAPTER 22

THE EMPLOYEES RETURNED TOGETHER. NOT because lunchtime was over, but because the company attorney had rounded them up and brought them in. They had assumed—or hoped, from the look of them— the new owner would fire them to end their suffering. The attorney did a lot of talking, mostly in English. He told me my employees learned it in school and fortified their skills with heavy doses of American TV. The guy sounded like a defense attorney cooking up a reason the employees shouldn't be given the death penalty. Something about no convictions and no current investigations caught my ear.

A middle-aged couple, Sokol and Geldona, did the accounting. They looked sullen and defeated and plump and round. Geldona had purple hair and an expression like Eeyore's. Her balding husband, Sokol, hid his pessimism a little better with a smile he turned on when someone spoke to him and turned off the instant after he answered. When he thought no one was looking at him, his eyes swept the desks and floors, as if he were looking for something of value to take home.

The company secretary was a bouncy young woman named Megi, fresh from the University of Tirana. Constantly in motion, she stood throughout the conversation and bobbed in place. In America, someone would've prescribed Ritalin to make her act like the rest of us depressed lab rats. I was glad that hadn't happened to her. She added a visceral energy to the room the others lacked. Where everyone else saw grime and hopelessness, she heard music and frolicked with unicorns. The world needs more Megis.

The last introductions were the operations guys, two Syrian refugees named Mardik and Firas. They could've been twins: thick black hair and trimmed beards, muscular shoulders, and rough hands from handling cargo. They were compact and strong with visible scars and the hard look of war veterans. They stared at me with soldier stares darker than mine. At some point in the not-too-distant past, they'd escaped the flames of hell. Their attitude changed when I addressed them in Arabic. They still looked suspicious but also a touch more hopeful about their future.

When Mason and the attorney left, I waited a beat.

"I don't care about the money you stole," I said to the group. "I only hope that you divvied it up equally between you."

They looked back and forth at each other, questioning who among them ratted them out. Which told me it had been equal. If it hadn't, all eyes would've turned to the one who took the most. I'd rather they worked as a team than resent each other. I tossed a banded stack of €100 euro notes on the table. "You get to split that as a bonus if you come clean about what happened to this company. Why did it go bankrupt in only a few months when it had been profitable for years before that?"

Their glances darted amongst each other until they silently elected Mardik to speak for them.

He squared his shoulders. "We did not steal from you."

"Not me, technically," I said. "The petty cash in that safe—" I pointed to the yawning iron behemoth in my office "—belonged to the bank at the time it was stolen. Same for the cash reserves in the bank accounts. But I said it doesn't matter, so don't fudge things with me. We won't succeed if we're not honest with each other. And don't worry, the bank threw in operating capital for me. Your paychecks won't bounce."

They smiled and nodded at each other. Steady paychecks in a country where the average household income is near an American teenager's allowance buys a lot of loyalty.

Mercury leaned between the accountants. *Uh, dude. You don't have a year's worth of operating capital. They gave you enough for a few weeks.*

I said, *You're the god of commerce. Think of something.*

Mercury said, *Maybe you don't remember me shouting 'don't sign those papers' back in London. I warned you. Did you listen to me? No, you went ahead and signed up for the debt that put the last guy in bankruptcy.*

I ignored him. What does god know anyway?

The employees weren't quite ready to level with me, so I upped the ante. "As soon as we get back to making money, everyone gets a ten percent raise. Then we'll work out bonuses."

The smiles grew and they nodded to each other more enthusiastically. I was winning them over.

Mercury said, *Where you getting bonuses and raises from, bro? In two months, you're back in London handing the keys back to the bank along with your house and car and 401(k).*

I said, *But the company made a big profit for years, then things fell apart. I'm going to return it to its glory days.*

Mercury said, *If we're going to make a Caesar out of you, you need a thriving business. Maybe you should ask these people where it all went wrong. Just a thought, homeboy.*

To the employees, I said, "You were making money a year ago and then it stopped. Something happened. Give it to me straight."

They spoke in Albanian and everyone tapped Mardik with their eyes. He resisted, so they nudged him forward with their hands. He ended up standing two feet in front of me.

"I will be honest with you, mister." He looked over his shoulder. His people nodded for him to go ahead. "We used to run guns to the Syrian rebels."

That was something I didn't expect. Detit Exports was an arms dealer? Just my luck. And I was leading the company back into bankruptcy without it. I asked, "That was profitable?"

"The ships carry grain, medicines, commodities, but those did not bring in enough to pay the bank," Geldona said. "Arms business was very profitable."

"Is there something else we could do for profit besides running guns?"

"Drugs?" Mardik asked.

No one flinched when he offered up that option. They were anxious about making money and not exactly picky about how.

Mercury stepped into my line of sight. *Don't go getting all high and mighty right now, homie. I know you just had a bad experience with some gunrunners in Paris and Greece. But you could make some serious coin, ya feel me?*

I looked at the floor. *Where does the Dii Consentes draw the line on morality?*

Mercury looked hurt. *Same place as everyone. On the far side of profit.*

If I was going to take down Ra for Nate's sake, I needed a lot of resources. That meant I needed Detit Exports to make money. Which meant I could deal drugs or guns. Criminal life sucks if those are your only options. Arms dealers had far fewer—albeit more deadly—enemies, and it was a business I had a passing familiarity with.

I said, *I could get in for a few deals. I'll only sell arms to the good guys. Make enough money to pay down the loans and then go back to the legit shipping business.*

Mercury said, *Now you're talking. That's just what Nate Hale was going to do, so you know it's a slippery slope. But if you're going in—go ALL in.*

After doing a doubletake at my long-abandoned idol, I stared down Mardik. I said, "Tell me about arms shipments."

"Each ship has a false hold. There, we kept guns." Mardik thought a moment. "We only sell guns to good guys."

Exactly what I wanted to hear. Except that the definition of "good guys" in Syria was a moving target last time I was there. Allies became enemies, bystanders became allies, NATO nations became invaders. If there had once been good guys by American standards, they were long gone. With refugees like Mardik and Firas guiding the deals, at least I knew the weapons would be sold to the little guys, the underdogs.

I glanced out the window. The Port of Durrës handled ferries from Italy. Plenty of freight came and went on trucks carried on those ferries. At that moment, there were no ferries. Only one cargo ship waited for containers on the docks. A pair of binoculars lay on the windowsill.

"That brought in all the cash," I said. "So what happened to the gunrunning business?"

"*Frieden Adriatic.*" Mardik spat on the floor, then nodded at the window.

I crossed to it and looked out at the end of the long pier. I picked up the binoculars for a better view. Containers rose off the dock and swung over the side and lowered to the deck where they were strapped into place on an aging freighter. Across the back end were the words, *FRIEDEN ADRIATIC.*

I turned back to the employees. "Are you telling me Baron Konrad von Frieden stole your business?"

"You know that son of a bitch?" Sokol the accountant asked in a hate-filled voice. "Yes. He stole what belongs to us."

"Well, then," I grinned. "I'm gonna steal it back."

CHAPTER 23

IT TOOK THE AFTERNOON TO sort out duties. Megi had orders to get the office cleaned up, painted, and redecorated. She loved the idea of having something useful to do. Sokol and Geldona were equally glad Megi was being useful rather than bothersome. That left them the quiet needed to face the arduous task of calling our suppliers and customers—the legal ones—and coaxing them back into business.

While they got to their tasks, my Syrians uncovered the *Frieden Adriatic's* next stop: Bari, Italy. A straight shot across the sea from Durrës. Bari was a town I had come to know all too well. That much was under control.

That left me time to prioritize. In the background of my crowded mind, there was a low hum of hatred toward Ms. Sabel. Sure, she gave me a head start in the world by giving me a company. But it was one that could only stay afloat by going to the dark side. I wondered if she knew that. She was a girl scout when it came to ethics, so I didn't think about it for long.

What I did think about was her secrets. Her words, *I'm glad you can read my mind, Jacob* replayed in my head. I had failed to read her mind and that's why she publicly fired me like a diseased rodent? And Jenny. She needed space, which meant I was dumped. I should know; I've been dumped a few times. In my experience, fighting to win her back would work better in a week or two after she realized her jealousies were misplaced. Of course, waiting to fight for her can backfire too, I can never tell with women. No matter what I did, I was screwed.

But it meant my dance card was wide open—to avenge the deaths of Dimitris and Nate. That could take up a lot of my anger-energy.

I would need to move fast. I hired a H155 helicopter for the trip to Bari, Italy. I asked Ansi, the pilot, to bring along a parachute rig for me, which he took as an insult to his skill. When I asked for two hundred-foot mountaineering ropes, he took additional offense. When I waved some money around, he turned his wounded pride into a smile. Mardik and Firas were skeptical but curious when I invited them along for the ride.

As we approached the bird, Mercury leaned against it. *You are spending a lot of money, homes.*

I said, *Are you telling me the god of commerce won't back me up?*

Mercury said, *For success in business, you need two things: something to sell, and someone to sell it to. You need to remember the Via Roma and the virtues of Roman life.*

I said, *And which virtues did you have in mind? Because sacking and pillaging to pay for things doesn't work anymore.*

Mercury said, *Yeah, that's why it's all gone to the dogs, bro. I'm talking about Frugalitas. The economies of life through simplicity. You don't need a big fancy helicopter.*

I said, *What if I plan to use it for sacking and pillaging?*

Hmm, Mercury said. *Now pillaging might be useful on the road to your first billion.*

I shrugged and climbed in with my Syrians.

Missions rely on mutual trust to succeed. I was heading out on a mission with two men I didn't know at all. I could tell they'd seen some action. It scars a man for life. And I could tell they'd survived enough to be eternally cynical. I figured I could trust them, but how much and with what information was sketchy. Money is the worst motivator for soldiers. If they were working strictly for cash, someone could buy their loyalty out from under me. I needed to build a strong rapport. I also needed to assess their strengths.

Halfway over the Adriatic, I asked Mardik, "Why Albania?"

"The Germans closed their border before we could get there." A sour expression crossed his face. He didn't want to talk about it. Firas avoided my gaze as well.

I nodded and looked ahead, indicating I wouldn't pursue the topic.

There were deeper stories inside these rough men. Having a few stories of my own, I knew how painful digging them out could be. Like the seventy-eight pieces of shrapnel the doctors decided would be best left inside me after twelve operations, there are some things men don't need removed. As long as it doesn't fester, let scar tissue hold it in place.

Many young men find themselves attracted to the passion of war. Mardik and Firas had the look of men who had gone like moths to a flame—and considered themselves lucky to exit singed but alive. Mother Nature instills a desire to protect what's "ours" from those who would destroy it. Then the bombs go off, the buildings crumble, the parks you once played in become craters. Your friends die in your arms and your officers lead a suicide charge. Things don't get better, they get worse. As time marches on, the inevitable lesson of war becomes clear to everyone fighting it: victory and defeat are equally impossible. The future becomes a gamble over whether you will die or lose a limb.

The war in Syria had been raging for eight years with no end in sight.

All of which explained why they left home and joined a smuggler on hard times. My only question was whether they initiated the idea of gunrunning or if my Canadian predecessor had been ahead of them.

Mardik turned to me and said, "Frieden has guns. We could not stop him. We have nothing."

"You have a US Army Ranger." I looked him in the eye.

Firas and Mardik exchanged glances as if the Canadian had said something along those lines before a string of defeats led him to the bottle.

We stayed silent after landing and made our way to the Riva Club, an upscale bar near the marina. It was on the other end of the city from a secure warehouse that had lost several hundred crates of Beretta AR70/90s. Still deadly, the fully automatic rifles used by the *Esercito Italiano,* the Italian Army, were being replaced by the smaller and lighter ARX160. They chose to stockpile the old weapons until they had accumulated enough for an auction. An enterprising officer had pilfered weapons and sold them to Konrad von Frieden.

I strolled into the Riva Club with my Syrians following me like a pair of mobster-bodyguards. In a booth by the wall, wearing a suit he couldn't afford on a lieutenant's salary, sat Federico. He looked up from his friends as I approached.

"No, no." He waved his hands between us. "We are finished."

Federico had been nice enough to provide some critical information for me. A couple weeks earlier, it had taken only ten punches in the gut to make him nice enough draw a map of Konrad's estate on Corfu.

"Not finished until I say." I grabbed a fistful of his shirt and hauled him to his feet. "One call to the investigators and your party life moves from the clubs to the cellblock. Tell your friends you'll be right back."

Federico glanced around for an escape route. Mardik and Firas did a fine job of impersonating immovable objects.

Federico shrugged and laughed and waved nervously to his friends as if we were going outside to snort coke. No problem.

In the alley, I shoved him against the wall. "I need to know everything about Konrad's operations. How many men are on his ships, how many ships, where they are at the moment, and where at least one of them will be at 0300 tonight."

His mouth dropped. "I cannot do this. I know only little about Konrad."

"Maybe I didn't make it clear." I punched him in the gut and yanked his head back up by the hair after he doubled over. "There are few things I hate as much as a corrupt lieutenant who sells weapons to mass shooters."

I punctuated my statement with another punch.

Federico spewed his drinks and the remnants of a pasta dish on the ground. I let him retch and catch his breath. Then he said, "He will not tell me these things. It is not possible to call him and ask."

"Start by telling me about his security arrangements. Then we'll get creative on the other part. I have faith in you."

Behind me, Mardik and Firas covered me like a well-oiled machine, constantly in motion. Wordlessly, they turned their gazes in opposite directions from each other, calculating every possible angle of attack. They checked the building cornices and the street beyond the alley. They tracked the noise level around us, silently observing every loud person or noisy car passing by. I could feel their nervousness at being unarmed.

"You turned him to the Greeks." Federico's eyes were wide as he panted out fear. "What more do you want?"

"Yours is not to question why, Federico. Answer me." I made a fist.

He held out his hands to block a punch. "The ships carry three guards, armed. They have ten or twelve crew. The bonus waits for them on delivery, they will not give it up willingly. He has five ships."

"Good start." I gave him a menacing smile. "Where are the ships?"

"This I do not know."

"Let's try a broader generality. How many are in the Adriatic?"

"I do not know this."

"Where are they stationed in general terms?"

"The Black Sea. Most days, they run Bari, Corfu, Istanbul, Alexandria, Odessa."

I said, "You left out Durrës."

Federico looked like he was going to be sick again. Turning a ghostly shade of white is a liar's worst problem. I knew one of Konrad's ships was on its way and so did he. Which meant he had gone back into the business of selling Italy's retired weapons to Konrad. I found that disappointing. He had sounded so convincing when he begged me not to turn him into the authorities, I thought he had started a new page in his life. I had trusted the man because he had been nice enough to tell me there was a stash of rifles hidden in Konrad's garage on Corfu after a surprise inspection of the *Frieden Adriatic*. My mistake.

"You're coming with me." I pushed him toward the street.

On the way to the helipad, I had him text his friends so they wouldn't worry about him. Then I confiscated his phone for the duration. Mardik called the captain of my nearest ship, Captain Rafia of the *Detit Fatma*, and had him sail to a point roughly fifty miles off the coast of Italy and as far from law enforcement as possible. He was instructed to let us know his coordinates, turn off all identification signals, and wait for further instructions.

Mardik and Firas did well in their first operation with me. They instinctively knew their places and never asked questions. But a man with little more than a frozen daiquiri for self-defense is hardly a test. The question in my mind on the flight over remained. Would they be an asset or a liability in my next operation? What concerned me most was their desire for firepower. Just because the other guy carries a rifle doesn't mean you need to carry one. People who carry weapons tend to over-rely on them for solutions.

For the next operation, I would go in alone. They could join me after I secured the landing zone. Once I formed the basic plan in my head, we had dinner. Federico abstained from eating. Still smarting from his punches, I guess.

Then we waited.

CHAPTER 24

FEDERICO CONVINCED HIMSELF I WOULD toss him out of the H155 chopper once we reached our cruising altitude of fifteen thousand feet. The thought never crossed my mind until he mentioned it. While it had a certain appeal, long ago I'd learned that, until the battle is won, you never know when a live hostage might come in handy.

I climbed into my skydiving rig and watched while we approached the *Frieden Adriatic* from above. My companions stared at me as if I were totally insane for jumping out of a helicopter in the dark. I gave them detailed, specific instructions. I could only hope they wouldn't decide to call it a night and go home. I bailed out into the night sky.

On the way down, I thought about Jenny.

Mercury floated alongside me. *Dawg, quit thinking about sex and keep focused. You miss the flying bridge and you're done.*

I said, *I know. But why did she want space? Does she really believe I slept with Ms. Sabel? Does she plan to even the score? Even though I didn't do anything? I mean, I've been there, done that—cheating doesn't work out for anyone.*

Mercury said, *She doesn't know what you did or didn't do. It doesn't matter. PAY ATTENTION!*

I flared to a perfect landing on the roof of the bridge. Minutes later, I introduced myself to Captain Akbaba at knife point. He cooperated and summoned his crew to the bridge for an important meeting. Which they were nice enough to attend. Given the trade they were in, they were understandably suspicious and arrived fully armed.

Which left us in an awkward position. As they lined up in front of the control panel, I said, "Some of you figured it out, but for the dim ones,

I'll explain why I'm holding this knife to your captain's throat at such an odd angle. You see, if you shoot me, my falling weight will plunge this knife into his jugular. Naturally, if I kill your captain, you will kill me. Which leaves us in a bit of a standoff. These things tend to get boring after a while. But luckily, I have a plan. I'll need one of you to flick the running lights off and back on."

No one stepped up to do as I asked. I pushed Captain Akbaba to the control panel and pressed my blade a little harder against his neck. He leaned over and pressed a button twice, which did what I asked of him. The lights blinked off and back on. I made him stretch to reach it to prevent any foolish attempts to break free, but this led to him losing his balance and smacking the panel. He righted himself and we settled in to wait for what would happen next.

Ansi set his chopper down gingerly on the deck and offloaded my Syrians. They brought Federico, which wasn't part of the plan but wasn't a bad idea either. Mardik and Firas joined us on the bridge and started stabbing Sabel Darts into Akbaba's crew. I had to explain the way the darts put guys to sleep for a few hours when Federico freaked out thinking they were all dead.

Once the *Frieden Adriatic* boys were sleeping like babies, we began the second part of the operation. Stealing the rifles.

The *Detit Fatma* pulled alongside and Captain Rafia sent some of his crew over. I watched from the *Adriatic's* bridge as they began locating and extricating the weapons from the holds. Frieden hadn't been as clever as my people. There were no hiding places for the large pine crates. The pilfered rifles were below decks and easily accessed after moving a few tons of leather goods. The men worked quickly and soon had everything lined up to transfer to my ship. Then we had a problem.

Both ships were built to load and unload on a nice, solid dock—on land. Neither were set up to hand off heavy crates to another ship while both heaved on the swells of the open ocean. Several crew members stood on the deck discussing methods and arguing the case for safety versus speed.

Then my plan fell apart altogether.

My man, Captain Rafia, radioed that the *Guardia Costiera*, Italian

Coast Guard, was on its way. Apparently, the poorly balanced Captain Akbaba had activated a distress signal while pretending to fall on the console. Sneaky bastard. Captain Rafia guided me over the radio on how to use the *Frieden Adriatic's* radio system to communicate with the Italians. That was something that couldn't possibly go well. I'm no sailor and don't know starboard from port. They would see through me right away. If I spoke to them, then left before they arrived, many questions would arise. It was doubtful the Italians would shrug off a freighter with a crew asleep on the bridge. They would want to know what happened and who did it.

My Syrians ran to the bridge out of breath. They reported it would take sixty minutes to get the rifles transferred. Captain Rafia radioed the Italians would arrive in twenty.

There were risks worth taking. This wasn't one of them. We were out of time.

Mardik and Firas had been invigorated by the idea of stealing Konrad von Friedens' cache. I watched their faces sink as they realized that wasn't going to happen. They looked at me the way they must have once looked at the Canadian who had also failed them. Desperation crept into their posture. Defeat clouded their hopeful faces. They could see the grime of the office and the bottle that would consume me, just as it had my predecessor.

Mardik asked, "We lose?"

I rarely fail in a battle. It broke my heart to disappoint them.

Then Mercury's advice sank in.

I put a hand on Mardik's shoulder and shook my head. "We didn't win, but we're not going to lose. We're going to make Frieden pay."

I radioed Captain Rafia back and told him to have his men lash the rifle crates to the *Adriatic's* deck as if they'd been there all day. When they finished that, they dragged the *Adriatic's* crew to their bunks and tucked them in. Mardik and Firas followed my orders to confiscate the *Adriatic* crew's weapons. I sent my people to the chopper. They were to be ready to lift off as soon as I joined them.

Next, Captain Rafia evacuated his crew. He moved the *Detit Fatma* a short distance, then radioed the Italians that he was near, ready to render

SEELEY JAMES

aid to the *Frieden Adriatic* if necessary.

I turned to Federico. "This is your last chance, lieutenant. You get on the radio and tell the Coast Guard these guys forced you to steal the rifles. You tell them you jabbed them with Sabel Darts then disabled the ship. You can be the hero here, Federico. Only if you sell your story. You play this right; you can keep your career and your freedom. Point out what happened to Dimitris and Nate Hale and ask for a new identity, new assignment. Get out of this while you still can. If they don't believe you, if you fail, you'll go to jail and the man they call Ra will find you."

He puked on the bridge. Then he grimaced and took the radio mic I handed him.

I held up a hand to stop him before he called in. I said, "Federico. If I ever hear of you selling anything that doesn't belong to you, I will find you and drop you out of a helicopter."

CHAPTER 25

I WOKE TWO HOURS AFTER hitting the pillow. Movement in my room. I reached for the light. A hand grabbed mine.

A familiar voice said, "No lights."

I sat up in the dark, exhausted but glad to see the silhouette of my best friend, Miguel.

I said, "'Sup, Dude."

"Sorry about the way things went down," he said. "Bum deal."

My eyes adjusted to Durrës' city lights coming through my film-thin curtains. It was definitely him, and he was alone. It felt good to see a friendly face. I popped out of bed and gave him a bro-hug.

"Dude. You give a man a hug without warning him you sleep in the buff?" He pushed me back.

"Sorry. Caught up in the moment." I grabbed my jeans and jumped into them. "Did Ms. Sabel send you? Am I back in?"

"Uh." He looked away. "You're not back in."

Until that statement, all my misfortunes felt reversible. I half expected Ms. Sabel to knock on my door and beg me to come back. Not half, fully expected. The air in my lungs left me. My world turned black. This whole trip to Albania wasn't a diversion? A set stage? My future was really tied up in a few rusty ships?

I asked, "Did she tell you what I did wrong?"

"Not a word." He shrugged. "We can't say your name in front of her. Sucks."

"Yeah. So. Did you come here to join me? I could use some help."

It was a reasonable expectation. He'd left the Army and joined Sabel two weeks after me. But it was more than I could hope for. Only people fleeing civil war in Syria or billionaires in Davos worked for Detit Exports.

"I'm not here." He dropped something heavy on the floor. "I gotta stay on Pia's good side. This is the best job I've ever had."

It had been mine too. But those days were over. Apparently.

"The CIA sent a warrant to trace your phone," Miguel said. "As you know, Sabel phones are encrypted beyond what the NSA and CIA can hack. So, they got the warrant. They don't know you're on a regular phone right now. But the incident made me wonder what the CIA wanted to know. I checked your location logs because, while the service is off, the GPS tracking remains live. I figured out where you were last night. I lined that up with an Italian Coast Guard call to a freighter. I'm not going to ask. We're not going to tell them about your new phone until start of business today, DC time. You've got four hours to get another new phone."

Did that mean the CIA wanted to make sure I was off the Alvaria case? Or did they think I had something to do with it? Maybe they were worried I was ahead of them. Few things in life are as frightening as knowing the CIA is interested in your movements. A new phone would free me of that—as long as I kept changing them every couple days. If I was important to them, they might send someone to tail me.

Miguel patted my shoulder. "Tania, Dhanpal, and I feel bad for you, bro. We pulled together some old stuff; odds and ends we had lying around. Thought it might come in handy. All decommissioned. All of it is legal somewhere." He paused a beat. "Not here, though."

He went to the balcony and checked the beach below, then he looked back into my suite. "Nice place."

When I found out hotel rooms in Durrës went for $18 a night, I opted for the best suite at the best hotel on the beach. It cost as much as a Holiday Inn back in the States. It helped take the grit out of the city and the depression out of my circumstance.

"I can't come back." He climbed out on the balcony railing and started to climb down like a spider. He stopped a few feet below. "Forgot to mention. If you see a young black guy, kinda short and walks with a limp, check out his ride. He never locks it."

DEATH AND BETRAYAL

He crawled down all five floors and vanished in the dark.

As he disappeared, so did my hope of being a Sabel Security employee. On the bright side, I was free of the CIA and Sabel. Now I could honor my oath to Nate. I'd go after Ra and his sniper on my terms. Konrad von Frieden would lead me to him—and I would make the world a safer place.

I crawled back in bed and caught as much sleep as I could. Then I went to Detit Exports.

The duffel Miguel left me weighed a ton. I lugged it into the owner's office and left it near the door. Captain Rafia, Mardik, and Firas were waiting for me. Rafia sat in the only chair that wasn't behind the desk. My Syrians leaned against the wall near the door. The new furniture hadn't arrived yet, but the place was a lot brighter. Clean windows make a bigger difference than one might think. I called out a thank-you to Megi. She bounced on her toes. Everyone gave her a round of applause.

Then I leaned my butt against the edge of the desk and turned my attention to my operations people.

Rafia was an old Turk with a big belly. He sat in my office like a Buddha, hands in his lap, solemn look on his face. Tobacco and coffee stained his breath and teeth. He dressed like Bogart on the African Queen, with a beat-up old cap too small for his head, baggy pants, and a shirt his wife should've thrown out a long time ago. If he had a wife.

What he lacked in presence he made up for in expertise. He began my education.

Rafia explained to me what an idiot I am—in a nice way. Apparently, transferring cargo at sea is not something you tell your captain about ten minutes ahead of time. The operation is called STS transfer, ship-to-ship. It's best done when both are stationary and at least one of them has special equipment. There are many ways to accomplish the task, but all incur a good deal of risk. The best risk is losing the cargo. The worst is losing both ships.

He said, "If you insist on playing the pirate, habibi, let us make plans."

Mercury said, *Pirate, homie? Are you ready to become a Caesar? I'll give you a hint: you need the fucking money, bro.*

I said, *This is the slippery slope?*

Mercury said, *Top of the hill, dawg.*

I said, *I'm in, just for a couple deals until I get some bills paid and an introduction to Ra.*

"I insist on playing the pirate," I said to Rafia. "What plans do we need?"

"I have ordered the necessary equipment for STS," he said. "If you can pay for it, I will be ready by dark."

I reached over and slugged his shoulder. "You da man, Rafia. Make it happen."

Mardik raised a finger to get my attention. "The *Frieden Arabia* is halfway between Tunis and Latakia, Syria. We believe they carry mortars, rifles, and missiles to Ahar al-Sham."

I tried to recall the shifting sands of the al-Sham groups: Tahir, Ahar, and a few others. Then I decided it didn't matter much. While they fought against Assad, which should make them an American ally, their goal was to form an Islamic state. Just like ISIS. Only with a different guy in charge. Which made them not-an-ally.

"Can we intercept the ship?" I asked.

Rafia nodded. He rose and crossed to a map on my wall. He pointed and said, "Halfway between the northern coast of Libya and the western end of Crete."

"They will be ready this time," Firas said. He had the look of defeat on his face.

"Let's come back to that," I said. "Who would we sell these weapons to?"

"To friends in Tartus." Mardik pointed to a speck of a town on the southern-most coast of Turkey.

"Who?" I asked.

Mardik shrugged.

"We have to be honest with each other, Mardik." I watched his eyes fall to the floor.

"Peshmerga," Firas said.

There was a silence that stretched long enough for everyone in the outer office to notice. They looked over their shoulders.

DEATH AND BETRAYAL

What Mardik didn't want to say was, the port of Tartus was in Turkey. Turkey was under the control of a dictator who hated the Peshmerga and everyone associated with them. Which meant we could lose everything, including the crew and ship, if we were caught.

"Captain Rafia, are you willing to land in Tartus and deliver the goods?" I asked.

He shrugged as if it were no big deal. I watched his eyes. The last thing I needed was a jailed or dead captain. I doubted he would be any happier about it. He avoided my gaze by sweeping his around the office. When he came back to me, he said, "There may be a need for some—what do Americans call it?—grease."

"How much grease?"

"A thousand euros." He shrugged again. "Maybe two?"

Mercury leaned over Rafia, giving him a close inspection. *You ever get the feeling Jason and the Argonauts aren't the only guys in the Aegean who could fleece you?*

I said, *How do I know the money isn't going into his pockets? How do I know he won't land in Turkey, take the Peshmerga's money and walk away forever?*

Mercury said, *To become a Caesar, brutha, you have to know who to trust and when to trust them.*

I said, *And?*

Mercury said, *What are you looking at me for? Sometimes you gotta make your own decisions, dude.*

"I'm going to trust you on that, Rafia." I gave him my soldier stare. When he flinched, I continued. "I'm going to give you three thousand. Bring back what you don't use." I pointed to Mardik and Firas. "All our paychecks depend on it."

The three of them exchanged nods agreeing to the risks. Which made me feel better. If the Syrians trusted him, I could too.

Firas was our skeptic. He said, "They will be ready. They will double the watch. It will be risky AF."

Mardik agreed with a grunt and a scowl.

I said, "Then we will need to be better armed."

Captain Rafia squinted at me.

I pointed to the bag. Mardik opened it. Rifles, body armor, Sabel vision, secure comm links, Sabel Darts, and 9-mils greeted them. Enough weaponry to liberate Aleppo. Almost. Their grins spoke volumes. Mardik pulled out something he didn't understand. He held up a black box with several dials and six antennae sticking out.

"Signal jammer," I said. "No one's calling the Coast Guard this time."

When my Syrians finished admiring the toys, their glances at each other carried more unspoken thoughts. I'd been on a few sketchy missions; I knew those thoughts. Can I trust our leaders not to walk us into an ambush? Can I rely on the guy next to me to cover me? Can I hold up under fire?

What separates the American military from most is the pre-engagement training. US soldiers walk through scenarios with variables until each man has his part memorized. We didn't have that luxury.

Mercury said, *Then all you got is the god of eloquence. Open your mouth and let my words flow through you.*

That arrangement had worked on several occasions. I trusted my mythical deity and gave them a soul-searching stare. Channeling Mercury, I said, "Trust, commitment, and brotherhood are not just words. They're a soldier's bond. We trust each other to find courage when fear fills our souls. We commit to have faith in each other when there is no reason to believe. We are the brotherhood we can turn to when every exit erupts in flames. Trust, commitment, brotherhood. We cling to those three little words, not because we're family or friends, but because we have, each of us, burned in our own hells from battles long over. We each have heard the agonized screams of those who gave their lives to save ours. We have marched to save our friends only to arrive a minute too late. Each of us has woken, drenched in the sweat of nightmares best forgotten. We have traveled the same roads, Mardik. We have aimed at the same enemies, Firas. You can see it in my eyes as clearly as I see it in yours. Now we take down Frieden together. I trust you, I am committed to you, I offer you brotherhood."

Captain Rafia watched the three of us. We sized each other up. We silently committed to each other with a glance. Firas the skeptic opened his arms for a group hug. Even Captain Rafia joined in.

We had done well the night before, but Firas was right. This time, they would be expecting us.

CHAPTER 26

FOR WHAT I PAID HIM, Ansi, my favorite chopper pilot, didn't mind lashing his craft to Rafia's deck and sailing south of Greece for a whole day. Nor did he mind taking off at 0300 again to ferry me high above a freighter. Ansi didn't ask questions about why I needed to jump out at fifteen thousand feet. I liked that.

What I hated, though, was that some ships have a monkey island above the bridge filled with radar domes and wiry antennas. My chute caught on something as I flared out above the *Frieden Aegean's* bridge. I dangled from an antenna with a four-foot drop to the roof of the bridge.

Fifteen feet below me, an armed guard scanned the well-lit decks below from the wing. He was alert and watching everything except the sky above him.

I had to cut my way out of my rigging. That landed me on the roof with the thud of a full-grown adult male.

So much for the element of surprise.

I flattened myself and waited for the guard to come up the ladder. I held my breath and listened. Nothing.

A split-second before the bullet pinged off the metal next to me, I realized they were coming up the other side. I rolled. With one hand on the ladder, I swung down to the deck below and stabbed a dart into the guard there.

That left me standing on a wing of the bridge staring through glass at three men with pistols. The good news: all the lights were on inside. They couldn't see me as well as I could see them. It wasn't much of an advantage, but it allowed me to scramble back onto the roof.

I liked the one-to-one odds up there better.

The trigger-happy guard who nearly shot me came at me. I pulled another dart out of my pocket. As much as I wanted to reach for my Glock, I was the pirate in this scenario and the punishment for murder would be worse than knocking them out and stealing their illegal cargo.

He aimed his rifle. I ducked behind a radar mast barely wider than a tree trunk. He came looking for me. I grabbed his rifle barrel as he came around the corner and used the mast for a fulcrum. It launched him sideways, causing him to fire. Which made the barrel hot as a griddle. I held on and shoved it backwards toward him. He wouldn't let go and fell on his butt. I jumped on him with a dart and jabbed his leg.

Two down. But the three from inside were now outside, climbing to me. I scrambled up the mast and readied another dart. The three came up, one on my right, the other two opposite, but behind the diesel exhaust stack. Which created a tactical problem for me. I could jump the one, or the two, but not all three.

They hadn't seen me, so I scrambled higher.

On the comm link, Mardik said, "We are coming in for landing on deck."

I couldn't respond without giving away my position, not even a whisper. The three guards stood two feet below my boot. One of them looked up. He aimed his pistol at me. He couldn't pull the trigger because the radar scanner a few inches over my head spun at a good rate and taking it out by accident would be catastrophic to the ship's navigation.

He fired anyway.

The round buzzed my ear. That left me no choice, I had to jump on him before he killed me and wrecked his radar. My feet shoved his arm away, dislodging his 9-mil, giving me an opportunity to jab him in the neck.

Before I could roll over and make a getaway, two pistols pressed against my back.

They hauled me to my feet and spun me around. One pinned my arms behind my back while the other kept a pistol jammed in my nose.

The one with the weapon said, "You come with us."

"No thanks."

They answered my snark with a powerful punch to the gut.

In my comm link, Firas said, "We are coming, brother."

My worst nightmare was the heroic but tragic end to my Syrians. Misguided tactics were never a good battle plan. I'd let them down by letting myself get captured.

The ship's crew led me down the ladder to the bridge.

Inside, the captain greeted me with a smug smile. He stood six inches shorter than me but thought it was the other way around. Strikingly young for a captain, he had premature gray hair and beard. He folded his arms and assessed me from a safe distance. Sounding distinctly American, he said, "I asked them not to kill you. I'm guessing you're the guy who put my friend Salah Akbaba in jail?"

I shrugged. In the distance, the unmistakable noise of the twin jets powering the helicopter reached my ear.

The captain couldn't hear it because he wasn't expecting it, but the chopper was moving in. I squeezed my eyes closed and tried to will my team away. They would be an easy target from the ship. Saying anything out loud would only give them away.

"Don't be modest," the captain said. "Tell me who you are and what you're up to."

The men with pistols shoved me into a chair with my back to the wall of glass overlooking the cargo deck. They took up positions on either side of me, just out of my reach.

"I'm a weapons inspector," I said as much to him as to my Syrians on the other end of my comm link. "I tracked some shipments and watched you load them onto this ship. I would advise everyone in the shipping business to avoid you and your freighter."

Hopefully, Ansi, Mardik, and Firas were smart enough to figure out my warning.

I counted his people in my head and figured there must be more armed men aboard than the two on the bridge. The ship had listed eleven crew with the port authorities but not all of them would be willing to grab a rifle. Outside of the navy, cooks and engineers aren't interested in laying down their lives for the ship's owners. Which meant there were between five and eleven firearms and only three of those down.

Mercury looked over the arrogant captain's shoulder. *Say, homie, you don't look like Scipio Africanus.*

I said, *Who was he?*

Mercury said, *Weren't you doing his thing back there in Durrës? Rome wouldn't give him an army to attack Carthage, so he went to Sicily. That's where Rome sent the soldiers who took part in defeats. Sicily was considered a punishment for failure. But Scipio knew generals were responsible for losses not soldiers, so he offered them a chance to redeem themselves. He ended up with a big ol' army full of veterans on the edge. I thought that was what you were going for.*

I said, *Yeah. Uh. Something like that.*

Mercury said, *Then how come you got captured right off the bat and your boys Mardik and Firas are nowhere around? How you planning on getting out of this one?*

I said, *Y'know, now that you ask, I could use a little divine intervention.*

Mercury said, *Huh. Well. About that ...*

Oh, no, I said. *You didn't bet the other gods I would die, did you?*

Mercury said, *Not exactly. There's a bet going down about the outcome of your Syrians. I'm here to assess the situation.*

Great. Having god on your side must be different for people in other religions. David counted on his God to defeat Goliath. Same for Moses versus Ramses. I wonder if they had to beg for help. I wasn't in the begging mood. Besides, I actually had read up on Scipio Africanus. He was the Roman general I was emulating.

I just miscalculated the timing a little, that's all. Or a lot.

The chopper came close enough to hear. In a second, it grew loud enough to cause everyone concern. The captain ran to the windows. His men lost their concentration on me.

The H155 swept by level with the decks, inches from the waves. Without warning, it swooped up high, crossed over the side, and came down. Its rotors scattered every speck of dirt from the deck.

Crew from below popped up from hatches and fired at the bird.

The captain pulled a radio and shouted, "Don't shoot. Hold your fire. The last thing we need is a chopper crashing into the deck and bursting into flames. Wait until they come out."

My maritime knowledge is pretty sad, but I understood his concern. Not only is fire a ship's worst nightmare, any ship in the vicinity would have to render aid. Authorities would be called. A firefighting ship would arrive. The whole boat would be combed to make sure no embers or hot spots remained. His smuggling operation would be exposed. And that's if the ammunition didn't catch fire.

Two black-clad figures in the open bay of the H155 figured out why the shooting stopped. It gave them a big tactical advantage. The chopper held a position twenty feet above a large cargo hold. They fired on the exposed crew members.

Mardik and Firas were smart, I had to give them that. They were just like me. We'd seen so much horror, we didn't care about risking our lives anymore. I would've preferred they stayed a safe distance out while I secured the ship, but they did what they thought best—and cut a couple hours off our operation. They were going to work out just fine.

"Damn it," the captain said. He faced me ready to turn me into a hostage.

But his plans were not going to work out the way he hoped. The first thing he noticed was the 9-mil in my hand. The second was his men lying unconscious at my feet. The third was the hulking silhouette of a large ship rigged for running dark pulling alongside.

I pressed the pistol to his temple and said, "Tell your men to surrender. We're going to take a few crates off your hands, then you can be on your way."

CHAPTER 27

THE MEETING WAS IN PROGRESS when Pia rolled in. Sabel agent Tania Cooper was in the middle of delivering the formal operations update to Reggie Forrest at the State Department. Eva Gomez sat at Forrest's right. Bradley Hopkins sat on a third side of the large, square table. Next to him was a man she didn't know. The fourth side was empty.

Reggie Forrest interrupted Tania to address Pia. "You're late. That is unacceptable."

"President Williams requested a meeting on short notice." Pia dropped her purse and a tablet on the table, pulled a chair and sat. "Address your displeasure to the White House. Bring me up to speed on attendance." She looked at the new man. "Who are you?"

"I'm Collin West, Weapons and Counterproliferation Mission Manager. I'm Bradley's boss. Pleased to meet you."

West's tone didn't indicate his last sentence was accurate.

She turned to Hopkins. "Mr. Hopkins and you, Ms. Forrest, are involved in two separate high security contracts with different agendas. Why are you both in the same meeting?"

"The Director of National Intelligence put us here," West said. "Our complaints about your personnel align with Ms. Forrest's, and one meeting is better than two."

Bradley didn't take his eyes off Pia.

"That was what I was told as well," Forrest said.

"By whom?" Pia asked.

The Assistant Secretary looked at her nails, then at West and Bradley.

After the silence became uncomfortable, Forrest said, "It was my idea."

Tania continued her report mid-sentence. "... who refused to acknowledge the product was on his ship. After rechecking the structure of the shipment, shipped as 'incognito,' his answers were plausible. RSAT, a department reporting to Ms. Forrest, shipped the product, meaning the captain knew it only as a series of containers. RSAT has not provided details about the nature of the incognito shipment to us. We have no information on dimensions, quantities, color or markings. In other words, we have no idea what we're looking for."

Tania slapped her copy of the report on the table and sat back.

"Ms. Forrest," Pia said with a quick glance at West, "why haven't your people responded to our request? A general description, a dimension, anything that would help us identify the Alvaria container you lost. It should not be hard to come by."

"Wait a second!" Hopkins nearly jumped out of his chair. "Are you telling me the system has been stolen?"

"No one said that," Forrest said. "It's not that big a deal, the ammunition is shipped separately."

"It did not arrive at the destination," Pia said. "RSAT refuses to answer questions about it and my security division has been engaged to retrieve it—sounds 'stolen' to me."

"Misplaced in transit." Forrest looked at her notes while Hopkins fumed.

"We're off track," Collin West said. "The topic of this meeting is your control of your employees, the quality of those employees, and their adherence to their security clearance requirements."

Pia sat still.

Forrest said, "The issues we've identified with Sabel personnel revolve around Jacob Stearne. We understand he has—"

"Jacob Stearne is no longer an employee."

"Let me finish." Forrest distributed a single sheet of paper to each attendee. "On this sheet, you will see several areas of concern. First, several websites report that you had an affair with him, a subordinate employee. Is this true?"

"That websites reported an affair?" Pia's voice rose. "I cannot speak to the trash you read on websites."

"Did you have an affair with an employee?"

"None of your business."

"Spare us your salacious interests, Ms. Forrest." Bradley raised his hand between the sparring women. "Pia, Mr. West and I are concerned that Jacob was read into this project ten days ago and just a few days later, he left Sabel Security. That means he has a deep understanding of the value of this system and now, no one can trace his movements. We know he arrived in Durrës a week ago where he took over an export company with a jaded history. We know he didn't have the financial resources to buy an export company. That raises red flags. Last night, he was seen in the company of two Syrians, an Albanian helicopter pilot, and a Turkish freighter captain, all of whom were inebriated and singing in loud voices about trust, commitment, and brotherhood."

Pia reeled from the news. She hadn't expected Jacob to associate with Syrians and Turks. Bradley was right to be concerned on that score. But she wasn't going to let them jump to conclusions. She asked, "And?"

"Jacob is a potential problem with a capital P." Bradley's voice heated up. "He bought an export company and now he's consorting with foreign nationals. If that doesn't concern you, it should."

"He's a veteran with more than one Bronze Star and a Distinguished Service Cross. If you have reason to doubt his patriotism, provide one sliver of evidence."

"Didn't you shoot him once?" Forrest asked.

"Irrelevant. He healed."

Across the table, Eva Gomez's eyes blew open.

Pia turned to her. "Friendly-fire incident. Kind of."

Forrest said, "A man in possession of highly classified information is drinking with foreign nationals. Our concern is not about his patriotism when he's sober. He could get drunk and—"

"Drinking is not his problem. He never drinks much or for long."

"Pia," Bradley said, "you know him better than anyone. How much should we worry about this guy? Your country deserves to know."

Pia hesitated and gulped.

West pointed a pen at Pia. "What do you mean? If drinking is not his problem, what is?"

The question Pia dreaded more than any other: What is wrong with Jacob?

He had been a long and loyal friend to her. He'd saved her life on several occasions. He'd always been there for her. His presence kept her grounded—even when his presence upset most other people. On the other hand, national security was at stake and there could be a problem. Betraying him made her feel terrible. But then, lying to federal employees, even obfuscating a little, was a criminal offense. That could represent a risk to Sabel Industries. She had to tell them the truth.

"His mental health has been questioned," Pia said. "There have been several psychiatrists involved going back to his time in the service. Their opinions are deeply divided. In my opinion, he's fine. I'm satisfied—"

"Whoa, now." Bradley looked stunned. "You are not qualified to gauge mental health by any stretch of the imagination. Who are these divided opinions from? Who is the most qualified to answer the question about whether he would sell out his country?"

"He would never—" Pia began.

Forrest cut her off. "What kind of mental health issue are we talking about?"

"As you are well aware, medical conditions are private. The net result is: he disclosed everything on his e-QIP and the NBIB cleared him. What is under my control is who leads the project. These contracts are led by equally decorated veterans, Miguel Rodriguez and Tania Cooper."

Pia watched Eva jotting notes, trying to get the acronyms right, presumably for later research. Pia caught her eye. "e-QIP is the online form you filled out for your security clearance. NBIB stands for National Background Investigations Bureau, one of many pieces in the process under the Defense Counterintelligence and Security Agency (DCSA). They cleared Jacob Stearne for this project before he left the company."

"Thanks," Eva smiled. "There are so many abbreviations and acronyms to keep straight."

"I demand to see that clearance," Forrest said.

"I'd like to see that as well," West added.

Bradley glared.

"Take it up with DCSA." Pia gathered her things and rose. She headed toward the door with Tania right behind her. "I have no control over that. If you want to worry about which imaginary gods talk to him, that's your business."

Bradley Hopkins shouted, "You let me give a full briefing to a man who talks to imaginary gods?"

West rose. "Stop right there. Answer one question for me. Do we need to terminate him?"

CHAPTER 28

THE MAN THEY CALL RA lay on a chaise lounge on the *Savannah's* upper sun deck in a sweat suit, sharpening his grandfather's V-42 stiletto. A heater built into the deck kept him warm on the sunny but chilly day. He looked up from his whetstone when Bonham arrived.

"How did it go, sport?" Ra asked.

"Better than I expected." Bonham looked around. "Where is your darling girl?"

Ra chafed at his insolence and pointed his knife at his associate. "She's not my 'girl.' She's an incredible woman. I told you once, and I won't again, your attitude towards her is unacceptable. Show some respect."

"Still in the full blush of rapture, are we?" Bonham tilted his head. "I thought you'd get over it. I miss my old friend. The one who used to tell me, 'You can have your fantasy girl if you have money.' What's happened to you? Please, go back to being the man with a stripper pole in front of the five-person bed belowdecks."

"What good have those girls done you, Bonham?" Ra put down the dagger and patted the lounge next to him, gesturing for Bonham to sit. "I've heard how her father, ravaged by his disease, left her mother destitute. And the cost of her mother's dementia drained my darling's pitiful public service salary. She cares for them, you know. She cares deeply. Watching her changed me. I've seen the light. After her mother leaves this tarnished world behind, she'll care for me. No one has before. They've only cared about what I might buy them." He paused and looked across the sea. "Who's going to care for you, Bonham? Do you think those college girls are going to stick around?"

Bonham sat sideways on the nearest lounge, not committed to lying down. "Topic for another day. I'm concerned about your darling detective overhearing us."

"Ex-detective," Ra said. He held up his phone showing a live stream from the gym deck. "Not to worry. I know where she is at all times."

Satisfied, Bonham stretched out on the lounge. "Our friends were not pleased, but they appreciated your caution. Too much risk with the CIA breathing down their necks. They agreed on that point. I have a new date and time for the big deal that works for everyone involved. If we can recover the shipment, we will be raking in some big money. I plan to buy a lot of fantasy girls with my stake. What about you?"

Ra smiled. "I have my fantasy girl. After this, I'm done. She wants to travel. Antarctica, Mayan ruins, the Rift Valley, Siberia, the Great Wall. All those places I've been before but never with my eyes open. I'm going to retire."

Bonham sat up on his elbows. "You? Retire? You'd go mad. You can't live without the danger. How are you going to get that adrenaline rush ogling the Crown Jewels in the Tower of London?"

"Maybe I'll steal them." Ra laughed at the thought. Then he said, "While you were gone, I've encountered another wrinkle in our plans. The Italians impounded the *Frieden Adriatic* with $200,000 in stolen arms. Seems the man who sold them to us ratted out Konrad. Can't trust anyone these days."

"Would he be the same man who turned Konrad into the Greeks?"

"I wondered the same thing. Konrad says the Italian lieutenant reached out to him for the second deal with no clue about the Greeks."

Bonham scratched his jaw. "What if they're working together? Konrad could've made a deal with Europol to trap the Italian."

"Again, something I considered. But my lawyers got his charges dropped in Greece. A friend of a friend dropped in on Interpol and found nothing leading back to me. Word is, there are no other cops or prosecutors willing to step up after what happened." Ra chuckled. "Nothing like a good sniper, right?"

"If I had a drink, I'd toast you on that one." Bonham held an imaginary glass up to clink. "I guess it could've been bad luck. Perhaps the Italians did an audit, figured out who was stealing, tracked the *Adriatic* with beacons?"

Ra snapped his fingers. A steward appeared. "Orange juice for me. You Bonham?"

"Same thing but make mine with a little vodka. No, make that a lot of vodka."

The steward disappeared.

Ra tilted up his sunglasses. "My analysis was similar to yours until three more of Frieden's ships were robbed at sea."

"Three ships? Pirates in the Mediterranean? No way. He's stealing from us."

"That theory has been disproven," Ra said. "Fido and Spot hung him upside down from a yard arm they fashioned just there." Ra pointed to the lower deck. "They beat him for an hour. He cried like a baby, but he never changed his story."

"An hour should do it," Bonham said.

The steward returned, set the drinks down in silence, then retreated.

"That leaves us in a sticky spot." Bonham sipped his drink. He sighed with satisfaction and smacked his lips. "We're left with the Estonians for the big deal. The Egyptians are shit smugglers and the Romanians would snake the whole project."

Ra sipped his orange juice in silence.

"You're not drinking?" Bonham asked. "That's not like you. It's almost lunchtime."

"Strange things happen when you fall in love, sport. You discover sex is exponentially more gratifying when sober."

Bonham snapped a look at his boss as if the man had stuffed used toilet paper in his drink.

"It's true," Ra said. "You drink to forget the ridiculous, impossible promises you made to your girls, Bonham. I have no guilt to mask."

His phone beeped. He picked it up and looked at the live stream. She'd moved from the gym to the shower in the owner's suite.

"All this love business aside," Bonham said. "Who is going to bring in the cargo for the auction?"

"What if someone is displacing Konrad?"

"What do you mean?"

"Remember Konrad's captain who ran aground off Naxos? We had him beaten, then fired him. He disappeared in Turkey and we never found him again. He was mad enough to go to the authorities, wasn't he? But what if he came back to take over Konrad's business?"

Bonham slurped more of his drink. "You might have something there. If not that guy, it could be someone like him. There are a few ungrateful wretches out there."

"If that is the case, I have a choice. I can prop up Konrad, give him beefier security, more guns, that sort of thing. Or I can figure out who wants his business. Someone who shows that kind of initiative—piracy in the modern age—is my kind of man."

Bonham gasped. "Dear God. That is risky. Taking on a newcomer at this late stage?"

"Which course is riskier?"

Bonham sipped his drink. "Sticky. Sticky indeed."

"Be that as it may, a new partner might be better than Konrad in many respects. Unknown to the Greeks and Europol is a good thing." Ra finished his juice. "If the new man checks out, I'll simply do a little loyalty test. Speaking of which, have you brought me the head of the man who stood in Konrad's garage and called the police?"

CHAPTER 29

I BROKE DOWN AND CALLED Jenny. It was a terrible idea. But, in my defense, I was drunk. What else are you going to do after you wreak havoc on the smuggling industry? Me and the boys cut loose in Athens one night. Talk about bonding with your squad. Even Ansi the chopper pilot got in on the act. Turned out, Captain Rafia knew every bartender in Piraeus, the port city within Athens. But, after half an hour on the dance floor at El Chapo, I felt lonely. Can you believe it? Surrounded by beautiful young women and I was lonely. So I called my girl back in the states.

Bad idea.

She'd been over-eager and talked too loud. The drinks in my system slowed my thinking but I figured it out after a minute. There was a man's voice coming from another room, asking her what was going on, who she was talking to, and so on. *Bring more crackers. You make a helluva artichoke dip.* Stefan Devoor's voice. Stefan had been Ms. Sabel's high-school squeeze. That meant Stefan was in that same rich-kid circle growing up. Stefan knew Jenny. Jenny knew Stefan. When she knew I knew Stefan, she tried to sound even more chipper. Which made it worse. I clicked off in the middle of her saying she didn't need any more space. Yeah. Well. Now I did.

Why did I care about anyone on the far end of the Atlantic? I'd given my soul to my country, to my employer, to my girlfriend, and what did it get me? I found more loyalty in my fellow pirates. Screw Jenny and Stefan—all of them.

I resolved to focus on my oath to Nate.

And that's how I ended up pissed off at the world and standing in

Konrad von Frieden's bathroom. I waited until the lather in his short silver hair needed rinsing. He leaned his head back. I opened the glass door, pressed my M9 bayonet knife to his neck, and turned the water off.

His eyes bugged out. His knees gave out. Which sank his weight into the point of my knife. Which caused him to renew the strength in his knees. He even managed to rise up on his tiptoes.

"Hopeless," I said. "I mean, look at you. You really let yourself go, Konrad."

He didn't say anything. His eyes strained to the right so hard to look at me it must've been painful.

He started to ask, "Who are—"

"Now, now." A quick little jab stopped him. "The guy with the knife asks the questions. Everybody knows that. OK then, Konrad. We're going to step out of this nice marble-lined shower and have a chat. If you make a wrong move, or say something I don't want to hear, your life is over."

I stepped back and guided him out with pressure from the blade on his neck.

He reached for a towel. I jabbed him. "Did I say you could cover that limp noodle?"

We stepped into his bedroom. Lather dripped from his head and rolled down his shoulder. I made him stand in the center of the room and walked around him in a circle. My knife trailed around his skin. He was substantial in height, chest, and girth. Not terribly fat, but big enough to have a permanent belt indentation. He was covered in bruises a day or two old, judging from the colors. Whoever banged him up did a remarkable job of hitting everything that hurt but leaving important areas, like the kidneys, untouched. It took medical training to pull that off.

"Who killed Nate Hale?" I asked.

"I don't know." His voice quaked with fear.

"Who killed Dimitris Bakakis?"

"I don't know." He closed his eyes.

"Who beat the crap out of you?"

"I don't know."

DEATH AND BETRAYAL

"Who turned in Captain Akbaba to the Italians?"

"I don't know."

"Oh," I said with a playful voice. "Let me help you with that one. It was—ME!"

His eyes popped open and found me. "Who are—"

The knife stopped roving his skin at the base of his cock. "Remember who asks the questions?"

"Yes," he squeaked.

"You can call me Osiris." I watched his reaction.

He just about lost his lunch.

This was not the arrogant man who threatened Dimitris two weeks ago. This was a guy who would piss himself if I dropped another bomb on him. To get anywhere with him, I needed to bring him down a notch. I pointed at the bed. He ran to it and sat. I put my boot on his crotch and pressed lightly but firmly. The knife went back under his chin.

"We have to be honest with each other, Konrad. It's the only way you're going to come out of this with your pecker attached."

"I don't know." His words came out fast. "I swear. I don't know who killed those people. I was in jail at the time. You can check the records."

"Dimitris told me you threatened him, downstairs in your dining room."

"You were here?" Konrad's eyes flashed to me. "With him? You're not Greek."

"Who asks the questions?" I pressed the knife harder and drew blood. "I'm not with the prosecutor's office. If you're trying to piece my motivations together, it's really simple: I'm an avenging angel. I came here to avenge the deaths of Nate Hale and Dimitris Bakakis. I know you didn't do it. That's why your manly bits are still swinging around. What I want from you is the name of the sniper."

"I, I, I can't." Tears filled his eyes. "It doesn't matter. If I tell you, he'll kill me. If I don't, you'll kill me."

"He?" I pressed my foot down harder on his balls. "I thought you said you didn't know who killed them. Sounds like you lied to me. I'm going to offer you a little transaction. You tell me the names of people you know, and I'll make promises I might keep. Let's try it, shall we? Do you know who killed them?"

"No, but I know who paid for it."

"Would this be the same guy who paid for your attorneys?"

Konrad choked.

"Talk to me, Konrad. Or you sing soprano with the castrati."

He looked at me with watery eyes. "You think you're so scary. You're nothing. You're a loner. You're one man. He chews up people like you every day. You might threaten a man in his house—he threatens whole cities. He threatens national economies. At a word, he could have this town rise up and hunt you down. You'd have nowhere to run, nowhere to hide. One phone call telling them that you destroyed the biggest employer on the island, and they would come for you like a medieval mob with pitchforks and torches."

"Seen those mobs, doused those torches. I've been unpopular with certain factions from Kabul to Mosul. They got over it. So, if this guy's so big and mean, why hasn't he come for you, Konrad? You lost ten million dollars this week."

"I'm a problem to be fixed. Like a car with a flat tire, a setback to be dealt with, then it's back to running down the road. He'll send better security and track down where things went wrong. His security man, Bonham, has an army of hardened criminals working for him. They'll figure out who stole the goods and then they'll track you down. Like I said, I'm just a problem." Konrad's eyes narrowed. "A man like you is a threat."

Mercury cocked his head to one side. *Y'know what, homes? I like the sound of that. You should be the guy who threatens cities.*

I said, *I did. Fallujah.*

Mercury said, *That don't count. You were part of the American war machine. If we're going to make you into a Caesar, you gotta start thinking big. We gotta meet this guy. Join forces, learn how he does things, then stab him in the back and take his stuff.*

There was a kernel of truth in what my used god said. Talking to this scary guy might lead me to the sniper and, since Ms. Sabel kicked me to the curb, I could take his stuff. Mainly his business. I could make sure we were selling arms to the good guys. The underdogs. Then I could get my own jet. My own Ferrari. My own yacht. When I promised Nate, he never said I couldn't get rich along the way.

"I never threaten, Konrad. It's do or don't for me." I pulled his chin up with my blade. "So, you're counting on this guy to help you with a penis transplant? Now that is a powerful man. Understanding, too."

"What?" It took him a second to catch up. He didn't like the idea of asking his friend to help him out with a new penis. "No. I meant the operations. He can fix the operations."

"Why would I let him fix what I tore apart?" I paused for a moment. "Are you proposing a merger, Konrad?"

"I didn't say anything about—"

"Say, that's not a bad idea. Instead of just stealing shit off your boats, I could just steal your boats. Merger. That just might work."

"Wait … he's not going to let you—"

"Who said anything about let? Put your pants on Konrad. You've got some papers to sign. Then you're going to introduce me to this friend of yours. Is he the man they call Ra?"

CHAPTER 30

KONRAD WAS ONE OF THOSE guys who wouldn't consider life without his manhood. He caved to my merger idea without a lot of protest. And then, just twenty-four hours later, we were going to a party on Ra's yacht. I wore one of my formal t-shirts. It read, "Duty called—I answered" over the 75th Rangers insignia. And a leather jacket. We arrived on a Zodiac and had to tie it up to the sport deck ourselves. Some yachts just don't have the staff to properly greet guests.

SAVANNNAH was written in big letters across the stern. I'd heard one of Ms. Sabel's billionaire pals crowing about a yacht with that name. I couldn't remember which guy. For a moment, and purely out of habit, I considered calling her to tell her she had been right. Ra was someone she knew. Someone she'd invited to her party. Then I remembered she blocked my calls. And she kept secrets from me about the CIA guy and Alvaria.

Screw her and her CIA contract.

I turned to Mercury. *I'll work my way into Ra's operation instead. I'll get a piece of the arms deals and always sell to the little guys.*

Mercury said, *Now you're talking, homes. Go big when you can't go home. But why just a piece of the arms deals? Why not work your way into the big deal?*

I said, *I don't want to get greedy. Gotta keep focused on avenging Dimitris and Nate first.*

We were met by some beefy guys. They insisted on taking my pistol. I turned it over quickly to prevent a search of my outfit. It worked. They led us up one level. Two of them waited with us while another ran to fetch Ra.

One deck above, a party with a DJ raged. Laughter, clinking glasses, and chatter rose above the horrible EDM their DJ played. If that was all the music they could offer, I was glad to wait below. Konrad looked anxious. He appeared to be evaluating Ginsberg's Laws of Thermodynamics. Or maybe he was thinking about the Paradox of Existential Nihilism. I get confused.

A middle-aged man in a casual suit soft as butter trotted down the staircase behind the big beefy guy. A younger, handsome man in an equally expensive suit and the kind of smirk that only comes from a safety net made of trust funds came up behind. I recognized the older guy. I'd met him before. He recognized me at the same time.

"Jacob Stearne?" he said with enthusiasm. He stuck out a hand and shook mine vigorously. "We've met, you know. On the *Numina* back in the good old days, when you were in Princess Pia's good graces."

"A night I'll never forget," I said. "Every commodity except health food, you told me."

"A real-life hero, Bonham." He spun to face his younger friend. "The man who saved Paris. Can you believe it? He's the one who's been robbing Konrad blind."

Bonham stepped up with a smile that wilted women and a handshake that crushed lesser men. I recalled Ms. Sabel telling me, *Nothing, not even a handshake is exchanged without a calculation of value.* As strong as he thought he was, he'd never had to lug seventeen pounds of M249 around a battlefield all day. When he gave me pressure, I squeezed back until his knees gave out and he twisted in agony. I let go and he stepped back. To his credit, his grin only faltered for a second. No one else knew the paralyzing pain he'd just felt.

Except George Falconer, the marathon-thin hungry guy. He said, "Are you two done figuring out who has the biggest dick? Let's talk business. What is this proposal you have for me, Jacob?"

"There's no proposal, George." I patted his shoulder. "New terms and conditions. You see, Konrad and I? We've merged our operations."

"Call me Falconer," he said. "Only one person calls me anything else. So then, a hostile takeover is it? Amusing. I trust you've gotten a golden parachute, Konrad?"

Konrad shrugged. As he had already determined, his life had run its course. It was only a matter of time before it ended.

"Of course, I gave him a golden parachute," I said. "I prefer silk myself as the gold tends to fall at a high rate of speed, but we'll see how it turns out in the morning. Plane's chartered and waiting."

Falconer grinned and faced me. "What does this merger stuff have to do with me?"

"There's a new reporting structure. I want to make sure you understand who to call when you need something shipped."

Falconer pulled a face of disinterest. "I don't ship anything, sport. I'm a financier. When Konrad wants to pick up €5 million worth of wheat in Marseille and sell it for €6 million in Kosovo, I provide the financing. Shipping is what freighters and exporters are for."

Mercury put an elbow on Falconer's shoulder. *Now you get how the Caesars work it, homie? They don't do anything illegal. They finance it. Let the little guy twist in the wind if he gets caught.*

I said, *How am I going to tie him to the sniper then?*

Mercury said, *Who cares about that? Kill him and take over his finance operation.*

I said, *Maybe Caligula got away with that when he killed Tiberius, but it doesn't work that way anymore.*

Mercury said, *World is falling apart, bro. I blame the Christians.*

"Whenever you want to finance some wheat," I said to Falconer, "just let me know."

"And we're supposed to believe the 'Hero of Paris' is willing to carry 'wheat' these days?" Bonham's sarcasm dripped off his chin like sloppy beer.

"Bonham," Falconer laughed, "stand down. If you'd been at Davos and seen this poor sod get dumped by the most arrogant little bitch since Katyonak Yeschenko, you'd understand what's happened to him. He's undergoing a reemergence. Jacob Stearne is tired of risking his life for a sparkly medallion hanging from a colorful ribbon. He wants everything Pia Sabel has. He wants what I have. He wants to make a splash—pardon the awful pun—in the export business. He wants to buy a yacht just six inches longer than the *Numina* so he can anchor it next to that scow next year. This is not a man to be trifled with. This is a man who has the power to take what he wants. I admire that."

Bonham did not look satisfied. He all but growled like a dog as he eyed me. "Where do his loyalties lie? Who does he work for?"

"That's a good question. Before we finance any 'wheat' he may want to ship, you can do a thorough background check on the man." Falconer turned a discerning eye on me. "See if any of his old army buddies are working in law enforcement or foreign intelligence agencies, that sort of thing. But his fortitude—just coming here tonight—is remarkable. If Konrad had balls as big as Jacob's, we wouldn't be having this conversation."

Falconer gave Konrad a death-ray glare.

"As it is," Falconer continued, "there might be a few wheat shipments in our future. As a matter of fact, I'm aware of a very big shipment in need of a capable exporter."

Behind him, my eyes caught movement. The figure of a beautiful woman descended the stairs. Yumi Shibata, dressed in a thousand-dollar party dress with diamonds circling her neck, stopped cold when she saw me. She moved slowly, inching her way closer.

It hadn't been a dream. She had been on the *Numina* in Monaco and at the hotel in Davos. She had asked for help. But help for what? She appeared to be living the good life.

Falconer saw her and followed her gaze back to me. He cut an angry glare at Yumi, then cut off her approach. Putting both his hands on her shoulders and turning her around. He said, "Darling, we have some business to discuss here. Nothing to worry about. If Mr. Stearne has time, I'm sure he'll come up to pay his respects. Now run along. Make sure the guests have enough to drink."

Yumi stole a glance over her shoulder on her way back up the stairs.

Two years ago she walked out on me. I was heartbroken for a while. Then I got over it. I moved on and met Jenny. But what happened to Jenny? What was Stefan doing at Jenny's place? Or were they at his? Where did that leave me? But that look on Yumi's face. Angst of the condemned. Did Yumi still feel something for me?

Falconer was looking at me with a growing fury when my gaze

swung back to him. He said, "We had a talk about you after the party on the *Numina*. I could tell something bothered her. She confessed she was in love with you a couple years ago. Even went to America and lived with you while she recovered from a traumatic incident in Tokyo." He stepped close and nosed up at me. "Tell me something, Jacob. Does it bother you knowing I'm inside of her every night?"

Konrad, Bonham, even the big beefy guys tensed up and leaned away from us as Falconer and I exchanged glares.

"If you think you're intimidating me—" I pushed him back an inch with my index finger "—consider this: when I killed two intruders and dropped their carcasses at her feet, she left me because I was too violent for her. Yet she lives here with you—in peace and harmony. So, Falconer, which one of us should fear the other?"

The waves lapped gently at the hull. A breeze flapped our jackets. Falconer stood still, unwilling to pull his stare from mine. The others watched, ready to hoist whoever lived through the confrontation on their shoulders and shout, "Long live the king!" But unwilling to pick a side prematurely.

Falconer blinked first. He turned to one of the beefy guys. "Benji, Yeller, Cujo, take him to the sport deck and feed him to the sharks."

Three beefy guys pulled their pistols and pushed me one way, while Falconer, Bonham, and Konrad went the other.

I smiled at a guy who weighed fifty pounds more than me. I pointed at the sport deck a few steps below us. I asked, "This way then?"

CHAPTER 31

THE FOUR OF US TROTTED down the steps with Yeller leading the way and the other two behind me. I decided they were working men. Not murderous serial killers who needed to be put down. I wouldn't kill them unless they left me no option.

All three of them were born big and had spent every day since lifting weights and looking in the mirror. If prisons have mirrors. No doubt they ate their cellmates' food to keep up their bulk. Weight makes a big difference in wrestling. Which meant I couldn't wrestle with them. It's also a big advantage in boxing. So, I wasn't going to box with them either.

Since raiding all of Konrad's ships, I was low on secret weapons. But I had five darts left. And this was why I'd saved them.

For people unaware of how a Sabel Dart works, the effect is confusing. When the first guy fell face first into the Zodiac, the second guy looked over my shoulder out of concern for his friend. When he landed on top of the first, the third guy became problematic. He didn't know what was going on, but he sure as hell knew who was doing it.

He swung at me. I ducked and tried to stab him. Missed. We sparred for a minute. He was musclebound and slow. After several swings and misses, I managed to dart him under the arm. Then I had to heave the meaty monster onto the Zodiac, which was a workout all by itself. When I finally got the boat's load balanced, I untied it, fired up the motor, and sent them out to the open sea. Given that it was nighttime, and the seas were calm, I estimated a minimum of two hours tooling around in the dark before someone found them. But that wasn't my problem.

My problem was that there was a party in progress and I didn't have a drink.

I trotted upstairs and introduced myself to a nice Swedish couple. They owned a chemical plant and exported their chemicals to Germany. As luck would have it, they had their own tankers for transport across the Baltic and didn't need my services.

A steward brought me a pomegranate martini. Delicious.

Another couple I met were social media entrepreneurs from Moldova. I couldn't remember quite where that was, so I faked it. I was listening to them rave about their software when I felt a tug on my elbow.

Falconer and Bonham appeared to be worried about something. I turned to the Moldovans. "Will you excuse me? We have a few details to work out on our new business venture."

I pushed both men around a corner where I found a few chairs lined up in front of a hot tub. Three bikini-clad young women lounged in the water sipping champagne.

Falconer seethed at Bonham. "Get your girls out of here."

"They're going to put on a show…" Bonham protested until Falconer looked ready to explode. "All right. Fine. Ladies, give us the deck."

Once the girls were clear, I tugged at Bonham's lapels. "Your boys stole my dinghy and left this little tub without any protection. You're in charge of security, right? Go out there and guard these good people before someone steals a tiara. Here, take this pistol."

"There were three of them." He looked at the SIG I held between us with astonishment. "What happened to the other two weapons?"

"Well, Bonham, I'm keeping those." I looked at him like he was a little kid. "They still have bullets in them."

Bonham looked like he intended to deck me. Having only two darts left, I didn't want to escalate things. I gave him my soldier stare. He backed down.

"Off you go, sport." Falconer gave him a push.

Bonham gave me a visual death threat and left.

As he rounded the corner, I called out, "Don't worry about their health or anything. They weren't dead when I last saw them."

The man gave me one more glare.

When he was out of sight, Falconer laughed loud and long. "You are something special. There's no doubt about that."

"Tell me about your wheat shipments, Falconer."

He crossed his arms. "Keep up, man, I told you this once. I don't ship anything. I finance deals."

I said, "Cut the pretense. You guys think using encrypted text messages like Whatsapp saves you from law enforcement, and you're right. It does. What you're missing is that I'm not law enforcement. I don't need a warrant because I'm not going to use this in a court of law. I stole Konrad's secret decoder ring. I read your messages. How do you think I found my way to you so fast?"

He snapped his fingers and a steward appeared. He said, "Apple martini for me. Jacob?"

"That pomegranate martini was the bomb. I'll take another one, please."

The steward nodded and disappeared.

Falconer crossed to the railing next to the hot tub and looked out at the lights of Monaco. "I may be interested in doing business with you. Before I do, though, I require a deep background check. You'll have to spend some time with Bonham. He'll look right up your ass. If you don't let him, I don't need you."

I tracked closer to him and realized the hot tub had a glass bottom. There was a large bed directly below it. I wondered what kind of show Bonham's girls had been planning. And for whom.

"That's fair," I said. "I've already found all I need to know about you."

He looked up quickly. "What do you think you know?"

"Everyone fears you for no reason. Bonham is the one they really fear. As soon as Bonham figures out you're all bark, you're a dead man."

He arched an amused eyebrow. "Go on."

"Relying on Bonham keeps you awake at night. You want me in your circle because you can see the potential rivalry. Bonham versus me, playing us off each other, maintains a balance for you. With me, you can see a brighter future."

"That's where you're wrong." He yawned and stretched. "I'm near the completion of the biggest deal of my life. When it's done, I'm going to retire. When I do, the entire enterprise will be his. And he can do to you whatever he likes. Maybe he'll give you his old job. Maybe he'll have you fed to the sharks. But don't underestimate him because of your little triumph over one of his dogs. Benji leads the light squad, the one we use for parties." His voice dropped to a hiss. "He has others, meaner and tougher. We call them 'Bonham's dogs' because they'll sink their teeth in your neck and rip out your jugular."

I shrugged.

Mercury stepped between us. *Dude, tell me you heard what he just said.*

I said, *I heard. One big deal and he's out.*

Mercury said, *And what big deal would that be? The one everyone's looking for? Alvaria? Hey, did I mention alveare is Latin for hives, as in bees and wasps?*

I said, *I'll worry about his big deal after avenging the deaths of my friends.*

Mercury grabbed my jacket and tugged. *Homie, think about marching through the Porta Triumphalis, your parade led by senators, the route lined with cheerleaders and fans, all calling for you to be made emperor. You could be just like Pompey, adored by everyone. I'm telling you bro, you steal Falconer's show and you can be Caesar. You could use the Alvaria to eliminate your enemies and take over a small country or two. Places like Belarus or Myanmar are desperate for a man like you. A Caesar's fortune lasts a lot longer than thirty-two years in those places. From there, you could build an empire.*

I said, *Yeah, yeah, yeah, calm down.*

Unfortunately, the words of my forgotten deity stuck in the back of my mind no matter how much I tried to shake them loose. The math fired off in my head. Spending a dollar per second is $86,400 per day for thirty-two years. That's $2.5 million per month, over thirty million a year. And that's if you have only one billion. Imagine these guys with fifty, eighty, a hundred billion. No wonder they blow half a billion on a yacht.

Falconer stepped back. "Everyone who works for me must complete an act of loyalty. A little something that proves how much my patronage means to him. You joked about a golden parachute for Konrad." He turned to the hallway leading to where we stood. "Konrad, come here a moment, will you?"

Konrad dragged himself out of the shadows like a condemned man.

Falconer pushed the Austrian to me. "Prove your loyalty to me, Jacob."

Falconer pulled out an ancient-looking dagger. The kind that was sharp on both sides for slashing back and forth, and pointy on the end for stabbing.

I frowned at his offer and pulled the razor thin blade concealed in my belt buckle. "Brought my own."

I pushed Konrad to the railing. He didn't fight. I glanced over my shoulder to see Falconer holding his camera up.

Twisting back to Falconer, I grabbed it from his hands and tossed it over my shoulder. It splashed in the sea. "Pull a stupid stunt like that again and you're going over the edge next."

He shrugged. He didn't care about the phone because rich guys always carry spares. "My testimony would be enough to convict anyway."

I returned to Konrad. I wrapped my arm around his neck and held the blade high where Falconer could see it over my shoulder. I whispered in Konrad's ear. "I'm going to slice your ear off and drop you in the ocean. It'll look like your throat's been slashed. If you can swim to the next yacht without being seen, I'll see you in Corfu. If you can't swim that far, leave me a note on the Pearly Gates."

CHAPTER 32

FALCONER HAD BEEN RIGHT ABOUT Bonham's dogs, Fido, Spot, and Rover. They'd grown up reading *Soldier of Fortune* magazine, went mercenary in tenth grade, and had been living it up as professional killers for drug cartels and dictators ever since. Bonham wasn't one of them. He wasn't a killer. He was a man who knew how to keep killers under control. Barely.

Bonham went over my books for two days. No one in Detit Exports liked him. Not Sokol or Geldona, the accountants. Not Megi, who had turned the office into a clean, professional-looking business. Not Mardik or Firas. As a matter of fact, no one in Durrës liked him. That might have been due to Megi having the city's largest Snapchat following where she posted angry memes about him every few minutes.

The day of reckoning came. Bonham met me in my office. He sat in my chair.

"Did you want to leave here with a limp?" I asked and reached for his collar.

He jumped out of my new high-back executive chair to deprive me of the satisfaction of chucking him out.

"No need to get in huff, soldier," he said. "If you want your chair back just ask nicely."

Bonham had no value to me. I wondered how far the new pirate-me would've gone to get him out of my chair. Probably too far. I had to pull back on my calculations. I needed Bonham to give Falconer a good report on me.

"Find anything?"

"An export company running on financial fumes." He smirked. "That merger with Frieden was a terrible business decision."

Mercury sat cross-legged on the new sofa. *Remember when I told you not to spend like Caracalla? In case you didn't read the book on him, he devalued the denarius and nearly bankrupted Rome. He didn't listen to me either. Stabbed to death at age 29 by one of his soldiers.*

I said, *How was I supposed to know Frieden was in debt up to his eyeballs?*

Mercury said, *Why do you think he was smuggling guns? And you stole his guns, so, when you bought his company, someone had stolen the money he was going to use to pay back his loans. In other words, you robbed yourself. Running a business isn't like working for Pia-Caesar-Sabel. You can't spend her petty cash fast enough to even get noticed. Here, money comes in, money goes out. You have to watch the bottom line.*

I said, *Oh.*

Bonham looked at me funny. "Are you all right? You look sick."

"Fine. What else do you need to report to your boss?" I dropped into my chair and checked my laptop. All the emails were ads from lonely writers desperate for me to buy their next book. I passed on the Ta-Nehisi Coates offer. When you read that high-brow stuff, people just make fun of you. Maybe it's the company I keep. I checked Bonham. He wasn't reading Coates.

"What did you find at Konrad's place in Corfu?" he asked.

"No hoard of cash, if that's what you're asking. Other than knickknacks from his travels, he didn't own anything of value." I went to Konrad's hoping to find him, but the gardener said the man hadn't shown yet. Maybe he drowned in Monaco. Maybe he went into hiding from me as well. "You went there, Bonham, you've seen the place. And your boy, Spot followed me everywhere I went, so you know I'm not hiding anything. Just so you're aware, I fired Konrad's security team because they sucked. But I kept his gardener. His house is owned by the company, and since I own the company now, I need it looking nice in case I want to sell it."

"His security people work for me."

"Well, won't they be happy to hear that. You better call them because they don't know where to report for work tomorrow."

Bonham clenched his jaw; tension filled his face. "Did you find his body?"

"Last time I saw it, he was bleeding profusely and doing a swan dive off the upper deck of Falconer's yacht."

"Funny his carcass never turned up." Bonham circled my desk until he faced me across it. "Usually they float up a day or two later and some fisherman hauls them ashore. Always makes the news in Monaco. That's why I make sure they have a heavy stone attached to their feet."

I pulled my M9 bayonet out and cleaned under my fingernails. "Zat so?"

"Handing Konrad's ear to Falconer was disrespectful in my book." Bonham leaned across the desk.

"Zat so?"

"Not the kind of thing war heroes do, either."

I absentmindedly pointed the tip of the blade at him. "Tell me everything you know about war heroes, Bonham. I'd love to hear about your experiences. Like, how many do you know? And if you ever met one, how did you manage to stay alive? Cuz, people like me ... we don't like your kind."

"Oh? What kind of guy am I?"

"You're the heel-spurs kind."

I scratched the blade across the stubble under his jaw.

He swallowed hard and backed up. "I still need your phone."

Mercury said, *Did you ever delete those texts to Jenny, homie?*

I said, *No, but what's he going to do with them? They're just a couple lovers questioning each other.*

Mercury said, *Make an excuse, go to the bathroom, delete all those things.*

I said, *Too late now, he's staring at me. And I want to get inside Falconer's circle. I want to know who's decision it was to pop Nate and Dimitris. Then I want to know who pulled the trigger.*

Mercury said, *Do not give him the phone. This is the voice of god talking.*

I tossed the phone to Bonham. "Your audit goes on any longer, I'm going to find another partner."

He caught it. "Once you apply for Falconer's financing, there is only one way out." He gave me what he thought was an evil eye. "What's the passcode?"

I told him the code. He started going through my texts. I finished looking at books on sale in my emails. *Death and Betrayal* was out. I clicked on it and started to order it. Then I remembered: I was in Durrës, Albania. Which meant I'd have to get the ebook version. I hate those things. If you can't hollow it out to hide a pistol in it, what good is it? I closed the browser.

"I know Pia Sabel," Bonham said. He hoisted a hip on my desk, half-sitting on it and leaning across to intimidate me. Fail.

"Funny," I said. "And we never met in all those years I was her personal bodyguard."

"Well, I know someone who knows her. They went to school together. I'm going to check into this fight you had with her. I think the whole thing was staged." He bounced the phone in his hand. "This phone of yours is only a couple weeks old. Hardly any calls, no browser history. Just a few drunk-texts. Where's the one you had before this?"

"Owned by Sabel Industries." I shrugged. "They kept it."

"So this one's a burner." He tried that evil-eye again. "I'm going to keep it, check your browser history, erased apps, that kind of thing. You can buy another one."

"When you're done exhausting yourself trying to prove your bizarre fantasy, what happens next?"

"Falconer will summon you to Tuscany."

"Tuscany?" I asked.

"Yacht season in Monaco is over. It's all about Tuscany now. He has a sprawling estate there. If you get an invitation, we'll supply an address."

CHAPTER 33

PIA PARKED HER MCLAREN, TURNED off the engine, and listened to the engine tick as it cooled behind her head. In front of her, the classic brick Methodist church was dark. The attached fellowship hall showed signs of life. She considered her plan. It would be an intrusion, and it might go badly. Probably would go badly. Still, it was something she should've done a long time ago. She squeezed her eyes shut, took a deep breath, grabbed her plate of gingersnaps, and got out.

The meeting was well-attended. Three leaders sat facing twenty others scattered in the sixty chairs lined up classroom-style. Pia took a seat near the center aisle, a row back from the last participant. She scanned the crowd to make sure he was there. He was. Front right. He didn't see her come in.

The meeting concluded with a prayer. Everyone stood up for it. That's when he noticed her. He was not happy. But he held hands with the others and prayed. She waited it out. As everyone else went for cookies and coffee, she kept her eyes on him.

Bradley Hopkins was checking his options. Going the long way around to avoid her would be too obvious. He sucked his lips in then blew out a breath and marched to her. He stopped a couple paces away, his face and posture rigid with tension.

"You got the cancellation letter," he said.

"My people did."

"There's nothing I can do about it. Collin West didn't do it. That came from over Bergstrom's head. The official reason was they didn't like the way you changed personnel without notice, and what those people, namely Jacob Stearne, did after they left your employ. I warned you about that. It's out of my hands now. No need for you to come here."

His statement caught her by surprise. CIA Director Bergstrom reported to the Director of National Intelligence, who reported to the president. She knew Williams didn't quash Bradley's contract. Which meant the DNI was responsible. That struck her as odd.

She nosed over her shoulder at the table behind her. "I made gingersnaps."

Bradley measured her words. He glanced where she indicated. A few people were pouring coffee and scarfing cookies off a plate. "You made them—or your chef?"

"I did. But she supervised. That's why they're not burned."

He relaxed just a little.

"Look, Coach, I have to apologize and—"

"Is that why you came?" He scowled. "You want me to grant you absolution so you can go back to your mansion and think everything's going to be all right?"

"No."

He huffed, his fists clenching and unclenching. "You ruined my life. My career. I had to start over."

"I know. And I want to make it—"

"That's all words. There's nothing more to say. Just stop calling me 'coach.' You're the only one to use that word in years." He moved around her and went for the coffee machine.

She watched him pour the last drops from the pot into a paper cup. He looked around for filters and grounds to make a new pot.

He wasn't going to make it easy, but she had committed to stick with it until she could crack that tough skin of his. She owed him. The biggest improvements in her youth soccer career came from him. For years he yelled instructions from the sidelines as she played against girls three and four years older. *The bruises hurt less when you win. The faster player wins the ball. You're better than she is, prove it. Go around or go through—but go.* And one night she let her worst instincts get the better of her. The recollection made her cringe.

She tracked around to him, picked up the cookies, and held the plate to him. "I need your help."

Bradley froze, the last scoop of coffee held above the filter. He stared at her for a beat, then dropped the scoop in. He closed the lid and pressed the button and the coffee machine started brewing.

He reached for a cookie. "How is it you need help?"

"Step five," she said quietly.

"To admit the exact nature of our wrongs." He paraphrased the fifth of the twelve steps to sobriety. "Why?"

She was being manipulative, she knew that. She also knew he couldn't refuse her. His face eased back a little. At least he respected the research she'd done.

"So I can move on to step eight."

"To make amends." He sighed. "You can't go back in time. Lindsey came clean, admitted she made the whole thing up. But no one heard her. Everyone was talking about what you did. That story raced around the world twice. I couldn't get an interview at a rec league."

Pia felt her face flush. She looked at the floor. Fighting tears, she took a deep breath and raised her head. He stared at her with cold eyes. Her heart raced with something she rarely felt: remorse.

"No, there's no going back. But." She took another deep breath. "There are other ways to make amends."

"Such as?" He took a bite out of the gingersnap.

"When the Security division told me you'd cancelled the contract, it caught me off-guard. You were so passionate about finding the bidders. So, I sat down and figured out why you hired us in the first place. And then the cancellation made sense."

He nodded slowly, solemnly. He glanced around the room. Three people chatted in a far corner. Two more talked in the doorway. The rest of the hall was empty. He tossed the uneaten half of his cookie in the trash.

He said, "I can't talk to you about a classified project. I can neither confirm nor deny the existence of a program to uncover anyone or anything. But I'm willing to listen to your theories."

He gave a nod to his left and led her to the middle of the grid of chairs.

She looked around. No one could get close enough to overhear them without being obvious.

Pia said, "I believe you didn't want to go through the Company to uncover the people bidding on Alvaria—let's call them 'the buyers'— because you had reason to believe someone within the federal system reported to the buyers. Let's call that person 'the mole.' You hired Sabel Security to keep the search at a distance. Enough of a distance that the mole and the buyers would be unaware of your search."

"Interesting theory," he said. "Go on."

"Then Reggie Forrest pulled you into that meeting. Her—"

He held up a hand to interrupt her. "Collin West pulled me into that meeting."

Pia frowned. "He should know better than to mix briefings on sensitive topics like that."

"Go easy on him," he said. "Collin was involved in the waterboarding thing. He did what they asked of him. When it became public, he became a scapegoat. Chucked out of Clandestine and sent to manage the lowly analysts. Now he's just a family man trying to put his kids through college."

"Noted," Pia said. "Anyway, Forrest's contract to have us find the missing system is not a conflict with your old contract, but they were separate issues and didn't need to be combined. By doing it anyway, she and West broke basic rules of secrecy. She might've done it out of malice because you questioned her in a big meeting, or she might be the mole, or the mole might've put you guys together to test a theory that you had a contract to find the buyers. I don't know which. But. Not long after that, the DNI cancelled the contract. Which means the DNI could be the mole, or he could be oblivious and cancelled the contract on the recommendation of the mole. I could call President Williams, tell him what's going on, and get the contract reinstated. But that would alert the mole. You'd be back to square one."

"Those are very interesting theories. You're still a brilliant strategist, even off the field."

"I've instructed my people to continue the search for the buyers and the auction. I've also told them to expand the search to include a mole. We don't need a contract. This one is on me."

"Making amends." Bradley looked around the room. "That would be a patriotic thing to do."

"That leaves me with two questions. What do we do once we find them? And, is Forrest incompetent or is she the mole?"

"What you do depends on who they are. But Forrest? I've been asking myself that question since I met her. I have a question for you. Do you realize your man Jacob has become a criminal?" He got up and went to the coffee machine.

"He's not a concern." She spoke too loudly. People noticed her. "Nothing to do with me."

Pia crossed the space and waited behind him, uncertain of what to say next. She didn't know what she had expected. An acceptance of her apology? Absolution? A punch in the nose? Or a simple answer about how to proceed with the project?

He picked up a paper coffee cup and offered it to her. She shook her head. He poured himself one.

He said, "You're too high-profile to ever come in here again. If your theory is right, if there is a mole, that mole would keep tabs on you. You're easy to follow. Me, I'm just a guy whose contract got dunked in the trash. I'm here every week. When you find something, send one of your people. An unknown with a plate of gingersnaps."

He turned away, took a few steps, then stopped. He craned over his shoulder. "Have your chef make them."

CHAPTER 34

WHEN THE INVITATION TO TUSCANY came three days later, I took Mardik and Firas with me to counterbalance Bonham's dogs. We checked out the Leaning Tower of Pisa and took the requisite photo of us appearing to hold it up. Firas went contrarian, trying to push it over. It was the first genuine smile I'd seen on either man. Sometimes it's the simple pleasures that make us forget the horrors. We rented a car and followed the map Bonham had provided. The area was too remote for Google Maps, they said. We wound our way from the coast deep into the hilly countryside.

We drove through a town made of stone buildings that spilled down the hillside like a medieval train wreck. Streets so narrow they were navigable only by scooters. When we neared our destination, the homes looked more redneck. Trailers were parked in a back corner and the Fiat was up on blocks.

Mercury flew alongside the car, just outside my window. *You know you're going to sell your soul to Orcus, homes. Just like Nate Hale.*

I said, *Nate got greedy. I won't make that mistake. I won't take their first offer. I'll counter. I only want a piece of the puzzle. Enough to get Detit Exports out of hock and go legit. Then I'll figure out which one of these guys gave the order and which one pulled the trigger. They're dead.*

Mercury said, *Be careful, my man. They'll make you sign up to be an arms dealer for the rest of your life.*

I said, *I'm not stupid. I won't sign anything. I'm not an arms dealer. I just enable transactions. Some impoverished farmer wants to protect himself from despots, I'll facilitate the firepower. That's it.*

Along the road, I called my gardener at Konrad's old estate in Corfu. No sign of the Austrian. The gods must have given him what he deserved for selling rifles to mass shooters. I wrote him off as dead. Although that left me with the problem of Falconer having witnessed the man's murder. He could hold that over me. At the back of my brain, I felt Mercury would've bragged if the gods had finished off Konrad. Bonham mentioned they never found the body. Could Konrad still be alive?

Falconer's estate sprawled over several square miles. It featured several wineries, a hunting lodge, a few small farms, and four hotels. The hotels weren't Hiltons, more like oversized eighteenth-century farmhouses converted to lovers' getaways with a few rooms each. We passed the remnants of a twelfth-century castle awaiting restoration. Near there, a fully restored chapel with three windows and fresh paint waited for the faithful. We came to the main estate as dusk settled in the trees. Eight buildings, all large and each seemingly cut from a cube of stone, were scattered along a winding loop of a driveway.

Rover waited for us with a Heckler & Koch G36 slung on his shoulder. He bared his teeth at my Syrians. They smiled back at him, as instructed. Mardik flashed a bottle of arak he kept in his duffle and shrugged. Rover softened his growl. We went inside.

My men were disarmed and given bunks with Bonham's dogs. I was given a room in the third building from the main house. It was smaller—only four bedrooms, one of which looked occupied. My room had a view of the Syrians' digs. That filled me with confidence for my survival. I had only two Sabel Darts left, and this would not be the place to blow them.

Falconer summoned me to the main house to hear Bonham's report on my trustworthiness. He stood in a blazer before an oversized hearth as if he were posing for a magazine photo. He held a green martini in his hand. The place had great wooden beams crossing low ceilings, hand-plastered walls, and polished stone floors. Windows and doors were set in walls three feet thick. Bonham lounged on a sofa.

"Ah, our hero returns." Falconer threw his hands wide. "Welcome to Radicondoli, Jacob. I trust your journey made you thirsty. Lorenzo, bring this man one of those pomegranate martinis he likes so much."

Charmed that he remembered my favorite drink, I shook his hand. He pulled me into a bro-hug, releasing me a second before it became awkward.

"No matter how much Bonham hates you, he couldn't find anything wrong with your operation." Falconer turned a sour face to Bonham, who rolled his eyes. "And he tried. He looked for any communication you might've had with authorities in the EU or the US, any contact with your old pals at Sabel, any tricks up your sleeve, and he found nothing. So, he's cleared you and now we can do business together."

"That depends on the business," I said. "What are we talking about?"

"Making money." Falconer looked confused. "What else could possibly matter? It's a simple transaction, really. You're going to recover something of value and bring it to a place where I can sell it. You do that for me, and I'll pay you five hundred thousand dollars."

I laughed. "If it needs that kind of background check, there's more to it than simple shipping. Which means we only talk in numbers with two commas."

Falconer's expression sank for a moment. Worrying I'd pushed too hard, I tried not to show it. Then Falconer leaned back with a roaring laugh.

"Balls, Bonham," he said. "This guy has balls of steel. You've got to admire that in a man."

Lorenzo came in with my drink and handed it to me. He disappeared.

"He still has to get rid of the Syrians." Bonham sipped an amber drink.

"Why?" I asked. "So I can hire your dogs? Not happening. A transaction must have value."

"You don't like Bonham's security team?" Falconer sipped his drink.

"Three of them stole my dinghy and never gave it back. Four of them let me kidnap Konrad right under their noses." As I spoke, I saw a lightbulb go off in Bonham's head. I'd bragged too much. "Not very effective security from what I've seen. They can't be worth whatever you're paying, Falconer. Let me scrounge up a few more Syrians and I can handle your security for less."

Falconer clapped my shoulder and turned to Bonham. "You hear that?

He's trying to steal your business right in front of you. Like I said, balls of steel."

I shrugged. "I've kept generals alive in war zones."

To his credit, Bonham stayed calm. Behind his stone face, calculations were in progress. He might've been calculating the size of stone needed to take me to the bottom of the ocean and keep me there. Maybe he was calculating the depth of grave he'd need his men to dig in the Tuscan forests. But he was working on some deep calculation in that evil mind of his. That was for sure.

Falconer sipped his martini, then extended it between us. "When you're ready to break out of your pomegranate rut, try one of these. Green apple, a little sweeter with a delightful sour bite. Quite nice." He stepped back and drew a serious face. "Did you know the CIA is watching you?"

I shrugged.

He dropped his voice a little deeper to underscore his concern. "You did something in Athens that caught their attention. Now what could that be?"

"Hard to say. I first caught their attention at the Battle of Najaf. They've been watching and learning ever since." Which was true, but the mention of Athens caught me by surprise. I should've fallen off their radar after being unceremoniously shipped to Durrës. Here he was telling me he had access to CIA information. I'd been warned he had friends in high places.

"Consorting with Syrian intelligence officers," Bonham said. He waited for me to look surprised.

I wasn't surprised. I was shocked. I had no idea. My Syrians' background began to flutter in my mind. I'd figured them for rebels of a lost cause. Intel officers meant they'd worked for Assad. There were untold stories in those guys. Stories I had wanted to leave buried. Now I wasn't so sure that had been a good idea. I'd have to dig around a bit with them. The CIA and several other groups within the US government didn't like people like me, with many secrets in our heads, consorting with agents of the nation's enemies.

I didn't let my concerns show. Instead I gave Bonham my soldier stare. He squirmed on the couch.

"I'll take an intelligent officer over prison rabble any day," I said.

"Intelligence," Bonham said, "as in Assad's Secret Po—"

"He knows, Bonham." Falconer waved a dismissive hand between us. "Your sibling rivalry is getting weary, boys. Put it aside so we can work together. The most important problem you face, Jacob, is operating capital. You don't have any. And you're going to need a lot."

"Don't worry about it. I can get capital any time I need it."

Mercury sat on the arm of the couch opposite Bonham. *Oh, really, homeboy? Where you going to get the money he's talking about?*

I said, *From you. Weren't you bragging about being the god of commerce?*

Mercury said, *The god of commerce is one thing. You're going to need the god of fantasy, bro.*

Falconer said, "Bonham's review of your books led him to believe you don't have enough to pay the loans on Konrad's ships next month, much less mount an underwater salvage operation."

"I have sources," I said. I felt sweat building between my shoulder blades and on my forehead.

"Who?" Falconer leaned to me. "Sabel Capital? The CIA maybe?"

"Uhm, no." I tried to project confidence I didn't have and wasn't getting from Mercury. My mind raced through options. Where had my god gone now that I needed him? This whole business world was like going to Oz for me. Put me on a battlefield and start tossing grenades. Screw this operating-capital bullshit. Whatever that means. "I have sources."

"I'm a financier." Falconer finished his apple martini, standing close enough for me to smell the tart sweetness. "All those loans Konrad owed—he owed to me. I'm not interested in refinancing those old rust-buckets of his. Or yours, I guess, as is the case now."

"I'm working on an early payoff for those loans." I have no idea where that sentence came from. I was hoping it was Mercury, but he sat on the couch trying to wave me off. "And arranging for some operating capital too. Your rates are excessive."

"I'll be damned." Falconer leaned back to admire me from head to toe. "If you can pull that off, I'll have Bonham go over your books again, make sure you're not holding out on me. But where are you going to get the three million you're going to need for the salvage operation?"

When life hits you with huge, unpleasant, and expensive surprises, the first thing you do is turn to god, right? When I turned to Mercury, he put his face in his hand, shook it back and forth, and said, *No, no, no.*

"I know a guy in London," I said. What was his name, Martin? Morgan? Marty?

Lorenzo stepped in the room and tapped a small chime.

"Good to hear, sport." Falconer clapped my shoulder again. "London banks finance anything, but if you think my rates are high ..." He laughed. "We're having dinner with a special guest. An expert in maritime recovery operations. Bonham found her. If I like her, and we hire her, she'll be running your expedition. In the meantime, you can have dinner with your Syrians."

He smiled and walked out. Bonham took his time rising from the couch. He tracked the long way around just to get in my face. He stopped toe-to-toe with me.

"You might've won a couple rounds with your parlor tricks," he hissed. "Don't underestimate me, Stearne. I always take out insurance on guys like you."

He left a cold breeze in his wake.

I tried to puzzle out why he looked so surprised when I mentioned Corfu. It came to me. I'd accidentally told him I was the guy who led the Greek SWAT team to Konrad. There had been four guards that night and only two on my last visit. That was a problem. But there was something else in his smugness about insurance. What was that about?

I headed for the front door. As I crossed the small foyer, Yumi Shibata descended the tiled staircase. We wound up face-to-face, close enough for me to smell her perfume and feel the heat of her breath. She wore a dark red off-the-shoulder satin dress that gave away her pounding heart.

Something erotic and painful and confusing and disorienting burns in your soul when you run into someone who walked out on you and never looked back. I stood still, unable to breathe or move.

She took my hand in both of hers and kneaded it. A pleading gaze rose from her upturned face. "Jacob. He won't let me go home. He would kill me before he would let me leave. I must get out. You have to—"

Behind us, the sound of footfalls pacing across the tiled living room cut off her words. She fled, her satin dress rustling as she went. I took a deep breath and pulled open the front door to head out. I crossed the brick driveway and followed the path to my Syrians.

Mercury paced alongside me. *Nothing like a damsel in distress to upset your train of thought, huh, homie?*

I said, *As far as I'm concerned, she made her bed with a murderous billionaire, she can lie in it.*

Mercury said, *Dang, that's cold, brutha. Why do you mortals get so bent when somebody leaves you? I mean, every time a mortal gets dumped, they pray to the gods to bring back their darling. And if we grant their request, y'know what y'all do?*

I said, *Why do I have a feeling you're going to tell me.*

Mercury said, *You trash 'em like soiled diapers. Stomp on their hearts in a nasty, right-back-at-ya kinda way. Y'all are some sick puppies.*

I said, *Word is, you made us in your image.*

I kept walking and called Josephine Seligman, the banker who sold me Detit Exports. When she answered, I said, "I've bought another shipping company and need to refinance some loans."

She asked me about assets, accrued interest, charge-offs, collateral, debt-to-income ratio, guarantors, loan-to-value ratio, right of offset, and a whole lot of other stuff. I had no idea what she was talking about. I asked her to call Geldona.

Josephine said, "I will. I'll let you know in the morning. Don't get your hopes up. I had to repossess that company once and I don't want to do it again."

On that happy note, I met with my Syrians. We ate and plotted and went to our separate rooms for the night. Mardik and Firas had one mission on this trip: befriend Bonham's dogs.

I stared at the plaster ceiling and watched the hand-swirled plaster not move. It was a little like watching the corn grow back on the farm. The farm where my girlfriend said marriage sucks. I rubbed my face with my palms. I wanted Jenny back. How was that going to happen while I'm living in freaking Albania and visiting criminals in the Italian hills?

Getting her back was so remote, I focused on the present. If I could get inside Falconer's operation, I could figure out which of these bastards would die for the sniper attack on my friends. That wouldn't bring Jenny back, but at least I'd feel better about Nate and Dimitris.

Maybe I could catch a glimpse of what the big fuss was about along the way. Maybe Alvaria was a weapon that should be sold to the highest bidder. Maybe I could return them to the government and get my life and my girlfriend back. But if she was off living happily in Stefan's arms, maybe I didn't need my old life. Maybe I needed a life where you can spend $32 million a year until Social Security kicks in. Come to think of it, I didn't want my old life back. Fuck 'em all.

Maybe I could push Falconer off a cliff and sell Alvaria to his highest bidder myself. Then I could have his yacht and his girlfriend. What did I care?

Mercury lounged on the ceiling with a golden goblet of wine. *'S what I keep saying, homie. Why can't you have a yacht? Why can't you have a jet? Is there some rule says a man risks his life for years on end ain't allowed to become rich and powerful? And what's with that CIA thing anyway?*

I said, *Yeah, why are they tailing me? Haven't I yanked their agents out of danger often enough? And how does Falconer know what they're doing?*

Mercury said, *And that's not the worst of it. Pia-Caesar-Sabel treats you like that? Who does she think she is?*

I said, *Yeah. That was like demon-possession or something. She trashed me so bad, Falconer noticed. Who needs her? I can do this billionaire stuff.*

CHAPTER 35

IN THE MORNING, I WAS summoned to the main house. We met in a spacious office with a substantial fireplace. Falconer stood behind a desk littered with papers, drawing a map on a whiteboard with a blue marker.

Bonham had found another couch to lounge on and was beside himself with glee.

Falconer stood up straight and faced me. "Jacob. So good to see you again, sport. Slept well, I trust. Bonham here is still against me bringing you in. He says decorated veterans don't turn into international smugglers. He thinks it's more likely you've turned into an international spy. What do you have to say about his allegations?"

I turned to Bonham and gave him my soldier stare. "Prove it."

Bonham gave me a dim smile and picked up a glass of orange juice. He tilted it my way in a silent toast, then sipped.

Falconer clapped his hands and laughed. "Exactly what I said. He had his chance, he dug into your records, and he couldn't come up with a shred of evidence against you. He had you followed for days. No dead drops, no cutouts, no coded messages. You never met with anyone he didn't like. I'm beginning to think he's jealous."

Bonham slugged back the OJ and smacked his lips and looked at us. "I'm over it. Besides, I have several insurance policies named Fido, Spot, Rover, and ... well, you get the picture." Bonham stood and reached out to me. "Welcome to the family, Jacob."

He didn't try his bone-crusher handshake a second time. I went easy on him. All friends here. I'd won.

"Now then," Falconer pointed to his whiteboard. It had a crude map of the Mediterranean with arrows to a cruder outline of the Black Sea.

"Here's the project. There is a package, consisting of several submersible containers, lying in five hundred feet of water not far from the island of Linosa. That's halfway between Sicily and Tunisia. You'll mount an operation to recover the containers and take them fourteen hundred nautical miles to the Black Sea. Your final destination will be revealed once you arrive at a certain spot unaccompanied. If you're stopped by authorities along the way, you are to dump the containers overboard. When you're clear of the authorities, you will recover the containers once again, and continue on. All recovery operations will be at your expense, so try not to dump them."

Most customs inspectors are land-based. Coastal enforcement agencies are ship-based. I'd never heard of any law enforcement operation that owned a submarine. Which made his method nothing short of genius. He'd stolen Alvaria by dumping it overboard. Then he waited for the NATO search teams to give up. Now he was ready to proceed. All he needed was a fall guy in case the plan fell apart. Otherwise, he would've hauled it up and put it on his yacht.

I'd need an underwater expert of some kind. Captain Rafia didn't strike me as a submariner. I wasn't even sure he could swim.

"Nice plan," I said. "What's in it for me?"

"What did I tell you, Bonham?" Falconer faced his friend. "This man is no hourly wageworker. He wants in. He wants a piece of the action." Falconer swung his arms between us. "I figured as much, Jacob. I reconsidered my previous offer. I'm now prepared to give you five percent of the auction price."

"What auction?"

"The package will be offered to the highest bidder. Commodities exchange. You deliver the package and prove authenticity, and you're done." Falconer shook a finger at me. "Then the winning bidder will deliver two hundred thousand barrels of oil, or two hundred million bushels of wheat, or some other untraceable commodity, and you take it back to port on your little boats and sell it. We split the profits, five percent for you, another percentage to Bonham, and I keep the rest."

"It's worth more than five percent then," I said.

"Nope. That's it, I'm afraid. Not a penny more, so help me god."

"Five million guaranteed."

"Where did you get that number?" Bonham laughed.

"Out of thin air. You need someone dumb or desperate. I'm not dumb."

"I'll give you a three million minimum guarantee," Falconer said. "But the five percent will bring you more than five million. Much more. Don't worry about the recovery aspect. We've hired a naval salvage expert to assist you. She's top in her field and is—as you so delicately put it—desperate. In her case, for redemption."

"You'll want to consult with her," Bonham said. "She can give you a better estimate of what you're up against."

Bonham trotted out of the office and returned a moment later. A woman in a business pantsuit followed him.

My world stopped turning for a long, agonizing moment. My knees buckled. I was suddenly cold.

Jenny Jenkins stepped out from behind Bonham.

CHAPTER 36

MY HEART BEGAN SPINNING AND pounding and caving and revving. It was all I could do to keep calm.

She extended a hand. "Nice to meet you Mr. Stearne." A cold demeanor faced me despite her jovial greeting. "I'm Jenny Jenkins, salvage specialist formerly with the US Navy. I recovered lost encryption systems from sunken ships."

I could feel her chill before our hands shook. Few things in life are as scary as a woman suppressing her anger. And she was angry. I played along pretending it was our first meeting. She could explain later.

Her hand was clammy, sweat on her palms. Nervous. I shook her hand slowly. Bonham couldn't wipe the grin off his face. He said he knew someone who knew Pia Sabel. Most likely, that same someone would have known Jenny Jenkins as well. Worse, I had given Bonham my phone with her number in it along with a whole lot of drunken texts. She was his insurance policy.

"We have a quick meeting with the estate manager," Falconer said. "You two get acquainted, discuss the details, make some rough estimates, and we'll close this deal."

He and Bonham stepped out and shut the door behind them.

I pointed to a door leading to a grassy hillside just beyond the office. We strolled out like strangers. She clasped her hands behind her back.

"What the hell are you doing here, Jacob?" she hissed.

"What were you doing at Stefan Devoor's house?"

"He was at mine. What are you implying? You were all over Pia."

"Those websites doctored the photos for clickbait. They're called deepfakes. We were just dancing."

"Same here. Stefan came over to watch the Redskins lose again." Her voice was barely under control.

One more accusation and she'd hit the shout-button. And I would respond. Escalating things wouldn't help either of us. I walked and she kept pace beside me. I said, "Let's stick to business. What are you doing here?"

"Bonham offered me a job." She looked around. "My specialty in the Navy was underwater recovery. That's what they need done. I got here last night. They told me about the project over dinner. This is right up my alley."

"You think so? Do you have any idea what they want to recover?"

"It doesn't matter. Salvage is salvage as long as it isn't antiquities of some kind."

"How did they pick you?" I asked.

"Why do you say it like that?" She pouted her question. "Bonham heard about my situation and offered me a job. I'm qualified and I'm ready to get back to work."

"Did he say anything about me?"

"Bonham? He's aware we're dating … if that's what we …" She pulled a curious face. "He asked me not to mention it to Falconer and not to fraternize with you. I thought that was odd."

"These aren't nice people, Jenny." I held her by her shoulders and looked into her eyes. "You need to turn this job down and go home."

"You're not very supportive." She wriggled out of my hands. "I land my first consulting gig and you want me to go home? You prefer the helpless me who has to rely on you for survival? Well, forget that. Wait a minute." Anger flashed in her eyes. She fisted her hips and stuck out her jaw. "Do you have a girl here? Is that what's going on?"

"No. You're the only woman I want." I waved my hands at Falconer's house. "This is what I do now."

"I thought you said they weren't nice people."

Her combative tone made my blood boil. She couldn't still be pissed about me dancing with Ms. Sabel. Someone would've clued her in by now. She must've given up on me. Maybe she figured if Ms. Sabel dumped me, I wasn't worth keeping. Maybe she didn't like the company

I kept. She must've written me off as a lost cause. That pissed me off.

"Gotta make a living."

"There you are." Falconer called from the open door to his office. "C'mon back. We have some papers for both of you to sign. A little indemnity for all of us."

As we reentered his office, I paused in front of him. "Before we sign anything, my cut is twenty-five percent. You need this thing delivered and you picked me to deliver it because, in this unreliable world, you know I will."

We all moved inside.

Falconer said, "Nope. Five percent, that's it."

I turned on a heel and headed for the door. "Good luck then. Let me know how it works out."

"Wait." Falconer chuckled. "I did reserve a little extra. You'll have an arduous task so … ten percent."

"Twenty-five," I said and continued walking.

"I'll split the difference with you. Fifteen percent."

"Split would be seventeen and a half." I held the doorknob in my hand. "Twenty."

"Fine." He blew out a breath. "But you pay Ms. Jenkins."

I looked at her. She appeared to be deciding between signing her contract and throwing a punch at me. She opted for both. The punch would come later.

Mercury, in his holy wisdom, decided this was the perfect time to appear behind Falconer. *Homie, you're about to sign an agreement that could make you a fugitive for the rest of your life.*

I said, *What life? I don't want to spend 15,873 years accumulating a billion. I want it now.*

Mercury said, *What happened to not getting greedy like Nate?*

I said, *I know what I'm doing. I'm not selling my soul. Hey, what happened to you wanting me to get rich?*

I'm just making sure you know what you're getting in to, Mercury said. *This is not the old you. You're always wanting to be the unsung— and unpaid—hero. You go this route and you'll wind up killing innocent foot soldiers like Benji or Cujo just to save your own skin.*

I said, *I would never do that.*

OK, don't pull up later blaming me, Mercury said. *When you throw in with these guys, there's no going back. But. If you put your back into this, you could wind up sitting on the deck of a yacht cruising on your way to Caesar-ville.*

I glanced at Jenny again and said, *Yeah, I like that idea. Falconer thinks I'm stupid. He went to twenty percent because he's planning to kill me at the end. He's got another thing coming. This pirate life suits me. I'm good at it. I get to put all my skills to use. I'll dig up his crates, steal his customers, and stab him in the back long before he can get to me.*

Falconer pushed a plush folder across the desk. A small stack of documents lay on top with a pen. There was a place at the bottom for my signature. I scanned the words; it was all about companies with names I'd never heard. I guessed they were shell companies. Near the bottom was a small section called "liability." In it, I agreed to accept all liability for any product or equipment transported on behalf of Falconer's shell companies. I was attesting to having acquired the goods from legitimate sources and bore all responsibility for legal ownership. Nice.

Bradley Hopkins of the CIA once warned me that talking about Alvaria could land me the death penalty. I hadn't said a word about it to anyone. I was clean. He didn't say I couldn't steal it and sell it to the Iranians.

I signed.

CHAPTER 37

FALCONER GAVE JENNY A STACK of reports on the containers and the approximate location. We retired to an unused office in another building to come up with an expedition plan. What I really needed was a plan to get Jenny fired and sent home. In any scenario imaginable, this didn't end well for her. She had plenty of trouble in her life; she didn't need to get mixed up in this. But then, she didn't trust me enough to heed my warning. Maybe I would let her suffer the fate she'd brought on herself. Maybe I wanted her to stay so we could patch things up.

The office they assigned us was in a bungalow undergoing renovations near a large garden. It had a finished kitchen and dining room. Two empty rooms had tools laid out, unfinished flooring, and various construction crap lying around. Jenny scattered the reports on the dinner table and started reading.

I took the time to text my banker for a status on my loan. Josephine texted back, "My first answer is no. My second answer is hell no. My third answer is, let me check on something. I'll get back to you tomorrow."

I texted her, "Let me guess, you went into banking when your career as a motivational speaker didn't pan out?"

She texted back, "I like smart heroes. That's the only reason I'm checking on something. Give me 24."

Jenny looked up from her reports. "This is odd. The containers are cylindrical. Twelve meters by three meters in diameter. That's close to a 40' ISO container. And they're sealed on both ends with pressure domes and pressure seals."

"All of which means nothing to me," I said.

"Every year, several thousand shipping containers fall off freighters. Bad weather combined with inadequate lashing is the most common cause. You know the kind of containers I mean. They're the big rectangular things that go from truck to train to ship."

"And?"

"These are round."

"And?"

"They're made to withstand pressures of the deep. They can survive falling overboard and sinking to the bottom of the ocean."

I studied her face, wondering if she'd made the connection between what I said about Falconer's moral fiber and the type of container they were using. If she figured out they were doing something illegal, she would leave on her own. I wouldn't need to talk her into it because she never wants to go back to prison.

She continued as if I were the one who didn't understand yet. "If these things catch on, ships could recover their losses from heavy storms. They could keep valuable cargo intact down to 5,000 feet or more and still recover them. This is genius."

Right about then, I noticed the video lens buried in the chandelier. A wide-angle lens about the size of a pen trailed a special wire up the fixture into the ceiling. Not very sophisticated but highly effective.

Jenny tapped a pen to her chin. "I wonder if this is a proof-of-concept project."

"Not likely."

Before I could explain, someone came in the back door and walked down the hallway.

Yumi stopped at the edge of the dining room in a floral dress and a floppy hat. She looked at me. Then at Jenny. Jenny looked at her. Jenny's face sank. She turned a scowl my way.

I don't know how women do it, but if you find yourself in a room with two women who once exchanged body fluids with you, they both know it instantly. Does it matter that you hadn't thought about one of them in two years? Does it matter that one of them had zero chance of ever getting back into your life?

Jenny slapped her reports closed and slammed them on top of each other in a growing stack. When they were all under her control, she stormed for the door. "I'll be in my room."

It was a good thing the renovations were still underway. The front door would need some attention after Jenny slammed it behind her.

"You should take a look at the garden," Yumi tossed her glance toward the hidden camera. "Many organic vegetables there. Maybe you would like to cook something for Georgie."

We strolled out into the midday gloom of an impending downpour. The garden had been winterized. Straw covered half an acre of plowed earth. A few melons remained behind, ready for harvesting before the next frost.

She pointed to the ground a few feet away. "You are not the kind of man to associate with George Falconer."

"Things have changed, Yumi." I almost complimented her on the strides she'd made in her English.

"I was good detective in Tokyo." She moved her pointing finger along the row as if explaining something to me. "I know what these men do. I know what kind of men do these things. You not one of those people. Worlds can change, volcanoes erupt, seas rise, but Jacob never change."

I was glad I'd refrained from commenting on her accent. "Then what the hell are you doing here?"

"Georgie was very nice man when we met. He treated me respectfully. We went on many date. He even visited my mother. She was having problems. Dementia. He was moved and he helped pay for best home for her. Full-time care. Nothing I can afford. Then I find out. Too late I find out."

My knowledge of elder care was limited. But I was aware special care units for dementia patients run from cheap and horrifying to hideously expensive for slightly less horrifying. The difference in price reflected the dignity of the patient's family; there's nothing to be done about the entropy of the patient's life. The family felt better about a place with fresh paint, new carpets, and friendly staff. And dignity meant everything to Yumi.

I pointed to some melons that looked frost damaged.

Yumi said, "I read his papers, emails, texts. I know what he does. Most things he does perfectly legal. Some things, not legal at all. One day, he caught me. He acted like I dumb detective. He told me blood on yacht not human, just shark." She looked up with angry eyes. "Shark blood. On a yacht deck. I said, the shark jump twenty feet in air to land on deck? He got mad. Very mad. I back down. He would kill me."

I leaned down and tugged at a dead vine. "What do you want me to do, Yumi?"

"You help me get out of here. I have no passport. No transportation. No bodyguards to stop Bonham's dogs."

I stood up. "I'm not sure I'm getting out of here, to tell you the truth. Bonham has me cornered."

"He knows you spy on him?"

"Shh." I shook my head. "Yumi, I'm not spying."

"And that was not shark blood. Don't tell me what I already know. True is true, lie is lie."

Mercury rose out of the ground like a time-lapse of a blossoming flower. *Everything's a transaction, young blood. You want information on Falconer and Bonham. She wants a ride out of town. Sounds like a fair trade to me.*

I said, *I'm not going to put her at risk like that.*

Mercury said, *You don't want to risk her like that. But you're going to. Because. You have to.*

"She is your girlfriend?" Yumi asked.

"She's the salvage expert."

"A half-truth is a whole lie."

"Yes," I sighed, "she is my girlfriend. She's also the salvage expert. But she doesn't know who Falconer is. And Falconer doesn't know she's my girlfriend. But Bonham does."

"Oh." Yumi inhaled sharply. "Bonham is most evil man. He will use that against you. Why do you bring her here?"

"I didn't. Bonham did."

"And I ask you for help." Yumi paced down the garden. "When you get out, you take me with you?"

"I'll do my best. You have my word."

Yumi nodded and started to walk back to the main house.

"Wait," I said. "In order to get out, I need to find out some things."

"Tonight." She spoke so softly I could barely hear—and neither could Spot, just twenty yards away. "Oh-two-hundred at the chapel."

Giving her hope, lying to her, felt wrong. Just as wrong as leaving the world behind and becoming an arms dealer. She was like Bonham; neither of them would believe I'd turned bad. I'm not sure I believed it either. Revenge for Nate and Dimitris would be a byproduct of my new direction instead of an ending.

I was going for Caesar now.

Why not? With a shipping company up to its waterline in debt, no job, and a pissed-off girlfriend, how many options did I have?

CHAPTER 38

ALL AFTERNOON AND EVENING, JENNY gave me cold glares and snippy answers. She was making me pay for not being supportive of her job. And for dancing with Ms. Sabel. And especially for Yumi. Giving her time and space was my best bet.

Everyone retired for the evening. Fido, Spot, and Rover, the three daytime dogs, had taken a liking to the arak Mardik and Firas plied them with. Bonham's estimation that my Syrians had been part of Assad's intelligence service made sense when I saw how well they befriended the enemy. They were experts at losing my money in poker games. And excellent drinkers who poured five times as much of the Syrian version of ouzo for others than they drank themselves. They never noticed me slip out of the bunkhouse.

But the three dogs on the night patrol, Benji, Yeller, and Cujo, were still pissed about that little boat ride I'd sent them on back in Monaco. Unlike Fido's team, they were not going to drink with the Syrians. Instead, they spent all night watching me. Ducking out had required a bed stuffed with pillows. But I made it.

The grounds were quiet. I snuck through the cold, damp brush at two in the morning. Then the rain started.

The chapel was not close to the estate's main buildings. It was half a mile down a sweeping and empty drive that Bonham's dogs used for patrols. I stayed twenty yards deep in the woods where the afternoon rains had left mud and wet branches. I finally found the old building. The clearing around the chapel looked significantly larger when I had to cross it in the dark.

I waited and listened, watching the area from behind a retaining wall.

One of the dogs strolled down the lane near the chapel. He was outbound and would return this way at some point in the not-too-distant future.

Moments after he disappeared around the bend, a hooded dark-velvet cape crossed the clearing. Yumi trotted straight for the chapel door, too far for a whisper to stop her.

Made of white limestone with red-brick framing for the doors and three small windows, it contrasted her like a billboard. Without moonlight, she was difficult to distinguish as human, but her movement would draw any casual observer. She creaked open the heavy wooden door and went inside.

I ran to the entrance, hoping to get in before she closed it. The guard might miss one loud creak in a forest full of swaying branches but a second would stand out. And a third, me going in after she closed the door, would warrant an inspection.

She closed it on my hand.

It was all I could do not to bark in pain. She heard me breathing hard and opened the door quickly, which gave rise to the loudest creak yet. I pressed a finger to her lips for quiet, grabbed her hand, pulled her out, and stuck my foot under the door. Lifting some of the door's weight with my toe, I closed it softly.

I led Yumi around the back and waited.

She whispered, "We should go inside. They will not see us."

The sixteenth-century architecture featured a single door at one end, no windows along the sides, six stone benches, and a stone altar. A guard could stick his pistol in the window beside the door, fire blindly three times and get six hits due to ricochets. Brilliant detective that she had once been, they never trained her to sneak into an ISIS stronghold and take down the watch one by one. Instead of explaining all that, I just put a finger back to her lips.

The guard jogged up the lane seconds later. He flicked a flashlight to life that seemed like a Klieg light in the darkness. It swept the area, leaving us in shadow by inches. He opened the chapel door and must have recognized the creak. His light filled the small space and reflected back into the trees behind him, leaving a monster shadow. Then he flicked the light around the grounds beside the chapel, nearly illuminating us.

I pulled us around the corner to the back of the chapel just in time. He came down the side, intent on having a look at the back end and the graveyard beyond. We shuffled quietly along the chapel's far side, playing cat and mouse.

He rounded the back as we rounded the next corner, barely one step ahead. He could sense our presence. The light beam played over the grave markers, most of which were toppled. Then he flicked it off.

I could hear him move. Which way he was going was unclear as his shuffling echoed off the tombstones in all directions. I pressed my back to the chapel's side wall. The footsteps became clearer, easier to hear, which meant he was coming closer. He made it to the corner and stopped. Most likely listening.

Yumi was smart enough to hold her breath. I did the same. I could feel the heat of his body three inches from mine, only a right angle of wall between us. My left arm was raised, ready to slam into his face should he turn the corner.

He didn't. He flicked his light back on and trained it on a marmot at the edge of the graveyard.

Then he turned the corner, his light splashing into my eyes. I slammed my fist into his face. He barely noticed. He reached for a pistol. I slammed my elbow hard to his temple. That caused him to stagger back a step without gaining me much advantage. I kneed him in the nuts. He raised his pistol to my chest.

I slammed my forearm under his, forcing his pistol skyward. We struggled. He was bigger than me and stronger than me. He attempted to shove the muzzle in my eye. I kneed him in the nuts again. The pain searing through his groin bought me enough time to shove him against the chapel and plant my back foot. He grabbed my hair and tried to pull my head back.

I keep my hair buzzed short to prevent his kind of attack. His free hand went to my face. His fingers found my eye socket. He shoved his finger in. His strength would overpower me in another second.

Yeller pushed off the wall to throw me off him. Instead, I grabbed hold of him, taking him with me, and spun as we went down. I landed on top of him which led me to believe I had the upper hand. But I knew enough about wrestling to feel his attempt at an arm bar. A move that would land me in a headlock, my arms useless. Then he would shoot me in the head and crow to the boss about having caught me with Yumi. They'd give him a medal. I didn't like that scenario.

He had a weight advantage and a skill advantage, leaving me only seconds. I had one option left. One I didn't want to do. But I had to if I wanted to live.

I shoved his arm and pistol under his chin. I squeezed my finger inside the trigger guard. Since there wasn't enough room for two fingers, his finger mashed the trigger.

The bang reverberated off the gravestones and church walls.

Instantly, he went limp.

The forest would damp the noise before it reached the main buildings. If I had any luck at all the other dogs would be at least that far away. But even a distant and muffled gunshot is a unique sound on a quiet night.

I picked up his flashlight and checked. It illuminated a neat hole in the bottom of his chin. And a big one at the top of his head. I estimated the round went straight through his cerebral cortex. Instant death.

Yumi gasped in horror.

Mercury leaned into the light. *Not going to kill innocent foot soldiers, huh, homie?*

I said, *You saw it. I had no choice.*

Mercury said, *I saw it all right. You went and killed Ol' Yeller just to save your skin. Just like I said. You've now become the man you didn't want to be. You are your own worst enemy.*

I said, *Thanks for the guilt trip. I feel bad enough about it. But, he brought it on himself. What do I do?*

Mercury said, *I dunno. Dump his body in the cistern?*

A few yards away was a capped cistern. Probably hadn't been used since the seventeenth century.

With tears streaming down her cheeks, Yumi helped me move the heavy cap and throw Yeller's body into the well. We replaced the cap and sat quietly on top of it. I took a moment to mourn the unfortunate death.

We waited a moment to regain our composure. When I let out a breath, she wrapped her arms around me and hugged me tight. She was shaking with fear. I allowed the hug for a moment. Then I pulled her back to look in her eyes.

I couldn't see her eyes. It was too dark.

"They will look for him," I said. "You have to walk back up the lane and meet them as they're coming back. Tell them you went to the chapel when you couldn't sleep but didn't find comfort. Then you walked the woods, but it was too wet. You decided to just go home."

She nodded. I think. It was still too dark.

"What do you need from Falconer?" she asked.

"He has a big deal coming up. It's going to be an auction. I need to know who the bidders are. Can you find out?"

"Why?"

That was a question I didn't want to answer. I couldn't tell her I planned to steal his customer list and hijack his auction. While trying to come up with something to fit the narrative, her hands slid inside my unzipped jacket. She put her cheek on my chest.

Mercury took that inopportune moment to appear behind her, creating a three-way embrace. *Ah, dawg, ain't this just like old times? Can you feel her heart beating against your chest?*

I said, *Get off her. And get her off me.*

Mercury said, *Y'know how in all the movies the hot chick has to put out so the good guys can sneak past the guards?*

I said, *What does that have to do with anything?*

Mercury said, *It's time you take one for the team, bro. Time for you to put out.*

I said, *I'm in love with Jenny, not Yumi.*

Mercury backed up. *Uh-huh ... sure you are.*

I pushed Yumi back. "We're not going there."

She slapped me.

"What was that for?" I whispered loudly.

"You made me believe you help me escape this place."

"I will. I ..." I took a deep breath. "We're not getting back together,

Yumi. You left me. It took a while, but I got over it."

"My mistake, I know. You won't hold that against me." Her hands slid over my pectorals.

I would've walked away except I needed the information if I wanted to beat Falconer at his game. There was no way he would leave his laptop unguarded in my presence. Which meant Mercury was right—I'd have to take one for the team. But I would only allow harmless fondling. No clothes removed, no bare skin. A guy has to draw the line somewhere.

"Look, can you figure out who he's dealing with?"

Her hands cupped my cheeks. "He changed his passwords after he caught me."

She drew away three steps, then faced me again, her cape swirling around her. "Jacob, he was going to kill me last time but stopped himself. It's too dangerous."

She was right about that. If he wanted me to kill Konrad for the crime of losing three shipments, he would forget all about how much he cares about Yumi and decapitate her for crossing him.

On the other hand, if she could be careful and get the bidder's list without tipping him off, then I could send Jenny and Yumi both back to the States. Once they were safe, I could deal with Falconer and Bonham.

"There's a way to steal passwords without getting caught," I said.

"He is very suspicious."

"You watch him type the first three letters, then make a show of looking away. Write those three keystrokes somewhere safe. Then you wait a day and watch him again. The second time, you watch him in the middle of typing. Don't look, then look, then look away. Catch the middle three letters. And so on. You do this step five or six times, overlap some letters to make sure you have it. He notices you are turning away halfway through. He suspects nothing."

She took three quick steps to me and wrapped me up. This time her hands went under my t-shirt. "I can try. I will do this for you."

She looked up at me and waited for a kiss. The red-blooded, all-American heterosexual male in me wanted to kiss her. The smarter guy who wanted to marry Jenny Jenkins pulled back on the reins with all his might.

Flashlight beams swept the road, still a good distance away. They weren't running, which meant they hadn't sensed any reason for alarm. We had a chance.

"Go." I pushed her. "Like we planned."

She nodded and moved swiftly toward the lane.

I leapt the graveyard wall a second before a light beam flashed by. I jogged through the trees and dense underbrush.

When I got back to my cottage, I rinsed mud off my boots in the kitchen sink, then snuck upstairs in my socks. I entered my room in the dark and tiptoed to the bed.

The light snapped on.

Jenny asked, "Where have you been?"

CHAPTER 39

FALCONER SAT UP IN THE dark, pulling his pistol from under his pillow. "Who's there?"

"It's me." Yumi took off a cape and hung it. "Sorry to wake you. I could not sleep. I went for a walk. Your guards are animals. They would not let me, they told me to go home. Still I cannot sleep."

He quickly stashed the pistol before she saw it. It would upset her. He flipped on the bedside lamp. "Why can't you sleep, darling? That's what happens to old people, not the young and beautiful."

"People go and some never come back. Where is Konrad? He never send thank-you note. It is not like him to disappear."

"Strange," he replied. "Now that you mention it, I've not heard from him since our yacht-closing party at the end of the season. He was unhappy about losing my shipping business to this Stearne fellow."

"You are awake?" she asked. She dropped her clothes in the hamper with a slosh. "Something bothers you?"

This is what he loved about her: that she cared enough about him to ask. All the other women he'd spent time with cared only about when the next shopping trip started and when the champagne would flow again. How he hated champagne. It thrilled him that Yumi hated it as much. They shared a love of all things sweet and sour.

"Business ventures always bother me," he said. "New people, new risks. Like your friend, Jacob Stearne. The CIA keeps tabs on him for me. Bonham went over everything that man owns and didn't find a hint of tracking or communications. So why did the CIA report he was drinking in Athens?"

"How do you know what CIA knows?" she asked. She came out in the silk teddy he bought her.

"I've told you," he laughed, "I'm a very important man. They email me updates on all my business partners."

She pulled back the sheets and slipped in. "I can never tell when you joke."

"No joke. I am an important part of the American economy. There are many things they need done off the official books. I champion revolutionaries and freedom fighters."

"One man freedom fighter is another man terrorist."

"Exactly. And what's keeping me up this evening is wondering which one is Jacob Stearne."

"Jacob is hero. They gave him medals in America. They gave him medal in France. He saves the little guy whenever the little guy is in trouble. He is always there to save the people."

Falconer sat up on an elbow and watched his darling as she snuggled into her pillow. "Why is your hair wet?"

"It was raining."

"Earlier it rained. Not in the last few hours." He reached an arm around her, felt her stiffen. "Who did you walk with?"

"No one," she said.

He felt an evasion in her voice. A deception. From his darling? It couldn't be. He kissed her cheek. "Did you meet your 'hero' on this walk of yours?"

"No, of course not. I walk down road and find Benji shining flashlight in my eyes. He asked me many questions as if I was a criminal. I am not a criminal. I am a detective from Tokyo. Honorable in my work and dedicated to public safety."

Falconer held her close. Her heartbeat was unusually quick under the smooth silk. Was he growing paranoid? A certain level of paranoia was warranted, especially since he'd gone into business with a war hero. One who once captured Yumi's heart. Bonham had found nothing to indicate Stearne was contacting any American or European agents. All his associates were new and sketchy.

Everything about Jacob's story added up to being cast out by an impetuous young woman who had either tired of his advances or had her own advances refused by him. But neither Falconer nor Bonham had considered Yumi, a detective from Tokyo who was honorable in her work, as a conduit for Stearne. Could she be acting as a cutout, transmitting messages from Stearne to authorities somewhere?

Yumi rolled over and touched her lips to his. She wrapped her arms around him and wiggled her nose across his. It angered him that she would try to manipulate him with sex. He had been fooled by women in his youth. No longer.

"Not right now, darling." He rolled over and switched off the light. "I'm much younger in the morning than I am this late at night."

She sighed, dissatisfied.

It had taken a good deal of his will power not to fuck her brains out. Holding her in his arms always made him hard as a rock. But not this time. Now he was concerned. Distrustful. Wary. And he didn't like that.

He also didn't like the idea that he may need to slice open that pretty neck and toss her weighted body overboard.

He slammed the brakes on his thinking. He couldn't let his paranoia run wild. Yumi was someone worth saving from his usual capricious decision-making. He would give her a quest.

"I need you to do me a favor, though," he said in the dark.

"Yes. Of course."

"When Stearne and his crew go to Albania to provision their expedition, I'd like you to spy on him for me. You're a detective and you're very good at it. You are someone who can question and search him. We know he has a communication device. We've not found it, but we know he must have one. I want you to find it and bring it back to me."

She lay in the dark, lit by the dim green light from the clock on the bedside. Her eyes searched his.

"This is difficult. I walk out on him two year ago. He hurt very badly. He does not trust me today. He hates me. He will not let me search or question him."

"He is not a saint. You have a power over men. You can use that to get close to him. I need to know who he reports to. It is very important to me."

Yumi's voice softened to a whisper. "What if he does not have a device?"

"He must have one. The CIA knew he was in Athens."

CHAPTER 40

PIA LOOKED UP FROM HER email at the executive assistant holding her office door open. "Yes?"

"Do you have time for Eva Gomez? She said you blew her off twice this week. I told her not now, you're preparing for the board meeting."

Pia looked at the two hundred emails flagged for her attention in her inbox. She calculated the time she needed to prepare for the next meeting. No, she didn't have time for Eva. Pia said, "Send her in."

No one knew better than Pia what it was like to come off the soccer field into the real world. And Eva's recent heartbreak made it that much harder. Pia felt sorry for the kid.

Eva stormed around the assistant and planted herself in front of Pia's desk with crossed arms. Pia offered a hand which Eva reluctantly shook. Pia pointed to a chair. She looked back at the assistant. "Could you ask Miguel to join us, please?"

"Your people are giving me the runaround." Eva pouted like a petulant child. "In the last ten days, I've learned more from internal reports than from you. It's supposed to be the other way around. This morning, I saw a report that Stearne, your ex-employee, is trying to get insurance for a 'suspicious' project. I don't even know why that's relevant."

Pia tossed her an inch-thick stack of papers, clipped together with a binder clip.

"What's this?" Eva asked.

"A report on FTE requirements estimating the cost for Sabel Industries to expand maternity leave from twelve weeks to eighteen." Pia tossed another large report at the State Department's liaison. "This is the actuarial table for a deployment of eight hundred security agents in the Nigerian oil fields. We need to self-insure on that project since we can't get an insurance company to offer our people life insurance at any price. The assignment's too dangerous."

Eva tossed her hands up. "What's this got to do with me?"

"At Reggie's request, we gave you an office near mine so you could work directly with me when the Alvaria project came up. It hasn't come up. This is what I do all day. I review and accept or reject actuarial tables, FTE provisioning, build-out costs, long-range planning. Welcome to the world at the top of the food chain. It sucks."

Eva crinkled her nose as she glanced at the report in her hand. "What is FTE?"

"Full-time equivalent. You can staff a position with two people working twenty-hour weeks or one person forty-hour weeks. Either way, that's one FTE."

"Oh." Eva took a breath. "What about the Alvaria project? Has there been any progress?"

"Yes and no. I'm not being evasive. We use methods to uncover secrets that we cannot divulge. My people have set in motion a series of operations that will eventually uncover where Alvaria went. Right now, I am not aware of the progress of those methods. I've asked Miguel Rodriguez to join us because he's in charge of them. Ah, here he is, right on cue."

Miguel joined them, shook hands, and took a seat.

Pia said, "What's the latest?"

"RSAT created a set of special containers for the Alvaria. They were built to withstand high pressure should they fall off a ship. Apparently, shipping containers fall off ships from time to time. The percentages are tiny, but the risk is real. This time, the Alvaria containers fell off the ship. Video footage from the ship's monitors show them rolling off into the sea. All the Alvaria containers were lost. And only the Alvaria containers were lost. According to the logs, they were somewhere off the coast of Tunisia. However, the ship's navigation system stopped working several hours prior and started working again several hours later."

"That was convenient," Pia said.

"Even more convenient, the ship was Libyan flagged. A significant number of the crew retired mid-cruise and went ashore when they were not far from Tripoli."

"What did the captain have to say about them?" Pia asked.

"Not much. When the ship docked and the shipment was noted as missing, he also retired. After a short inquiry, he returned to his home in Algiers. He has not responded to calls. The Algerian embassy refused a visa for me to visit."

Pia turned to Eva. "That's where we are. Any questions?"

"You can't be telling me everything." Eva's naïve-but-earnest face turned from one to the other and back. "You know more. What is it you're not telling me? Why not? What's going on?"

Miguel canted his head to Pia. "Should I give her the details?"

"Do you trust her?" Pia asked.

Miguel looked at Eva. "Do you want to know secrets that are so critical to the lives of agents in the field that telling anyone, even your boss, could get someone killed?"

Eva squirmed, glanced at Pia, then back to Miguel. Without an ounce of conviction in her voice, she said, "Yes."

Pia took a long, deep breath. She felt the young graduate's pain. Knowing the adults in the room didn't trust you with something was almost as bad as the pressure of actually knowing the secrets they withheld. Here was a young, untested person, eager to be a contributing member of the team. Pia had been that same eager person once. Pia's heart ached. To trust Eva would endanger lives and careers. She felt better about trusting her soldiers. They knew firsthand the risks involved. They understood how the slip of a word at a party or a simple brag at the office could endanger more than they understood. Yet, Pia felt she could trust Eva. Maybe it was their shared background in soccer. Maybe it was seeing that fresh, eager face, still a few years away from the cynicism of life in the real world.

"Give us a minute, Miguel. I'll send her to your office, then you can fill her in on the details."

Miguel nodded at Eva and left.

When the door closed behind him, Pia said, "Use your imagination for a moment, Eva. Think about what kind of person would want a weapon system that lets you upload a photo for facial recognition, send it into the sky within a few miles of that person, and know the weapon won't stop until that target is dead. What kind of person do you see using it?"

Eva watched her closely for a moment before answering. "Pretty evil dude."

"Don't underestimate our gender. Could be a pretty evil woman as well. But, let's look at existing dictator records. Since Vladimir Putin came to power, ten opposition leaders and over a hundred sixty journalists have been murdered. Imagine what those numbers would look like if whoever was killing those people had Alvaria. Italy has made remarkable strides in clearing the Mafia out of Sicily. Imagine how hard that would be if the Mafia got hold of Alvaria. Think of the countries struggling under brutal dictatorships like Egypt and Syria. Now, think about how much they would pay for a system like that to rid themselves of revolutionaries."

"A lot. I get it. I know it's valuable—"

"Not just the dollar value. Think about the arms race. If Iran has one, does Iraq need one? If you're a hero in Kurdistan but a pariah in Turkey, do you have to worry about being targeted?"

A light went on in Eva's eyes. "Border crossings aren't set up to stop them. There could be open warfare between countries. And within countries. Genocide and civil war. Oh my god, these things are terrible."

"Now I want you to look at container ships." Pia searched the term 'container ship' and turned her laptop to face Eva. "Describe these."

"Neat, rectangular, stackable containers." Eva shrugged.

"And RTSA put Alvaria in cylindrical containers, stuck them on a ship like this—and they rolled off." Pia waited until their gazes met. "Who thought round was a good idea?"

Eva thought for a moment. "Are you saying it was intentional?"

Pia didn't move.

"It could've been stupid." Eva's eyes rolled to the ceiling as she thought. "But it's more likely intentional. And you mentioned in a meeting that RTSA didn't cough up the shipping information right away.

Only the Alvaria containers fell off. Then the captain and crew retired. Which implies they caused the system to fall off. But they would only do that if they knew what was in the round, pressure-resistant containers. The shipment was supposed to be incognito, so they shouldn't have any idea what was in them. Huh." Eva stopped for a moment. "And that means someone told them, and the only people who knew were RTSA people. Someone in the State Department is working with the hijackers."

"Back in my playing days," Pia said, "lots of people treated me like a dumb athlete. I hated that."

"Yeah," Eva said absently. "Me too. Wait a minute. You and Miguel are keeping me out of the loop because you don't want State to know what you're doing. You want to catch the guy."

"Someone outside of the State Department could be manipulating RTSA. Someone might've paid the captain and crew to lose the funny-looking containers. We can't barge in, tossing accusations around, wrecking careers, without proof."

"When you asked me why they picked me, you were checking to see if I was in on it." Eva chewed nervously on a thumbnail.

Pia didn't move.

Eva's bright face clouded. Her shoulders slumped. The shine of naïveté was gone. "Now that I know, I can't tell anyone. Not even Forrest."

"Lives and careers are on the line," Pia said. "There are Sabel agents sneaking around warehouses looking for clues. If the mole finds even a hint about what warehouse they might sneak into, they're dead. If we accuse the wrong official at State, we could ruin a career. You can't say anything to anyone. All you can say is, you've reviewed the work in progress, and you're satisfied."

"I don't like that." Eva looked wounded, as if the coach had blamed her for losing the championship.

"Your boss fired you up, told you to come in here and read me the riot act. She wants an update. She's not a career official, but even she should understand the sensitive nature of this investigation. Was her request out of ignorance or malice?"

Eva shook her head slowly. "I don't know."

"One last question before I send you to Miguel, who will fill you in on a lot more things you can't talk about. Who authored the internal report you mentioned about Jacob Stearne's insurance problems?"

"The CIA."

CHAPTER 41

JENNY WASN'T SPEAKING TO ME. She spent all day poring over her notes and making the provisioning list. After she saw me sneak out in the middle of the night, she'd seen Yumi follow. That was all she needed to know. Why Jenny was watching people come and go in the middle of the night was a question I wasn't allowed to ask. There was no way I could defend our clandestine meeting without putting Yumi's life at risk. I didn't answer her. Which left Jenny with only one reaction: I was dead to her.

After an entire day working without me, she produced a list of the requirements and extra equipment we would need. She presented it to Falconer, Bonham, and me in his office. She covered all the details. A crane system retrofitted to Captain Rafia's ship. Several remote operated vehicles, ROVs, for locating and attaching cables. A system for lashing the round containers to the deck. And so on.

Her estimate: $2.3 million.

When I finally stopped gasping, Falconer said, "That's not a problem for you, is it sport?"

"No," I squeaked.

Mercury said, *Remember when I said you can't spend money like you were still working for Pia-Caesar-Sabel, homes? And remember when you laughed at me? Maybe you remember hiring a helicopter to take you around on your swashbuckling pirate tour? Remember when I said, 'Don't buy Konrad's company?' And how did you treat the god of commerce?*

I said, *Yeah. Sorry about that. So. Can you come up with $2.3 million?*

Mercury said, *Will you conduct a Lectisternium in my name?*

He referred to a seven-day feast in which I would make public offerings to him and otherwise embarrass myself worse than a street-corner evangelist. I said, *Probably.*

Mercury said, *You're not filling me with confidence, brutha.*

Falconer leered at me. "Are you making all your payments on time?"

Bonham leaned to my ear. "If you don't make your monthly, we snip off one joint at a time. First the fingers, then the toes."

I tossed him a weary look.

Bonham grinned and whispered, "Not yours."

He tossed a glance at Jenny.

"Time is critical for this venture. We need to recover those containers and get them to the Black Sea in less than a week. If your fantasy banker isn't coming through, I'll insist you use Falconer Capital for the operation."

I turned to Mercury. *Y'know, I was thinking. I could do a massive Lectisternium. Yeah. Next couple days. In Durrës.*

Mercury scoffed. *Durrës? You think I wanna go back there? The Albanians never believed even back in the day when they were called the Ardiaei. No, homie, gotta be done back in Washington, DC with an audience.*

I said, *C'mon, don't push me. I need Falconer to see me as an equal. Not a subordinate like Bonham. And definitely not someone who will let his girlfriend lose her fingers and toes. This is serious. Please! Why are you looking at me like that? OK, fine. I'll do the whole rite when I get back to DC.*

Mercury said, *And why do you want him to see you as an equal?*

I said, *Because Jenny's never going to take me back now, so there's no reason to impress her. I'm going to stab Falconer in the back and take over his operation.*

Mercury said, *Now you're talking, homeboy.*

Jenny watched me thinking. She had questions about the conversation that just took place, but she was too polite to ask. Falconer looked at me funny. Bonham gave me his version of the soldier stare. It wasn't half bad.

"Give me a minute, folks," I said. My heart pounded like Santana's percussion section. Give me a rifle and I'll charge into a machine gun any day, but these business sessions were scary as hell. I tried to keep my voice from cracking. "I gotta check with my, uh, private banker in London."

I texted Josephine Seligman at her bank in London. "Remember me? I thought you were going to get back to me, the smart hero."

Everyone watched me, waiting for the answer. Seconds ticked by.

I said, "Maybe she's in a meeting."

During the lull, Fido stepped in and whispered something to Bonham. Falconer saw them and glared. "What is it, Bonham?"

"Yeller ran off again." Bonham looked sour. "They're checking with that girl in town—"

"Don't bother," Falconer snapped. "We gave him a chance last time. He's fired."

Fido fidgeted as if he wanted to plea for leniency. Bonham cut him off with a glance and he retreated.

I scanned the room expecting Mercury to show up and take credit for my lucky dodge. Oddly, he wasn't around.

Then my phone chirped. Josephine texted back. "Didn't Mason call you? He'll be in Durrës tomorrow to sign the papers. Those ships were mortgaged to the hilt at usury rates. We have you covered on all existing loans and an additional line of credit up to €10 million."

While reading, I felt Falconer's determined and piercing gaze waiting for me. While this was good news—Josephine's line of credit spared me from his Mafia-debt—there could be advantages to using Falconer to finance the project. For one, if I tossed him overboard, I wouldn't have to pay him back. Then I'd be ahead. If I failed—nah, I wouldn't fail. But if the authorities caught them and then their lawyers got them off, I'd be in a sniper's crosshairs.

I'd just have to win and destroy Falconer and Bonham. With what I made from Falconer's big deal, I could become the King of Albania. Maybe even Emperor of Albania. Yeah.

I glanced at Jenny. She stared out the window with her back to me. Not a care in her mind about the project's finances or my well-being. I followed her gaze outside. Yumi strolled across the hillside in a different hooded cape. Then I saw Jenny's reflection in the glass. If I didn't get Jenny calmed down, she might commit her second murder. And this time there wouldn't be any 'justifiable' angles. I'd work on that later.

Then an odd thought struck me: what if I can't pay Josephine back? Do private banks have goons like Bonham? No. As we learned in the 2008 debacle, they have taxpayers to bail them out, so no need for muscle. Which made her offer look much better. Besides, if I should fall to a sniper's bullet, the banks would send more detectives to find my killer than the Greek government ever did. So, I was actually safer going that route.

I showed the text to Falconer.

I expected him to be impressed. Instead, he was pissed.

"Bonham," he rasped in anger, "go back to Durrës with him and go over everything again. No one could be dumb enough to refinance those rusted old tugboats. First, go to London and give this Josephine a serious going over. Find out if she's funneling CIA money to him somehow. Don't stand there with a smug look on your face, damn it. This isn't you winning over Jacob, this is you failing to find his connections. CIA, State, Sabel, Europol, he must be working with someone."

Bonham fled.

Jenny's mouth dropped open.

Falconer stepped to me, nose to nose. "You are loyal to me, aren't you, Jacob? Is he going to find anything connecting you to some clandestine outfit trying to ruin my big deal? You need to come clean now, Jacob. I know what you did."

"What did he do?" Jenny tried to squeeze between us. "What did you do, Jacob? What's going on here?"

Falconer backed up a step and seethed. "He's a hero. They gave him medals in America and France, god knows where else. Someone told me, 'the little guys can count on Jacob to save them.' If that's the case, why does the CIA follow him around Athens?"

"Who cares?" Jenny asked. Curiosity creased her brow. "The CIA tracks everyone with high security clearances when they go abroad. Why does it matter?"

Jenny watched Falconer and I stare each other down.

"What the hell is going on here?" she asked. "What's in those containers?"

CHAPTER 42

IN JENNY'S MIND, I'D GONE from being dead to being damned-in-death. Not only did she think I had cheated on her, she was now aware I associated with criminals. And that meant she also associated with criminals, which was somehow my fault. Reminding her I'd recommended she drop the project and go home only made things worse. She flew to Oslo in search of suitable ROVs. The university there was the only institution with used ones on the market for sale. Apparently, ROVs are not available at hardware stores in rural Italy.

My only defense would jeopardize lives: mine, Yumi's, Mardik and Firas, the rest. So, I made no defense. I let her think angry thoughts on her trip.

My Syrians and I flew to Durrës under the watchful eyes of Rover and Spot. Bonham took Fido with him to London. The engagement ring, still in my jacket pocket, felt more like a lump of coal. I ran the pocket's zipper open and closed the whole flight, burning off nervous energy.

It was easy to tell when Bonham arrived in London because Mason, Josephine's representative, texted me seconds before we landed. "Ms. Seligman has some concerns about your associates. Apparently, they were quite rude to her."

"Tell her not to feel special," I texted back. "They were quite rude to me too."

Mason picked us up at the airport and noticed my traveling companions. Two former intelligence officers from Syria and two men whose portraits probably hung in post offices back in the States. Luckily, Mason had only rented a four-seater. I shrugged at the dogs and told them to meet me at the office.

As soon as the papers were signed, Mason shot out of Albania like a human cannonball.

Bonham came in from London the next morning for an extended review of all my spending. Geldona and Sokol were nice people but they were accountants. They spoke in English, but it may as well have been Albanian. It was all accounting-speak; I had no idea what they were talking about. Although I did get the message that there weren't going to be any more helicopter flights with huge bonuses paid to the pilot if I wanted to pay my employees. Also, drinking binges in Athens were restricted.

And accountants wonder why no one likes them.

No one had to tell me that to pay back the €10 million, I would need to make a huge profit in the next four weeks.

Bonham continued to pore over my texts and travels. He asked the hotel for security footage. To prove my sincerity, I paid the staff to show him whatever he wanted to see. My friend Miguel grew up climbing his ancestral cliffs in Canyon de Chelly on the Navajo reservation. I was confident his midnight visit to me would never show up on video. The staff gave me a new suite while Bonham took over mine so he could search it down to the carpet fibers.

Before he began his final sweep of my suite, he said, "I'm going to find out who you're dealing with. Don't think my visit with your nice banker proves anything. No one with your derelict assets gets that kind of money out of a bank."

"Knock yourself out." I said. "I've got nothing to hide."

He shoved me against the wall. "Tell me how you got the money. Tell me now and I'll make your death easy."

"Mercury, the god of commerce, has smiled upon me. If you had an ounce of faith, you'd be running the show instead of being Falconer's fool."

He scoffed. "Don't ever disrespect me again."

"Or what?" I turned my back on him and walked down the hall. "Will your dogs steal my dinghy again?"

Shortly after landing, Jenny began working with Captain Rafia on refitting his ship to create a salvage vessel. Her Nordic trip did nothing to change her mind about me, but she had come to terms with the contract she'd signed. Falconer's excuses didn't add up. The covert nature of the operation combined with Bonham and his dogs told her to limit her involvement and get out. The professional redemption angle was gone.

Jenny avoided me and my office. Although she hadn't said so, when this project was over, so were all my hopes of reigniting our flame.

Maybe I could get a refund on the ring.

Captain Rafia didn't mind working all day with a pretty young woman. He and my Syrians threw themselves into the task. From my office window, I could see the ship's contour change throughout the day. Cranes and crane jibs were modified. Winches were added. Materials and workstations were brought on board. Geldona stood in my office at one point, watching the work in progress, then gave me a look that said, *This better pay off.*

Working with Ms. Sabel had given me a glimpse at her level of responsibility. She weighed the risks not just in dollars but in the livelihoods of her employees. It was my first experience walking the financial tightrope business owners tiptoe every day. Everyone in the company looked to me for their daily wages. Money was flying out of my office, down the pier, to workers who hammered and welded and wrenched in the cold and damp of a November day.

Would this pay off? Would I keep Sokol and Geldona employed long enough to reach retirement? Would Megi save enough to go to graduate school? I wasn't worried about Mardik and Firas. They'd landed on their feet a couple times already. Worst-case scenario for them, they become Bonham's new dogs. But they looked to me to keep them from that wretched fate.

The next day, Bonham came to the office to say goodbye. He plopped in a chair, landing his briefcase on the floor beside him with a thunk. "Don't think I've given up. I'm leaving Fido here to watch your every move."

I toyed with the idea of darting Bonham and his dogs, but I only had two darts left.

His phone rang. When he took the call, I caught a brief flash of the caller ID: Falconer. I only heard Bonham's side of the conversation. He said, "Yes, I spoke to each of them this morning. They are calling our integrity into question. We can't have any more delays." He paused and listened, then glanced my way. "If you wish. Stearne won't mind at all."

He clicked off and faced me. "Falconer's on his way here. He thinks I missed something and wants to check it out in person."

I tossed my hands up. "Fine by me. Where do you head to next?"

He pointed out the window at Rafia's ship. "I'll look over all the communications gear. We'll monitor everything you do from the *Savannah.*"

"Darn, I won't be able to contact my Russian overlords without you knowing." My voice dripped with sarcasm.

"We know it's not them," he said. Anger crossed his face when he realized I'd tricked him.

"Don't worry," I said, rising to show him out. "I won't tell Falconer you gave away the country of origin for one buyer."

He stood and met my gaze. "I did nothing of the sort. And don't try to say otherwise."

He stormed out of the office.

I hoped he was the one who gave the order to kill Nate and Dimitris. Slicing him open would be a pleasure.

Fido remained behind, one leg draped over Megi's desk. He flirted with her. She tolerated him. I considered stepping in on her behalf. But then Fido would spend the day with me instead. I was done saving the meek. She could deal with him.

When I retook my chair behind my desk, Mercury was sitting in the chair Bonham just left. He pointed at the floor by his foot. *Bonham left his stuff behind, bro. Wanna have a look?*

I said, *What's in it?*

Mercury said, *Really, dude? You need a god to tell you what you could find on your own in a few seconds?*

I rose and grabbed the sleek leather messenger bag. A password-protected laptop in the center compartment. An unused notepad and pens in a side pocket. A three-page printout with names and phone numbers. At the top, the words, "Segreto List."

I may not speak Italian, but I knew *segreto* means secret. I also knew it should be *Lista Segreta*. But then Bonham spoke French, not Italian.

It had to be the list of bidders for the Alvaria system. One click of my phone and I could send Ms. Sabel and the CIA guy exactly what they were looking for. Maybe that would bring me back into the fold. Maybe a good deed would be considered a form of redemption.

Mercury leaned over my shoulder. *Sure thing, homie. The last three weeks, you've heard from Pia-Caesar-Sabel how many times? Oh, that's right. None. Maybe a good deed would be appreciated? How about all those times you saved her overprivileged ass from getting killed? OK, I take that back. She did give you a fleet of rust buckets and a couple washed-up Syrian assassins. And how much help did she give you since? None.*

I said, *Total screw-over. I mean, sure, she gets pissed off and blows up, but weeks later, not even an I'm-sorry call? And she's keeping secrets from me. Something about Alvaria.*

Mercury said, *Don't forget the CIA. What have they ever done for you? Remember that time in Kandahar when they said the chieftain was in with the Taliban but you found out later they'd been duped by the rival tribe into killing the only guy who wasn't selling opium poppies on the black market?*

I said, *Yeah, that was a pure CIA fail. The Rangers had to ship me to ISIS-held territory until the Afghans forgot about me.*

Mercury said, *And they want you doing them favors?*

I wiped my fingerprints off it and put the messenger bag back nice and neat where I'd found it.

"Yo, Fido!" I waved him into the office.

Megi gave me a look of appreciation when he trotted toward me.

The man stopped in my personal space as if his size would intimidate me.

I pointed to the bag on the floor. "Your boss left his briefcase behind. Be a good boy and take it to him."

Fido grinned at me, baring his incisors, which had been filed to sharpened points. Perhaps to give him the look of a real dog. Whatever the intention, it was creepy as hell.

"Did you touch it?" he asked.

I rolled my eyes. "He won't want it left lying around long. I've no idea what's in it, but no businessman wants his papers in plain view. Pick it up and take it to him at once."

Falconer stepped out from behind Fido with a suspicious glare. "Give me that."

CHAPTER 43

ONE SERIOUSLY PISSED-OFF FALCONER GRABBED Fido and the briefcase and left to chase down Bonham. Then the trouble started.

Yumi swirled in.

She wore yet another velvet cape over a dress with a floral print that brought it to life. How many velvet capes does a woman need? Her arrival spelled nothing but trouble for me, but I couldn't think up a reason to get rid of her before she ran into my office.

The staff craned over their shoulders with surprised, gossipy looks. I waved them off and they faced front in unison like a school of fish.

"You missed Falconer," I said. "He went to the ship."

"I can't do it." Yumi approached me with far more familiarity than I wanted.

Normally, I don't mind a woman's roving hands. But when my almost-marriage was in trouble it was an unwelcome problem. Then I remembered my almost-marriage was as real as Tinker Bell riding a unicorn down the streets of Durrës. Even so, I grabbed her hands and held her a respectable distance from me.

"Can't do what?" I asked.

"The password. I have the first four letters of Falconer's password, but I never get the middle. He does not use it as much as his phone and that works on facial recognition."

"The phone might work instead." My hacker friend, Bianca, told me several ways to get into someone's phone without facial recognition. The easiest involved dialing up Sabel Technologies' special phone number and letting them hack it directly. That wasn't going to happen. The next method involved an accomplice at a phone company. While that might work, it was highly illegal—and I didn't have an accomplice at a phone company. The least effective way was my only option.

"Turn his phone off when he's asleep. Do the complete shutdown. You know how to do that? Good. Then, next time he turns it on, he can't use facial recognition, he has to type in his passcode. Get that the same way we talked about getting the password. You might have to pull this trick two or three times to make—"

"I don't want to." Her gaze hit the floor. "He caught me looking into his business. After that he does not trust me. When he saw me look at you, he not trust me at all. He told me to find your comm device. He thinks you talk to authorities on some device."

"Here," I said. I handed her the three primitive bugs Bonham tried to hide in my office. "You found them."

She looked at the microphones, then at me.

I said, "They're his, but I have a jammer that prevents them from working in here. Take them and join him on the *Fatma*."

She nodded, reluctantly accepting them. "Also, I found out, he gets CIA reports on you. He says they consider him important part of off-book operations."

That was the worst news I'd heard yet. I said, "No big deal. I knew that."

She said, "The other night, I say nice things about you. He got very angry. He yelled at me."

"Did he hurt you?"

"Not physically." She wrapped her arms around me. "Georgie is not a nice man."

I pushed her back a step. "I know."

My employees were looking over their shoulders at me again. I waved them off again. "I think he's involved in the killing of my friends. I'm not leaving here until I find out. I can't help you until I'm ready to leave, so we're both stuck for now. I need you to get his password for the laptop or the passcode for the phone."

She started to whimper.

My anger rose. "You got into this deal two years ago. You can stick it out a few more days. I'm over you, so don't try pushing those buttons.

242

When I see you in a new thousand-dollar cape every day, I don't get the feels."

Her eyes flared wide and angry. "I hate them. He fills my closets. Throws away everything of mine, whatever he does not like."

"What a sad story." I took her elbow and led her out of the office. We made our way to Rafia's ship half a mile down the wharf. The long walk did her good. She calmed and puffed up her resolve.

Near the ship, she promised to try the phone.

We boarded.

We crossed the decks and were guided to the superstructure that housed the bridge and crew quarters. A crewman reported that Bonham, Rafia, and Jenny were inspecting some cranes elsewhere on the ship. I took Yumi to Falconer on the bridge.

The first officer was in the middle of reviewing the work in progress with Falconer when we stepped into the main room.

Falconer glared at me and crossed to us, leaving the first officer uncertain where to go.

"Where the hell have you two been?" Falconer barked.

Yumi stopped in her tracks. "You told me meet you at office. But you were not—"

"Don't give me that." He grabbed her forearm.

I grabbed his. "Think, Falconer. We haven't had time to do anything since you left my office. Don't act like an obsessed schoolboy."

He shoved Yumi aside and aimed his ire at me. "The biggest deal of my life is coming down the pike this week. Hundreds of thousands of downtrodden peoples will benefit. I need to keep focused on this project every step of the way. Nothing will distract me from what needs to be done. I will not have you making little unwanted passes at my woman. No one fucks her but me."

Yumi blushed and snuck away while we faced off.

"I'm the last guy you need to worry about, Falconer. Keep an eye on Bonham if you want to get jealous. He's handsome."

He pushed his nose up to me and jabbed a finger in my chest. "My success flows from eliminating people I need to worry about." His volume dropped. "Don't think I can't eliminate you at this point. One of

Bonham's dogs is a terrific sniper. We don't need you."

I used my height advantage, pushing my chest into his face as I barked down at him. "You don't know how perilously close I am to calling that bluff. One more threat and your whole crew of little wannabes gets tossed on the dock where you can watch me sail away."

He snarled. "Don't push me, Stearne."

Mercury stepped between us. *What in the name of Mars are you going to war about, homes?*

I said, *He's an asshole who thinks he owns Yumi.*

Mercury said, *There you go again, getting all hopped up about the little stuff. You said she made her bed and she can deal.*

I said, *I should grab Yumi and Jenny and get out of here. This isn't going to end well.*

Mercury said, *If you think this isn't going well, try sticking two jealous women in the same car. You won't get halfway to Tirana. C'mon, dude, let's get focused on the two things you need: the exact coordinates of the containers, and the bidder's list. Then you can toss him overboard. Right now, you need to back down.*

I said to Falconer, "I give you my word, I've no interest in Yumi. When a woman treats me the way she did, I never go back. She's all yours."

He backed off an inch with death still in his eyes.

I needed to get him back in my corner. Ms. Sabel told me billionaires like special treatment.

"Most people love hanging out with heroes." I smiled at him. "Have you told your friends and family you're besties with the 'Hero of Paris?' Probably not because they wouldn't believe you."

He cocked his head, curious for the first second, then amused after that.

When I saw him lighten up, I said, "You know, we inked a big deal back at your crib in Tuscany, but we never celebrated it. I'll give you something no one else has. Gimme your phone, step in here, we'll get a selfie together. You can post it on Instagram."

He frowned. "Do what?"

"Remember that party on the *Numina?* Everyone wanted a selfie with me—but I refused. I'll make an exception for you. You'll be the only guy to have a picture with me. Off the dance floor, that is. C'mon, step in here."

He squinted, eyeing me with suspicion. He needed an excuse to back down. He knew I was trying to bridge the gap between us. He warmed up to the idea and whipped out his phone and unlocked it. I grabbed it out of his hands, held it high, and snapped away. He grinned like a kid on Christmas.

CHAPTER 44

EVA GOMEZ SAT UPRIGHT AND attentive in Reggie Forrest's office, letting the sharp rebuke roll off her back. She'd been through worse. Like Walmart. As Forrest began repeating herself, Eva let the words stream past her ears. Her mind and her memories floated back to that sunny summer morning.

El Paso had been her family's home for a hundred and fifty years. The red brick of Sacred Heart Church in the Segundo Barrio, on the US side of the river, had been a second home. Her great-grandfather had been baptized there. Her grandparents and parents had been married there. It's where she was baptized. And where her sister and cousin's funerals were held.

Eva, her sister, and two cousins went shopping that day. They heard pops outside that sounded like firecrackers. They were near the door and curiosity drove them to look toward the sound. The shooter walked in, aimed his assault rifle at them and fired five shots. Eva's sister fell backward into her, knocking her to the floor. The shooter continued past them into the store, shooting at anyone whose skin was darker than his. Before going on his deadly rampage, the killer had posted a hate-filled screed decrying a perceived invasion of his country.

Ever since, the nightmare replayed in her head when someone overreacted or ranted without cause. There were events in the world worth getting upset about. Walmart was one. Reggie Forrest was not.

As Forrest continued berating her, she began to understand why the great and powerful Assistant Secretary Forrest had chosen new and inexperienced Eva Gomez to work with Pia Sabel. A mole had worked to steal Alvaria on Forrest's watch. While the Assistant Secretary made moves to recover the system, she needed a scapegoat in case everything blew up in her face. A new, inexperienced employee might inadvertently send messages about deliveries and cylinders and shipping dates and contractors. Could someone plant evidence on her? Make her look corrupt? It sounded like a bad spy movie, but was that kind of thing possible? Eva wanted to run to her desk and check her sent folder.

Finally, Forrest began running out of steam. Eva tuned back in as Forrest said, "That's why there is no reason for you to ask RSAT any questions. You are not to go back there. If there's any digging to be done in their records, I'll do it. And, as I've mentioned more than once this morning, I don't have time for it right now. So, unless you give me a good reason to ask these questions, you will stop pestering the RSAT people."

"Yes, ma'am."

Forrest tilted her head as if Eva's answer had been too easy. "Why were you asking these questions?"

Eva considered her reply carefully. One wrong word could tip Pia's hand and risk lives. "Their reluctance to help the people at Sabel struck me as odd and unprofessional. I didn't mean to step on any toes. I thought they would tell me and then I could relay the information."

"Are you spying for Pia Sabel now? Is that what you think is the right thing to do?"

"I just thought it would help find Alvaria. Isn't that what you hired them to do?"

"I didn't hire them to blame my division and I didn't hire you to spy for Sabel."

"Sorry, ma'am. I won't do it again."

Forrest dismissed her with a wave of her hand.

Eva walked the dull corridors of the State Department back to her gray cubicle. She'd been away from her desk many times to visit Sabel Industries headquarters. Someone could have hacked her computer. She thought through what someone trying to frame her might do. She recalled a high-ranking military officer who'd sent classified documents to a reporter using Gmail.

Eva opened her browser and checked the history for the most recent date when she'd gone to Sabel HQ. Sure enough, there was an entry for accessing Gmail. She didn't have a Gmail account. She was still on USC's email system. The access was date and time stamped minutes after she'd left the office two days ago. It usually took her most of an hour to reach Sabel on the Metro, which meant an investigator would conclude the entry could be her work. Holding her breath, she opened Gmail. In the sent folder were several emails with documents about Alvaria's shipping details. They were sent to an account name that was a jumble of letters and numbers.

She looked at the surveillance camera over her head. It sat on a bracket extending a foot from the wall, putting the lens forward of Eva. You didn't need to be an expert to know her desk was in a blind spot. Was her desk assignment intentional too?

With only a few months on the job, she hadn't developed a mentor other than Forrest. She fell into her chair, put her elbows on her desk, and ran her fingers through her hair.

That's when she saw it. That guy's business card tossed under the monitor. The CIA guy. She picked it up: Bradley Hopkins, Weapons and Counterproliferation Mission Analyst. Without thinking about what she would say, she called him. He answered. She reminded him they were in an odd meeting together with Pia Sabel. He said he recalled it.

"What can I do for you?" he asked.

"I need some advice about Alvaria and how bureaucracies work. Something strange is going on—"

"Can you come to Langley this afternoon?" He shuffled papers around in the background. "Say, two this afternoon?"

Though caught off guard by his abruptness, she detected anxiety in his voice. "I guess I could get there by then."

"See you," he said and clicked off.

She stared at her phone for a moment, digesting how quickly he'd changed a phone call to an in-person meeting. Should she worry about him? She didn't recall him being creepy at their previous meeting. And nothing bad could happen at CIA headquarters. Maybe he was just in a rush.

She called IT to report unauthorized use of her computer. They walked her through changing her password before referring her to the Inspector General. The lady at the OIG's office took her statement over the phone with little interest and told her someone would contact her in a week or so. As she hung up, Eva heard the woman say to a coworker, "James Bond's messing with another newbie."

Eva checked the files in the sent folder again. They weren't classified documents. She hadn't run afoul of the espionage act. But they were revealing of the shipment. Did Forrest have something to do with all this? She remembered Pia cautioning her about ruining careers on too little information. She took a deep breath and hoped Bradley Hopkins could help.

She figured out how to get to Langley using the Metro and a bus. On the long ride, she wondered how people afforded Lyft rides everywhere after they paid rent in DC. When she got off at the Visitor Center, she noted the return bus was two hours later. This was the part of public transportation she hated. Waiting for busses or walking the extra mile to a different bus stop. Maybe it was time to buy a car.

Bradley met her and walked her back through the cube farm of his mission—the term they used instead of team or group—to a meeting room. Few people looked up as they walked through. No one spoke to Bradley. No one asked who she was. She expected more from the CIA than a purse inspection and a phone locker at the front desk. She guessed that meant he was as far down the ladder as she was. They were equally unimportant.

They took seats on opposite sides of a laminate-topped table in a small, drab room.

Bradley said, "What troubles you about Alvaria?"

"That no one at RSAT will answer questions about how it was shipped."

"And how was it shipped?"

"I'm not sure how much I should tell you." She hesitated. "I'm new to security clearances, sorry. So, I won't answer that. I'm hoping you can tell me why the CIA has such a huge interest in Jacob Stearne."

"You're referring to the report on his drinking companions in Athens?"

She hesitated to tell him about the second report. If she expected to get something out of this meeting, she'd have to tell him something. He seemed like a nice guy. Something about him felt right to her. Someone she could trust. "There was another one about his insurance problems."

Bradley looked surprised. "From the CIA?"

"Right. I understand the first one. You guys like to keep track of people with security clearances. You're probably tracking me." She snickered at that thought. He didn't. Which sobered her. Of course someone was tracking her. That's why he wanted a meeting on his turf. He didn't know if he could trust her. "Uhm. So, why would they care about his insurance?"

"What kind of insurance?" he asked.

"Something to do with a salvage operation. He couldn't get any in Albania, but got insured by Lloyds of London."

Bradley leaned back, a concerned look clouding his face. "I don't know what that's about. Are you sure it was a CIA report?"

She nodded. His concern deepened.

"I don't know how the government works." She felt a floodgate open and her questions pour out. "Why would Reggie Forrest stop me from asking RSAT about shipping containers? Why would someone use my computer and a false Gmail account to send unclassified documents? Why won't people be honest with each other about what's going on? Why not just tell the world we have Alvaria and then destroy it? I know, I know, someone will build it. But why all the secrecy?"

She stared at the wall behind Bradley, unable to meet his cold stare. She felt he was measuring her or looking into her soul for something.

He leaned forward, his forearms on the table. "Did you bring gingersnaps?"

"Gingersnaps? No." She thought it an odd question.

"Did Pia Sabel send you? She was supposed to send someone to a meeting with a plate of gingersnaps."

"No, Pia doesn't know I'm here. Look, I'm new. I don't know anyone around here, and I have a lot of questions about a system I can't talk to my friends about. I found your card from that meeting a couple weeks ago. I thought I could talk to you."

"You can," he said. "I'm just ... never mind."

"Why did you ask about Pia Sabel? You don't like her, do you?"

"I liked her once," he said. "That was a long time ago. It doesn't matter. I have even more questions about Alvaria. I'm honored you thought you could talk to me. But I don't know any more than you. Here's something to ponder. I'm the least senior guy in this office. You're fresh out of college. We've been handed responsibility for the most dangerous weapon in the American arsenal—and someone stole it. Why did they pick us?"

"Exactly what I was thinking." Eva sat up straight and met his gaze. "Someone wants to blame us."

"Nothing pisses me off more than being underestimated."

"Yeah." She started to like this guy. "Me too."

"Let's drop this conversation for now." He shot a suspicious glance at the cube farm outside the room, then he stood. "Let's have lunch tomorrow. There's a food truck called *Carolina Wings* that parks outside Air and Space on 7th Street."

She rose, still a little uncertain about the confusing swirl of events. "I've seen that one. Always parks next to the Jamaicans."

He held the meeting room door for her.

As she stepped out, a young man almost ran her over.

"Sorry," he said. "Ryan Wheeling. Are you all right?"

Another man approached from the other direction. "Who's this, Bradley?"

Bradley said, "This is Eva Gomez, a liaison from State on a project. Eva, this is my boss, Collin West, and my co-worker, Ryan Wheeling."

"Nice to meet you, Ryan. Mr. West, we met in a meeting with Reggie Forrest." She shook hands while noticing strange glances bouncing between the men.

"Right," West said as he squinted at her. "You're Forrest's liaison to Sabel. What brings you to Langley?"

"Sorry, gotta run," she said. "If I miss the bus at the Visitor Center, is there another bus stop near here?"

Ryan backed up and waved a hand as if she could see where he indicated. He said, "Dolly Madison stop on Dolly Madison and Potomac

School Road."

She glanced at the other two men and realized they were older and drove cars. She and Ryan were younger and walked a lot. Cars were far down the priority list for young people. She smiled her thanks at him and walked down the hall.

Bradley hung back with his boss and Ryan huddling in a hushed discussion. Then Bradley trotted to catch up and escorted her to the exit where they shook hands and said goodbye.

She picked up her phone and checked Google Maps for the bus stop Ryan mentioned. It showed her the quick way out on a perimeter road that skirted the CIA parking lots. The stop was a quarter mile down Colonial Farm Road, a lane nestled in the trees between the CIA maintenance yard and Langley Park. She set out hoping the gray skies would hold off the rain for another hour. It was a pleasant walk despite the late November cold.

Halfway down the tree-lined lane, the first vehicle to take the obscure road barreled toward her from behind. The noise of the engine indicated acceleration beyond what the sleepy lane could safely manage. She stepped off the pavement into the grass.

The vehicle slammed to a diagonal stop inches in front of her. Two men in balaclavas jumped out. They raised bats and rained blows on her head.

CHAPTER 45

CAPTAIN RAFIA DECLARED THE REFITTING of his ship almost done on the evening of day four. We'd sail in the morning. He took Jenny and his sailors out to dinner to celebrate. I thought that was generous of him until he gave me a wink that told me he planned to expense it. Being a business owner had a lot of unexpected decisions. I waved him on. They had worked hard and deserved appreciation.

Since Jenny was going with him, and she wasn't speaking to me, I took my Syrians to a different restaurant. A nicer place on the beach. Ansi, my favorite helicopter pilot, joined us. We ordered what looked like lobster. Only the lobsters weren't red and pretty like Maine lobsters. They were brown and had white spots. But Mardik and Firas's eyes and grins were big. To them, they were the finest lobsters on the planet. I could picture Geldona shaking her head like Mercury and tsking her way through my spending. But I could also see the pleasure rich people get out of giving people things. The smiles of others make you feel good. Even if it's temporary. Even if the reason you feel good is because, as a provider, giving things to people grants you a certain amount of power over them.

When my men began devouring the dish, I started in on some long-ignored questions. "You worked for Syrian Intelligence. Why did you leave?"

They stopped eating instantly. Their eyes swung to mine quickly. Butter dripped from Mardik's fork. Ansi froze, the question catching him by surprise.

"Why accuse us of working for Assad?" Firas, the angry one, asked.

"Because you're too smart for foot soldiers."

Mardik finished chewing. "Firas is my cousin. His father and my father, brothers like that." He held up two fingers close together. "Firas had two sisters, I had a brother and sister. Our families grow up on the same block in Homs. Have you been to Homs?"

I had visited under the cloak of night, but that was a secret the army made me promise to keep until 2059. "No. Is it nice?"

"Was nice. When we grew up, our street had trees. Now, rubble."

Firas leaned forward and stabbed his knife into the table. "Our families are buried in that rubble."

"Our mothers, our fathers, our sisters, my brother—all dead." Mardik leaned in quieter than his cousin. "We left the country in uniform. We were captains, so no one stopped us. We gave every penny we had to Rafia. He took us to Greece but the borders beyond were closed. He came back to our refugee camp two weeks later and brought us here. Now, we have nowhere else to go. And no one else to go with."

Firas said, "We are with you. You are a good leader. You trust us. You are good to us. But we don't like these dogs, Fido, Spot, and Rover. We don't like Bonham. He is just like Assad. He demands your loyalty, then kills everyone you love. If you want us to stay, we stay. But we don't like it."

"I don't like it either. But hang in there another week. I have an endgame planned."

"These are very dangerous people." Mardik let me know with his dark glance they were entrusting their lives to my endgame. "The kind who kill in the night."

Because they had been Assad's intelligence officers, they knew why I didn't elaborate my endgame. If Bonham tortured them, they would have nothing to say. As long as I didn't tell my Syrians anything, they could pass polygraphs and resist truth serums. They nodded and went back to enjoying their dinners.

I didn't tell them Fido had followed us to dinner and Spot had taken over surveillance halfway through. We were being watched, just as Bonham promised. When we finished eating, I told them I was going to my hotel. They returned to the ship to double-check the work. We parted ways in front of the restaurant.

I caught Ansi's elbow. I said, "After I leave, there may be a young black man who walks with a limp near the office. Tell him I sent you and ask where his car is parked. He will tell you. Go there, it'll be unlocked. There will be a duffel bag in the trunk. Keep it with you. I may have another operation like the ships and we'll need that duffel."

Ansi grinned. "Working with you is like being in a spy movie. I will do as you say."

Miguel had promised to send Cody, the new kid on Ms. Sabel's personal security team, with more cast-off weaponry. I'd been watching for him every day. He hadn't shown. I trusted Miguel to send him when the time was right, when they wouldn't get in trouble with Ms. Sabel. I didn't know when that was, but I was praying it would be soon. Some things you have to leave to the gods. As dangerous as that may be.

I started walking. After two blocks in my hotel's direction, I made a hard left into a narrow alley. Spot followed about a hundred feet back. I looked over my shoulder without turning all the way to face Spot. It gave him the impression I hadn't seen him. I made my way deeper into the heart of Durrës, giving him a little room and confidence as I turned left and right at every street and alley. In the spy trade it's a process called *getting clean* and is used to shake surveillance. My suspicious moves made Spot think I was making a clandestine rendezvous.

He picked up his pace, closed the gap.

People on their game will walk wide around a corner. Not up close to the edge. It allows you to see someone hiding behind a building or wall. Spot had done it well for the first seven corners. Then he began to feel confident. I quickened my speed. After turning two corners in rapid succession, I trotted loudly around a third corner, then waited for him close behind the fourth.

He came around it tight. As he trotted around the edge, I slipped my knife under his chin and hugged him from behind. I said, "What's your real name, Spot?"

"Does it matter?" He squirmed and wriggled.

"I guess not." I pressed the blade harder and pulled a 9mm SIG Sauer P226 Legion with an Army star on the grip out from under his jacket. I held that to the base of his skull, stashed my knife, then searched him.

"Friends or enemies?"

"What?"

He had a Velcro ankle holster with a Beretta Nano. I shoved the holster and weapon into my jacket pocket. He had a knife in his pants pocket. That went into a trash can nearby.

"Friends or enemies?" I asked impatiently.

"What do you mean?"

"Choose one. Here's a hint: my friends are alive."

"Friend?"

I turned him around and gave him a big hug, never taking the barrel of his pistol from his skull. "Aw, dude, I knew we were going to get along."

I pushed him back. "We're going for a walk. You're going to stay an arm's length to my left. That way, I can shoot you if you change your mind about friends or enemies."

We started back toward the row of hotels on the beach.

"In case you're wondering, I'm not meeting anyone. There's no one to meet. I know Bonham doesn't believe that, but you've been watching me for days. What have you found?"

"Nothing. I get it. But, I'm just doing my job, man."

"Where're you from?" I asked.

"Ithaca."

"Greece or New York?"

Spot gave me a curious glance. I grinned. He hadn't expected a touch of humor in the tense situation. He shook his head to hide his grin. I asked him about his favorite subject: him. We chatted about his childhood for several blocks. The events that shaped his life, the people he blamed for his failures, the successes he believed he achieved. Psychopaths love it. And this guy charted high on the psychopath scale. By the time we strolled onto the beach, he was waxing poetic about his youth. He led a daring escape from juvenile detention and killed a man in Juarez when he was eighteen. I killed a lot more than that in Iraq when I was eighteen, but I didn't brag.

After catching up on his failed marriage (who could've seen that coming?), we moved on to current events.

I asked, "If I go back to Bonham and hand him your pistols, what's he going to do?"

"Nothing. He'll go ask Falconer."

"Bonham isn't calling the shots?"

Spot laughed. "Hell no. He likes to pretend, but he's just Falconer's fall guy. Something catches up from one of my hits, Bonham gave the orders."

"Clever. OK, so I give your gear to Falconer. What happens?"

Spot turned a shade of green. "I get dumped in a shallow grave. Probably with my throat slit, maybe buried alive."

I clapped him on the back. "Well, buddy, I don't do that to my friends."

We sat in the dark on the pilings of the old wharf. Behind us, giant dunes of coal waited to be shoveled onto trains and taken to market. A quarter-mile through the coal mounds was the new wharf and Rafia's ship, the *Detit Fatma*.

"So," I asked, "when Bonham bragged to me about killing a Greek lawman, he didn't really do it?"

"Ah hell no. That guy couldn't stab a drunk whore. I'm the sniper in this outfit."

That was all I needed. Nate Hale and Dimitris Bakakis would be one step closer to resting in peace when this dog was gone. Although finding out Bonham wasn't involved was a terrible disappointment. Killing him would've made my whole week.

Mercury popped out of the water. *Hold on, homie. Don't be killing this guy yet.*

I said, *Why not? He told me the orders come from Falconer. I don't need him anymore. It's time for Spot to atone for his sins. And don't tell me he was just following orders. We put that excuse to rest in Nuremburg.*

Mercury said, *You'll never make Caesar if you kill everyone but don't bring home the spoils of war. Who are the bidders? Where is the auction? How do you get paid?*

As the heat of anger rose from my chest to my head, I realized my derelict deity had a point. I needed Falconer for another week. But Spot wouldn't know any of those things. Spot had killed my friends. He was proud of himself and his marksmanship. He did what others told him without discerning if it were right or wrong. Leaving him alive would endanger countless others.

I considered several ways to dispatch him. Paying him back with a sniper hit sounded appropriate, but I had neither the time nor the resources. What seemed most poetic was to follow the rituals of his tribe: going for the throat.

I pulled the knife from my belt buckle and turned to Spot. "Wow, were you the guy who made that incredible shot in the prosecutor's office on Corfu? I mean, that was a spectacular feat of marksmanship. I thought there had to be two snipers involved."

He laughed. "Piece of cake that one. All by my lonesome. Two shots fired, two targets down."

I held up a hand for a high five. He turned to slap it.

I slit his throat on the far side from me so the arterial spray wouldn't splatter my nice clean clothes. I wiped the knife on his shirt before putting it away.

Spot sat on the piling, one hand to his throat, blood flowing between his fingers in a stream. He knew he couldn't stop the bleeding. He knew he was dying. He spluttered and said, "Why?"

"Because you killed good guys, Spot. That's bad. The world will be a better place without you in it. Now that you're gone, I'm moving on to Falconer. He'll be more of a challenge."

He slumped as the blood loss weakened his muscles. I pushed his body into the sea.

Mercury watched the man's wool coat become waterlogged, dragging him down as the tide pulled him out to sea. He said, *Seneca wrote, 'All cruelty springs from weakness.'*

CHAPTER 46

WAS SHE RELIVING WALMART? EVA'S brain felt scrambled with fear and pain. Doctors fussed and nurses bandaged and people spoke and nothing made sense. Beaten with bats. Why? Was it another racist attack? Was there no end to those people? Or was it related to Alvaria? They wheeled her to a dark room. She fell asleep.

A nurse woke her while checking on her. "Are you ready for visitors?"

Through her swollen eye, Eva could see her two saviors standing in the hall outside her hospital room. They were uncertain about knocking. Her gratitude overwhelmed her; she wanted to cry. She started to speak but her voice wasn't ready. She nodded at the nurse. The nurse waved them in as she left.

Eva took a breath and swallowed and tried again. "Come in. Please. Oh. Do I look that scary? Thank you for saving me. Sorry, I can only see you if you both stand on my left."

Bradley Hopkins came to her side with Ryan Wheeling right beside him. Bradley asked, "Are you OK?"

"No. Everything hurts, one eye is swollen shut, and the other is almost. Concussion but no broken skull, they told me."

"Thank god," Ryan said.

Bradley said, "Did you know those guys?"

"They wore masks. How did you happen to come down that lane?"

"After we talked about bus stops," Ryan said, "I overheard something out-of-place about you. I told Bradley and we decided it would only take a minute to check it out. We scared them off. But, damn, that was off the charts."

Bradley said, "Have they called your family?"

Ryan backed up toward the door and canted his head as if listening for a faint sound outside.

She nodded her head yes, but that hurt worse than talking. "My family lives in El Paso. I couldn't hear them on the phone because of my ears."

"Friends?" Bradley asked.

"My roommate's on vacation in Chicago. Back on Tuesday. Forrest keeps me working all day and night. I don't have a social life."

Ryan came back close to them and pointed his thumb over his shoulder. "Then you're not expecting visitors? Cause I just heard the nurse give out your room number."

They exchanged worried glances.

Bradley said, "We've got to get her out of here."

Eva's adrenaline began to flow. The guys were thinking the same thing she was: The hit men were on their way to finish the job. That scared her more than the surprise attack. She pressed the nurse button.

"We can scare them off," Ryan said. "We did it once before."

"If they're willing to come back, they'll be more determined." Bradley and Ryan checked each other out, sizing up the argument. Bradley cut off the younger, clean-cut kid. "This ain't the movies. The bad guys don't fall down when you blow on them."

A nurse came in and checked the monitors as she spoke. "What's the matter, dear?"

"Could I get a different room—quickly?" Eva asked.

"Oh, no. This one's fine for you. Everyone's really busy right now." The nurse swept out of the room a second later.

Bradley shook his head and checked the closets for something he could use as a weapon.

"Ever heard of white privilege?" Ryan looked at the two them. "It ain't fair, but I'm willing to try it."

He stepped out into the hall. Eva couldn't see him, but she heard him. "Ma'am, Ryan Wheeling, CIA. Could you do your country a small favor? Could you move the young lady into a different room for about two hours? Please?"

Eva didn't hear the answer, but Ryan came back in with the nurse and an orderly. The nurse tapped the brakes for the bed casters with her toe and together they grabbed the machine cart and bed and wheeled her out the door.

Ryan shrugged as she passed by him.

They took her to a room diagonally across the hallway from the old one. When she sat up, she could see inside the old room. Bradley and Ryan followed.

When the nurse finished setting up Eva's monitors, Bradley stopped her and held out his CIA ID. "Do you have a mop handle or anything I could use defensively?"

The nurse looked him over suspiciously. Then she turned to Ryan. The young man nodded solemnly.

The nurse said, "I'll find something."

After she left, Bradley tossed his hands in the air and shook his head in exasperation. "I'm thirty years older than you but she needs your approval."

"I don't make the rules," Ryan said. "I just abuse them."

The orderly returned a minute later with a length of white PVC pipe and an aluminum broom handle. He gave them to Bradley. "Sorry, brother, all I got. This isn't the armory."

"Thanks," Bradley said. "Could you do me a favor and keep your ears open? You hear anything violent, call the cops immediately. We could be worried about nothing, but just in case."

"You got it." The orderly pulled out his phone and punched in 911 without pressing dial.

Bradley passed the broom handle to Ryan. They closed the door to a crack and kept watch.

Long minutes ticked by. Eva noticed the dark outside the window. The doctor had told her she'd been unconscious for a while. It must've been longer than she thought.

Her new heroes took turns at the door to keep alert. She chatted with them about movies and music, nothing that took their attention off the coming battle they considered to be a certainty.

Just as she lost interest and felt sleepy, Bradley stiffened. He snapped his fingers at Ryan.

Both men looked nervous. They weren't soldiers or fighters, but they were willing to risk their lives defending her. She felt deep gratitude.

The men took a couple breaths and bolted across the diagonal space. They raised their weapons and brought them down hard as they burst into her old room. Eva sat up on her elbow, despite the pain that shot through her shoulder.

The first thing she saw was the plastic pipe, shattered and splintered come rolling out of the room. She heard grunts and groans and smacks. The aluminum mop handle flew out of the room bent like a paperclip.

Hospital staff came to the hallway. Some looked into the room but must have decided the fight was too violent. Eva saw the orderly with a phone to his ear. He glanced her way, saw her looking at him, gave her a thumbs-up.

The staff parted for the tiger-like figure of Pia Sabel striding down the hall. She carried a vase of flowers in one hand and gave a curious glance at the staff. When she came level with the doorway and looked inside, she handed her vase to a bystander, shrugged off her winter coat, and stormed in.

She backed out almost as quickly, followed by a large, rough man swinging a black baton. Eva marveled at the woman's height advantage. She ducked under his first swing and rose back up with lightning speed, delivering a powerful blow with the heel of her right hand to the underside of his jaw. As he reeled backward, he swung again and hit her in the ribs. By then she'd twisted far to her left, coiling the muscles in her legs and core, then unwound in a blur that landed her left elbow on her assailant's temple. He banged into the metal door jamb, his head bouncing like a tennis ball, and collapsed on the floor.

The staff pounced on the man, landing four pairs of knees on his back.

Pia picked up the baton and disappeared inside the room. Eva heard the baton crack from where she lay. A second later, Bradley and Ryan staggered out. Blood dripped from their faces. Bradley held his arm in pain. Ryan limped. Pia came out holding the wilted form of a man by the collar as if he were a rag doll.

Suddenly, police filled the hall, guns drawn. There was a lot of shouting. Eva lay back down and rubbed her shoulder.

Half an hour later, after the police questions were answered, Eva's new heroes came in.

Bradley said to Pia, "What happened to the low-key thing, sending a guy with gingersnaps to my meeting?"

Eva jumped in. "I told you, she didn't send me. I'm working on something of my own. But I need help."

Ryan looked at Bradley with a glance at Pia, as if asking the older man if she should be included.

"We're all on the same team here," Bradley said. "We're all read in on Alvaria. But it appears the four of us are the only ones who want to retrieve it. And someone—" he tossed his nose toward the fight scene "—wants to keep it lost. We should compare notes."

They discussed the nagging questions that puzzled each of them. Including questionable activities such as the CIA's exaggerated interest in Jacob Stearne, the RSAT's reluctance to help Sabel Security, Forrest's combative defense of her department, and the original sin: who came up with the crazy idea to ship Alvaria to Albania?

Pia said, "Given the events of this afternoon, let's move Eva and the conversation to Sabel Gardens where I have a doctor on staff and plenty of trained guards."

No one argued with that. Invitations to the legendary mansion were the hottest ticket in DC. Eva couldn't believe she would be a guest at the home of the greatest player in women's soccer. The pain of her injuries almost melted away. Only Bradley appeared less than enthusiastic about it.

While the orderlies packed up Eva for transport, Bradley took Pia aside where he probably thought Eva couldn't hear. He asked her, "What have your people found?"

"I had a plan," she said sheepishly. "I set things in motion. It all went haywire. At the moment, I have no idea what's going on."

"You may not want to admit it," Bradley said, "but your man Stearne has joined forces with Ra. That's for damn sure."

CHAPTER 47

THE SAILOR ON WATCH WORKED for me, so he didn't say a word when I told him not to log that I was coming aboard the *Detit Fatma*.

Having seen me from the bridge, the first mate ran down the steps to greet me. He intended to ingratiate himself to me. Which was not what I wanted. But, being the owner, I had to let him give me a tour and tell me what a great job he was doing. Finally, he led me to what would be my accommodations for the voyage.

It wasn't a cruise ship, nor was it a yacht. The cabin was spartan but spacious. Square, curtained windows lined two sides, a flat screen hung on a wall, and it had a cramped but fully functional bathroom. Since I was on a ship, I should call it a head. The bed was made, a vase of flowers stood on the coffee table before a nice sofa, the desk was clean. I turned to the first mate and said, "Is this the master suite?"

He hesitated long enough for me to understand.

"Captain Rafia has the nicest suite," I guessed, "which means this is yours when I'm not here?"

Again he hesitated, which answered the question.

I said, "Where is Jenny staying?"

He led me to a room down the hall. It was identical to mine but noticeably smaller and more cramped. Her suitcase was shoved into a corner.

"The room doesn't look lived in," I said. "Hasn't she been staying aboard the last two nights?"

"Yes, but Mister Bonham requested her room a couple hours ago. He didn't want this one." He noticed my displeased look. "His dogs made it sound like the orders came from you, sir."

"Does Jenny know this happened?"

"She found out an hour ago."

"Was she pleased?"

"No, sir. Quite angry."

"Have their rooms swapped back immediately. Where are his dogs staying?"

"With the crew, sir. Several decks below us." He pulled a radio and ordered people to the guest deck.

The workers came in numbers. Everyone wanted the owner to see them hard at work. I didn't mind the attention. In fact, it's good to be the king. If I pull this deal off, I'm getting a yacht and following my fleet around the Adriatic. Maybe we could start hauling arms to places like Venice and Florence. Does Florence have a port?

Mercury appeared between the mates, making a big show of carrying an imaginary vase. *Holy Bellona, does Florence have a port? Save me, Juno, save me. Can I get a mortal with a brain? Can I get the Scarecrow from The Wizard of Oz?*

I said, *How am I supposed to keep track of every town in Italy?*

Mercury said, *Not just a town, homie. A city built by Julius himself. He called it Fluentia, because it was at the confluence of two rivers. It was on the Via Cassia halfway between Rome and Genoa. And—until the Christians showed up—they had a nice temple dedicated to yours truly.*

Since the whole crew had shown up, they carried one item each. It took all of twenty seconds. I gathered them and swore them to secrecy. No one was to know I was there. They agreed. I think. Most were Singaporean with limited English. The first mate promised my secret was safe with them.

When they left, I slipped into Bonham's room and looked for a good place to stash Spot's pistols. His closet held a suit and a few shirts, none of which fit a working ship. In the corner were two medical oxygen canisters connected to some kind of regulator. I guessed they were left there by the previous tenant, since Bonham didn't appear to have emphysema. His top drawer held a few designer t-shirts and a workout set. His underwear drawer seemed like a good option in an oddly fun kind of way. I buried the weaponry at the back and closed the drawer.

DEATH AND BETRAYAL

I went back to my hotel and strolled in without thinking. Before he saw me, I spotted Rover watching TV in the lobby, Barcelona versus Dortmund in the Champions League. I backed out and jogged to the corner of the building where Miguel had climbed the outside. What he'd made look easy gave me vertigo just looking up.

It wasn't going to climb itself. I grabbed a piece of trellis and started up.

The first two floors had vines and lattice work. The next three offered only quarter inch fingerholds spaced far enough apart to make climbing them the scariest thing I'd done since I got tangled up in that Monkey Island at sea. As I rose above the third floor, I realized I was passing Bonham's room. His lights were on. I scrambled higher and faster when I heard the sliding glass door open. I froze and looked down.

Two feet below my right foot stood Bonham. He sipped an aperitif of dark liquid and gazed out to sea. I felt the sweat on my fingers building up, loosening my grip. One tiny move could send some of the hotel's cheap cement down on Bonham's head. If he saw me, I'd have to kill him. As satisfying as that idea would be, it would jeopardize my grand plan. I took a deep, silent breath and slowly tried to reposition my fingers. It wasn't working. I needed all four fingers on both hands to hold my weight.

I felt myself falling and tried to will myself to stick to the wall like Spider-Man. That wasn't working either. My fingers burned with the agony of spent muscles.

Then I felt a pair of hands push my butt, helping my weight hold. I didn't need to look down. It could be the hand of god helping me. It could be the power of positive thinking. If I looked down and saw him, Mercury would make me sing songs of praise and thanksgiving. Which would give me away. So, I thought nice thoughts about him. Just in case this god thing is real.

Finally, Bonham went inside. I resumed my climb.

Just as I climbed over the railing to my balcony, I spotted Yumi sitting on the balcony next door, her chair turned to face me, sipping tea with her eyes glued to mine. A pair of binoculars sat on the side table next to her. I glanced over my shoulder. Our respective balconies had the only view of the wharf where Spot's karma caught up with him.

I said nothing. I tipped a salute her way. She sipped her tea without any expression.

The only reason Falconer didn't stay on his yacht in the harbor was to keep an eye on me. That he left it to Yumi was an indication that I'd passed his suspicious test. Thank Mercury, I hadn't opened the briefcase Bonham left as part of that test. Still, it gave her the power to report Spot's killer. If she told Falconer, I was cooked. My Syrians were brave, but Bonham's dogs were savages.

I went in and went to bed and hoped to hell Yumi was still on my side.

As my head hit the pillow, I thought about the questions still rattling around in my head. What happened to Konrad? If he was dead, why hadn't his body washed up in Monaco's heavily traveled harbor? How did Falconer get CIA briefings? Was that just a brag to Yumi? Did I owe the CIA a report on the man they call Ra? Hardly. I was no longer an employee on a contract to find the auctioneer and his bidders.

I turned off the light.

I slept well. Killing a bad man has a soothing effect on me.

Except when Mercury quotes Seneca.

CHAPTER 48

THE NEXT MORNING, I BOARDED the *Detit Fatma* to do what owners do, supervise. Jenny had thought of everything, calculating the weight and balance of each container. There were backup systems for the critical equipment. She'd outfitted the ship with separate winches for the rovers so we could recover them while the last container was still being raised. That would speed up the process.

The operations center, occupying half the mess, hummed with people testing equipment. Jenny supervised the tests.

Captain Rafia and I walked in. Jenny gave orders and crewmen plugged things in. My mouth ran dry at the sight of her. She went out of her way not to look at me. I guess absence had not made her heart grow fonder.

Falconer, Bonham, and the dogs followed along behind us. We went to the bridge in a group, climbing the stairs up seven levels. Rafia proved more agile than expected. Once we arrived, Rafia went into full captain mode. His casual, friendly, humble persona disappeared. The master and commander came out. He barked orders. He dished out compliments and rebukes in a quick, businesslike voice. As he ran through the checklists for departure from port, his crew jumped to their assigned duties.

Off to one side, Fido and Rover would whisper to Bonham, then trot off to different parts of the ship. After the fourth such subterfuge, Bonham approached me.

"Say, Stearne." He poked me. "Have you seen Spot this morning?"

I shrugged and went back to watching Rafia with avid interest. Durrës doesn't need harbor pilots and Rafia had left the driving to his navigation officer. They worked like father and son.

"He was following you last night." Bonham stepped close to my side.

"Until I went to my room," I said. "I didn't invite him in."

Falconer watched us with concern.

"Captain," Bonham called over my shoulder, "we cannot leave port until my man is aboard."

"Proceed at your leisure, Captain." I faced Bonham and crossed my arms. "This man has no standing here. If he's lost one of his sheep, he can fly the guy out to meet us later."

"Why not wait?" Bonham asked. "He should be along in a few minutes. Unless you know something different."

"I know my crew is here on time. If you can't maintain a basic level of discipline in your people, that's not my problem."

"Don't get cute with me." Bonham fumed. "The three of them are inseparable. He never turned in last night. They searched the city for him. He's not late. He's missing."

I lost my patience. "Are you suggesting we hold up the entire expedition and lose the tide so we can look for your employee?"

I had no idea if modern ships could lose the tide, but Rafia backed me up with a scowl. I was beginning to understand why Mercury had lobbied against killing Spot. His death was becoming a problem.

"I agree with Stearne." Falconer formed a triangle with Bonham and me. "Let's not hold up the expedition."

Captain Rafia had the lines cast off, the last step before getting underway.

Jenny stepped onto the bridge, saw me, and found her way to the opposite corner. My heart pounded loud and hard. I could only hope Bonham couldn't tell because he'd mistake my reaction for regret at killing Spot.

"I'm telling you," Bonham said, "Stearne killed him."

Jenny's eyes went wide and swung to Bonham and me.

"This isn't the first employee you've had run off," I barked at Bonham. "I recall one of your men escaped back in Italy."

"Yeller was different. He was a binge drinker. Spot never went missing. This was his life."

"Enough of your bullshit, Bonham," I said. "Search the ship, bring me a shred of evidence I'm remotely connected to your man's tardiness."

The ship began pulling away from the dock. Despite the ship moving carefully and slowly away from the dock, the sheer size of the thing was impressive. From our vantage point, and realizing the weight and momentum involved, it felt frighteningly quick. A small boat in the wrong place at the wrong time could go under the bow and never be seen again before you could reach for the brake pedal. Or whatever you do to stop a big ship.

"I saw him with you." Fido decided to speak up. "You were talking."

"When it comes to following me, he was almost as bad as you." I rolled my eyes as dramatically as possible. "I talked to him until I was bored. So, a minute or two. Then I went to my hotel."

"You never came in," Rover said.

I began to feel a bit hemmed in. Had they followed us to the wharf? No. If they had, they would've jumped me when I tossed him in the drink. They didn't have a body, but they knew.

"Just because you didn't see me doesn't mean I didn't come in," I replied to Rover. "I saw you watching Champions League on TV. I watched Barcelona score from a foot behind you, not that you noticed."

Bonham ground his teeth. Rover was ready to beat me up for outing his terrible surveillance skills.

"You killed him, I know it." Bonham yelled. "I can prove—"

Falconer raised his hand and lowered it. Everyone fell silent and turned to him. He said, "Darling saw him on his balcony last night. That gives some credence to his claim." He looked at me with an undetermined amount of menace. "What time was that, sport? Never mind, it doesn't matter. We will do as Mr. Stearne recommended. Bonham, search the ship."

He turned to leave. Then he stopped and turned around. "Say, Captain Rafia, lock Mr. Stearne in your brig and make sure he doesn't interfere with the search or plant evidence. I'll be returning to the *Savannah* now. Send me updates."

Captain Rafia turned red and inhaled, ready to unleash his wrath on the landlubber who didn't know the captain represented all three branches of government once they'd left the dock. Anyone confined to quarters would be at his command and not the suggestion of an interloper.

I held up my hand to cut him off.

I said, "Falconer isn't aware that you give the orders here. Forgive him for his demand. And forgive him the ignorance of thinking a container ship would have a jail cell. However, I understand his concern. If you can spare them, please have two crew members accompany Bonham and his boys as they scour the ship. Open every hatch for them. Make sure they're satisfied. One of his people can stand at my door to make sure I don't leave or plant evidence."

Falconer turned to Bonham. "Search Stearne's room first."

CHAPTER 49

TWENTY-FOUR HOURS CONFINED TO QUARTERS would've been unbearable had it not been for the fact that I always travel with books. Captain Rafia and the first mate stayed busy running the ship. My Syrians brought meals to my suite. Bonham's dogs took turns standing watch outside my door. They managed to rig a mechanism that kept me from opening my door from the inside.

The search turned up nothing and they eventually tired of it. Naturally, they never searched Bonham's room. Just my luck. I spent the time slogging my way through *The Twelve Caesars* by Suetonius, because you-know-who keeps pestering me about Roman history.

Jenny never dropped by even though her suite was across the hall.

My discarded deity lounged on the sofa. *Like I was saying, home boy. You got yourself locked up and that's not helpful for the endgame. Seneca teaches you gotta balance life in theory with life in practice. This is a time when you should reflect on the murder of an innocent foot soldier—*

I said, *Spot was not innocent.*

Mercury shrugged and ate cheese from a plate that hovered mid-air in front of him. *So he murdered a few people. He was just living in the moment. I mean, c'mon, homie, who hasn't done that? The point is, you can't go around killing these guys until you have what we came for: Alvaria. Dang, dude. If we had them things back in the day, the Christians woulda never taken over. Anyway, we needs these dogs alive and kicking, because when someone kills them, someone gets locked up and taken out of the action, ya feel me? So don't go all superhero-mode, tossing everybody overboard. Falconer's gonna get suspicious.*

I said, *I'm not worried about Falconer.*

Mercury said, *You should be. Out of Seneca's fifteen virtues, you blew through severitas and veritas like they didn't even matter. You're on the road to Acheron. That's a river in Hades.*

I said, *I know what Acheron is. What're the other two things?*

Mercury rolled his eyes and his little wings flapped in frustration. *Severitas, severity, or how well you keep yourself under control. Slicing a hole in that guy's jugular wasn't whatcha call self-control. You coulda done that later. And veritas is truth, as in you should always tell it.*

Before he could wax poetic on truth, I heard voices in the hallway outside. I'd been barefoot all morning, so I tiptoed to the door. The walls were thick, but the doors were hollow. I heard Jenny and Bonham.

Jenny sounded angry and suspicious. She was in the middle of saying, "He's different, that's all. What did you guys do to him?"

"Your boyfriend came to us. He wanted in. Why, is that so bad?"

"You guys discuss a man missing, you accuse Jacob of killing him, but no one says a word about going to the police. Why is that, Bonham?"

"What's different about Jacob since you broke up?" Bonham asked.

When he said that, my heart stopped. She was mad. Mad about Ms. Sabel. I was mad at Ms. Sabel too. Then Jenny had Stefan over for some unexplained reason. But—when did we break up? Was it over? Somehow, I'd clung to the hope there was a chance, as distant as it might be. Hearing the words cut like a Ka-Bar slashing through my ribs. The ring was still in my jacket pocket, hanging in the closet. Her answer could gut my will to live.

"I didn't say we broke up." Her answer was defiant, but her follow-up question was anxious. "Did he say we broke up?"

That little bit of uncertainty in her voice filled me with hope again.

"Why did you say he's different?" Bonham became more insistent, angry. "What's changed?"

"He was a hero. Now, I don't know, it's like … I feel like he's gone off the deep end. He doesn't care about anyone else anymore. He only cares about himself. Maybe it's the war. They say PTSD catches up with you."

"You think he killed my man?" Bonham's voice dropped to barely audible through the door.

"I never said anything like that." Jenny's voice rose in pitch and volume. "If you think someone killed that guy, why don't you go to the cops? What're you afraid of?"

"I'm afraid … you're in it with your boyfriend."

"You're an asshole." Jenny's feet pounded down the hall. "I have work to do."

"Bad things happen to little girls who cross me."

I tried to twist the doorknob silently. It was still barred on the outside. Lucky for Bonham—I would've ripped his head off.

From the end of the hall, Jenny snarled at him. "What's that supposed to mean? Are you threatening me?"

I heard Bonham stride after her. "I'm telling you. I take security seriously. If there's something you and your boyfriend are hiding, I'll find out and there will be hell to pay. What did he tell you about Spot?"

"Nothing!"

"Then you should ask him."

I couldn't hear her answer. Quiet words were exchanged. I heard the hatch at the end of the hall slam. I heard Bonham's feet padding down the hallway to his cabin. I tried the door again. Still no use. I never should've allowed them to lock me up. Bonham threatening Jenny never crossed my mind. She was in danger from the moment she agreed to take the job, but I never thought it would come because of something I did.

I looked at Mercury. He shrugged and had the good sense not to say told-ya-so.

When the steward brought my lunch, Jenny came with him. She'd taken on Ms. Sabel's fondness for form-fitting athletic fashions. While they gave her complete freedom of movement, they also showed off her body in vivid detail. She was fit and trim and understated in a way that drove my imagination wild. But her real sexiness came from confidence, not curves.

She didn't speak while the crewman laid out places for two on the coffee table and dropped two plates. He sensed the tension between us and left. She closed the door behind him.

She remained at the door for a lingering moment, her hands still behind her on the knob. I pointed an invitation to the sofa.

"Did you have something to do with the disappearance of that man?" she asked.

A lifetime of disappointments didn't form a foothill compared to the Himalayan-sized disappointment I felt in her question. Yes, I killed Spot. She never batted an eye at the horrific piles of bodies I stacked up in war, but she wanted to know if I had something to do with a man named after a dog? Where were her loyalties now, with Bonham or me? Should I trust her with the truth?

"I heard your conversation with Bonham." I watched her gaze drop to the floor in shame. "He demanded you ask me. What would you like to tell him?"

"I'd like to tell him the truth." She ran to me and wrapped her arms around me. "That you didn't have anything to do with his disappearance."

I felt gentle sobs well up inside her. Slowly, I moved my arms around her. It took a minute to feel like it was real, that she was in my cabin, that she wanted me again. That she wasn't running to me because Bonham was worse. None of that made me feel any better about trusting her. The Syrians knew why I didn't tell them things. It was for their own good— and mine. She served in the Navy. She should know that. But if she pressed me on the issue, she would know the truth no matter what I said. She knew me that well.

Considering the risk of telling her the truth made me realize how deep I had fallen into Nathan Hale's nightmare. In short order, I would have the most terrifying weapon system in the world on the deck of my ship, ready to deliver to the world's worst tyrants. And I was locked up. If I didn't get a grip on the situation, I would end up just another dog on Falconer's leash.

The ship started slowing. Rafia's voice came over the PA: we were arriving at the coordinates for the containers. Jenny's job started now.

We looked at each other. I felt the warmth of her body pressed against mine. The curve of her waist felt good in my hands. The light pressure of her breasts against my chest added more feels. Her face turned up to mine. I could feel the heat of her breath. Our lips grazed each other's. I searched her liquid brown eyes for any hint of "no." They were all "yes."

We kissed.

All the anger and jealousy of the last few weeks fired our resurging flame. The kiss lasted a wonderfully long time. Finally, we came up for air.

"What happened to you, Jacob?" She looked up at me with pleading eyes. "Did you kill that man?"

Veritas.

One too many questions. Was she kissing me to get herself out of danger with Bonham? Did she realize we were both dead if she told Bonham anything? Or was she trying to understand me better? I figured if it was anything other than the latter, I didn't want to live.

I held her tight, clinging to hope.

"After Spot bragged about killing a Greek prosecutor and a damn fine lieutenant, I stabbed him in the heart and dropped him in the harbor."

CHAPTER 50

ONCE RAFIA DROPPED ANCHOR, JENNY'S crew got moving. Their search was quick and easy. The coordinates had been spot on. Whoever "lost" these containers managed to feed Falconer latitude and longitude that put us within half a mile of their location. Her ROVs found the first of ten containers before dinner.

That evening, Captain Rafia and my Syrians sat in my luxurious prison, playing poker with 100 Lekë coins. I can hold my own in most poker games, but these guys had grown up playing for grocery money. They concentrated hard on winning. Since Lekës coins are worth ninety cents each, I didn't mind losing. My concentration stayed on the sound of the winches.

The second one came up a couple hours later. Smooth as silk. The next three came up an hour or two apart. Then something went wrong. The pitch of a crane changed. Rafia and my Syrians cocked an ear to the noise. A second later they ran out, leaving their cards and drinks on the table. They left the door wide open.

Neither of Bonham's dogs stood guard outside. They probably wanted to see the action at the cranes since standing in the hall had to be the most boring detail on the ship.

Before I could entertain the idea of walking out, Bonham walked in.

He leaned against the jamb looking quite drunk. "You might've taken out one of my men, but I'm still coming out ahead."

"If I cared about whether you live or die, I'd ask how you figure. But I don't, so save your breath." Remaining on the sofa, I peeked at the poker hands on the table. Firas's looked best with two pair. "Why do you keep me confined to quarters after you've searched the ship?"

"Because I can." Bonham swayed his way into the room and flung himself in a chair. "I'm going to make $200 million extra on this deal."

"Good news," I said. "You can use the money to buy someone to do some thinking for you."

"You're so arrogant." He ticked a finger at me. "I went to St. Andrews, you know. And Dartmouth. I'm quite good at thinking. Say, do you have something to drink other than that Turkish crap?"

"Raki? I have some fine aged Scotch and a bottle of Hennessy XO." I got up and found the Hennessy. I poured two fingers of it straight up, took out a second glass and filled it with raki. "But raki is good enough for you."

I handed him the milky anise-flavored drink and sipped from my glass.

Bonham sneered and snarled. "I come from old money, you know. St. Andrews was the best private school in Washington. I was a member of the best country clubs, too. My father was a member of the Georgetown Club."

"Do you hear yourself?" I sat and leaned in so we wouldn't be overheard. "You use the past tense. You 'went to private school,' you 'were in a country club,' and your best line, 'my father was a member.' What happened, *sport*?"

He sipped his raki and gave me his best death-glare. I sipped my cognac and gave him a superficial smile.

"I'll be back there again." He grew smug. "I'm going to get your share. That's how I'm getting so much more."

I did the math. Falconer and I agreed on 20 percent for my share. If Bonham was right, that made the deal worth a billion.

Mercury tapped my shoulder. *Dude, only governments and ginormous corporations have that kind of cash.*

I said, *When Bradley told me about it, I was thinking the whole deal was fifty million. When Falconer told me I'd get five million, my math said that made the deal worth a hundred million. But I didn't believe him.*

Mercury said, *Big money, bro. $86,400 per day big. $32 million a year for thirty-two years. Big money means big bidders. You're up* *against Walmart and Volkswagen and Compass Group.*

I said, *Why would they want Alvaria?*

Mercury said, *Haven't you noticed, brutha? Companies like Walmart have more employees than the Chinese have soldiers. George Orwell was right, the world is controlled by corporations. Next time Volkswagen wants to do a merger, they just put Toyota's board of directors into their little drone swarm and—bang—problem solved. I'm telling you, if we had one of them things, Augustus would never have had problems with Antony and Lepidus in that ridiculous Triumvirate thing.* Mercury got dreamy-eyed and looked to the ceiling. *And we coulda dealt with those damn Christians. None of this crawling-around-in-the-catacombs bullshit.*

I said, *You're not filling me with a lot of confidence here.*

Mercury said, *Homie, if you're going to be a Caesar, you gotta make your own confidence. Puff up your chest, attack anyone who crosses you, forget about everyone else. Hey, what's that sour look for? Don't get scared now. You're going up against China's Red Army, ain't no big thing.*

I said, *Yeah, no big ... You've got me on this one, right?*

I looked around. Mercury was gone.

"What's that?" Bonham looked at me funny.

"I said, how're you planning to get my share?"

He grinned big, this time because he knew something I didn't. There was even a maniacal twinkle in his eye. He tilted his glass my way as a salute, then chugged half. He set the glass down and exhaled with satisfaction.

"OK," I said, "I'll bite. What is it?"

"When the *Savanah* gets here, you and I are going over for a little visit. You're going to sign your company over to me. I'll take it from there."

"Because I'm a generous guy?" I sipped my cognac.

"Because you stabbed my man in the heart and dumped him in the harbor." He gave me that smug grin again and sipped. "And because you don't want anything bad to happen to that sweet girl of yours."

CHAPTER 51

I LEAPT ON THE BASTARD, pounding my forearm into his face. He and the chair he was in went over backwards. His drink went flying. I sat up on him and raised a fist ready to pound into his face.

Mercury caught my arm. *Not yet, homie.*

I said, *Why not?*

Mercury said, *You already killed one guy and that got you locked up. Where's killing a second guy going to get you?*

I said, *He threatened Jenny. I'm saving her.*

Mercury said, *Why? She told him exactly what you told her. She betrayed you.*

I said, *I don't care. I'm going to get her out of here. She's going back to the states where she belongs and I'm going down with these bastards. Starting with this guy.*

Mercury said, *That doesn't stop the other two dogs or Falconer, who's on his way here with three more dogs. You need to think. This guy is your insurance. If you want to live through the week, get a new plan.*

Bonham squirmed and looked at me funny. "There's something wrong with you."

"Damn straight. You're using Jenny for your insurance. I'm using you for mine." I pulled out my second-to-last dart out and stuck him.

His dogs could return to their duty station at my door at any minute. In a rush, I dragged his considerable frame down the hall to his cabin. I found a piece of rope, tied him up, and gagged him with underwear.

Satisfied, I went back to my room and broke the mechanism that locked my door from the outside. I propped it up so the casual observer wouldn't notice the dysfunction and waited.

The noise of the winches had started back up. The fifth container came aboard to much cheering on deck. Without delay, the cranes resumed their task, sending lengths of steel cable down five hundred feet to the bottom. There, Jenny and her robotic submarines attached the lines to the next container and hauled it up.

Fido and Rover returned.

I had only one dart left. I stood by the door listening to them talk about how they were going to kill me as soon as Bonham told Falconer what happened. They were debating decapitation versus multiple stab wounds. One of them came up with an idea involving gasoline and a match. That didn't appeal to me.

Waiting too long would allow time for Bonham to come to. I had to make a move.

The lamp on the desk had a good solid base. I held it in one hand and reached for the door. A couple of practice swings gave me some confidence. I ripped the door open and slammed the lamp around the corner to the left.

Unfortunately, that was the exact moment Fido chose to bend down to tie his shoe. My lamp bounced off the wall, sending shockwaves back up my arm. Reflexively, I swung it back with all my might into the side of Rover's head. He had that stunned look on his face: mild concussion. I tossed the lamp in the room and pulled my last dart out of my pocket. I stabbed Fido as his fist slammed into my ear. Fido collapsed.

Reeling backward with my head ringing, I saw Rover regain his senses. He lunged for me. We tumbled into my cabin. He clutched at my throat with both hands. I clawed at his face with one hand and felt behind me for the lamp with the other.

Rover's mass overpowered mine. He rolled himself on top and began choking me. His thumbs worked hard to crush my windpipe. The lamp was out of reach. I tried counter-choking, but his big, steroid arms pushed mine out of the way. My best defense was slapping at his muscle-bound head with little effect.

My air supply dwindled. Silver sparks appeared in my peripheral vision as I finally landed one blow to his chin. He shrugged it off and redoubled his efforts to wring my neck.

DEATH AND BETRAYAL

I felt my consciousness ebbing. I fought to stay awake as the blood flow to my brain dropped and the oxygen supply forced corners of my brain to shut down.

My arms felt like noodles, no longer striking with any purpose. I was fighting a phantom in a nightmare. I couldn't even see Rover's face. My vision narrowed to dark slits.

Suddenly, he reared back. His hands came off my neck.

I gasped and spluttered. Rover kicked me as he backed toward the hall. I rose up on my elbows, my vision coming back as blood pumped back into my brain.

Rover was half in the hall, half in my room. A white sock with two oranges stuffed in it pounded down on his stomach, blow after blow. The oranges-in-a-sock is an old trick used to beat the crap out of someone without leaving a mark. Rover's internal injuries would last days.

I took a deep breath and staggered to my feet.

In the hall, Mardik had Rover in a headlock while Firas took big overhead swings with the sock. I watched for a moment. Not for the joy of watching the bastard get his, but to observe the practiced technique of my Syrians. They had learned some horrifying methods in the course of their careers.

They decided Rover was no longer a threat and released him. He rolled over looking sick.

"Don't puke on my ship." I grabbed him by the hair and forced him to the toilet in my suite.

While he let it all out, I turned to my Syrians. "Thanks guys. Do you always carry a sock with oranges?"

Firas cracked a grin on one corner of his mouth. "The last container comes up at dawn. We were tired of you being absent."

We dragged Fido and Rover into Bonham's room.

"You should have called us," Firas said.

I said, "I didn't want you getting in trouble should it turn deadly."

"We are with you, boss," Mardik said. Both of them nodded their heads in unison. "All the way."

We trussed the dogs up with rope Mardik found in a storage locker. We used more of Bonham's underwear for gags. I'd left Spot's pistols in the drawer. I wasn't sure what it would take to make them look in there for evidence.

Captain Rafia joined us a moment later. He glanced at—but didn't mention—the bodies tied up and gagged. Only Rover was awake, and he was about as active as a frozen snake. We moved the card game to Bonham's room so we could keep an eye on them.

Near dawn, Rafia was down by several thousand Lekë, about fifty bucks, when his first mate came in to let us know the last container was located and would be on deck in half an hour.

Mercury said, *Tough negotiations ahead, homeboy. You need to get the auction location and bidders out of Falconer before you can bump him, Bonham, and the dogs off.*

I said, *Nothing tough about it.*

I dialed Falconer. A sleepy voice picked up. I said, "I have Bonham and his dogs tied up. I have all eight canisters retrieved and on deck. It's time to renegotiate our deal."

Falconer took a long slow inhale. He blew out a breath. "Toss those pricks overboard if you'd like, sport. We're not renegotiating. Not while I have an ace up my sleeve."

He clicked off.

My mind raced through possibilities for his cockiness. Was he threatening Yumi? Possible, but unlikely. Jenny? No, she was with us. Some other connection? A bomb maybe?

The medical oxygen tanks I saw in Bonham's room flashed in my memory. What were those things?

CHAPTER 52

IT WAS THEIR THIRD MEETING in as many days. Bradley and Ryan enjoyed coffee while Eva sipped tea in a nook at Sabel Gardens. Eva's swollen eye had gone from grapefruit-size to tangerine. It began to let light in. She could feel it. The swelling in her other eye and her lip were down considerably but still hurt.

Bradley took another gingersnap off the tray and wolfed it whole. "Sabel's chef makes the best cookies in the world. Have you tried these?"

Eva took one and nibbled a corner. The cookie melted into a sensation of sugar, ginger, and a few unidentifiable but wonderful spices. She wolfed the rest in one bite. Ryan watched her cautiously until he saw her satisfaction spread into a smile. He took one.

A few seconds later, the plate was empty.

"I never liked gingersnaps before," Ryan said. He licked his fingers.

"Wow." Eva considered licking the crumbs off the plate. "Back to business."

"We have to be careful, guys," Bradley said. "I know what it's like to be young and out for blood. We have little evidence and no proof. I don't want to ruin someone's career by accident."

"Pia said the same thing," Eva said. "You two think alike. Why don't you like her?"

Ryan watched while she and Bradley stared each other down.

Ryan said, "Let's stick to the plan. Don't get sidetracked."

"You're right," Bradley said. He met Eva's gaze. "We'll talk. Some other time."

They went their separate ways. To avoid detection or casting doubt on innocent people, their strategy required each of them to pursue a different piece of the puzzle, covertly interviewing different people for clues that would lead them to the mole.

TWO HOURS LATER, REGGIE FORREST stood at the window in Eva's guest suite and looked over the winterized gardens. "When will you return to work?"

"The doctor said a couple more days," Eva replied. "I'm sorry to miss so many days, ma'am."

"It's nice of Pia to give you such nice accommodations, but I've seen nothing from her people." Forrest kept her gaze outside. "At least your weekly reports gave me something to pass up the ladder."

Eva prayed for someone to call her boss and demand she attend some meeting on the other side of town. The last few days had been a pleasant recovery until the visit from Forrest. But Eva had suggested the visit since she and her confederates were after information. The sooner she started asking her questions, the sooner Forrest would leave. Eva took a deep breath.

"You came to DC not long ago," Eva said. "You didn't have any civil service background. Who was your mentor?"

"I don't see what that has to do with anything."

"Everything here's so complicated." Eva recalled Pia advising her to use flattery like butter on corn. "You managed to learn so much so quickly. How did you do it?"

"I did have a little help early on." Forrest turned around with a smile. "A nice old guy gave me some ideas and always picked up the phone when I had a question."

"Who, that CIA guy? Isn't he a level below you?"

"Please. The man I'm talking about is still married, so let's not talk names." Forrest crossed her arms and turned back to the window. "But my mentor was, or rather still is, connected, you know. He knows all the right people. He and the DNI are in the same alumni association. I forget what college they went to. He helped me navigate the treacherous waters of political-military affairs. He pointed out high-profile projects that got me noticed and helped me keep my job when the administration changed."

"Giving Alvaria to Albania, that was his idea?"

Forrest faced Eva with a sharp scowl. "That was my idea. And it would have been a good one if these damned Sabel people had taken care of security from the beginning. I don't know who wrote that contract, but they weaseled out of their responsibilities on a technicality."

"Before it turned into a nightmare, wasn't it in the pipeline before you came to State?"

Eva watched Forrest's fingers tapping impatiently on her upper arms. Then Forrest faced Eva. "Are you suggesting I should blame this whole fiasco on my mentor?"

After she snapped that question, Forrest looked to the ceiling and appeared to warm to the idea.

"Not at all," Eva said. "I was just wondering where it originated."

"Well, it was lying low. Apparently, the project had stalled because neither the Albanians nor the manufacturer endorsed the plan."

Eva wondered if Forrest heard herself. "Then you got behind it and made it happen. That must've taken a lot of effort."

"Did it ever," Forrest said. "My mentor was a huge help. He pointed it out to me. It would be such a great gesture to the smaller, defenseless nations to give them better weapons than the Russians or the Chinese. For once, the little guys could stand up and defend themselves."

BRADLEY HOPKINS PUT HIS TRAY down next to a dour older woman in the CIA cafeteria. She looked at the empty tables nearby then gave him a once-over.

"Dana, right? Bradley Hopkins. Mind if I join you?" He sat down without an answer.

She sat motionless.

She looked different from her company directory picture. He checked her short, white hair and wondered if it was a natural color. It was her, though.

"I came across some of your work recently." He picked up a forkful of chicken Caesar. "Thought I'd drop by and tell you how much I appreciate your quality of work and how I love the detail."

Dana picked at her meatloaf.

Undaunted by her recalcitrant personality, he continued. "You've been summarizing reports for as long as I've been here. And they're all top-notch."

"Which one are you talking about?" Her voice was husky, like a lifetime of smoking had caught up with her. She took a bite of meatloaf and studied him while she chewed.

"We're tracking a guy, used to be a decorated veteran. He went to Athens and you got the details of his drunken texts to his girlfriend." Bradley chuckled. "That was subtle, Dana. But very fun to read in a classified report."

She snickered with him. "They do tend to get damn dry after a while. There were more than texts in that one. We got transcripts of his conversation too. I left the salacious bits out. But that wasn't me. Thank the NSA for listening to the private lives of our soldiers."

Bradley pointed his fork at her and laughed. "Aw, see there? Now, you know the report I'm talking about. That was a good one. No idea why they thought we needed to track that particular guy, but thank you for at least making it fun to read."

Dana smiled. "I don't pick these people. I just listen to hours of recordings and flip through hundreds of texts and chats, then summarize."

"I thought you were in counterintel, no?" Bradley asked.

"That's my mission, why?"

"The guy in Athens isn't in the service. He's been civilian for a few years. Now he's overseas with his own company. How could that possibly fall under counterintel?"

"Beats me," she said. "The whole deal was off. The field guys weren't regular Company officers, stuff like that. What's this really about?"

Bradley looked around them. He took another bite of salad and made her wait. He patted his lips with his napkin. Then he said, "There are a few of us who see strange things going on. Like tracking a veteran who doesn't need to be tracked. We're thinking we might have a problem. We might not. See, from where I stand on the ladder, all I see are butts. If I bring this up and I've read it wrong, there's a whole world of shit raining down on an innocent guy. If I read it right, the Company has a problem. Not Aldridge Ames, but still a billion-dollar problem."

Dana frowned in thought. She didn't say anything but dug into her meatloaf in slow and steady bites.

When she finished, she looked at him with sad, weary eyes. "Your questions are reportable, you know."

"I do. But I'm working a hunch and I want to be careful before I wreck a decent guy by accident."

"What do you want from me?"

"There was a report about Jacob Stearne's problems getting salvage insurance. That's outside a counterintelligence scope by a mile." Bradley pulled a strip of paper out of his pocket, put it on the table with his palm covering it. "All I want from you is this: if the name on this piece of paper came to you for a favor on that insurance research, scrunch this up and toss it out with your trash. If he had nothing to do with it, leave it here on the table."

He lifted his palm and finished his salad.

Dana stared at him for a long time while he ate. She pulled on her glasses and took a discreet glance at the strip of paper. She pursed her lips and made a face. What was it? Anger? Disappointment? At him? At the guy whose name she read? Bradley wasn't sure.

Dana scrunched up the strip, tossed it on her tray, and rose. "I hate that guy."

RYAN WHEELING PEERED ACROSS THE main room at Tachibana, the sushi restaurant in downtown McLean. The young lady from HR waved to him from a table toward the back. He smiled, waved back, and picked his way through the chairs to reach her. As he walked, he realized two things. First, she was wearing a dress that implied she considered this a date. Second, she had a car. His use of public transportation was a badge of eco-honor. Sometimes. But when the girl involved thought they were meeting as the prelude to a date, being car-less made him feel insignificant. But Ryan was the kind of guy who would never let that show.

He smiled and pecked the cheek she offered when he sat.

"Have you ordered yet?" he asked.

"Sashimi plate," she said. "I thought we could split it."

He smiled at her despite having seen the price tag. Even split it would cost twice his lunch budget.

"And Bento Box B," she added. "Sashimi never quite fills me up."

"Same," he said. He choked at the price of that as well. "That's perfect. You've got this down."

"I come here all the time," she said. She added a shoulders-caved giggle that showed off her dimples.

Who the hell was Mikayla and why did he think inviting her out to lunch was a good idea? Why not the cafeteria at Langley?

"Oh, hey, those people you asked about? Nothing in HR about harassment. No complaints." Mikayla leaned in with a conspiratorial wink. "What do you think she did? Did she do something to you?"

"Asking for a friend," he said with a wink. She laughed.

A dead end. And he was so sure there would be something in there. Maybe giving her three names had been a bad idea, like Bradley said. But Mikayla was the kind to blab and that would expose them. Maybe making it sound like sexual harassment had been too far off-topic, like Eva had said. But asking HR direct questions could also unmask their inquiry with disastrous results. He would just have to dig a little deeper.

"No, really," she said, tugging his arm. "What's your interest?"

Ryan looked over both her shoulders and behind him, then leaned in to whisper. "I think they're a polyamorous triangle."

"And you want in?"

He gave her a sly glance and leaned back as the sashimi plate arrived. She popped her chopsticks in two and picked a slice of tuna. He picked a slice of pickled cucumber.

"Seriously," she said, "you think they're snogging it up after work?"

"When someone brags about partying with the rich, you ever wonder if they're full of it? I just had that feeling after walking in on them before a meeting. They shut up too fast. It's no big deal."

"You just needed an excuse to ask me out?" She batted her eyes at him.

He hesitated too long. Her gaze fell and she slurped up some salmon. If he expected to find anything of value out of the young lady, would he have to take one for the team? He looked her over. She was not hard to look at. Since Emma left him, he hadn't done more than go to football parties and get drunk. He'd done a lot worse than Mikayla many times. But, since they started working together, he couldn't get Eva off his mind.

"OK, you caught me. I needed an excuse." He shoulder bumped her.

He would play her, he decided. Enough to get the intel they needed, then he'd cut off anything with Mikayla. The more he thought about it, the more he realized he needed to ask Eva out. He wasn't going anywhere with Mikayla after this lunch.

Mikayla grinned with a piece of ginger stuck to her tooth. He couldn't help but laugh.

"There was something else in the files, though," she said. "One of your three suspects partied on a rich guy's yacht in Monaco last summer. Wanna guess which one?"

Pia walked into Eva's guest room holding the reports they'd written. "Eva, Ryan, Coach ... I mean, Bradley, these are all excellent statements. Before you act on this, I'd like you to consider your careers. The Whistleblower Protection Act is supposed to protect you, but as we've seen in recent years, it doesn't always do that. I'll defer to your decision—it's your work that will expose the head of the operation, but I'd like to take this up with my friends at the FBI."

"We appreciate that," Bradley said. "We prefer to see if the system works the way it's supposed to. We'll report it via Whistleblower. If we don't see FBI agents coming in a couple days, we'll let you know. They should show up to ask questions at least."

"We discussed it," Ryan Wheeling said. "We appreciate you offering to help. But if you pull strings for us, it'll send the wrong message.

Either people will come to us to settle scores through our connection to you or they'll lock us out, fearing we'll use our connections to get ahead."

"We know it's not going to be easy," Eva said. "We're committed."

CHAPTER 53

FROM HIS EXPERIENCE IN ASSAD'S military, Mardik confirmed what I suspected. The tanks weren't medical oxygen. They were Syrian nerve agent containers. Sarin gas to be specific. Syria destroyed their nerve agents when they destroyed their stockpile of chemical weapons in 2014. Except for the ones they didn't. For example, the Agent 15 they unleashed on a rebel village in 2017. And the innocuous-looking canisters we were staring at in Bonham's cabin. I tested Mardik's theory by placing one cannister in front of Rover and watching his eyes bulge as I pretended to open the valve.

Mardik had been trained on them and what to do in case of a sarin attack. The short version was, you say your prayers because there was no way to survive without the atropine antidote.

"Captain Rafia, does the ship's infirmary stock atropine?" I asked.

"Three injectors of 2 mg." He shrugged. "Not enough, habibi."

Firas examined one of the containers and bounced it in his hands. "These are empty."

His short pronouncement shocked us all. If the cannisters were empty, where the hell was the gas? Was it a bluff?

"The seals have been broken." Firas continued looking over the pressurized container. "There are markings on the fittings. They've been connected to something. They transferred the gas."

"They weren't searching the ship for their friend," Rafia said.

I yanked Bonham's undies out of Rover's mouth. "What did you do? Where did you put the gas?"

"Fuck you," Rover said.

I punched him and pulled back, ready for a second blow. Rafia grabbed my arm.

"Fire suppression system," he said. "We use gas-type. Their search of the ship was to find the access points for refilling the system."

Rover grinned.

I gave him a black eye.

"Can we clear it?" I asked as I rose to face Rafia. "Pump it back in the bottles?"

Rafia shook his head. "Too risky. Probably impossible anyway."

We left two crew to watch Bonham and Fido sleep. They were told to kick Rover every few minutes for exercise. Captain Rafia, my Syrians, and I went to visit the fire suppression system down in the engine room. Most ship fires occur in the engine room, with the kitchen as the runner-up. The fire suppression system covered the whole ship.

In a small room near the engine room were four bright-red cylinders. They were marked as high-pressure CO_2. A refilling valve at the far end was missing its rubber cover. The brass threads were exposed. A length of flexible tubing lay nearby. Pressurized lines connected all four cylinders to each other with one end running to a plenum. From there six lines exited in different directions. Five disappeared into the bulkhead.

The sixth had been refitted to include a remote-control device with a handwritten note taped on it, "Tampering can trigger system." Implying it would go off if we tried to disconnect it. Falconer had us under his thumb.

"This is where they filled the system." Rafia tapped the brass threads on the end. "And that line runs to the bridge and living quarters."

"There is no alternate bridge?" I asked.

He shook his head sadly.

My first thought was to abandon ship, but I was in debt for tens of millions, the company was virtually bankrupt, and my people would lose their livelihoods if I didn't do what Falconer wanted. Once again, I understood what Ms. Sabel was talking about when she considered risks.

We went back to the bridge to think, even though it would be the first place to fill with toxic gas should a fire break out anywhere on the ship.

Jenny joined us and reported the containers were all stowed, all the equipment recovered, and her operations were complete. She expected a pat on the back from the captain. He didn't even acknowledge her presence. She looked at me.

My gaze must've telegraphed my mood. She'd ratted me out to Bonham to save her skin. Instantly, she knew I'd figured it out. She staggered back as if I'd hit her. I looked away.

My phone rang. Falconer. I put it on speaker.

"You've figured it out, sport?" Falconer asked.

"Yes," I hissed.

"Drop anchor twenty-five miles south of Odessa. You can get there in three days. I'll be in touch." He clicked off.

For a moment, back when we were kissing in my stateroom, my plan was to get the last container up and send her home. She could've called the CIA, Europol, anyone besides Bonham, and I wouldn't have cared. I considered calling the authorities myself now that we had Alvaria on deck. There was a good chance I would wind up in jail, but at least Jenny would be safe.

Mercury said, *You're going to betray me, homes? The god of commerce? You're on the verge of making a billion dollars!*

I said, *Jenny's worth ten times that. Plus, there's the moral question.*

Mercury said, *Morals are as flexible as blades of grass, brutha. People in your country voted for a guy who proved that point in spades. Nobody cared because the economy was good. Even if you did clean up and go home, you don't have the bidder list. That's what the CIA guy asked for.*

He had a point. Governments don't care if you come back with something. They only care if you come back with what they sent you out to find. I said, *The only thing left to do is go to Odessa and get my money.*

Mercury said, *Now you're talking. Plenty of pretty women looking for Caesars in that part of the world.*

Jenny left the bridge.

We discussed it for a few minutes. Call in people to fix the system? It was a problem that required specialists with specific equipment. If we brought someone on board, Falconer would notice and pull the trigger. Same problem if we turned off course.

No one could come up with a plan, so Rafia set a course for Odessa.

At least I had a backup plan for Jenny. We needed her for the remainder of the trip in case we had to drop the containers overboard then recover them again. After that, she was going home. I called Ansi, the chopper pilot, and told him to meet me in Odessa.

CHAPTER 54

CAPTAIN RAFIA DROPPED ANCHOR FAR from the shipping lanes just before dawn. A sunrise we would never see for the low clouds and fog. Too far from shore for phones, the captain alerted the *Savannah* of our arrival via radio.

I turned my collar up and tugged my jacket tight around me as I scanned the horizon from the wing of the bridge. My coffee mug was cooling fast in the chill. My mind calculated how and when I could kill Falconer without endangering anyone else. So far, all my ideas were suicide missions.

Falconer had arrived the day before. We didn't have his coordinates and didn't see the *Savannah's* profile on the ship's radar. He was out there somewhere in the haze. Lurking like a gray shark.

Jenny made her way toward me in tentative steps. She stopped ten feet short of where I stood. "I'd like to see this through, if that's OK with you."

"It isn't."

"Look, Jacob, we can work through whatever you're mad about." She moved a little closer. "Could you talk to me?"

I pointed at a small speck in the air above the horizon. "That's Ansi. He's going to land here in twenty minutes. He's taking you to the airport in Odessa. You've been paid. Geldona has already transferred funds to your account. You're going home."

"Nothing happened with Stefan."

"Nothing happened with Ms. Sabel."

"Jesus, Jacob, it's weird that you call her Mizz Sabel. I know, it's a sign of respect for you, like calling an officer 'ma'am.' But everyone else calls her Pia."

"Not me."

She leaned her elbows on the railing and watched Ansi's H155 turn from a speck to a blob above the fog. "That's not why you're mad at me."

"You ran straight out of my room to Bonham. What did he threaten you with that Mardik and Firas couldn't save you from?"

She faced me. "He didn't threaten me."

"Oh, he threatened me?" I scoffed. "And you have so little faith you thought he would beat me?"

"He had all the power behind him."

"Only because I let him."

The ring—still in my jacket pocket through all my adventures—jumped into my fingers. I turned it over and considered flinging it into the sea.

Mercury floated down from the heavens and landed between us. *Who poured the mean-sauce all over you, dawg?*

I said, *She betrayed me. Could you leave us alone?*

Mercury said, *Seneca wrote, If a man knows not to which port he sails, no wind is favorable.*

I said, *We don't use wind anymore. We use internal combustion engines.*

Mercury said, *You were going to marry her, bro. Sure, you're pissed. Won't be the last time either. If you don't know where you're going with her, you'll always be pissed. What good is that? Figure out which port you're sailing to with her so we can get on with the show.*

I said, *I like being pissed off. Especially when I have a right to be. It makes me feel ... powerful. Now, leave me alone.*

Mercury said, *All right, homes. Before I go, how about a little Marcus Aurelius? 'How much more grievous are the consequences of anger than the causes of it.'*

Damn that god of mine. He always makes me think. I hate that.

"I didn't want to risk it." Jenny had inched close enough to touch me. "Besides, you appear to have weathered his storm."

I faced her. "The storm hasn't begun. That's why you're going home."

"Come with me, then."

Her invitation—or was it a demand?—tugged at my heart. If she wanted me back, why should I stay here? Why risk my life? Why not sell everything and move to an island and live like bohemians? Then the reality crept in like an unwanted guest. Sure, she'd renounced her father's wealth, but how long would the daughter of a billionaire live in poverty on a filthy beach? All the pristine beaches with white sands were taken up by Hiltons and Marriotts. The bohemians get trash-strewn coasts of gravel.

I took a deep breath. "I can't leave until I deliver the containers. You're not safe here."

"Neither are you or the others."

"Falconer contracted you to this point. He knows you're leaving."

"I can't leave, not like this."

And I couldn't stay mad at her, no matter how hard I tried. Mercury was right about the consequences of anger. She'd survived her own hell, she deserved better from me.

My arms slipped around her, pulled her close. She put her face on my chest and squeezed as if at any minute we were going to be blown overboard. We stayed like that in the cold and damp, oblivious to the world and all its evils. I enjoyed her embrace until the noise of the chopper came to my ear.

"Apology accepted." I kissed her forehead. "I love you."

Then I kissed her on the lips. And she kissed back with the same kind of hunger and lust I felt. We kept it up like lovers in the final scene of a bad rom-com for what felt like an eternity. The music swelled. Or was that the chopper? Finally, when the rotor wash nearly blew us overboard, we broke off.

"I want to stay," she said. "Until I know you're safe."

"I can't be safe knowing you're vulnerable. Bonham knows that and will use it against me. The best thing you can do for my safety is go home. I'll send for you when this is over."

"Send for me?" she asked. "Aren't you coming home?"

"I'll call you. Whatever."

Below us, Ansi set down the H155 on top of the forward hold. It had become his second home.

She squeezed me hard one last time, then ran from the bridge. I chased after her, but she threw hatches closed in my path to slow me down. After the third one, I got it. She wouldn't leave if I escorted her all the way. She wanted me to wave goodbye from the bridge. In case anything bad happened, her final memory would be that long, windy kiss on the bridge wing.

CHAPTER 55

WE NEVER UNTIED THE DOGS during the three-day voyage. Bonham, Fido, and Rover stank like wet versions of their self-inflicted nicknames. We shoved them in Falconer's launch and tossed their duffels in with them.

Mardik held the line in his hand, ready to cast us off. "You sure you don't want us coming with you, boss?"

"I got this," I said. "Probably."

"You usually do." Firas waved me off and trotted up the long aluminum stairs hanging off the side of the ship.

"We still have the containers," I said.

Mardik nodded and tossed the line to the cockswain. He followed his cousin up the stairs.

The little tender drove up and over the growing swells. Whitecaps began to form. Drizzle fell on us. My captives shivered without jackets. I faced forward and felt the cold rain wash my face.

Sending Jenny away moments after our reconciliation was one of the most painful things I'd done. My sternum felt as if it had been torn down the middle and my rib cage split open. She asked if I was coming home. Was I? If I did the right thing and turned in the bidders, their bosses and partners would come after me the same way I was going after Nate's killers. They couldn't let something like that stand. It would encourage others to turn on them. She would have to join me on the run. I couldn't ask her to do that.

Mercury had a good point about cashing in. If I pulled off this deal, I could be set for life, live like a king in Baku on the Caspian or Varna on the Black Sea. Maybe Argentina, Brazil, or an island in the South

Pacific. Would she come with me then? There was no way to know. But it was the safest course of action for me and anyone who wanted to live with me. It was better to be King of the Bad Guys than informant on the run.

Halfway across the stretch of Black Sea separating my ship from the *Savannah*, I held up three clear plastic bags in front of my captives. "I was planning to give these back to you when we reached Falconer's boat. But I think I'll toss them."

I did a big, dramatic wind up to fling the bags—and all the pistols in them—into the ocean.

"Wait!" Fido yelled.

All three of them stared at one of the bags.

I paused and said, "I'm sure you have plenty more aboard the *Savannah*."

I re-enacted my dramatic wind up.

"No! Wait." Fido was beside himself. "Let me see that. Not to hold. Just to look at that pistol on the left. The one with the Army star on the grip."

I held Spot's pistol in front of him.

He examined it. Then he glared at me. "Where did you get that?"

"These toys were in your rooms." I shrugged. "I'd have to ask the crew which one came from which room."

All three leaned in close. Then Fido and Rover turned to Bonham with hate and death in their eyes.

"What is it, guys?" I asked. "You're scaring me here."

"That was Spot's pistol." Fido never took his eyes off Bonham. "It's in the bag with your Glock."

"Whoa, dogs." Bonham began to sweat despite the rain. "He planted this on me. He killed Spot. His girlfriend told me he stabbed Spot in the heart."

"Dude, don't go blaming me." I did my insulted act. "When you didn't want to call the cops, I found that suspicious. You didn't call because you didn't want him found. So, I asked the Durrës police to look for him. They found his corpse floating in the harbor. But, no knife wounds in the heart." I looked each of them in the eye. "When we get to the *Savannah*, you're free to call them and ask the manner of death."

The dogs tried to live up to their names. They jumped on Bonham, biting and snapping because their hands were tied behind their backs.

I watched. Shoulda brought popcorn.

They were still going at it when we arrived at the sport deck where Falconer waited for us.

"Ahoy there," he said in a quiet voice. He nodded at the dogfight. "Not very nice way to treat your guests."

"Fuck you and your dogs."

I climbed aboard his ship and looked around while he and his crew pulled my captives from his tender and untied them.

Yumi appeared a deck above us. She looked down at me, saw Bonham, and repressed a smirk. Then her demeanor went back to morose. She held up her phone and gave me a half-hearted thumb-up. She had Falconer's code. That was a good thing. Now all I needed was to steal his phone. Like all modern humans, he carried it in his hand or pants pocket. He never left it on the couch or table and walked away. I'd have to think of something clever.

When someone made the mistake of untying Bonham's hands, he leapt at me. I twisted as he approached, casually slamming my elbow into his face. He fell into the sea. The crew raced to grab life rings from a storage bin. They tossed him a lifeline.

Falconer sighed and stood next to me. "You're doing this just because I put your crew's lives at risk?"

"This—" I waved my hands at Bonham thrashing in the sea "—is a wellness treatment he's been asking for. At the best spas they call it a cold plunge and they charge $500. He's getting it free. But I ask you, does he look the least bit grateful?"

Falconer chuckled before catching himself and turning serious again.

I climbed the few short steps to the main deck. It had a swimming pool in the middle of it. Steam rose from the heated pool. I just wanted to get out of the rain. It was coming down now at a steady pace.

Falconer followed me up. "You're not out of the woods yet, sport. You still have to deliver the goods. And don't get any funny ideas about handing over empty boxes. You'll need to authenticate the merchandise.

SEELEY JAMES

Anything less and your ragtag bunch of refugees will be corpses on a ghost ship."

I figured his demand was meant to justify killing me instead of paying me. Which meant, he'd do the same for Rafia and the crew.

"Authenticate?"

"You don't think I'm going to accept your word that what's in those big, dark containers is worth all that money, do you?"

"I don't know what's in there."

"You didn't peek?" He gave me a menacing glare. "You didn't take the items out and replace them with fakes? No, dear boy, you're not going to walk away until you authenticate."

The handoff procedure hadn't entered my mind before. All I wanted was his bidder list so I could stand in for the man they call Ra and take their money. It made sense they would want to know that Alvaria was real. But how the hell would I pull that off? Give me an M4, an M249, a Mk 19, anything with a trigger and iron sights, and I'm good. Alvaria? I didn't know if I could spell it.

Time to change the subject. I said, "What I peeked at was the trawler two miles off your starboard side."

He turned and looked. It was a speck in the distance. Too much fog and haze.

"What's wrong with a trawler?" he asked.

"ELINT trawler dressed up to look like a fishing boat. Someone's watching you."

He spun to face me. "What's ELINT?"

"Electronic intelligence, like SIGINT, signals intelligence. Hidden on that trawler are great big ears prying into your phone, your radio, your internet connection. Anything electronic is being monitored."

"Who are they?" he asked.

"Beats me. All I know is my ship is that way, too far for them to be watching me. And we're too far from shipping lanes for it to be anyone else."

Falconer snapped his fingers and told the steward who materialized out of thin air to bring him binoculars. Three seconds later, he scanned the horizon until he found the ship. He studied it for a long time. He said

308

to me, "Something's fishy about that round dome in the middle."

"Dad jokes?" I asked. "Take it seriously. That thing hides a big parabolic dish, looks like a satellite dish. It's listening to us talk."

"Isn't that illegal?"

"In international waters? No."

"Who are they, Russians?" he asked. "Chinese?"

"That's an American radar mast."

"I don't like that. Not one bit." Falconer handed me the binoculars. "You need to do something about it."

"Me? I just told you, they're not listening to my ship."

He pointed to the tender. "I've had enough of your arrogant little displays of power. If you think I'm intimidated by your pathetic trouncing of my pawns, you're forgetting who holds the remote to your fire suppression system. Start thinking. And think hard. How would you dissuade them from sticking around?"

In modern warfare, where most of the combatants are mixed with the local population, you learn to search a man's eyes for his intent. Falconer's intent was to kill my crew if I pissed him off. Having seen him take a sick pleasure in watching me kill Konrad von Frieden, I knew he had zero empathy for anyone but himself. He was right. I'd been strutting around, proud of my hand-to-hand skills, not seeing the bigger picture. He still held all the cards.

At least Jenny was off the table.

I held up the binoculars and hoped to Minerva they were listening to us right then. "I'd tell them to call Vice President Anne Wilkes to ask her if they should take operational orders from Jacob Stearne. Then I'd go over there and ask them nicely to return to port or go harass that Russian destroyer on its way to Sevastopol."

He took the binoculars and checked the destroyer barely visible in the distance.

"And if they refused your request?" he asked.

Asking me to take on the US Navy was brilliant. He knew I'd either die in the attempt or commit atrocities that would prove my value to him. They didn't staff a spy ship with fresh recruits. There were most likely six to twelve men on that ship who'd had the same training I'd had. My methods of surprising a poorly trained, underpaid Panamanian freighter crews weren't going to work on a spy vessel.

I said, "Then I'd send it back to port the hard way."

"Good." He handed the binoculars to his steward. "We leave this time tomorrow. If you care about that pitiful crew of yours, that trawler better be disabled when we get underway."

CHAPTER 56

I HAD THE CREW OPEN the containers. There were large wooden shipping crates inside. No markings, no invoices, no numbers, no barcodes. That was good. I had the crew take the crates below decks and lay them all out in a covered hold. They rigged up enough lights to simulate daylight. That operation took all day. I left two men in charge of securing the hold; no one was allowed to enter before I returned from dealing with the trawler.

The rain let up after dinner. Ansi and his H155 were ready to go at 2 AM.

Ansi had followed my directions back in Durrës and found a care package from my ex-friends at Sabel. NightVisors, a new batch of darts, a satellite phone fed by Sabel Satellites, and a few other toys. It was enough gear to keep me in or out of trouble, depending on how I used it. All of it was standard issue at Sabel but claimed as lost by my friends. Nice of them to risk their careers to help out an exile. I owed them a big round of drinks. Maybe new cars if this deal really paid off.

To minimize the chopper noise that might alert them, I calculated 17,000 feet altitude and a mile distant. That gave me enough room to circle a few times to pick out a landing zone. Somehow, I expected the deck of the trawler to have a wide-open space for bringing in the nets. But this deck had eavesdropping hardware all over it. And it was old gear, rusty and broken in spots. There was only one place open to the skies. The bridge roof. It was tiny. Just forward of the funnel and about six feet by twelve feet. One of the smallest pieces of real estate I'd ever attempted. And it was rolling with the waves.

Mercury floated along with me, stretched out with sunglasses as if he were on a lounge chair at a Caribbean resort. *Like old times, huh, homie? Remember that time I landed you in the courtyard of an ancient German castle?*

I said, *The time I almost got killed? How could I forget?*

Dude. Mercury sat up on his imaginary lounge. *How many times we gotta go over this? An attitude of—*

Gratitude, I said. *I know. What am I going to do with these guys? How am I going to get them to back off?*

Mercury said, *This is why we study history, my man. So tell me, why are we doing this?*

I said, *Falconer doesn't trust me. I've got to get rid of the CIA to prove my loyalty to him. Then I can get close enough to steal his phone.*

Mercury said, *And then we have it all. Hey, these guys are just foot soldiers in the grand scheme of things, so don't kill 'em like you did Ol' Yeller. That was dark, man. Really dark.*

Then he saw a goddess in a slinky nightgown fly by and he took off after her.

Or, I'm hopelessly insane.

Such is the nature of faith.

The night watchman stood on my landing patch. That was both good and bad. It meant I could let his body break my fall, which was good, but the noise when he fell would alert the crew. The good news, parachuting is pretty silent with the exception of the rustling of the fabric when you flare out.

The poor bastard heard me about two seconds before my feet hit his shoulders and shoved him, at eighteen miles per hour, onto the deck. For him, it was a 190-pound man crash-landing on top of him. For me, it was like landing on a pillow. Untangling the chute took as long as his recovery.

I had the advantage and jabbed a dart into his neck.

"Are you Jacob Stearne?" A face peeked above the cabin roof. "Whoa! Did you kill him?"

"He's asleep." I gave him a brief on the dart system. "Who are you?"

"Captain. We've been expecting you."

"I didn't need to waste a dart on him?"

Captain no-name—because the clandestine service doesn't like using them—took another look at his man. His gaze met mine. "He could use a nap. Come in here where it's warm."

"Not with your lights on." I pointed to the dark aft deck. "Meet me over there."

I crawled down the outside ladder. He waited for me next to a large drum that once rolled up the empty nets. He had a scruffy beard and longish hair. He leaned against a bulkhead, looking more like an undercover cop on the waterfront than a captain.

He said, "We called Admiral Wilkes."

"You mean, Vice President Wilkes?"

"Sorry. We sailor-types prefer her old title before her slide into the dark profession."

"You heard me, then." I gave him a once-over because I was impressed. "You are listening to every word Falconer says."

"My mission is not in question here. Yours is. What's this about?"

"Classified. Like your mission. But our two missions have become entangled. I need you to stand down for seventy-two hours."

"No can do." He crossed his arms.

"Get Wilkes back on the line."

"She doesn't have anything to do with my chain of command. She said you've gone off the reservation, you're on the lam. She told me to make an arrest."

I regarded him for a minute. There was something about him that struck me as odd. The CIA does some clandestine stuff, often way out of the ordinary, but a ship-based listening post they would've left to the Navy. This guy looked CIA. And that was being generous. Something about him was off. As if maybe he'd been CIA once but got kicked out for snatching purses in the parking lot at Langley. And there was another problem. The VP hadn't liked me since I started dating her daughter. But I saved her life once and she wouldn't forget that. She would've told this guy to accommodate me, not arrest me.

It took me a couple seconds to realize who they were and why they were there. Which gave me a little leverage with Falconer. But there was no sense negotiating anything with these guys. They had no value to me.

I stabbed a dart in his thigh. He dropped to the deck. When he fell, the pistol in his hand clattered across the steel surface. I picked it up and checked it: serial number filed off. He had an ankle pistol and a nasty looking knife. I've never figured out why people like ankle-holsters. Any halfway decent pat-down is going to reveal it. And if you need it in the middle of a firefight, what're you going to do, call time-out so you can kneel down and fish it out? Dumb. My philosophy: Take one weapon, use it well.

I peered around the corner and listened. There were two more on duty. One guy was in the day room. The other was on the forecastle deck. The sleeping quarters lay between the two men.

I walked into the dayroom where the man on duty watched the waves with outdated night-vision binoculars. They were big and bulky and heavy. He pulled a radio to his face and said, "Zodiac, half a mile south by southeast."

"Roger," the answer squawked. "Headed this way?"

All he said was, "Ack—"

I regretted not darting him a split second earlier because that "ack" must've alerted the other guy. Moving into the sleeping quarters, I counted four bunks but only two heads. Skinny crew. I darted them in their sleep. Hardly sporting, but they took the assignment. They knew it came with hazards.

Kneeling next to the dayroom door, I pulled a chair close to me for cover.

The last man squawked on the radio, calling out his shipmates' codenames and getting no replies. I waited patiently.

His boots pounded around the deck outside until he found the captain. Then he went into stealth mode. He crept past the dayroom door and checked the sleeping quarters. He'd figured out there was only one room left onboard where I could hide.

When he came from there, he would enter through a different door and see me before I could attack. If he had his pistol drawn, I could die instantly. I considered moving. The sea was calm and the night was quiet. There was a generator running below decks. But all it would take was one squeak of a shoe on the steel deck and I was done. I had to move.

I grabbed the metal leg of the chair and raised it off the floor to prevent it scratching when I shifted positions. I rose, anticipating facing him. He wasn't there.

I glanced around the room, the chair still in hand, and spotted him outside.

He raised a rifle out to sea and fired five rounds in rapid succession. He paused. Then he must've gotten a bead on Mardik and Firas in the Zodiac because he planted his feet and timed the swells for a more stable shot.

Bolting the hatch, I threw the chair at him. The hit stunned him long enough for me to leap on him and dart him.

Which left me with a ghost ship.

I signaled my Syrians to come in and pick me up, then ran from room to room, killing all the lights and shutting everything down. I think I dropped anchor. It seemed like the right button to press. Something big and heavy splashed into the sea. I made my way to the engine room, found a toolbox, and used the tools to smash the fuel line. They weren't going anywhere.

I made my way topside. Mardik and Firas held the Zodiac against the hull while I jumped in. We sped off across the waves.

Mercury floated out of the night sky and sat next to me. *What's wrong with you, homes? Here you are killing more innocent foot soldiers. I don't know if you're cut out for the Caesar-life after all. I'm seeing a whole new dark side of you and it ain't pretty.*

I said, *I darted those guys.*

Oh, is that how you're wanna play it? Mercury looked disgusted. *Your boys here planted explosives on the hull. They be pissed about getting shot at. If you're gonna lead, you gotta take full responsibility for your people.*

Behind me, a fireball lit up the sky a split second before the concussion wave slammed us hard.

CHAPTER 57

PIA SAT AT THE TABLE flanked by Tania and Miguel, her specialists on the contract. She nodded at Secretary of State Lincoln Coulter when he entered the Truman Building's meeting room. He tipped an imaginary hat her way and took the seat at the head. Reggie Forrest followed in his wake and took the seat next to the Secretary. Forrest brought five people with her, all of whom left an empty chair between themselves and Forrest. Pia nodded at Eva, who returned a minimalist acknowledgement.

Pia figured it must be hard for Eva, Bradley, and Ryan to keep quiet at this stage. They knew the enemy but couldn't say anything yet. The Whistleblower program took time to filter through channels and complete the required research.

"A few hours ago," Forrest said without preamble, "a former employee of Sabel Security led an attack on a CIA vessel off the coast of Odessa in the Black Sea. Is he part of your operation?"

"If you're referring to Jacob Stearne, he is not." Pia reminded herself to be patient. "I've told you this before. I have no communication with him, nor do I have any idea what he's doing."

"I think you're working with him to steal Alvaria. Corporate espionage."

"Do you have a shred of evidence to back up your bullshit?" Pia asked.

Secretary Coulter frowned and patted the air in front of him. "Let's keep this civil, Pia."

"She just made a baseless allegation." She tried and failed to look chastised. "I thought we were done with that crap after the last administration."

Coulter shook his head and nodded at Forrest to continue.

"The State Department engaged you to locate and retrieve the Alvaria system." Forrest sniffed with attitude. "To date, all of your updates have contained little substance and no progress. What do you have to report today?"

"Nothing new. As I've explained in the past, our sources and methods—"

"It's been a month, Ms. Sabel," Forrest snapped. "Your sources and methods mean nothing to me. We're talking about leaving the most advanced weapons system in the world compromised. It's out there somewhere—anyone could find it. And you've done nothing. Have your people cracked the bidder's list?"

All eyes at the table turned to Pia. She felt the heat of the question as much as she felt her company's lack of progress on that front. In her peripheral vision, she could sense Miguel sitting ramrod straight, eyes forward, giving away nothing about his team's work.

Pia said, "We do not have a contract to retrieve the bidders list."

Forrest shuffled through her papers. "Oh, yes, I see. Terminated by the CIA for lack of progress." Forrest flicked a glance at Secretary Coulter. "We may come to that decision as well."

Coulter eyed his Assistant Secretary with suspicion. "We have not yet, Reggie. Continue."

Forrest said, "Have you made any attempt to recover the Alvaria system?"

"Yes." Pia hesitated. "And no."

"What the hell is that supposed to mean?" Coulter asked. "Pia, I know President Williams is a friend of yours. I know he relies on your counsel from time to time, but that doesn't entitle you to a free pass at the expense of national security. I'll call the president myself and update him after this meeting. I doubt he'll back you up when he hears you've made no progress. This is serious business, young lady. Something very dangerous has been lost and we need to know if you intend to recover it or not. Now, explain yourself."

"Without exposing sources and methods, we know the containers have been recovered. They're not in Sabel Security's possession at this time. We—"

An audible gasp from all the State Department employees interrupted Pia. The only voice that hurt her feelings came from Eva Gomez. She had not yet explained this part to her protégé. The danger was too great. Pia could feel the young woman's anger without looking at her.

Pia continued. "We have reason to believe the entire system will be recovered within a week."

"What, by magic?" Forrest asked.

Pia stayed still.

"Next topic," Forrest said. "I assigned a liaison to your organization who was tasked with communicating progress reports to me. She has learned something of your sources and methods yet refuses to give me details."

"She is protecting the lives of operatives in the field."

"Who have not done anything in a month!"

"Reggie, there's no need to shout." Coulter patted the air again. "Pia, we need something. There must be something you can tell us."

Pia sensed a minimalist nod from Miguel. She considered the ramifications. To confront Forrest with the evidence could be premature. There was one critical question about the Assistant Secretary still unanswered. Forrest may have unwittingly answered it at the beginning of the meeting, but it was far from conclusive. She would need to ferret out the truth somehow. That aside, she still owed them an answer.

Pia looked directly at Coulter. "We believe there is a mole in the CIA."

"What does that have to do with us?" Forrest asked. "We're not the CIA."

"You're sharing information with them on this project." Pia turned her coldest gaze on the Assistant Secretary of State for Political-Military Affairs.

"When we can't get information from you," Forrest snapped, "or my employee whom you've somehow subordinated, I have to get information from someone."

"Who told you Jacob Stearne attacked a CIA vessel?" Pia asked.

"I'm not at liberty to say." Forrest crossed her arms and leaned back.

Lincoln Coulter cast a curious gaze her way, then back to Pia. He said, "We do have communications with the CIA for many reasons."

"It's a Top Secret mission," Forrest offered. "I'm not at liberty to discuss it."

"Is it your official position that you are read into a CIA black op focusing on Jacob Stearne?" Pia asked.

When Forrest nodded without speaking out loud, Pia leaned back and gave Miguel a nod.

Miguel leaned forward, holding his phone out. "Begging your pardon, ma'am. After you mentioned the attack, I texted Director Bergstrom. She checked. There are no CIA ops in the Black Sea. Further, she mentioned the CIA mothballed all SIGINT and ELINT ships decades ago. There are a few in that area for training purposes. None are deployed, either for covert ops or training purposes."

He slid his phone, open to the text thread, to Coulter.

All eyes turned to Forrest while Coulter read the text thread. He offered the phone to Forrest. She shook her head. He slid the phone back to Miguel.

Pia faced Forrest. "Why did you ask for all the intel on the arms dealer they call Ra on your last visit to Interpol?"

Forrest choked, then composed herself. "That was official business."

"The personnel there didn't think so."

Coulter turned to Forrest with a quizzical frown.

"We're losing sight of the meeting agenda." Forrest kept her gaze focused on her stack of papers for a long time. Then she drew a deep breath. "This isn't about me. This is about Sabel Security and their non-performance. Due to a lack of progress, we need to terminate this contract and hire someone else. Someone responsive—" she narrowed her eyes at Pia "—and competent."

No one spoke for several long agonizing seconds.

Secretary Coulter took in a long, loud, and attention-grabbing inhale. "I will talk to Bergstrom about this incident, Pia. I'm sure there's an explanation for it that doesn't fit in a text thread. On the topic of non-performance, we would be starting over. A great deal of time would be lost bringing someone else up to speed. That would be costly for us in many ways."

He looked around the room at his people, taking their pulse and measuring their mood. After another dramatic inhale, he said, "Pia, you said you would have the system back in a week?"

"Yes."

"You can't string us along on something this important. It's too dangerous." He sighed. "I'll give you until the end of the week to recover it. That's four days."

CHAPTER 58

FALCONER SLIPPED HIS ARMS AROUND Yumi Shibata's waist from behind. He snuggled her robe-clad body close to his and inhaled her perfume. Together, they stared out of the *Savannah's* master suite windows. Holding her reminded him of how much he truly loved this woman. He understood that deep in his soul. She inspired him. Her humility, her quiet soul, her disinterest in the fleeting happiness of money. Yumi's life was centered on the people she loved. And she loved him like no one before.

While nestling his cheek against the top of her head, he imagined their future travels together. As soon as this deal was done, he was gone. No more dealing with people and their fickle loyalties and their mutinous intrigues. No more Jacob Stearnes or Ross Bonhams or Konrad von Friedens. No, he would relax, enjoy the world, hold his girl the way he held her now. He would never let her go. They would do everything together. A private tour of the Vatican. Strolling through the Forest of Knives in Madagascar. Stargazing into the clearest skies in the world from Pisco Elqui, Chile. Visiting the Roman ruins in Timgad, Algeria. Who better to share it with than Yumi?

"What are you thinking, darling?" he whispered.

"Why we have prisoners." Her voice was cold, her body stiff.

"My dear, don't worry about the little things. In a matter of days, I will rid myself of this nasty business. It all goes to Bonham. Then we do nothing but travel, as I promised."

She tensed noticeably when he said Bonham's name. That surprised him. She hated Bonham and his misogynistic ways. Or did she? Perhaps she pretended to hate him. Didn't women like bad boys? Weren't romance novels filled with men who took what they wanted in a manner that would be considered assault in real life? Was darling Yumi one of those conflicted women who loved and hated Bonham's behavior?

"What bothers you, darling?" he asked. "You don't like Bonham?"

"Two people are kept in their staterooms with hands and feet bound. Why is this? What are you doing?"

"Business is full of bad characters. Sometimes we need to instill discipline in our partners." He turned her to face him. "They threaten our existence. Threatening me threatens your mother's aid. We have all this, the yacht, the jets, the estates—and these people put it at risk. That's why they're bound up."

She pulled out of his hands and stormed off to the kitchenette. He followed her. He couldn't stand it when she was mad at him. When she adored him, everything was right with the world. It broke his heart to see her angry.

"A few more days," he said. "Then, Angor Wat, as promised. Just the two of us. No Bonham. No dogs."

She ground coffee beans and poured them into a filter. "This is not right. This is criminal behavior. I am detective in Tokyo. I know what you are doing. I've had enough. I cannot stand by any longer."

"Perhaps we should see a doctor. Get a prescription to keep your emotions in check for these last stressful days."

She shot him a nasty glance, put the grounds in the coffee machine, then filled the pot with filtered water.

"Darling, have the staff make coffee."

She glared at him. "Easier to make than call someone."

He scratched his head and stared out the windows. "Must be this dreary weather has you in such a foul mood. Tell you what—after Angor Wat, we'll go to Ratua in Vanuatu for a few days. Get our fill of sun and beach."

She poured in the water and pushed past him. "Let those people go."

Falconer hated it when people told him what to do. It made him boil with anger. Who did they think they were, his equal? Anyone else would've been excoriated for such a challenge. He simply never allowed it. Was he seeing a new side of humble, obedient Yumi?

He shook his head to clear it. Maybe he misunderstood her. He followed her into the bedroom, where she finished dressing in stretchy athletic leggings and top. They drove him wild with desire. She knew that. He squinted at her as she pulled an outer layer over her top. She was doing it on purpose, distracting him to keep him from realizing the importance of her challenge.

"Criminal behavior," he said quietly, "is what keeps your mother in a decent nursing home. She receives valuable care in exchange for a few unpleasant situations. These are the transactions that fund our life. Never forget that."

He rushed across the room and grabbed her. She looked up at him with frightened eyes. Just like every other woman had. It always came down to the same thing in the end. A woman could be nice and pleasing for a while but eventually she wanted out of her contract. She stopped wanting to put out, but she never stopped wanting to receive her bounty. Whether it was a shopping trip in Monaco or a dementia ward in Tokyo, it was always the same.

"I don't," she snapped at him. "My mother is why I stay."

"Don't you dare say that!" he shouted. "You're just saying that to make me angry. Don't test me, little girl. Don't test my anger. You love me. You know you do."

"What happened to the man who brought me flowers?" she cried. "Where is the man who respected me?"

"I'm right here and it's time you showed me a little respect, damn it. Why should I keep paying for the old woman if you won't deliver your half of the transaction? If you value the elder care I provide, you owe me your love and devotion."

She struggled to free herself from his grip. "I hate you."

Rage erupted from his heart. His brain clouded with red heat. He shook her and threw her on the bed where she belonged. He jumped on top of her, his knees pinning her arms to her side.

"Take those clothes off." He tore the shirt from her chest. "Take that off right now. It's time you did what you do best."

CHAPTER 59

I FOUND A NEW RESPECT for Captain Rafia. He had the *Detit Fatma* anchored half a mile from Falconer's *Savannah* by the time I woke up. Overnight he'd had his smartest guys look at the fire suppression system. They came up with some ideas for unplugging Falconer's remote control unit. Unfortunately, they were all too risky for Rafia's taste. The basic problem remained: without proper testing and hazmat suits, the first man to go in could die if their calculations were wrong. And worse, they could all die if the wind changed direction.

Falconer's threat still hung over me and my crew. But I slept through all of that. Midnight raids demand plenty of beauty rest the next day.

Which didn't work out as well as I'd hoped. Falconer called my phone so many times I finally answered it. Sleepy voice and all. He demanded a face-to-face meeting. He didn't sound happy.

Mardik piloted the Zodiac across the gentle waves. We chatted about how killing people who shot at us was not always the best solution to our problems. In the end, we agreed to disagree. Cultural differences. Clouds began leaving the region without taking the haze with them. Mardik dropped me at the *Savannah*, then moved off, out of pistol range as I'd instructed.

A humorless steward led me to the main deck. Bonham and Falconer lounged under the upper deck, saving them from the occasional drizzle. They reclined on cushioned chairs wearing sweats and coats. Fido patted me down. When I passed his inspection, I approached the pair of arms-dealing overlords.

Mercury marched alongside me. *There it be, homie. The phone.*

He pointed at the little table between the two deck chairs. Two cups of coffee sat on either side of one shiny phone. It lay closer to Falconer than Bonham, indicating it was the phone with all the contacts on it.

Mercury said, *That's what we came for. Grab that, kill everyone on board, call the people on the list, and tell them there's a new dawg in town. Hey, you like that? See what I did there? New dawg. Get it?*

I said, *I got it. Wasn't funny. But you're overlooking the problem. I don't have his code. Back when I had Sabel Tech behind me, I could get them to unlock it. Now, I need the code.*

Mercury said, *Yeah, your girlfriend has it. And she has some bruises.*

I took in the hazy sky as a way of looking up without being obvious. Two decks above us, Yumi watched me from a perch only I could see. As soon as our gazes met, she gave me the thumb-up again, this time with sad eyes. Her wrist was bruised. So was her neck. She backed out of sight.

"You lied to us," Falconer said. "You planted those pistols on Bonham."

"How did I do that?"

"Don't play the sophist with me. I don't care if it was you or one of your crew. You killed Spot and you planted the pistols where his dogs would find them."

I shrugged. "Bonham never filed a missing-persons—"

"Drop the bullshit," Falconer said. "Just answer me one simple question. Why would Bonham kill Spot?"

"Beats me," I shrugged. "Was he using his teeth when giving blow jobs?"

"I don't give a damn about Spot or his tragic end." Falconer leapt to his feet and stuck his face in mine. "The biggest deal of the century is going down this week. Everything I own is on the line. I don't need your sophomoric jokes. I'm moving forward now—at warp speed. I need someone I can trust. Someone I can rely on to get the job done. I'm willing to pay handsomely for the best operator in the world. Do you have what it takes, Stearne?"

"Yes, sir." I hadn't been berated like that since I left the US Army. I nearly saluted. "That's why I took out the trawler for you."

"True." He circled me in a way I found unnerving. "That was quite a display you put on last night. We saw it from here. But taking on the CIA was not wise."

"Done it before, do it again. No big deal. They're a bunch of pansies."

He stroked his chin while he regarded me with a hint of disdain. "We still have that little problem between us—you killed Spot."

He let that accusation hang in the air and went back to his chair. He sat and picked up his coffee and sipped and smacked his lips and looked satisfied. Then he looked up at me. "I need to trust you and yet you've lied and murdered without owning up to it. How do I redeem you, Jacob?"

My eyes drifted to his phone. I could snatch it, dive overboard, hope to scramble back in the Zodiac and fly away over the waves before Rover and Fido could shoot me. A plan with a minimal survival rate. Especially since Zodiacs are big balloons easily deflated by 9mm bullets. And Yumi might have the code, but she hadn't told me yet.

I had to string him along and come up with a better plan. With rich guys, knuckling under and doing what they asked never won them over. Standing up to them in a respectful manner usually offered better results.

"I'm not a dog walker. You never mentioned protecting your pets as part of the deal. Something happens to them, take it up with your security team." I gave Bonham a sneer. He let it roll off. "You asked me to pull up containers. I did that. You asked me to bring them to the Black Sea. I did that. You asked me to prove the product is the real deal. I'm working on that. Your part of the bargain was $5 million or 20 percent of the auction, whichever was bigger. Quit worrying about 'redeeming' me. The real question is, will you live up to your part of the bargain?"

He stared at me with an unreadable expression for a long time. He sipped his coffee without taking his eyes off me. Bonham didn't move. In fact, he hadn't moved since I arrived. I began to wonder if his dogs had killed him and propped his mummified body in the chair.

Falconer finished his coffee with a slurp. Then he said, "No business deal goes well unless both sides stick to the whole and unvarnished truth at all times. I tolerate nothing short of that perfection." He waved his hands vaguely at his yacht. "It's the secret to my success. You and I cannot survive on lies and half-truths, Jacob. We must ground our operations in empiricism which leads us to realism—and that will lead us to success. Without a firm, proven grip on the reality we confront, we can only lose. Don't you agree?"

I had a bad feeling about his question. "Sure."

Falconer snapped his fingers. Out of the dark shadows behind him came Rover, pushing Konrad von Frieden in front of him. Konrad was bound at the wrists, shackled at the ankles, gagged, pale-white, and looked to have a fever and an infection. No doubt a dip in the Mediterranean was not the best thing for a man missing an ear.

"Realistically," Falconer said, "would you say you did everything you promised me?"

Mercury jumped in front of me. *OK, now's a good time to grab the phone and dive off the side. I calculated the odds. Your chances are nine million to one.*

I said, *Chances of what? Survival?*

Oh hell no, Mercury said. *Dying. But you do have that slim chance of making it. You stand here, I don't think you're going to live very long. That Falconer-dude does not look happy, not to mention Fido and Rover have their weapons out and are itching to pull the trigger.*

I said, *If I die, will anyone remember the Dii Consentes?*

Mercury deflated. *Yeah, uhm, no.*

I said, *What are the other options?*

Mercury started to shake his head.

I said, *What did Quintus Fabius Maximus Verrucosus do when he faced a superior force?*

Mercury smiled. *Did you really read up on the man who invented guerilla warfare? Homie, strike me down but I am impressed. Why, he would delay the battle. That's why they called him Cunctator, delayer. I cannot believe you invoked his name. You know, he defeated Hannibal by attacking supply lines. He only fought skirmishes and retreated to stretch the enemy lines, then he attacked from the sides. But, none of that does you any good. What you need to do is the guilty-wife-defense.*

I said, *The what?*

Mercury said, *When confronted with proof she's having an affair, the guilty wife denies everything and instigates counter allegations. He* raised his voice an octave. *I never went anywhere with Mike. But what's this I hear about Kayla? Everyone in town is talking about you two. How long have you been sleeping with her?*

I rolled my eyes at Falconer. "Did you really think I was going to kill a man just because you asked me to? Do I look stupid? What fool would do a thing like … Oh. Sorry, Bonham. From that glum look I'm guessing you fell for that one. Anyway, Konrad never did anything to me personally. I've got no beef with him. You're missing the real problem here."

"You had a beef with Spot, then?" Bonham jumped up, fists clenched. As if he could land a punch.

"Yes, as a matter of fact. He killed a friend of mine named Nate Hale." I turned my gaze to Falconer. "He said you ordered him to. I'll kill you for that later, after this deal is done." I enjoyed the look of shock on his face. "The only reason you didn't shoot me when I got out of the tender is because you need me. You can't pull this operation off without me. You know it. I know it. And now your dumb dogs know it. But again, I'm telling you, you're missing your real problem."

Everyone stood stock still on the deck. The breeze ruffled our jackets. The waves swelled under the yacht. The flag on deck three fluttered.

Finally, Falconer took the bait. "OK, fine, what is the real problem, sport?"

"That wasn't a CIA ship."

CHAPTER 60

FALCONER STOOD AND GAZED OVER the featureless horizon populated only by a large blue ship. "Oh? Pray tell, who was sneaking around on that trawler?"

"They worked for your partner inside the US government."

Falconer eyed me with what looked like a mixture of suspicion and concern. "How did you arrive at that conclusion?"

"They were not the kind of men the government keeps on the payroll. Let's just say they were less-than-professional. That and the equipment onboard dated to long before my time. The ship had been mothballed ages ago and stolen for this mission."

And, there was a good chance they were the same people who tailed me in Athens. But I didn't bring that up.

"If I had partners, why would they want to spy on me?" Falconer asked.

"Honor among thieves ain't what it used to be," I said. "Could be a couple explanations. The optimistic view would be they wanted to make sure you held up your end of the bargain. The cynical view would have them standing by to kill you and take over the show as soon as I delivered the goods. Since they were armed to the teeth, and asked questions about delivery, I took the precaution of eliminating that cynical probability."

Bonham scoffed. "He's just trying to change the subject."

"He's done it quite well," Falconer said. "I appreciate your solution to the potential problem, Jacob. That shows initiative and genuine concern for our partnership."

"You're not letting him get away with this," Bonham protested. He looked like a boy whining about fairness. "He killed one of our men."

"Indeed. But as he pointed out, he had a score to settle. We'll let that go because he was right about the other part. We do indeed need his expertise. Let's explain it to him now, shall we Bonham?"

At that, Bonham caught Fido's eye and the two of them left. In their absence, the forgotten hostage, Konrad checked left and right, hoping for an escape. Rover pressed his pistol barrel in Konrad's cheek and forced him to face front again.

"We have a problem," Falconer said. He grabbed some nuts from a small dish without offering me any and popped one into his mouth. "When I told you we need to authenticate the system, we actually need to demonstrate that it works."

I stood still. Good things come to those who wait.

Falconer went on. "Before you get any ideas about killing me with my own weapons, I've been told the system ships with non-lethal paper bullets. The real ammunition ships separately."

"Standard procedure," I said. "If the tank's ammo accidentally goes off, you don't destroy the tank as well."

"I'm told they sent targets that can be destroyed by these paper bullets."

I said, "OK."

Falconer moved in close for a confidential murmur. "I doubt Bonham could figure out the instructions for what's in those containers. They're written in army-speak and—"

"And they take a certain amount of intelligence gleaned from years of figuring out the latest army gear, radios, night vision, shoulder-fired missiles, that kind of thing. I get that. I know you're hoping to kill me before you have to pay me. And I'm planning to survive. So, we'll leave that contest for after the auction. Let's just get this deal done. I want my money."

"That's what I love about you, Jacob," Falconer said and slapped me on the shoulder. "Balls of steel. You want your money. I want my money. The customers want a functioning system. Indeed, let's get it done."

Yumi had appeared on the second deck above me earlier. Falconer stood under it and hadn't seen her. In my peripheral vision, I noticed something on that balcony flapping. I glanced around the decks and sea to get a good look at it without drawing attention. The flag flying from a mast on the third deck's outer wall snapped in the light breeze. Below that, three pieces of paper had been wetted and stuck to the outside of the second deck's outer wall. A place where only I could see them. Handwritten on each one was a large two-digit number, 26, 15, 93.

Falconer snapped his fingers. A steward appeared. He said, "Orange juice."

"I'll have one too, please—and thank you."

He observed me for a long moment after the steward trotted away. He pursed his lips and looked out to sea.

"The better the demo, the bigger the bids," he growled. "They have to want it. They have to be willing to kill each other for it right then and there."

"I'll get the demo working," I said. "Don't worry your pretty little head about it, Falconer."

He tilted his head, forming a question. "You said the trawler was CIA, had an American radar mast. But it wasn't CIA?"

"Not officially. It hadn't sailed in years. They don't use ships anymore, it's all satellites. Those guys weren't feds or Euro-cops, they were mercenaries looking to jump your auction."

This time his face showed the concern. He crossed his arms and looked out to sea. "You're sure they were American?"

"From their terrible fashion sense to their New England accents."

"That is a problem." He kept his gaze focused on the gray horizon. "Thank you for taking care of it. I doubt Bonham would've been so prescient."

I glanced up at the second deck. She was watching me. Yumi's sad gaze met mine. I couldn't tell from the distance, but I thought she had tears in her eyes. She peeled the papers off the deck's outer wall and disappeared again. Falconer's phone code. I glanced at the table. The phone was gone. He'd pocketed it at some point.

The steward returned holding a silver tray with two glasses of OJ on it. He offered one to Falconer first, then me. We clinked glasses as if toasting.

I said, "Whoever financed the trawler had deep pockets. Are they still a threat?"

"The downside to being successful." He sighed then scowled. "Everyone wants to drag you down. Even you threatened me. Or did you think I didn't notice? You were wrong. I hadn't planned to kill you." His voice lowered to an angry snarl. "But now that you've threatened to avenge your friend, you're in danger."

"I've lived with danger for a long time," I said. Since we were being honest with each other, I didn't see any reason to hold back. "I'm glad I don't have to face your sadness."

He frowned. "What sadness do I face?"

"You're alone. No one loves you. They love only what you give them when you give it. When the giving is over, so is the adoration. It's a pyrrhic victory that aged your face. I doubt Yumi loves you for anything more than her mother's welfare."

"Fuck you." He took a swing at me.

I grabbed his wrist. "Don't fuck with me. Just hold up your end of the deal. Bring the bidders and hold that auction. I want my money."

He wrenched out of my grip. "Bonham isn't the fool you take him for, you know. He insists we have insurance on everyone we do business with. We like to make sure we get every ounce of attention out of our business partners." He turned to the shadows under the deck. "Bonham, bring Jacob his ounce of humility, will you?"

Bonham strode out with a smug grin. Behind him Fido pushed a woman out of the dark recesses.

She came into view, bound, shackled, and gagged just like Konrad.

Jenny Jenkins.

CHAPTER 61

JENNY SHOWED NO EMOTION. SHE didn't flinch. She didn't cry. She didn't fold. She remained proud and held my gaze with unwavering courage. I knew what she was thinking. The helipad was a short walk from the terminal. They'd tricked her along the way, probably a plea for help. She knew she should've been more wary. But she was here, a pawn in a game she didn't fully understand. She took responsibility for her lapse in judgement. She didn't blame me.

I did. I should've forced her out the minute she arrived. Sure, she would've hated me for not allowing her a chance to work again. For treating her like a child. Back then, she'd had no clue about Falconer or the depths of his evil. And I did.

"Ah, I see we've finally dispatched that damned insolent attitude of yours," Falconer said. He turned to Bonham. "From the look of him, I'd say you were right. He is in love with this girl."

"Let her go," I said. "Take me in her place."

"You're a terrible negotiator," Falconer said. "I already have you in her place. I have both of you in your places. You little shit."

"What do you want?" I ran escapes through my mind in a frantic search for a way out of Falconer's vice.

Falconer stuck his aging, sun-dried face in mine with a nasty glare. "It's not about what I want, sport. It's about what you will do." His voice dropped to a mean-spirited growl. "You will stop lying to me. You will stop threatening my men. You will stop acting like my equal. You will prostrate yourself when I enter the room. You will kill whom I tell you to kill. You will do everything I tell you. Including—"

He stepped back an arm's length and let out an angry breath. He tracked around the back of Jenny. He took a 9-mil from Fido and pressed it to her cheek.

My heart pounded as I dreamed up ways to get out of this nightmare. There had to be something I could do. My eyes swept the decks, the dogs, the weapons. Falconer grinned as he watched me. He knew what I came to understand. I was out of luck.

Jenny stood still, ready to accept her fate. The finest of naval officers. Pride and courage to the end.

Three decks above me, someone hauled the ship's flag in.

Falconer caressed her face with the muzzle. "—killing Konrad."

Jenny shook her head, no. Like any good officer, she would never allow herself to live while someone else was sacrificed in her place.

Konrad von Frieden had no such dedication to protecting others. His eyes bulged with fear. If the tables were turned, he would gladly let Jenny die in his place.

I kept my cool but could see no way out of his sick game of loyalty.

"I don't doubt he deserves it." I shrugged as if none of this mattered to me. "He did sell rifles to mass shooters. Why not have Bonham do it? Insurance in case he was the guy behind that trawler. Whatever you do, don't ask me. If I take a life today, it'll be yours."

On that third deck, a white rope hung from the flagpole. A hand reached out to the loose end and hauled it back in. It was knotted in a hangman's noose.

"Quit screwing around," Bonham said. "Kill all three of them. I can do the demo. It can't be that hard."

Falconer's faith in his lieutenant showed in his disdainful glare.

"ROSS!" Yumi's voice called from above.

I looked up. Yumi teetered on the third deck's railing. She wore a cream silk teddy. Bruises covered her wrists and legs. A white noose hung firmly around her neck.

"ROSS!" she called again.

"What the hell?" Bonham ran out from under the decks, stood next to me, looked up, and muttered, "Nobody calls me by my given name."

"No! Yumi! Don't do it!" I yelled.

Hearing the strain in my voice, Falconer joined us in a rush and looked up.

"I can't go on living without you, Ross." Yumi wobbled on the railing. "You promised to take me away. You promised to get rid of those other girls. You promised to get me out of here, away from him."

She jumped.

Her body fell, the line snapped taught, the noose tightened, her head canted at an impossible angle. Her body swung back and forth from the flagpole. A broken neck. Instant death.

I stood frozen in disbelief while her body swayed back and forth. Sickness rose in my gut.

Falconer let out a shriek of pain and horror and anguish. He fell to his knees and threw up.

Bonham and his dogs raced to the stairs.

I tried to parse her words. She would never have an affair with Bonham. She had asked me to save her from Falconer. Had she given up and asked Bonham? He would've reported her. Why did she take her life?

To my right, Falconer retched again. He sobbed and heaved in personal agony.

I looked around the empty deck. Then I realized why she'd done it. She knew she would never get away from her evil overlord. She understood my predicament and bought time so Jenny and I could get away. Giving her life that others might live.

Guilt and regret slammed into my stomach. I couldn't breathe.

I ran to Jenny, ripped the gag out of her mouth and flailed at her wrists. The knots were too tight. It would take too long. The shackles on her ankles were equally impossible. With tears for Yumi flowing down my cheeks, I bent my knees, shoved my shoulder into her belly, and stood. From his safe distance, Mardik must have sensed the urgency and powered the boat toward the *Savannah* at full throttle. I turned to run down the steps with Jenny on my shoulder.

Falconer shoved his pistol in my eye. "Put her down, motherfucker. No one leaves!"

I didn't move. She remained on my shoulder.

Above us, Bonham and his dogs hauled Yumi's body in.

SEELEY JAMES

"No one's going anywhere." He moved the pistol from me to the back of Jenny's head.

"You pull the trigger, it'll be the last thing you ever do," I said.

"Think I care?" he shouted through rage and tears. "I've got nothing left. This is your fault. You think you're so perfect? How come I have the yacht and the jet and the women?" He teared up. "The women. Oh, Yumi. Oh my god."

He broke into sobs.

I ran through scenarios in my head. I still had Jenny on my shoulder, which limited my fighting moves. I had one hand I could free up. I couldn't guarantee success with one backhanded blow. Which left Jenny's life in danger.

Before I could act, Falconer choked in a breath. "You son of a bitch. Let's see if you die with that fucking flippant attitude."

He aimed the barrel at me and squeezed the trigger halfway. I kept my calm eyes locked on his. Jenny didn't flinch.

"We couldn't save her." Bonham called from a few feet away.

Falconer's rage moved with his glare, from me to Bonham. He dropped the pistol and pulled a V-42 dagger from his pants pocket, opting for a much more personal method of killing the man.

When he pulled out the knife, his phone clattered to the deck.

Falconer charged at Bonham. "You traitorous piece of shit."

"No, George. No. She made that up. You know I would never—"

Falconer's knife struck Bonham's throat with a wet thwack. He chopped and slashed and hacked at Bonham.

Mardik pulled the Zodiac up to the sport deck. He waved me over.

Behind us, Falconer's stabs continued making soggy, gruesome noises.

I shifted Jenny's weight on my shoulder and looked at the phone on the deck ten feet from me. I bent down to pick it up. I lost my balance and staggered. My toe inadvertently kicked the phone. It spun across the deck and splashed into the sea.

My heart broke for Yumi. Her sacrifice saved me. Because I'd taken too long to save her.

I ran for the Zodiac and fell in with Jenny as Mardik raced us away.

DEATH AND BETRAYAL

The yacht behind us bobbed gray and lifeless in the formless sea. For all its great expense and opulence, it was nothing more than a mausoleum of vanity.

I could see Falconer stabbing his anger into Bonham's corpse. He rose from his murderous task when he realized we were getting away.

"I still own you, Stearne," he called across the sea. "I still have your life in my hands."

CHAPTER 62

JENNY CLIMBED THE *DETIT FATMA'S* rickety aluminum stairs ahead of me, protesting the whole way as she had since we got the ropes off her wrists and feet.

"I don't care," she said. "I want to stay. I can help you. Just tell me what's going on."

Mercury flew alongside me, his little brass wings flapping like a hummingbird. *Yeah, homes. Tell her the truth. Tell her you're going to be the next Caesar by making a billion off that homicidal wackjob, Falconer.*

I said, *Exactly what I don't want my future bride to know. If she'll marry me, that is. Which is doubtful.*

Mercury said, *Are you telling me all this pining and moping about you've been doing is because you think she doesn't care about you? Dude, I'm telling you, that woman has a high degree of pudicitia.*

I said, *A high degree of what?*

Mercury rolled his eyes to the skies. *Brutha, read up on the sacred language of your gods. It's Latin, it means purity, as in chastity. It was what Romans aspired to.*

I said, *How does that work when you're always talking about orgies?*

Mercury said, *Oh, orgies, now that's different. Prostitutes and slaves don't count.*

See, this is why I'm convinced I'm insane and not blessed. His conversations don't make sense at all. Ask anyone who talks to a god, they'll tell you, it ain't easy. Maybe Christians and Jews get straighter answers, but I doubt it. I tuned him out.

I chased Jenny up the long stairs. "Ansi is going to take you to

Odessa—again—and this time you're getting on a plane and going back to the states."

"While you do what, Jacob?" She turned around, staring daggers into my eyes.

A thousand answers flooded my brain, from the outright truth to downright lies. I could tell her I'm about to open the world's biggest nightmare of a weapon and sell it to god-knows-who for a billion in wheat or oil. Or, I could tell her I'm bringing unicorns to the sick children of fantasyland. No story I could come up with would work.

Mardik was following us and bumped into me when we stopped. A quick glance at him told me he wanted the pretty lady to stick around. Not that he would make a move on my girl, but any guy on a ship full of men would appreciate the presence of a woman. He sensed I'd read his mind. He shrugged.

"I have a lot of work to do," I said. "And no time to explain it. It's going to be dangerous."

"I was a naval officer. I know danger."

"Can we talk about it when we get on deck?" I looked down.

Sea stairs on the sides of freighters are not like the heavy oak staircase in my ancestral farmhouse. They're thin, cheap, and sway up and down with the waves on rare occasions when the ship has small-craft visitors. The stairs were meant to be lowered onto a stable wharf.

She turned around and marched up double time. When we reached the deck, she gave Mardik a glance that made him scurry away while she stepped into my forward path.

"Thanks, Mardik. You're the best!" I called after him.

Jenny kept her scowl on me. "I don't know what's in those containers, but I already bet my life to help you with them."

That was true. I'd planned to put the whole thing together by myself because, while I trusted my crew as far as I could throw them, they were heavy and didn't fly far. That and the fact it was a secret weapon fewer than a hundred people knew existed. How would she react when she found out what was really going on?

"I'm not getting on that chopper." She pressed her breasts lightly to my chest. An act she knew would have me eating out of the palm of her

344

hand in a second. Plus, she meant it.

"You never even went to the terminal?" I asked.

"I thought I was being clever. My plan was to rent a boat and come back out here, follow you around if you wouldn't let me back onboard. But Bonham caught me."

"And Fido will too, if you give him a second chance."

"We'll fight them off together." Her hands slid around my waist.

My body warmed in the damp chill. She knew how to soften me up. One thing was clear: she wasn't going home. Which meant she'd be safer on the ship. Sarin gas and all.

Mercury squeezed Jenny from the other side as if we were in a three-way again. *That's right, dawg. Your woman will be safe on a ship in the middle of the sea with fourteen lonely men while you work all by yourself in that cold, dark hold for hours on—*

I said, *OK, OK. I get it.*

Jenny said, "You do?"

I realized my arms had slipped around Jenny's waist. I was holding her tight against me. How did that happen?

"You're right," I said, "we're in this together. You can't ask any questions, though. And I have to warn you … you're not going to like what you find."

CHAPTER 63

JENNY AND I WENT BELOW deck into the hold. I flipped on the lights. The crates were large and laid out for easy access. Two long tables and a tool chest were set up at one end. I found a crowbar and started opening the crates. Jenny worked behind me, looking for instruction manuals after I pried each lid off. We found two big binders. No markings, no insignia, no logo, nothing to identify who owned, designed, or built the contents of the boxes.

Next, we laid out all the parts. There were launch racks, refueling systems, and the long tubular drones that made up Alvaria's "autonomous drone swarm." There were exactly one hundred of them, each five feet long, made of carbon fiber and light as a feather.

I mansplained them to Jenny. "They use collective processing to produce artificial intelligence. They target based on facial recognition and draw on any known data on the subject. Each one can destroy a hundred cubic feet, everyone inside a Toyota Camry. They have a range of two hundred miles, and once launched, they're completely autonomous."

"Remote assassination," she said without the shock I expected.

We set the launch racks on the hydraulic floor that could be raised to deck level. We loaded the paper bullets into the drones. They were firm enough for show but not as firm as rubber bullets. We fit the drones into the launch racks. Each rail had an automatically seated fuel and electronics connection. When we loaded the last one, we stepped back to admire our work. Instead of being awestruck, we were shocked. It was a terrifying array. Ten racks with ten drones each, aiming upward at a 45°angle. Collectively, they looked ready to start Armageddon.

I'd been around M142 rocket launchers in the Army. They're huge trucks, twenty-three feet long, weighing eighteen tons, carrying six rockets each. They look heavy, unwieldy, and massive. They can fire missiles with a similar range and would destroy the whole Toyota, not just the contents. But they were easier to shoot down because they're big. If they missed, no one would know until the next surveillance satellite took a picture.

What Alvaria lacked in explosive power, it made up for in numbers, range, speed, and deployment. And autonomy. Once launched, Alvaria wouldn't quit until the target had been annihilated.

It took Jenny and me a little over thirty minutes to rack the first one hundred drones. And Alvaria could be recovered, reloaded, and sent back out to kill again in little more than an hour or two.

True to her word, Jenny never asked any questions. A fact I found strange as the magnitude of the system began to reveal itself.

She figured out the fueling process while I read the operations manual. It was long and full of features. Alvaria could be programmed on the fly. One frightening option: you could take a picture of someone or something with the included tablet and identify that person or thing as a target. Instructions, targets, and general locations could be updated in real time. The operator needed only to give general coordinates within a mile of open land or an acre of dense city, and the system would find the poor bastard. It would hunt him down, destroying anything that tried to defend him in the process. The numbers could be used to concentrate firepower on a single, hardened target, like a bunker or a tank. Or, they could be dispersed to target a hundred individual leaders at a May Day parade, editors in a newsroom, or the leaders of a civilian protest march. High-density cities like Hong Kong were named in the examples, as well as remote regions like the mountains of Pakistan.

We finished up and double checked our work. Everything appeared to be in place. We had only one crate of spare parts left over. I knew the military. I knew what was in the last crate without opening it.

I sent Jenny to get lunch. While she was gone, I confirmed the crate's contents. She returned as I finished checking the manuals. She set a plate of fried chicken in front of me.

"Are you ready to fire up the software?" she asked. Her voice trembled.

I looked at her. She smiled weakly. I noted her odd reaction. As if she were waiting for the other shoe to drop.

I turned on the tablet. It booted to a screen of satiny royal blue. Then the logo came up. I couldn't believe it.

There, in big bold letters, with the familiar look and feel I'd come to know and love was the name of the company that developed the most horrific weapon in the world:

Sabel Weapons Systems, a division of Sabel Industries.

Time stopped along with my heartbeat and breathing.

Deep in my brain, I heard Ms. Sabel's voice at the Rose Garden in Lyon: *We are our own worst enemies.*

My stomach flipped. My heart raced. My blood pressure rose and crashed. My body felt like an empty vessel moving through a void. My mind went blank.

The events of the last few weeks flew through my head like a movie on fast forward. Ms. Sabel introduced me to her peers as if I were her fiancé. She introduced me to her list of suspects who might be the world's most demonic arms dealer, Ra/Falconer. She had said, *I can't risk the jobs of sixty thousand employees.* Then she dumped me in front of everyone, including the paparazzi, like an heiress would be expected to: cold and heartless. She tossed me a shipping company as "severance." She cut off all communications with me. I had been fired. An exile in a lonely world. Why?

For this?

Bewildered beyond comprehension, I looked at Jenny.

A trace of fear crossed her face. She leaned back as if I might hit her.

Another movie played at high speed. Jenny reacting to salacious photos of me with Ms. Sabel. Jenny with Stefan's voice in the background. Jenny getting a job through Bonham. She stubbornly refused to go home. Not once, but twice. When I shipped her off, she tried to come back.

"You knew." I stared at her.

Her mouth opened and shut. Her lips trembled. She touched my arm. I flinched. She looked at her hands.

We sat in silence for a long time. My mind was blank.

Finally, she said, "Pia planted the headlines to help build your legend, not to make us jealous of each other. We should've realized the gossip headlines are always about her, not you and me. Neither of us stopped to think about that. Pia realized I was ticked off and invited me over when she got back from Davos. I refused. I didn't want to talk to her. So, she had Stefan invite me to his house. I didn't know him all that well, so I counter-invited him to mine. He came. Pia came with him. It was a ruse. She explained everything."

Another voice from the recent past echoed in my ear. This time it was Jenny saying, *I'm qualified and I'm ready to get back to work.* She took the job to help me.

Mercury rested his grinning head on top of Jenny's. *Easy now, homes. I know this looks bad.*

I said, *Ya think? What the hell is going on here?*

Mercury said, *Pia-Caesar-Sabel works in mysterious ways, bro. What can I say? You gotta think this through, because getting stepped on by a Caesar is an incredible honor for a little Mymaridae like you.*

I said, *What the Vulcan happened to making me into a Caesar? And what in Cere's name is a Mymaridae?*

Mercury said, *The smallest known insects, commonly known as fairyflies.*

I said, *And?*

Mercury said, *And what?*

I said, *And what the fuck happened to turning me into a Caesar?*

Mercury looked hurt. *Language. Please, there's a lady present.*

I said, *Since when did that—*

Mercury said, *OK, calm down, homie. No need to get excited. You got screwed, that's all. Have you ever noticed the gods just don't like some people? And. Yeah, that's right, by 'some people' I mean you. Not even the Babylonian gods want you to succeed, and they lost their last worshipper when Howard Hughes croaked. C'mon now, don't take it personal. It's just that we get a kick out of watching you flail along in your meaningless life. So, try to use your brain and do some thinking here. Maybe you'll get why Pia-Caesar-Sabel did it.*

At first, I didn't care why she did it. I hated her. I almost hated Jenny for not telling me she was in on it. I breathed slowly, trying not to explode. I mean, screwed over by the gods is one thing. Who hasn't had that happen? But screwed over by Ms. Sabel? I used to think she was a decent human being. Except for that time she shot me. Other than that, she's a decent human being. So, what was she thinking?

I said, *Wait a minute, you told me about existential nihilism. 'She wants you to complete the mission. But you can't exist.'*

Mercury said, *But why did she do it?*

I said, *Because Ms. Sabel never approved building this system in the first place. Her dad set it in motion before he was killed. When she found out, the contracts were already in place and irreversible. There was nothing she could do to stop it. Then someone sold it to the Albanians, which she knew—and her old coach knew—had to be a setup for industrial espionage. Plain old theft. That reminds me, what's with her and that old coach anyway?*

Mercury said, *You can read all about it in a back issue of People magazine later. Keep focused on Alvaria.*

I said, *Unmarked crates and containers you can toss overboard. That means someone in the federal government worked with Falconer to set up the theft. Ms. Sabel didn't know who was involved. She had to send someone under cover to stop the auction. Why me?*

Mercury said, *Remember when she weighed her responsibility to sixty thousand employees versus your responsibility to your fiancé? That's when she decided you were expendable. Because you are. If you die, Jenny would get over it and marry Stefan. The world keeps turning. So keep thinking, why did Pia-Caesar-Sabel pick you and not some other guy?*

I scratched my head. *She had to pick someone she could count on to figure it out. Someone who could get inside Falconer's operation while she worked to expose the government insider. To make sure I was protected, she couldn't have any knowledge of where I was or what I was doing. If the government mole was high up, she could pass a polygraph saying she had no idea who had Alvaria. Because they could get a national security warrant and find out who was working in the field. Then they could eliminate me. She needed someone who could work autonomously—like the drones.*

Mercury pressed his index finger to his nose. *See, brutha? She screwed you over because she loves you and trusts you and knows you'll get it done.*

"Bullshit!" I jumped out of my chair yelling at Jenny. "This is total bullshit. How could she do this to me? How could you do this to me? Why didn't you tell me this back in Tuscany? Did you and Ms. Sabel think you couldn't trust me with the truth?"

"There are different people competing inside of us all the time," Jenny said quietly. "There is the person we want to be. There is the person we can be when the need arises. And then, there is the person we never want to be."

I paced across the hold rubbing my neck. "The person we don't want to be? What's that supposed to mean?"

"You don't want to be an arms dealer."

"Oh, and that's why she had to fuck me over?" I paced back to her fast. "So I'd want to become an arms dealer?"

"Do you think Falconer would've ever believed you had turned bad ... if you hadn't turned bad?"

CHAPTER 64

I COULDN'T SIT STILL. I fumed and paced and ranted. "How could she risk the lives of my crew?"

"She doesn't know about them or the sarin gas," Jenny said. "She would be sick about it if she did."

"Put people's lives in jeopardy without thinking they might end up dead? Who does she think she is, the Pentagon?"

"You're right. She knew this project would come at a high cost but it turned out a lot worse than expected. We still need a solution."

"Yumi picked a solution that's making a lot more sense right now." I couldn't stop pacing up and down the hold. "If I didn't owe Rafia and everyone else onboard a way out of this mess, I might follow her into oblivion."

"Let's work toward that." She threw up her hands. "I mean, work our way out, not follow her into oblivion."

I kept pacing. What the hell was she thinking? I'd just waltz in, figure out who the bidders were, and waltz back out with a list? Like the nastiest arms dealers in the world were a bunch of kindergartners waiting for me to steal their candy?

Mercury sat astride one of the drones. *As a matter of fact, homie, that's exactly what Pia-Caesar-Sabel was thinking. You always made it look easy in the past. Why you chose this mission to fall apart is beyond me.*

I said, *I am not falling apart. I'm going to pieces. There's a difference.*

Mercury said, *What's—*

I said, *Don't ask.*

Mercury said, *You'll figure a way out of this. You have to. I've got a hundred denarii riding on you—to win this time.*

I said, *You used to bet a hundred aurei at a time.*

Mercury shrugged. *You kept living through tough times and I kept losing money. I'm down to my last few denarii.*

"Had it not been for Yumi's sacrifice," I said, "you would have a knife to your throat while Falconer made me dance to his tune. When his music stopped, we'd both die."

"Yes." She wrung her hands as tears filled her eyes. "I get that. And I'm grateful to her."

"OK, let's work on a solution." I glared at Jenny. "Here's one: I go over there and kill Falconer. Does he have the gas system rigged to blow if he doesn't enter a code every hour?"

"I don't know." Jenny shook her head. "Too risky."

"We evacuate everyone. We load up the chopper with the first batch of six people. He sees us, pulls the trigger. Eight people die instead of fourteen. What do you think—acceptable losses?"

She crossed her arms and looked into the corner. "No."

"Why don't you toss a couple ideas out there?"

"Well, we could ..." She shifted her weight. "Or, maybe we could ..."

She got up and started counter-pacing, walking forward when I went aft.

"Do we know how he accesses the gas?" I asked. "Did Rafia's crew figure that out?"

"It's radio-based," she said, "not the phone that went overboard."

"That sucks."

We had no way of knowing who holds the radio, what it looks like, or how it works. It could be sending a pulse that keeps the system from activating. If we blocked the radio signal, we could wind up dead. Or it could be the opposite. The risk of finding out was too great.

"We could buy a shitload of atropine," I said. "Would that work?"

"You did that. Ansi brought in thirty injectors. But it only works if the person administering it doesn't die first. And then it's not a hundred percent. And before you ask, gas masks don't work with sarin, you need an entire respirator system. They don't stock them in Odessa or Sevastopol."

My phone rang. I grabbed it. Falconer. I clicked on speaker.

In an eerily calm voice, Falconer said, "My guests are arriving now. We will serve them breakfast at eight and follow that with a demonstration at nine. You will come to the *Savannah* at ten of nine. No excuses."

"No problem, Falconer." I hid my growing anxiety under a layer of bluster. "Paper bullets didn't sound very exciting, so we poured kerosene on the targets. The demonstration will knock your socks off."

I clicked off. The pain of Yumi's sacrifice filled my head with rage. Add one more death to the list of lives I would avenge. Slowly, an image of Falconer dying in agony formed in my mind. I had the will to make it happen. And where there's a will ... A smile crept across my face. I caught Jenny's gaze. *"Flectere si nequeo superos, Acheronta movebo."*

She quizzed me with her eyes.

"It means, *If I can't bend the will of Heaven, I will move Hell.* In other words—I know how to win."

CHAPTER 65

FALCONER GAZED ABSENTLY AT THE big blue ship barely visible on the horizon as dusk settled over the Black Sea. The *Savannah's* lights came on, waking him from his trance just as the first guest tender arrived. He cursed not having a ship big enough for a helipad. Even Stearne's ratty old freighter had room to make a helipad out of a hold cover. He had nothing but his stupid yacht. Would his guests take the auction seriously under such shabby conditions?

Konrad—the fever from his infected ear barely under control—greeted the first guest and escorted him up the short flight of stairs. Falconer checked the steward next to him. The tray of champagne flutes sparkled. Yang Lin marched up the stairs beside Konrad with his gaze locked on Falconer.

Showtime.

"Good evening, sir," Falconer exclaimed with an excited voice and a slight curtsey. "It is a pleasure to meet you."

They exchanged small talk until Falconer could see the next tender's running lights. He sent Mr. Yang, or Mr. Lin, whichever was the surname, to his assigned stateroom to rest before dinner.

As Konrad passed Yang Lin off to the steward, Falconer saw the stain of Bonham's blood on the deck. How many times did he have to tell those stupid, lazy hands to clean thoroughly? A thousand? Too late now. He turned his position and repositioned the champagne-bearer to keep the guest's eyes away from that part of the deck.

Fyodor Dzyuba and Yasser Faraj arrived together. Konrad introduced them. Falconer gave them bubbly and flattered them. He sent them off to their rooms. The damned stain was bigger than he thought. It covered a quarter of the lower deck. Sweat broke out on his brow.

He snapped his fingers for a steward and was about to give instructions to rescrub the deck when Akram Al-Sheeb's floating whorehouse arrived. Konrad escorted the Arab prince up the steps before he could turn to avoid his guest seeing the stains. They chatted amiably. Al-Sheeb said nothing about the blood. Arabs understood the need to control employees.

He finally got rid of the prince and called the steward over. The man ran for a brush and bucket. He came back and set to his task with vigor.

The last guest, Frida Herlovsen, was late.

"Women always are," he said to Konrad without thinking.

"Yes, that's true." Konrad nodded.

It was a good thing he hadn't dispatched Konrad when he took care of Bonham. Someone had to make proper introductions. It wouldn't do to have the *Savannah's* captain acting as an important person. All his guests had a captain or two lying around. These people found Konrad's royal lineage impressive. They didn't know he was a loser. And who better to act as his butler than a baron, or duke, or whatever he pretended to be.

"Losing Ms. Shibata was a terrible blow," Konrad said with a sigh. "I shall miss her."

"She was just another insect crawling across the barren desert of existence alone and unloved. Nothing more than a speck of dust blown about by siroccos from North Africa to the Gobi. One of the minions whose lives are spent by others for their pleasure. She had her chance for a glorious life with me—but she blew it. How many have gone before her on that sordid path to extinction, Konrad? The world is full of insignificant people like her. Like flash-in-the-pan celebrities. How many pop stars, full of themselves, have strutted out on stage and sung their feeble song only to fade off the charts the next day? They're forgotten in a week and not heard of again until they overdose in a seedy hotel. Why waste time remembering the dead? Everyone gets there eventually."

"Yes, sir." Konrad blinked and looked away. He pointed at lights in the distance. "Frida, goddess of the north."

"She represents a very dark faction. Keep your eye on this one."

When all the guests had been flattered and sent to their rooms,

Falconer's exhaustion took hold like a hundred-pound weight. He headed for the master suite but stopped. He'd seen the steward scrubbing, yet it was still there. Bigger and darker.

"I told you to get this stain out!" he shouted. "Get back here and scrub it clean."

The whites of the steward's eyes grew large and shone with fear as he glanced where Falconer pointed. The man's gaze flicked between Falconer's and the spot several times. Then he said, "Yes, sir. Right away, sir."

Unbelievable. The captain hired these blind, deaf, and dumb Panamanians or Pakistanis, whatever they were, and just look at the pitiful results. Falconer stormed to his room.

The instant he slammed the door, he heard footsteps outside. A firm knock followed. He opened the door to find the biggest dog, Benji, staring at him with anger. Falconer said, "Yes? What is it?"

"The dogs are pissed about Bonham."

"You too? Good. We're all in agreement. He's better off at the bottom of the ocean."

"No, sir. We're pissed off about that."

Of all the impertinence. The last thing he needed was the biggest of the dogs being sent to lodge some form of complaint. What world did they come from that allowed the lowly foot soldier to talk back to the king?

He pushed his chest against Benji's. "Fond of the stupid lout, were we? Feeling lost and lonely without the man to hold your leash? Well, Konrad's your boy now. Cry and whine to him all you want."

"Oh no, sir." Benji looked confused, which was a constant state for the lug nut. "Bonham promised us bonuses. We didn't get them in our last paycheck."

"Is that right?" Falconer shot back. "You think you deserve some kind of bonus after letting your boss sleep with my woman? Well, talk to him about it. If you don't find him a good conversationalist—" Falconer slid his V-42 stiletto out of his pocket "—I can put you on his plane of existence."

Benji backed up a step and patted the air between them with his hands. "I didn't mean—"

Falconer slammed the door on him. Where could he find replacements for those morons? Argentina maybe. Myanmar? Iran? He could kill Stearne and take over his Syrians.

His bedside phone rang.

The captain. "The guests are complaining about their accommodations, sir."

"Who?"

"All of them. None of them like their staterooms. They say they're too small."

The indignities of hosting international VIPs on a 273-foot yacht were unbearable. They should've accepted his bid for the *Numina* over Sabel's. Then he wouldn't have complaints from Arab princes, Russian oligarchs, and Nordic supremacists. And what were they complaining about? They were on the verge of stepping out of obscurity and becoming the next Putin, Pinochet, Mao.

Falconer contemplated methods of dealing with the arrogant bastards. All of them commanded resources that could inundate his motley dogs. They were generals and princes and oligarchs. At the snap of a finger, he and everyone in his employ, was dead. Using violence would prove a losing proposition for him. He needed to turn things around. What he needed was a good auction with a high bid. He always believed a happy bidder bids the most.

There were ways to make bidders happy. And he knew how to do that. He looked in the mirror and gave himself a wink. He regripped his phone and said, "Captain, get that cook into his DJ outfit. Rig the big deck with heaters. Start pouring drinks. What these fools need is a party."

CHAPTER 66

PIA ENTERED THE ROOSEVELT ROOM in the West Wing uncertain of the agenda. Finding her co-conspirators Eva, Bradley, and Ryan waiting for her was a surprise. Pia looked around the room. Only the four of them but plenty of chairs for more.

"You said you'd let us do this our way," Eva said.

Pia shrugged. "They called me, didn't tell me anything."

Bradley looked her over with doubt written all over his face. He crossed his arms and leaned back.

Ryan shrugged. "Guess we'll find out."

Secretary of State Lincoln Coulter walked in, Reggie Forrest right behind him. He looked confused by the presence of the others. Close on their heels, Collin West of the CIA. He looked around as if he was in the wrong room. He checked the room's name on the door, then took a seat not far from the two men who worked for him, Bradley and Ryan.

Three imperious-looking suits came in, two men and one woman. One closed the door and stood guard in front of it. The lady stood behind Collin West. The last suit took up a position at the head of the table. He slapped a sheaf of papers on it and slid them to West.

"Dan Sherinian, FBI Counterintelligence." He noticed Pia, closed his eyes, shook his head slowly, then took a deep breath. "Should've known you'd be involved, Sabel. Anyway, we're not going to wait for the Director of National Intelligence. He just resigned." He faced Collin West. "Do you have a criminal defense attorney?"

"Why?" Collin looked expectantly at the faces around him. "What are you talking about?"

"You're under arrest for espionage," Sherinian said. "A report came forward under the Whistleblower Protection Act. We investigated and collected a trove of evidence against you. The NSA has recordings of your phone conversations with George Falconer, an arms dealer also known as Ra. You're going to need an attorney."

"Who is the whistleblower?" Collin rose from his chair. He glared at Bradley. "I demand to know who turned me in."

"Your guilt will be decided on the evidence, not the person who reported you."

"I demand to confront my accuser!"

"The Attorney General will be your accuser. The facts will speak for themselves."

Collin picked up his briefcase and headed for the door. The agent guarding the door put a hand up and shook his head.

"Agent Trier, cuff that man," Sherinian said.

As she did, Sherinian turned to Reggie Forrest. "Do you have an attorney?"

"I didn't have anything to do with it!" she shouted. "He kept telling me things that would be good for my career. I didn't do anything wrong."

"That's why you're going to need an attorney," Sherinian said. "At this juncture, you're a target in an investigation. We can't tell if your actions were self-serving, ignorant, or part of the conspiracy to commit espionage. We will find that out in the course of our investigation. It's one thing to take a job for which you have no qualifications; it's another to execute your duties with willful ignorance of the laws you swore to uphold. If you want to claim Collin West used you, your ignorance is criminal. You should retain an attorney and meet me at my office at 9 AM tomorrow. Your cooperation will go a long way toward determining which charges will be brought against you. You are free to go."

Reggie Forrest scooped up her things, turned an icy glare at Pia, then scurried out.

The FBI agents headed for the exit.

Secretary Coulter said, "Wait a minute. I was told this was a meeting with President Williams."

Sherinian shrugged. "I didn't arrange this meeting. I was told to come get these two out of it."

"I'm glad to see the FBI found a place for you and Catherine," Pia said.

"We would've thanked you for asking Director Shikowitz to hire us, but we would've preferred it if you hadn't fucked up our previous careers in the first place."

With that, the FBI agents exited, pushing West in front of them.

"Another career destroyed?" Bradley asked.

"I've made mistakes, Coach." Pia pursed her lips and looked at the table. "I've tried to atone."

Without looking, she could sense Eva Gomez's head swivel between Coach and herself. She kept her head down.

A moment later, President Charles Williams strode in. "Welcome to the West Wing, everyone. Sit, sit. Please. Lincoln, Pia, good afternoon." He walked over to the other three. "You must be Eva Gomez. It's a pleasure to meet you. Ooh. That eye doesn't look healed. I hope it gets there soon. Which one of you gentlemen is Bradley Hopkins? Sir, it is an honor. I can't believe I'm meeting one of the finest coaches to take the field. Truly an honor. And that means you must be Ryan Wheeling. Great to meet you, young man. The country is in your debt, my friends. Welcome, all of you. Without your hard work and dedication, a tragedy would have occurred."

All three looked at Pia.

"Did I say something wrong?" Williams laughed.

"Our reports went through the Whistleblower program," Bradley said.

"Aren't our identities supposed to be secret?" Eva asked.

President Williams turned to Pia.

"Sorry, guys." She blushed. "President Williams came to dinner at Sabel Gardens last night and I might have bragged about your work."

"What happened to keeping secrets?" Eva asked.

"She nominated you for the Presidential Medal of Freedom," Williams said.

All three faces lit up at the mention of the honor. Clearly, it was the last thing they expected. The highest civilian award the nation can bestow was given to fewer than eleven people a year. The honorees were most often celebrities or people of cultural significance. Never before had three low-level workers been given the prestigious award.

He turned to Pia. "You didn't mention anything about a whistleblower ..."

"That's OK," Bradley said. "We weren't hung up on anonymity. Were we, people?"

The other two shook their heads, still a little shocked and bewildered.

Williams warmly shook each of their hands. As he did, he said, "What makes this country great are the people who stand by their commitment to the Constitution, uphold the rule of law, and put their country ahead of their personal agenda. Were it not for people like you, Alvaria could be in the hands of our enemies this very minute. The nation thanks you for your service."

The three murmured humble thank-yous.

"My office will be in touch about awarding the medals. There will be one hitch, unfortunately. I will award them to you, but, due to the security surrounding Alvaria, you can't tell anyone how you earned it until 2045."

The President nodded at Coulter and the two moved off to a corner. "Lincoln, we have to take a close look at all the appointed cabinet positions. I'll need your help getting rid ..."

Pia and the others huddled at the end of the table.

"What did you do to that FBI agent?" Bradley asked.

"What is wrong with you?" Eva asked Bradley. "She nominated you for the Medal of Freedom."

Bradley stammered and tried to avoid the young woman's glare. He faced her. "You're right. Time to let it go."

"He was the best coach I ever had," Pia said. "He stuck with me through my middle-school career. Then he was picked by the National Team as defense coach. He was part of the reason the scouts found me at such a young age."

"What went wrong?" Eva asked.

"You asked why I left soccer at the height of my career? An underage teammate accused him of sexual assault. I took it upon myself to dispense justice by beating the crap out of him." Pia's eyes filled with tears. "He was a coach. He couldn't defend himself. Biggest mistake of my life. My teammate later admitted she was seeking attention. It was too late. His career had been ruined not as much by her as by what I did. People assumed the real allegations had been swept under the table to obscure my assault. I left the game in an attempt to prove that wasn't true, but people believe the worst."

They were quiet. Eva's surprise turned to embarrassment. No one knew what to say.

"Wow." Ryan's voice surprised the others. "I didn't know you played soccer."

Another moment of shock silenced the three.

Then Bradley Hopkins roared with laughter. "Oh man. Bring me down a notch. We needed that, didn't we, Pia?"

Pia caught his contagion of laughter a second later.

When he caught his breath, Bradley said, "Pia, apology accepted."

She gave him a big hug. "Thank you. I am sorry."

"Holding on to it doesn't do either of us any good." He leaned into her hug, then backed up.

"I trust those are tears of joy." President Williams approached. "I have to run. Pia, could you tell me where we are on recovering the system?"

Everyone faced her.

"At this point, everything is in the hands of Jacob Stearne. He's at an unknown location, working against impossible odds under the threat of instant death. Everything we've worked for, everything we've risked, is now in the hands of the gods."

Williams tensed. "Did you say gods, plural?"

CHAPTER 67

THE COFFEE KEPT ME AWAKE until first light. By then, we'd rehearsed the demo so many times I was asleep on my feet. Then dawn came and my body responded to the daylight. A second wind. We raised the hydraulic floor with one hundred drones and the four remote-controlled targets lined up on it.

Jenny and I went through the steps for the umpteenth time. Ansi would fly halfway to the *Savannah* to release the remote-controlled airplane targets on my signal. Jenny would stand by onboard to make sure the remote-controlled sea-based targets released properly. Everything else was controlled by the tablet. Target identification, timing sequences, recall commands, and anything the operator wanted the drone swarm to do would come from the tablet.

Once the targets were launched, Jenny and Ansi, plus Rafia and the crew were done. The demo, and all their lives, would be in my hands.

My life would be in the hands of a certain god who'd gone missing overnight.

Typical.

Captain Rafia toured his ship, going in circles around the deck and through the rooms, checking everything like a nervous bride. I met him on deck. A cold, damp sea breeze swirled around us. A seagull dive-bombed the deck before deciding the ship's rats were not worth catching. Falconer had set the rendezvous far from the shipping lanes, yet a big blue ship cruised on the horizon. Too big for another trawler, and too far away for us to worry about. I leaned back on the railing as if I hadn't a care in the world. Once you've faced death a few too many times, you quit worrying about it. While inevitable, in my profession it always comes as a surprise.

"Are you sure this will work, habibi?" Rafia asked.

"No," I said.

He put a hand on my shoulder and squeezed. "We will do everything we can to get you out of there."

"Don't risk anyone on my behalf. I'll be OK." I'd worked out the odds. There weren't any. None of us wanted to say that out loud. I looked across the waves at the *Savannah*. "What is that, a mile? I can swim that."

"I wish I could be so certain all the time." His sad eyes looked me over. "How is it you have no fear?"

"The truth?" I waited for him to nod. "I have god on my side."

He laughed. "You're facing certain death and still you make jokes. I wish I had as much faith as my mother. She was a Wali'Allah." He glanced at me. "Friend of god. What you call a saint. I've never been a good Muslim. I always cheat on the last day of Ramadan."

"Don't worry," I patted his back. "Knowing god is a gut-wrenching disappointment."

Rafia's suspicious glance my way was interrupted by Jenny's arrival. She looked more worried than the captain. She cared about me. Maybe I'd been too harsh about how she and Ms. Sabel totally screwed me over, endangered innocent people, and still seemed to think it was all for the greater good. My hand slipped into my jacket pocket and found the ring. Still there. I zipped it closed.

One by one, the crew converged on us. They didn't wish me luck in case it might jinx me. In silence, they gave me their support with pats on the shoulder and appreciation in their eyes. I was giving my life for a slim chance to save theirs. Their gratitude showed in their silence.

Mercury tiptoed along the ship's railing. *Gonna work up the nerve to ask her, dawg?*

I said, *If I live through the final curtain call—that she and Ms. Sabel set me up for—yes, maybe.*

Mercury said, *What ever happened to forgiving people?*

I said, *Forgiving someone is what you do after you survive the ordeal they put you through. And even then, it's kinda iffy.*

Mercury said, *Well, no matter what happens, just remember: it wasn't my idea.*

I said, *Is that a tear in your eye?*

Mercury sniffled and wiped his eye with the back of his hand. *Salt spray. That's all, homes. Neptune's giving me shit about the money I owe him.*

I started to laugh. *You old sentimental fool. You're actually worried about me, aren't you?* I studied him for a minute. *Wait a second—is this because you bet on me and now you're having second thoughts? Now I remember. You were complaining because this wasn't your idea. Holy Diana. Don't you have any faith in me?*

Mercury looked away.

At that moment, I was ready to go Zoroastrian. Whatever that is. I made a mental note to look it up. If I got back.

"We walked the routes ten times," Jenny said. "We triple-checked the equipment and everything looks right. We've run out of time for a live drill."

"We will deal with whatever comes up," Rafia said. "It's the best shot we have. Thank you for doing this, Jacob."

Firas slapped my shoulder. He started to say something when a tear formed in his eye and his voice caught. He turned away.

Mardik stepped in his place. He hugged me hard, letting his tears flow. "You're in the good fight, Jacob. We always thought you were the best boss."

A crewman ran up with a ship-to-ship radio. A call for me.

Falconer. "Ready for your big audition, sport?"

"On my way." I clicked off.

Mardik nodded toward the Zodiac. No more time for goodbyes.

Jenny threw herself on me in a big, wrap-around hug. She held on tight. "I'm sorry, Jacob. I'm really, really sorry. I … I love you."

"Hey." I put my knuckle under her chin and lifted her face. "No matter what, I'll always be with you."

There was little chance we would see each other again. In all the scenarios I dreamed up to kill Falconer and save Alvaria, I didn't see a way to live through it. There was no way off Falconer's ship. Swimming away from men with guns wasn't going to work. Ansi didn't have a rescue winch. Besides, helicopters are easy to shoot down. Short of a magic dolphin, it was a one-way trip.

"I know." She sniffled. "You're coming back. You have to."

I pulled away and trotted down the stairs. Mardik cast off and cranked the throttle. The morning mist had burned off. The sun was weak as tea, the air cold and biting. We arrived at the *Savannah* quickly since Rafia had moved the *Fatma* closer to the yacht for better observation. I sent Mardik off, reminding him to hurry, and trotted up the short stairs.

Falconer met me halfway. He stopped me with his hand on my shoulder and smiled. "I woke up this morning with a new attitude in life, dear boy. Everything I cared about is gone. I have no reason to live." He found that low hiss he liked to use. "Other than beating condescending little fucks like you. I own you. You will do everything I tell you. And you'll do it well." He flashed a radio transmitter the size of a TV remote. "If I press this little red button, or if the battery dies, or if the device falls in the sea, everyone over there dies." He nodded at my ship. Then he looked deep into my eyes. "Do we understand each other, Jacob?"

"Absolutely," I said in my extra-chipper voice. "I'm telling you, this demo is gonna be a blast."

"It damn well better." He led me up the steps where six chairs were set up to watch the demo off the port side.

Four men and one woman nursed hangovers with Bloody Marys. All the dogs were there—Fido, Rover, Benji, and some others whose names I never bothered to learn. They were all armed. I gave the dogs a nod. Fido bared his fangs.

Falconer introduced me and gave me the floor. He took the sixth spectator chair and played with his phone.

I noted the phone. He had a backup phone, probably downloaded the contents from the cloud. Probably had the same code.

I stepped up, considering my options. Jenny's plan was for me to jump overboard, swim under the yacht to confuse the shooters, come up on the other side, climb into the Zodiac, and make a run for it. I turned that plan down because Falconer would live and my crew might not. I considered the other option, the one I came up with. My plan was complex with many possible problems and a high probability of failure.

I took a deep breath and cranked my positive attitude up to eleven.

CHAPTER 68

I STEPPED IN FRONT OF the five bidders and Falconer. A diverse group of killers from all walks of life. Only the southern hemisphere lacked representation. No one from Antarctica wanted in on this? Their loss. I grinned and held up my tablet with the Alvaria logo prominently displayed.

"Lady and gentlemen, allow me to introduce Alvaria." I pressed the button to start the demo.

From the ship parked a mile away, we could hear the noise of 100 small jet engines firing up. One by one, they leapt into the air, three seconds apart. They formed a squadron in the sky, flying an oblong route two miles long. Each lap took less than half a minute.

"Alvaria drone swarms can reach speeds of 450 mph. That makes them hard to see, so today we've dialed them back to 300. They can range over 200 miles from home."

As a group, we watched in stunned silence while the awesome formation of drones flew in a tighter formation than a murmuration of starlings.

"They self-select altitude and create their own holding pattern while awaiting their targets. We will launch four remote-controlled targets the size of jet skis. Which of you would like to take the controls and try to outsmart Alvaria?"

They all raised their hands except Falconer and the Arab prince.

I handed out the remote units, giving the lady the special one. I told her, "Yours is a boat equipped with a Gatling gun that you can control here." I showed her the aiming-and-firing joystick.

To the group, I said, "My assistant Ansi will launch the two airplanes from the helicopter over there."

I pointed at the chopper half a mile out. Two RC aircraft jumped out and headed straight for the sea below them.

"Get your planes under control, gentlemen," I scolded them. They laughed and fought the controllers until they had them righted and flying in circles.

"Now for the boats," I said, pointing to the big ship where Jenny launched two sizable craft.

Having learned from the airplanes, the two RC captains took control quite quickly.

"Now, our first operation is simple." I stood before them like a carnival barker, holding my tablet in one hand and making grand gestures with the other. "We will attempt to shoot them down before they even have a mission. Madam, would you do the honors?"

I stepped to one side to give them the grandest view possible.

She laughed with girlish glee and pressed the Gatling gun's trigger. It fired into the waves on her first attempt. She figured out the controllers and got the tracer fire higher and higher with each burst. Finally, her stream of mini bullets came near the swarm.

Two drones left the flight pattern and swooped down.

"Run, dear lady! Get your boat out of there!" I shouted at her.

Now an expert with the remote, she swerved in a zig-zag pattern, pushing her speed to full power. Her tongue stuck out between her lips as she concentrated. She put body English on it, twisting in her seat as she zig-zagged the craft to what she hoped was safety.

One drone swooped left, the other right. The first one fired a direct hit. The target exploded. Nothing remained but a few remnants burning on the water. The second peeled off immediately to return to the flock. The first circled its victim, looking for survivors. When it was satisfied it had saved the swarm from danger, it too returned to the flock.

Falconer shot me a concerned glare. I motioned as if I were pouring something, reminding him of the kerosene.

I announced, "Automatic self-defense."

The bidders cheered and clapped and hooted.

The lady cried out with a Nordic accent, "My turn was too short. I want another!"

She tried to grab a controller from the Russian next to her. He laughed, pulling his controller away in the nick of time.

I realized that while the captain and crew had been complicit in many crimes, they didn't deserve the same fate as the rest of us. The same went for the dogs, although I had less enthusiasm for sparing them.

Behind the group, on the other side of the deck, the captain supervised a steward who scrubbed a portion of the deck with a brush. I slid over to them. In a quiet voice, I said, "Captain, get your people forward with all your life rafts. Stand by to abandon ship. Don't wait for the owner or the guests."

He stared at me blankly for a moment. I gave him my soldier stare. He nodded slowly, then tugged the steward's shoulder. They left.

As I rejoined the group, Falconer cut me off. "They were cleaning a stain for me. Why did you send them away?"

"You don't want this deal showing up on Instagram, do you?"

He shook his head, gave me the tiniest nod of thanks, and went back to his chair. I retook my position in front of the group, slightly off to one side.

The Russian asked, "This is just LOCUST, right?"

He referred to the current swarming programs under development by the five biggest militaries, an acronym for Low Cost UAV Swarming Technology. Palm-sized drones launched in large numbers. I said, "LOCUSTs aren't truly autonomous, they're pre-programmable with inflight options. They cost ten times as much and carry only three ounces of explosives. Not only are they slow and noisy, they have a fatal flaw that you already know about: you can catch them with fishing nets."

Everyone laughed at the last line.

"Who would like to set a target on this?" I held up the tablet.

The Arab shouted down all the others with his comment that he had no RC unit to play with. He came forward. I showed him how to take a picture with the tablet of any of the three targets left. When he picked one of the airplanes, he gave it back to me. Speaking in Arabic, I told him which button to press to create a target out of the fuzzy picture he'd taken. Impressed with my language skills, he pressed the button.

Right away, the swarm came out of its loop and dove for the target aircraft. In less than fifteen seconds, it was vaporized.

The bidders clapped and cheered again.

Behind me, the helicopter had reached the *Fatma* and taken off again. Its path took it away from us. Falconer noticed. He tracked around to me. "Where is your pilot going?"

I thought fast. "Recovery zone. Can't let these things go to waste and the *Fatma* can't accommodate their landing pattern."

He backed off with a suspicious look.

I addressed the bidders. "Faster, quieter, and collectively more powerful than sixteen Reaper drones, nothing can stop the Alvaria. Their economy is derived from off-the-shelf parts. The brains in these things are generic mobile phone boards, hardened to withstand electro-pulse weapons. They communicate collectively to produce true artificial intelligence over a proprietary communications system that will be revealed only to the highest bidder. Up to twenty-seven units can malfunction or be destroyed before the processing power is degraded. I'm telling you, folks, once the target is sent upstream, nothing can stop them."

"What about underground, parking lots, that kind of thing?" one of them asked.

"They're equipped with heat sensors that can see through walls up to two inches thick. If they can fly into the building in pursuit, they will. If they've determined the target entered a hardened bunker, they will send ten drones to open a hole in the bunker before flying in to continue the pursuit."

They nodded and murmured about the effectiveness of the system while I took a class picture.

"We have two more targets." I faced the bidders with a grin. "Who wants to pick the next one?"

The woman rose first and pushed the smaller Chinese bidder out of her way. He giggled as he fell back to his chair. They were like kids with a new toy. She picked the other airplane and clicked the button. Seconds later, despite the operator's best moves, it was nothing more than a puff of black smoke.

All the drones returned to formation. The bidders watched in fascination.

"One last target. Who wants it?" They nearly fought each other, with the Saudi winning out.

He targeted the boat and the drones peeled off. Another success. The drones returned to formation.

"You could hover swarms over a city to replace the police?" the Saudi asked.

My vision of the future turned drastically darker.

"That's a great idea," I said cheerfully.

"If these are off-the-shelf parts," the Chinese bidder asked, "everyone will have these in no time. There is no need to bid."

"It's all in the software. This is ten years ahead of any other AI in the world. It's ahead because it's a single-function AI."

Behind me, I heard the *Fatma's* lifeboat release from its launch pad high above the water and splash into the sea. That was the signal. The last part of my plan was ready.

Falconer tracked around to me again, pointing at the *Fatma*. "What the hell is going on over there?"

"Drills, I guess? Malfunction, maybe? I don't know. Shouldn't you focus on the bidding?" I turned to his guests. "Any other questions?"

"What kind of fuel?"

"Liquid propane," I answered.

"How far away can the tablet be from the swarm?"

"Without satellite options, about a mile with line of sight."

There were no more questions.

Falconer started to speak. I cut him off. Impressed with my sales pitch so far, he gave me the go-ahead nod.

"You're bidding on three important pieces of intellectual property. The first is the miniature jet engine. In the world of RC model aircraft, there are many jets in the four to five feet category. The fastest among them goes 451 mph. But, if you look that one up on YouTube, you will hear it. And you'll note that it has some heft. While we can hear the Alvaria drones, they emit a tenth of the decibels of propeller-driven drones and a quarter of other jet engines. On top of that, they get significantly better mileage off readily available fuels.

"The second is the software. This stands out as the most important advancement in artificial intelligence, harnessing the power of common circuit boards to create an autonomous supercomputer in the sky. And the third thing is the proprietary communications system that brings it all together." I gave them my best salesman smile and shook a finger at them. "But, if you want to know more about that, you must have the highest bid."

All the bidders thought about this for a quiet moment.

I stole Falconer's thunder. "Let the bidding begin!"

CHAPTER 69

FALCONER TOOK OVER THE BIDDING process, opening at half a billion dollars. I edged over to Fido.

In a quiet tone, I said, "I don't like you, but I'm going to save your life. I've targeted these six people. It's locked in. There's nothing you can do to stop it. If you stay here, you're going to die with them. If you go to the forward deck, you'll find the captain and crew preparing lifeboats. Whatever you do, don't let one of the big shots get in a boat with you."

He looked down at me with a scowl. I held the tablet in front of me with the class picture of Falconer and his bidders. I touched each face and clicked the set-target button. The next button to popup was the GO button. Fido's eyes bulged.

He said, "Why aren't you running?"

"To make it work," I said, "I have to go down with the ship." I patted his beefy shoulder. "It all goes down in minutes, so get moving."

I walked away.

No one picked Fido for his brain power, but even the dimmest functional brain can work through a difficult problem eventually. He took longer than I expected. To his credit, it was the moral questions that tripped him up. *Do I shoot Stearne and try to save the boss? Should I tell the boss what Stearne just told me? Do I leave in a dead run and save my skin? Do I bother to inform the other dogs?* I could tell that's what he was thinking because sweat formed on his forehead as his brain taxed its limited operational power to figure everything out.

I moved back to the bidders, standing in front and off to the side again, next to the railing. I listened to Falconer.

He said, "I'm going to give you a few minutes to think things through. If you don't have permission to raise your bid, perhaps a call to your boss might be in order. Or, if you'd like, create a co-op for a higher bid."

He strolled over to me with his Bloody Mary. He pointed at his dog. "What did you say to Fido, sport?"

"Just gave him a heads-up on his immediate future." I was staring at the clean deck where the steward had been scrubbing.

"Is that stain still there?" Falconer asked, following my gaze. "You can see it, can't you? Where is that damned steward? He needs to finish the job."

Below us, something large and oddly shaped swam in the murky waters. I glanced at it just as a revelation about the stain came to me. My head jerked up. I caught Falconer's gaze. "Where is Konrad?"

He eased his stare over the railing and out to sea. "He served his purpose."

"That's his blood the steward was cleaning up?"

"Hell no, they're still working on Bonham's. Konrad's corpse is in the master suite with Yumi." He sipped his drink. "They've all been disappointments. Those useless fucks."

That his death came at Falconer's hand fit. Konrad got his instant karma. Mourning him required more energy than I could muster.

Mercury popped up. *Hey homie, if Konrad got what he deserved, what do you deserve for killing ol' Yeller?*

I said, *Will you stop? I've never seen the movie. It came out long before I was born.*

Mercury said, *'Member when Konrad boasted about Falconer's power? He became Falconer's last victim. That's what happens when you associate with poisonous people.*

I said, *What're you saying, that's why I'm going to die?*

Fido chose that moment to wave his dog pack to join him. They were slow to leave their posts. Fido waved one more time, then ran forward. The others followed him more out of curiosity than understanding.

Falconer noticed the deserters. "Where do they think they're going?"

"Checking on the captain. He's doing a routine check of the lifeboats on this scow."

"Why did the *Fatma* release her lifeboat?" As soon as the words left his lips, he looked at me. "Jacob? What have you done?"

The large object I'd seen earlier swam out from under the *Savannah*, turned around in a slow, tight circle, and swam back under the yacht.

"Rafia dropped anchor out there." I patted Falconer's arm. "The crew opened every hatch and window, then abandoned ship. When you set off the sarin, it will blow away in the wind. It has a very short shelf life when exposed to air or water. We'll send in a crew with respirators tomorrow and wash it all down."

Falconer's expression changed from mildly amused to murderous rage. He pulled his remote out and pressed the red button.

"They're all gone," I said. "The chopper took Jenny and my favorite Syrians. Rafia took the rest."

Falconer pulled out his V-42 and tried to stab me.

Anticipating his move, I grabbed his wrist and wrenched the knife from his hand. I shoved him back and tossed the blade into the sea.

I leaned to his ear and hissed, "Yes, the military ships the ammo separately. You have to understand army-speak to get the joke. The explosive-tipped rounds were in a separate crate, on the same ship. It wasn't kerosene that made those explosions."

Falconer gasped and looked at the last bits of wreckage floating on the waves. He looked me over and realized he'd lose a fistfight. Behind him the bidders had taken notice of our heated discussion and short-lived burst of violence. They pressed back in their seats as if that would save them.

"Sit down," I told Falconer. "Did you know Yumi's suicide was a distraction to allow me time to escape? Bonham had nothing to do with her. She hated you so much, she asked me to save her, take her away from here. I told her about my endgame, this—" I swept my arm toward the Alvaria swarm "—and she wanted you to die so badly that she gave her life to make sure I would succeed."

"You're lying!"

"Remember when your guys had to search the chapel on your estate? That was when she and I first spoke. Yeller discovered us. He's at the bottom of the well. Remember how she wanted to stay in that hotel in Durrës instead of on your yacht? She watched me kill Spot from the balcony and never said a word."

The color drained from Falconer's face.

"Thanks to her," I said, "all your money and your murderous control of others is coming to an ignominious end. All your bling, your estates, your cars, and yachts—the stuff you thought made you important—will be sold at auction. The only reason people pretend to like you is to get some of your money. When that's gone, your name will be forgotten. I'm doing this for Yumi, and Nate Hale, and Dimitris Bakakis. Remember them?"

He was too stunned to move. I reached in his pocket and extracted his phone, then lightly pushed his chest.

He collapsed into the chair and watched me with the fear he'd instilled in others all his life. From the look of him, he didn't like the feeling of helplessness and vulnerability. He hugged himself.

I addressed the people remaining on deck. "Folks, I have good news and bad news. The good news is, you've all won the bid. You are going to get the full power of Alvaria."

I waited while they smiled suspiciously. Falconer didn't speak. The others were working out the logistics of when they might get it and how they would share it.

I said, "Your initial deposits of commodities are already consigned to Detit Exports. For that, I thank you from the bottom of my heart."

The Russian, looking suddenly pale, raised his hand. "And the bad news?"

"Ah, the bad news … it's very bad. When I say you're getting Alvaria, I really mean—you're getting Alvaria." I turned the tablet to face them. They could easily see their faces circled with the word "target" below each one. In the corner, a big green GO button waited.

I hesitated. Pressing GO would destroy the ship, the passengers, and any crew who hadn't cleared the area. That included me because the dogs would never let the man who killed Spot into a life raft. In all the endgame scenarios I visualized, there was no way out for me. Pressing the button was an act of suicide. It would be worth it to rid the world of people like George Falconer.

I said, "Thousands of innocent lives snuffed out by your arms deals are about to be avenged."

I pressed GO.

All six mouths dropped open at the same time. Accustomed to giving kill orders, they'd never come close to feeling threatened before, that much was obvious by their expressions.

"Nothing can stop Alvaria from annihilating its targets." I resumed my carnival barker voice. "There's nowhere to run, nowhere to hide, and the only way to recall them is via this tablet."

I held the tablet aloft and watched their frightened eyes follow it. Then I tossed it into the sea. "Good luck, and may the best man die first."

Their gazes followed the tablet overboard, then rose to see a hundred Alvaria drones turn in unison and scream straight toward us.

CHAPTER 70

I WANTED TO LIVE LONG enough to see it happen. I jogged down the steps to the sport deck to put a safe distance between me and the condemned. I watched as the swarm jumped into action. In situations where the target may hide behind walls, Alvaria forms squadrons of four to ensure each target is taken out. The first to arrive would remove the barriers; the next would remove the target. On paper, that sounded like a nice feature. In person, it was terrifying.

Six squadrons shrieked toward us at 300 mph. Crossing the mile of Black Sea between their position and ours took twelve seconds. In that time, the bidders moved faster than they ever had before in their autocratic lives. They scrambled to get behind a wall, a piece of furniture, anything.

From where I stood, I had a ground-level view of the attack. The drones had three explosive tipped projectiles each that destroyed the deck and furniture in the first pass. The Russian who'd thought he was clever by running to the far side of the ship and flattening himself against the wall discovered his Alvaria squadron had tracked him. In formation, they flew up and over the bridge, and rained death from above. The explosions ripped that side of the ship.

I heard the hull crack.

The Nordic woman attempted to swim to safety. Since we were a hundred miles off the coast of anywhere, and it appeared her swimming days were a distant memory of her youth, I couldn't figure out where she thought she would go. Her squadron fired, the bullets zipping by, inches from my shoulder, scaring the hell out of me. They circled her, firing one from each drone until she was nothing more than chum. On the bright side, sharks in the Black Sea are rare and endangered, and she would go a long way toward feeding them.

Falconer ran to his stateroom. No doubt to find a weapon of some sort. The maneuver managed to obscure him from his squadron's first pass. The downside was: he missed the Arab prince being obliterated along with the couch he was hiding under and a good deal of the main salon. Falconer reappeared on the second deck and took pot shots as his squadron circled the ship. He hadn't thought that through. He was no longer just a target—he'd turned himself into a threat to the swarm. Another squadron of drones broke from the main pack and headed straight for him.

He spotted me a moment before his death became inevitable. He aimed his 9-mil at me and fired.

The round whizzed past my ear.

I can't resist a chance to cheat death. Mercury needs me too much to let a dweeb like Falconer take me out. I stood up straight and stepped left. He fired again, going for a headshot. Those are the easiest to dodge. Especially from a handgun held by an amateur on a gently rolling deck. He fired a third and fourth round. I slipped and fell to the deck, almost in the water.

That big blob-thing was swimming below the ship again.

That's when I put it all together. The big blue ship on the horizon. The blob beneath the surface. My chances of surviving had just improved from impossible to maybe. I had a way out. A big smile creased my face.

Another of Falconer's rounds buzzed my hair. I jumped to my feet. As much as I loved taunting him, it was getting a bit tedious. I took a bow and called out to him, "It's been fun—but I gotta run."

"Think you're going to swim all the way to Odessa?" he shouted and fired another round.

"I only have to make it as far as the *Numina*."

His gaze crossed the sea to the big blue ship on the horizon.

Right then, the squadron looking for Falconer found him. They were behind him, swooping out of the sky. Unfortunately, that left me directly in the line of fire for every explosive bullet that missed. Falconer dropped to the deck. The first three bullets flew past my shoulder.

I dove off the sport deck. I swam down and under the *Savannah* as the bullets splashed through the water near me and exploded.

Then I heard the first muffled pops of Alvaria rounds ripping Falconer to shreds, deepened in tenor by the ocean. I came up on the far side in time to hear the little jets screaming overhead. Four of them in rapid succession with another four following an instant later. They were circling, checking the faces of the survivors against their target list. I'd chosen the "double tap" option to make sure no one survived. That was mean of me, I know.

The *Savannah* creaked and groaned from the damage in her midships. I'm not a naval expert but it sounded like she was going to split in two. Off to the front of the ship, the panicked captain and crew were climbing into life rafts. They hadn't understood the urgency until the shooting started. Then an orderly evacuation devolved into chaos. They dove overboard, often missing their raft. Fido glanced my way. He gave me a tiny salute of thanks before jumping.

Mercury popped up in the water next to me. *Whoo-hoo! Homie, you put on a better show than those Fourth of July parties at Sabel Gardens.*

You're in a good mood, I said. *Does this mean you won your bet?*

Mercury said, *For once, you came through for me. Usually, I gotta save your ass. But this time it worked out. No hard feelings about making you feel like you could actually be a Caesar, right?*

I said, *Is there a reason I can't at least be rich enough to retire early?*

Mercury said, *You think me and Jupiter and Minerva want to watch you sit around all day getting fat and sassy? Nah, that's as boring as watching reruns of* Friends. *That shit wasn't funny the first time around, why watch it again? No, brutha, what makes the gods squeal with delight is when you be teetering on the edge of a cliff.*

I said, *Great. Thanks. So glad my tribulations are your entertainment.*

Mercury pointed to the life rafts. *Their silence makes them complicit, don't it?*

I said, *If I know Ms. Sabel, she has Ukrainian naval ships headed this way to mop up.*

The big gray blob came up from the depths below me. The *Numina's* six-person submarine broke the surface. Water poured off the plexiglass bubble in sheets. Jenny Jenkins at the controls. The access hatch at the back opened.

She called out from inside, "Get in, quick!"

CHAPTER 71

AS SOON AS I HAD the hatch closed, the submarine dove. Jenny was all business, focusing on a small panel of controls. It looked intimidating, so I kept my mouth shut. She took us below the range of the stray Alvaria rounds zipping into the water and set out on a heading for the *Numina*. I picked my way through the three rows of chairs and took the seat next to hers.

The bubble was huge, and the view was awesome. Except the Black Sea didn't get its name from being pale blue like the Caribbean. It was dark green and murky.

Once we were away from the death and destruction, Jenny faced me with red, angry eyes and a shriek. "What the hell is wrong with you?"

"You know, the last thing you said to me was, 'I love you.' Can we go back to that?"

"You were standing there letting him shoot at you—like it was some kind of game!"

"You saw that?" I took her scowl as a yes. "Only fair to give him a sporting chance."

Tears ran down her face. "Jacob, I'm serious. I was worried about you."

"Why?" I held up my hands. "I'm fine."

"Jacob, people talk. They tell me things. Things I don't want to believe."

I patted my knees. "Oh-kaaay, looks like we're going there."

She slapped my leg. "I'm serious. People say things like, like you're crazy. You must be crazy to let someone shoot at you. Are you crazy, Jacob?"

Mercury squeezed between us. *Good question, dawg. Are you?*

I said, *Could you give me a minute here? You're not helping.*

Mercury said, *It's a serious question. She deserves a serious answer. You gotta tell her about me, bro. Then she'll understand why people think you're looney. They're simply mistaken because they don't listen to their assigned gods.*

I said, *What do you mean, 'assigned gods?'*

Didn't we go over this once? Mercury cocked his head as if I'd forgotten my lessons again. *All the gods talk to all the people all the time, but only a few can hear us. I mean, do you have any idea how frustrating it is for Jesus? He spends days on end waving his arms, jumping up and down, and who does the Pope end up talking to? Igaluk.*

Mercury laughed and slapped his knee.

I said, *Who?*

Still laughing, Mercury said, *Igaluk, the Inuit moon god. And the Pope is convinced he's getting it straight from his savior's mouth. Haven't you noticed, he's the first Pope to worry about climate change? Well, guess whose igloo is melting? Ha! Those Christians. They've been one messed-up bunch since they started waging war in the name of the Prince of Peace. But whaddaya gonna do, right? Hey. Look, you're missing the point. She's worried about your sanity. Come clean about me and she's going to be just fine.*

Hold on, I said. *How can all the gods be everywhere, for everyone, all the time?*

Mercury said, *We're like electrons, we're everywhere—* He spread his hands in front of him as if smoothing a tablecloth—*and nowhere.*

His voice and his apparition disappeared at the same time.

Jenny's head was tilted. Her eyes were filled with tears. "Jacob?"

"I just killed the vile arms dealers who supply murderous dictators and you think I'm not going to celebrate?"

"Celebrate? Is that how you celebrate? Letting someone shoot at you?"

"Well, duh." I was completely confused. "What do you do?"

She broke down in sobs. I guessed maybe other people celebrate an important victory in other ways. A fist pump seems kinda low-key, though. But it bothered me that she was bothered.

Through a wad of tissues, she said, "You know I have Adult Attachment Disorder as a result of my Rape Trauma Syndrome. I'm over-attached to you. You risking your life makes me just lose it all over again. Why would you do that?"

Mercury had his formal toga on, the full-length one with red trim. *This would be a good time to introduce us, dawg. We can be one big happy family. I'm ready. Go on now.*

I said, *You're not predicting her reaction accurately. A while back she said she doesn't want a wack job for a boyfriend.*

I patted Jenny's knee. "I'm pretty invincible. I get a kick out of it. That's all. No big deal."

"No big deal? You could be gone like that!" She snapped her fingers. "I can't deal with that."

She broke down into sobs again.

My anger rose. "You can't deal with it? But you could leave me out in the cold as an arms dealer because Ms. Sabel told you it was a good idea? Did she tell you the CIA only wanted us to identify the bidders, not do anything else? Instead of sending you into harm's way, she could've sent me a Sabel Satellite phone and I could've cracked Falconer's list a week ago."

She blew her nose and said, "The CIA cancelled that contract."

"What?" That was it. My gasket blew at that point. "I did all this for nothing?"

"Not for nothing. To keep Sabel Weapons Systems from losing their—"

"Proprietary technology. Nice. Risk my life and the lives of Rafia and Mardik and Firas and the whole damn crew—so Pia-Caesar-Sabel can make another million?"

I couldn't speak anymore. My blood boiled. My head grew so hot I looked for an air conditioning control.

Jenny regarded my outburst as dangerous. She leaned away from me in the small space and eyed me with fear.

"Did you just call her, 'Caesar?'" she asked with a trembling voice. "Are those people right? You are crazy?"

Jenny went into steaming-mad-silent mode. So did I.

I pulled out Falconer's phone and tried the code 26 15 93. It worked. The screen popped up with a picture of Yumi as wallpaper. I took a moment to remember her. Then I took a deep breath. A few seconds later, I found the paperwork for the commodities the bidders had relinquished as deposits long before the auction. They were stacked up and waiting for Detit Exports in Sevastopol. Perfect.

Outside the submarine's bubble, the sports bay walls on the *Numina* opened and welcomed us in. The crew attached the lift cables and brought us out of the water and slid us gently to the inside deck and opened the hatch.

I came out first, my anger growing with each step. I stormed up the steps to the main deck where a celebration was underway.

Ms. Sabel poured champagne for Rafia and the crew. She saw me and gave me a smile that withered as she assessed my feelings. Everyone saw me and gave a cheer. Then they noticed I wasn't in my cheering mood. They quieted. I stepped in front of them.

"Guys, be grateful for Ms. Sabel's hospitality, but don't get too drunk. Tomorrow, there is a lot of work to be done. Captain Rafia, as soon as the *Fatma* is ready, go straight to Sevastopol. We have many loads waiting to be shipped." I pointed at Ansi, Mardik, and Firas. "You three, come with me. We're leaving."

"Wait," Ms. Sabel said, shocked. "I want to tell you how much I appreciate—"

"Risking the lives of these good people for a few million dollars? You're welcome." I strode out, heading to the helipad. My ever-faithful squad right behind me. I prayed to a certain used god that I'd never endanger them for personal profit.

"No," Ms. Sabel called out. "I'm recalling Alvaria. It's going to be mothballed."

Behind me, I heard Jenny say to Ms. Sabel, "He needs space."

Yeah, how much space do I need to keep away from a billionaire who can cross the planet in a day?

CHAPTER 72

WHEN WE LANDED IN DURRËS, we went straight to work. Falconer had collected $150 million in commodities as non-refundable deposits. Oil, grains, metals, rare minerals, all kinds of things were sitting on the docks waiting for Detit Exports to pick up on Falconer's behalf. The winning bidder would've paid a lot more, but whoever it was died, so I planned to grab as much of it as I could.

The paperwork had my name on it, I had Falconer's phone for verification, and possession is nine-tenths of the law, so it was mine for the moment. The financiers of the dead bidders would try to claw it all back somehow, so I put every ship I could get my hands on to work. We brought those commodities to market as quickly as possible. Once it was all liquidated, the heirs of the arms dealers couldn't get it back.

A few days later, when the authorities in Sevastopol slammed the door shut, we'd made off with $75 million, give or take a few.

I used the money to pay off Josephine's generous loan. I learned that Ms. Sabel had guaranteed that loan to make sure I could complete the mission. I repaid Sabel Industries for the gift of the company to make sure she could never lay claim to it. I paid off Ansi's loans on his choppers and brought him into the Detit fold. The rest I put into a fund for operating capital.

When it was all set up and the lawyers had all the paperwork done, I gathered the employees in our little hovel of an office, decorated for the holidays by the ever-energetic Megi.

"You guys worked hard." I had Megi pour raki for everyone. "Some of you risked your lives. All of you kept your faith in me. I wish other people had done as much. As of tomorrow, this company will be yours.

I'm selling you the whole thing, debt-free. The only thing I ask is that you never again smuggle so much as a matchstick. Keep your noses clean. You're set for cash, so you never have to resort to gun-running."

All but one of them cheered and drank.

The ever-cautious Firas raised his hand. "You're selling it to us? How much are we paying?"

I smiled broadly. "From all our dealings over the last week, I took enough to pay off my mortgage back home and take a little vacation. Oh, and an old lady in a dementia ward in Tokyo is taken care of. The rest is yours. You're not rich, but you have the opportunity to become independent business owners."

It was a lie. They were rich. By Albanian standards anyway. I hoped they didn't spend it all on gold chains, cars, sunglasses, and houses with plaster replicas of Greek statues.

Geldona told them the bottom line. A round of enthusiastic cheers went up. Megi spilled raki as she bounced from one glass to the next.

We partied like college kids. We took over a bar across the street, singing and dancing and pissing off the locals.

I left them singing songs in a language I'd never heard before and went away for the rest of my life.

I WENT TO NEPAL TO find myself. My first stop was Jagannath Temple.

To meditate, I had to pay a local guide to talk a mile a minute to drown out Mercury. Naturally, my discarded deity was beside himself with jealousy. I had to ignore the famous erotic carvings. After a thorough investigation, of course. I had no idea they advocated fertility through threesomes and orgies with every gender combination mathematically possible. I learned it's impossible to meditate when you have so many innovative positions and combinations for lovemaking in your head.

At least, it was for me.

Instead of finding myself, I came away with a lot of questions. Questions like: Why in the name of Vesta do people flock to a poverty-stricken country where squatting over a bring-your-own-toilet-paper hole is the rule, not the exception? And why do people think religions in other countries are better than the ones they grew up with?

Mercury said, *What I been telling you, homie. Why be a wimpy Christian when you can run with Mercury, Mars, Minerva, Jupiter and the whole pantheon?*

I said, *I give up. I'm all yours.*

Mercury looked at someone or something over my shoulder. *You heard the man, Jesus. Beat it. You too, Moses. He's mine. We don't go around mutilating men's peckers, either, ya sick bastards. OK, see ya at the gods' convention. Bring some real money this time.* Mercury returned his gaze to me. *Oh, yeah, where was I?*

I said, *I'm circumcised. It's done before you come home from the hospital these days.*

Mercury put his arm around me. *We're gonna get you some help, bro. We can deal with this tragedy. But, while we're sorting out your weird American rituals, I need you to make up with Pia-Caesar-Sabel. She's rich. She said she's going to mothball Alvaria, so no harm, no foul, right? Besides, she wants to talk to me.*

I said, *She tried talking to you. It didn't work and she thinks I'm nuts, but at least she's nice enough not to say anything rude. Anyway, she used me like bait on a mousetrap. If I went back, it would be like—what do they call that—battered spouse syndrome? Is there a battered employee syndrome?*

Mercury said, *No way. You're not in that class at all. First of all, you have god on your side, so the only risk involved is when you piss me off. Second, she's not battering you. Don't go trying to grab attention when there are people who've really been hurt.*

I said, *She shot me once.*

Mercury shrugged. *Yeah, well, that was a little over-the-top. Not as bad as Poppaea, though.*

I said, *I'm going to regret asking, but who was she?*

Mercury sighed heavily and looked up. *Ceres, is he illiterate? Maybe he watches too much television. I don't know.* He faced me. *Poppaea was Nero's second wife. Nero divorcing his first wife, Octavia, wasn't good enough for Poppaea. She insisted on having Octavia's head. Literally.*

And she got it.

I said, *You're right. Ms. Sabel's not that bad.*

Mercury said, *Besides, you get back with the Caesar and you might win your girl back. By the way, did I mention Nate Hale's interment is tomorrow?*

CHAPTER 73

ARLINGTON NATIONAL CEMETERY IS BEAUTIFUL at sunset after a rain. The bottoms of the dark gray clouds glowed bright yellow, casting a warm light on the sacred grounds. I didn't get around the world quickly enough to make the church service, but I found the gravesite before the honors team and mourners arrived.

Feeling tangentially responsible for his death, I stood back from the family, off to one side.

Of all the things the military does well, Arlington is a masterpiece. With an average of twenty-three funerals a day, they run it with respectful precision. The Episcopal priest the family chose was experienced with the procedures and performed the graveside service with complimentary timing. He said, "Everyone the Father gives to me will come to me; I will never turn away anyone who believes in me…"

My concentration wandered.

As it always does when I visit, the weight of Arlington pressed on my shoulders. I'm overcome by the burden of the living when humbled by the sacrifice of 400,000 souls resting in peace. While the priest read from the New Testament, I thought of a different Bible verse. In John 15:13, Jesus referred to his imminent crucifixion in a striking parallel to the soldier's calling: "No one has greater love than this, to lay down one's life for one's friends."

Nate Hale might have lived if I hadn't convinced him to help the prosecutor. But for how long? Would I have been forced to destroy him with Falconer? Would he, like Bonham and Konrad, have fallen at the homicidal hand of Ra? Would he have been as brave as Yumi and given his life to buy my escape? He chose a violent world for reasons I cannot begin to fathom. Yet in the end, he chose the right path. I hoped and prayed that in my last days, faced with my bad choices, I would summon half his courage. It's never too late for redemption.

My gaze rose from Lieutenant Hale's small green temporary marker across the surging hills of gravestones. The markers of those who made their lives the barricade between our safety and our enemies. My days continued onward in peace because of their service and sacrifice.

The priest said, "O God, whose blessed son was laid in a sepulcher in the garden: Bless, we pray, this grave, and grant that he whose body..."

As we age, our conscience expands to encompass a wider understanding of duty and honor. With that broadened understanding comes the exhaustion of responsibility. Too often, we find ourselves comfortable and sated with our position in life. We forget the need to revolt against autocrats who would usurp our freedoms. We leave it to others to tear down those who would turn our liberties against us. We allow those who disregard our ideals of free speech, free press, and equality for all to take the reins of power. The waves of headstones remind us of those who held the line against authoritarians. Their lives of honorable service embolden us to do our part when we are called.

Nate Hale feared that to turn on the powerful would be a death sentence. Even so, he rose to stand against those odds.

Behind me, the firing party of seven soldiers stood in formation and fired three times. The bugler played his lonesome dirge. The flag was folded and presented to Nate's mother. The honor guard marched away. Soft words were spoken, then the mourners departed.

I approached Nate's casket and laid my fingertips on the crest. I felt a modicum of accomplishment. As if I'd made a small payment on a large debt. I whispered, "We got them, Nate. Your death has been avenged."

For a moment, I felt thousands of ghosts surround me with gratitude for caring enough to stand up for our brother-in-arms. I felt the late November chill seep through my clothes. I shoved my hands deep in my jacket pockets and shivered.

I sensed someone watching me.

A short distance away, hovering near an old oak, stood Ms. Sabel and Jenny. They wore black. They had attended the whole service.

Seeing Jenny filled me with warmth. Being in her presence, holding her gaze, sensing she still cared about me, made me understand how people can live their entire lives together. Somewhere in our rollercoaster relationship, I'd lost track of how she felt about me.

I approached them. Stopped six feet short.

Jenny's eyes were full of tears. The sight of her filled me with longing for her embrace. The warmth of her breath, the scent of her skin, the presence of her tender love. I'd missed her more than I realized.

My heart wanted to go home. My brain was too proud to speak.

Ms. Sabel said, "We want you back."

Did I want either of them back? They lied to me. Used me. No. It was not going to be that easy. No one was going to say "sorry" and go back to hugs and kisses. Too much resentment would fester beneath forced smiles. Too many recriminations would go unspoken. There was a lot of work to be done before anyone found absolution. Were either of them willing to make the effort? Jenny didn't believe in marriage. Ms. Sabel had lied to me before. If they swore on a Bible, would they keep their oaths? Were they worth it?

Jenny stepped forward, opening her arms.

I pulled my hands out of my pockets. The robin's-egg blue box I'd carried for weeks flew out and tumbled to the ground at her feet.

THANK YOU!

Thank you for choosing my book. I hope you enjoyed reading it as much as I enjoyed writing it. As an independent writer, I am dependent on word-of-mouth referrals and book reviews. If you liked this book, please tell everyone, and leave reviews all over the place. I will be eternally grateful.

When you do write a review, send me a link to it and I'll put you in the next drawing for an autographed book. I run at least three or four drawings a year.

If you can't get enough of Pia, Tania, Miguel and Jacob*, checkout the series at SeeleyJames.com/books. While you're there, join my newsletter to get discounts, drawings, fun, news, outtakes, and more about the Sabel Agents club on Facebook! Every week (or so, sometimes I'm lazy), I'll let you know about the book in progress, personal triumphs & tragedies, what I'm reading and other fun stuff. I even had one person write to me to say, "I don't like your books, but I love your newsletters." To which I replied, "Thanks, Mom." Yeah … whatcha gonna do?

I'd love to hear from you. Please write, message me on Facebook, let me know what you think.

*I like you already.

NOW THAT YOU'VE READ THIS BOOK, WHICH ONE SHOULD YOU READ NEXT?
HTTPS://SEELEYJAMES.COM/BOOKS

ACKNOWLEDGMENTS

My heartfelt thanks to the beta readers and supporters who made this book the best book possible.

- Certified StoryGrid Editor Leslie Watts whose brilliant coaching and critical diagnosis turned this book from just another great thriller into the greatest masterpiece of all time. Probably. Visit her website https://writership.com/
- Extraordinary Editor and Idea man: Lance Charnes, author of the highly acclaimed *Doha 12, SOUTH, THE COLLLECTION, STEALING GHOSTS and CHASING CLAY*. If you like beautifully written art heists, visit http://wombatgroup.com
- Medical Advisor and Character Diviner: Dr. Louis Kirby, famed neurologist and author of *Shadow of Eden*. http://louiskirby.com Without his help, the ending would've been a snoozer.
- Amazing Editor: Mary Maddox, horror and dark fantasy novelist, and author of the Daemon World Series and the fantastic thriller, DARK ROOM. http://marymaddox.com

A special thanks to my wife whose support, despite being a tad reluctant, has gone above and beyond the call of duty. Last but not least, my children, Nicole, Amelia, and Christopher, ranging from age twenty to forty-seven, who have kept my imagination fresh and full of ideas.

ABOUT THE AUTHOR

His near-death experiences range from talking a jealous husband into putting the gun down to spinning out on an icy freeway in heavy traffic without touching anything. His resume ranges from washing dishes to global technology management. His personal life stretches from homeless at 17, adopting a 3-year-old at 19, getting married at 37, fathering his last child at 43, hiking the Grand Canyon Rim-to-Rim several times a year, and taking the occasional nap.

His writing career ranges from humble beginnings with short stories in The Battered Suitcase, to being awarded a Medallion from the Book Readers Appreciation Group. Seeley is best known for his Sabel Security series of thrillers featuring athlete and heiress Pia Sabel and her bodyguard, unhinged veteran Jacob Stearne. One of them kicks ass and the other talks to the wrong god.

His love of creativity began at an early age, growing up at Frank Lloyd Wright's School of Architecture in Arizona and Wisconsin. He carried his imagination first into a successful career in sales and marketing, and then to his real love: fiction.

For more books featuring Pia Sabel and Jacob Stearne, visit: SeeleyJames.com.

f facebook.com/seeleyjamesauthor

instagram.com/seeleyjamesauth

BB bookbub.com/authors/seeley-james

Made in the USA
Coppell, TX
17 October 2021